Julia drew in a shaki___ ___ath

and blinked, striving to f___

She was pressed ___ ___all
and delicate against ___ her
any more tightly, son___ As
it was, the side of her ___ the wool of
his coat, and both the ___ weave were overpowering
and irritating.

"I've put something about your neck," she heard him
say, his voice low. "It's not merely a necklace, but a powerful
enchantment that will protect you. As long as you wear it,
you'll be safe from Cadmaran and all other magic. But you
must give me your solemn vow, Julia, that you'll not remove
it until I tell you to do so. That's of the greatest import. Do
you understand?"

"Yes," she managed. "I think so."

"It's all right if you don't. We'll speak of it later." She felt
him pulling away, and sank her fingers into his coat with
immediate desperation to hold him fast. "We must go," he
said, gently pushing until she reluctantly gave way.

With care, he grasped her chin and tilted her face upward. "Look at me, Julia, can you see me? Do you know
who I am and where you are?"

"Yes," she murmured, licking her dry lips. "I know you,
Mister Seymour."

He smiled faintly. "After tonight . . . Please call me
Niclas, if you wish it. You may well want to call me something far less appealing before this night is done . . ."

• • •

"*Touch of Night* drew me into a magical world from the first
page. Susan Spencer Paul is a master storyteller!"
—Ronda Thompson, *New York Times* bestseller

Touch of Night

Susan Spencer Paul

St. Martin's Paperbacks

TOUCH OF NIGHT

Copyright © 2005 by Susan Spencer Paul.
Excerpt from *Touch of Passion* copyright © 2005 by Susan Spencer Paul.

Cover photo of castle by Mark Stephenson/Corbis, photo of man by InMagine, and photo of sky by Photodisc.

ISBN: 0-312-93387-8
EAN: 9780312-93387-6

Printed in the United States of America

St. Martin's Paperbacks edition / August 2005

St. Martin's Paperbacks are published by St. Martin's Press, 175 Fifth Avenue, New York, NY 10010.

10 9 8 7 6 5 4 3 2 1

Dedicated with love to my wonderful sister, Rachel, who possesses the rare and welcome gift of making the lives of all those around her happier. Thank you for everything you've done for me, Rachel, and for all that you continue to do. I am truly blessed to be your sister.

Touch of Night

One

Dark night. Almost no moon showing through the fog-shrouded haze.

Still. Quiet. Peaceful. Lonely.

Just as Niclas wanted it to be.

Only those souls who haunted such nights were out now: prostitutes, gamblers, drunkards, and thieves. Those who were lost and those who sought respite in the black shadows. Even so, the docks were nearly empty, all saner folk keeping themselves well within taverns and gaming hells, out of the cold, damp darkness. The few whose steps and voices passed within his hearing wisely stayed away from Niclas Seymour's tall, foreboding figure.

The Thames flowed beneath his feet, under the dock where he stood.

Dark. Deep. Slow and steady.

Peaceful, aye.

That was what he sought. Peace. But it was impossible to find, no matter how often or desperately he pursued it.

Peace wasn't meant for people like him, who lived under

a curse; it was the blessing of the sinless and pure, and of those who sprang from untainted, earthly bloodlines.

He lifted his gaze toward the hazy stars, barely visible against the night's fog, and tried to remember what it felt like to be at peace. At rest. There had been a time, only a few short years ago, when he had known the feeling well, and had so foolishly taken for granted the happiness it brought to his days.

What wouldn't he give for even a few of those happy hours now? Just a few blessed hours of quiet nothingness. It would be worth every bit of his fortune, and more. But no amount of money could lift the curse that had been laid upon him. Niclas knew that full well. Money, for all the power it wielded on earth, held no value in the spirit realm. The residents who ruled that sphere demanded a far different manner of payment for wrongs done, usually like for like. Suffering for suffering. Loss for loss. Blood for blood. There was always a way, but only if the cursed one could find it.

And there, as the playwright had so aptly stated, was the rub. God alone knew how Niclas had tried and the lengths to which he had gone, but nothing had set him free. A saner man would have given way by now and either accepted fate or put his miserable life to an end, but Niclas, after three years, wasn't anything approaching sane.

Tonight he would put into motion one final attempt, and if it wasn't the answer . . . then, he supposed he would follow the course of so many who had gone before him.

Lowering his gaze, he turned to look across the Thames, where the lights of Mervaille glowed, their reflection shimmering on the dark surface of the slowly undulating water. It was one of the few remaining medieval palaces that still existed along the river, and had been a safe haven in London for generations of Seymours. His cousin Earl Graymar resided there for a part of each year, during the months when Parliament met and while the season was under way.

Mervaille was not the family seat of the Seymours—only Glain Tarran, their domain in Wales, could lay claim to such intense love and devotion—but it was a very close second. It was a well-situated property, beautiful, private, and surrounded by lush gardens and vast green lawns that rolled down to the edge of the Thames. The palace, which at its inception had been only a simple fortress, was built not long after William's appearance in England. The Seymour family had by then been wealthy landowners, but had kept themselves strictly within the borders of Wales, their beloved land. Following the Conqueror's arrival, however, it became expedient for the family to maintain a presence much nearer to the center of both trade and political power. A small measure of monetary persuasion, combined with a somewhat greater amount of magic, had been all the Seymours, or Symwrs, as the family name had then been spelled, needed to secure the valuable land to build Mervaille. It had been dangerous to risk exposure by using their powers, but necessary, for the Symwrs were then a rugged Welsh clan who had for centuries been a stinging thorn in the necks of all occupiers. Without the use of magic, William surely would have hung Baron Symwr rather than gifting him with a rare piece of property.

As years and ruling families passed, the Symwrs built their proper London estate, establishing a place of power among the very people whom they still stubbornly resisted in Wales. The family gained influence and grew wealthy, first as traders and then by building its own fleet of shipping vessels. Centuries passed, and they learned the art of politics, and how to use their money and friendships to gain safety. Other families like them, who were different and strange to common mortals, began to do the same, and before the day of Cromwell rose they had come together at last to form a bond of union. Seymour, Bowdon, Llandrust, Cadmaran, and others. They lent their various powers and skills for one common cause: to live safely in the world of mere mortals. They called themselves, simply, the Families.

By then Mervaille had been transformed from a simple fortress into an exquisite palace, the Symwr name altered to a more acceptable, Anglicized form, and the barony elevated to an earldom.

And all of it, the wealth, the politics, the rise in power, had taken place from Mervaille.

No, it was not the dwelling the Seymours held most dear, but it was surely the one for which they were most thankful. From Mervaille their kind had gained safety in the very midst of England's greatest city. Its walls enclosed a refuge that only Glain Tarran in Pembrokeshire could equal, for when its gates were shut, mortals could not touch them, and those of magical heritage could fully relax, not having to worry, or even think, about stepping wrong.

It had been three long years since Niclas had known that kind of peace and safety. He had been banned, on that long-ago night when the world had come crashing down on him, from both Mervaille and Glain Tarran. None of the cursed could pass their gates. It was forbidden.

Niclas hadn't realized, at first, just how greatly he would miss the family estates where he had spent so much of his youth, or that he would come to yearn for a presence at the family gatherings that had once made him so impatient, but time had proved him wrong.

How different he was now. How different everything was. He'd taken so much for granted in the happy, easy life he'd once lived. Like Mervaille. Niclas gazed at it with longing and thought of what it would be like to be there, just once more. To drink in its beauty and be at complete rest, free from worrying about being found out by the world.

But it was impossible. Instead, he had to stand here, across the river, and content himself with the sight of his family's estate. And wait for Malachi to come.

It wouldn't be long. The earl would have received his summons by now. Niclas had only to ready himself to lay out his proposal and prepare for the arguments that his cousin would be certain to present. He already knew what they would be; he'd been saying them to himself during the past several days.

A familiar pressure in his temples warned Niclas that someone was approaching. He sensed a series of faint emotions—curiosity, then surprise, then a moment's consideration, and then—Niclas sighed when he discerned it—pleasure. He didn't have to turn around to see the two men who'd seen and decided to rob him. He already knew that they believed they could easily overpower him.

Both their footsteps and their emotions grew more recognizable as they neared, and Niclas, too weary to fight any more this night, said aloud, "Be wise, gentlemen, and leave me in peace."

More surprise, and they fell still. Niclas could feel a touch of fear mingling with their growing excitement and anticipation. He made a tempting target, he knew, despite his superior height and build. His garments, dirtied and torn though they were from several earlier altercations, were the clothes of a gentleman. No amount of dirt or blood could change their fine fabric or cut, nor could a great deal of mud or scuffing hide the make of his expensive boots. And that meant money, jewelry, or at the very least a decent pocket watch. Oh, aye, he was a tempting target, indeed. But it was often thus. This was the fifth time in the past week alone that he'd found himself in such straits, and perhaps the hundredth or more since he'd taken up his nightly wanderings. At some point he would surely run through all of London's knaves and finally be left in peace.

He had tried to dress less conspicuously, but his manservant, Abercraf, had adamantly refused to let him out in public attired in anything less than perfection. Not that Niclas blamed him. The poor fellow had charge of him so infrequently these days that he had to make the most of every opportunity.

"What'd 'e say, Vess?" one of them asked in a bemused tone. "Is it a fight 'e's askin' for?"

"I dunno," the other replied. "I think 'e's drunk. Hey, mister," he addressed Niclas's turned back. "You drunk or some'at?"

Niclas sighed and briefly shut his eyes. God help him, he was weary of this.

Slowly, he turned to survey the men standing before him, and wasn't in the least surprised by what he found. They were markedly similar to the hundreds he'd faced down in the past three years: tough, thin, dirty. Their emotions were the same, too. Hungry, nervous, hopeful, a little giddy, and a good deal afraid. He gazed at them solemnly for a long moment, then said again, quietly, "Leave me in peace."

The shorter man licked his lips and, making two fists, took a step forward.

"Give us your purse, m'lord, and we'll do just that. There's no need for any trouble, is there?"

"No," Niclas agreed, "there isn't. But that decision is in your hands. It would be best and wisest for all concerned if you'd simply go your way now."

They stared at him.

"Stop gabbing and give us your purse," said the taller—and meaner—of the two. "We aren't 'ere to talk."

"I know that well enough," Niclas said with a small, unavoidable laugh. He didn't mean to taunt them, but it did amuse him to think of anyone with even a small measure of intellect wishing to attempt conversation with such unschooled ruffians. Certainly not he, who had once been famed for his ability with words. The sudden memory filled him with another stab of that painful and so familiar longing for all that he'd lost.

But he didn't have the luxury of wallowing in sorrow just now, for his would-be assailants were emanating far more fear than nerve, and that never boded well for wise decision-making.

"I am not going to give you my purse," he told them, "or anything else. I also do not wish to harm you. Come now," he said reasonably, "you're tired and a little drunk. One of you is worried about a woman, perhaps your girl?" He looked from one to the other and saw the shorter man's mouth drop open. "You're both wondering whether you can truly best me, and afraid that you can't. You're thinking of what you'll do if your friend is hurt and can't run away—and have decided to abandon him to his fate if that should be the case."

Niclas wasn't entirely certain of all the details, but he'd felt their emotions well enough to guess. It was sufficiently close to cause panic in both. That, at least, he felt quite fully.

"I don't want to harm you," he said once more. "But I promise that I can easily overpower you both. Go now," he advised, "before you do anything foolish and regrettable."

They almost did. Niclas could feel the indecision, especially in the taller one. Unfortunately, the shorter one possessed a great deal of pride and stubbornness. Niclas knew he'd made up his mind even before he pulled out the knife hidden beneath his ragged waistcoat.

" 'E might have a gun, Vess," the taller one warned.

Vess smiled, revealing gaps where teeth had once been. "Nah, 'e don't. 'E would've pulled it already. Wouldn't you, m'lord?"

Niclas was beginning to grow irate. Malachi would arrive at any moment, and dealing with him successfully would require every bit of mental acuity Niclas possessed. And God knew, it was far better for him to diffuse the situation than to let his cousin do so. If Earl Graymar stuck his nose into the matter one of these silly fools might inadvertently be harmed.

"I apologize," he said, moving forward with that suddenness that always seemed to take mere mortals by surprise; it certainly took his would-be assailants by surprise, for the one named Vess nearly dropped his knife. "But I haven't the time to entertain you any longer."

It was done quickly, with no harm to either of the men. Vess lunged at him with the knife, but Niclas easily turned aside and, before the fellow could even lift his arm up for another attempt, had twisted the weapon from his hand and thrown it to the ground. The taller one moved as if to leap on Niclas's back but, like his partner, couldn't match either the speed of Niclas's movements or his superior strength. Before either of them could divine what was happening he had them aloft, one in each hand, held by the front of their shirts. They struggled and shouted and cursed until Niclas gave each a hard, thorough shake, and then they fell still, more, he suspected, from shock than fear.

"You're much lighter than I expected," Niclas said, looking from one to the other. "Far easier to lift than the last few fellows who attempted to empty my pockets. I hope," he added severely, "that you will appreciate how often I am forced to endure such nonsense."

Vess attempted to curse at him again, but stuttered too much for the words to make sense. Still, Niclas understood his meaning very well and shook him again until his head wobbled on his short neck.

"Now, what shall I do with you?" Niclas turned about contemplatively, the men dangling from his hands. "Shall I toss you into the river? Take you to the nearest tavern and display you like shot pigeons to your fellows? Or should I simply knock your empty skulls together and be done with it?"

"My choice would be the river," said a voice from the shadows. "Only think what an entertaining splash they would make. Much better than the stones we used to throw when we were boys."

Niclas lowered his gaze to see his cousin, the earl of Graymar, walking slowly toward them.

"I do apologize," said the earl in his most gentlemanly manner as he came nearer, his light-colored hair easily visible in the dark of night. "I hope I'm not interrupting something important. I only came because I thought you wanted to see me."

Malachi Seymour was slender and tall, lithe and elegant as a cat, yet strong, too, in unsuspected ways, just as Niclas and other Seymours were. His long, silvery white hair was tied back in a neat tail at the nape of his neck, causing his sharp, elfin features to stand out even more starkly by contrast. Like Niclas, he was dressed in almost unrelieved black, tempered only by the white of linen shirts and cravats. Unlike Niclas's, the earl's clothes were exactly neat and clean. Not that it mattered. Regardless of what Niclas might wear, or how tidy he might keep himself, he could never match his cousin's perfection.

"I believe I'm the one who should apologize," Niclas said, and lowered Vess and his gasping friend to the ground. "I should have dealt with these fellows more quickly, but my nights are long and I must fill them with such amusements as I find. Go on," he said to his assailants, releasing them. "Console yourselves with the thought that as I'm no longer without aid, you necessarily had to leave me unmolested."

Within moments he and Malachi were alone, the sound of Vess's and his partner's frantic footsteps quickly fading into the night's mist.

"That," said Malachi, "was most unwise. They'll spend the rest of the night regaling their comrades with tales of your supernatural powers. You seem determined to end your days on the gallows or, worse, burned upon the stake as some of our more unfortunate ancestors were. They couldn't resist using their powers in public, either."

He lifted one gloved hand palm up, upon which a small flame suddenly appeared. Moving closer, he surveyed Niclas's attire with an expression of polite disdain. "You're filthy," he stated. "How long have you been out this time?"

"It's good to know that you follow your own advice so well, cousin. For pity's sake, put your blasted fire away. If the night watch should see—"

"Why? Is he coming?" Malachi asked. "Is *anyone* coming? I assume you'd give me warning far before any individual could make his—or her—way into view."

Niclas scowled. "No. We're quite alone as far as I can tell. Unless there's a Seymour or Cadmaran or anyone of our ilk lurking about. But if there were, *you'd* know of it."

The fire disappeared and Malachi tugged on his glove to rid it of creases. "We're quite safe from intrusions of that sort, I promise you. There isn't a Cadmaran anywhere near London, thank God. If there were, I'd be rather more occupied with them at the moment than with you. How long have you been out?"

Occupied. Aye, that he would be, Niclas thought. Malachi wasn't only the head of the Seymour family, but the most powerful wizard in Europe, as well. More than that, he was the *Dewin Mawr,* the recognized leader of the Families. As such, Malachi's life consisted of one burdensome responsibility after another. There had been a time when Niclas had helped him to shoulder those responsibilities, but that was before the curse, in those nearly forgotten days when his mind had been strong and his thoughts clear, and when his own powers had been so readily controlled.

"How long?" Malachi prompted.

Niclas sighed and ran a hand through his thick, unkempt hair.

"I don't know. Four days, perhaps."

Malachi raised one slender blond eyebrow. "You've stopped keeping track?"

"There's no reason to do so," Niclas replied. "Time is all the same for me now."

"You must *make* it different," Malachi said sternly. "I've told you time and again how vital it is for you to continue to mark your days and nights. You risk insanity, otherwise."

Niclas uttered a mirthless laugh and turned to pace back toward the water's edge.

"Risk," he repeated. "I believe we're nearly beyond that, cousin."

Earl Graymar followed him until they stood side by side at the dock's railing. "Have you taken that potion I gave you?"

"It was as useless as the rest," Niclas told him. "Everything is useless, Malachi," he said more softly, staring down at the water. "I'm beginning to think that nothing will ever make a difference. Perhaps the curse can't be lifted."

Malachi set a comforting hand on his shoulder. "You mustn't let yourself give way to despair, *cfender*. There is always a remedy for blood curses, even one so difficult as yours. We have only to find the way."

"I used to believe that," Niclas said. "I don't anymore. But I'm desperate, and foolish." He glanced into his cousin's face, so filled with concern. "I want to make one more try."

"Niclas—"

"Only one, Malachi, and then I'll stop. You've already divined what I'm going to ask of you."

The earl of Graymar straightened, his expression troubled.

"I'm sorry, Niclas. I would allow almost anything to help you be rid of the curse, but I cannot let you use a complete innocent for your own purposes. Miss Linley trusts me to lend her my aid in solving a difficult problem, not to put her in company with a man who can scarce control his behavior from moment to moment."

Niclas faced his powerful cousin head-on, all his weariness and desperation driving him.

"You think I'll hurt her? Or cause her distress? You know very well I won't. I realize that of late I've been, perhaps, rather erratic—"

"Perhaps?"

"Very well," Niclas admitted, "I've not been entirely stable for some time. I understand your concerns. But I'd never harm a woman, certainly not one who might hold the key to my redemption. Only think a moment and consider. She's his cousin—"

"Very distant," Malachi put in. "It's likely the relationship is far too minor to serve the purpose, even if you should shed blood on her behalf, which I pray won't be the case."

"The Linleys were Drew's relatives, regardless how distant," Niclas argued. "If I can avenge his death by performing a valuable service for them, I might end this torment. And," he added, moving quickly to face Malachi as he turned away, "our own uncle is the cause of their distress, which may add even greater weight to the deed in the eyes of the guardians. If I can be the instrument that will solve the trouble—only consider, cousin, the effort it would require to force Uncle Ffinian to give way—then it might suffice."

Lord Graymar shook his head. "I can't . . . Niclas, you know very well that I can't take the risk. If you had followed my instructions and taken the potions or even performed the exercises I asked you to do—"

"Chants and meditations," Niclas muttered dismissively. "They were useless."

"If you had done them as I asked," Malachi repeated, "they would have at least helped you maintain a more even temper. Instead, you choose to wander aimlessly for days on end, fighting and getting into all manner of trouble, creating the worst kind of rumors, which I'm forced to answer as best I can for those members of society who—"

"Society," Niclas repeated tightly. "I hope you tell them all to go straight to—"

"Blazes, yes, I know," said the earl. He closed his eyes and appeared to pray for patience, then looked at Niclas and sighed. "There was a time, *cfender,* when you understood what it means to our kind to keep the world from becoming too curious, and how vital it is for all of us to behave circumspectly. You even used to help me keep our wilder relatives in line. Do you remember?"

Niclas set fingers to his forehead and rubbed at the seemingly ever-present ache that throbbed behind his eyes, striving to put his exhausted thoughts in order.

"Of course I remember. If I didn't, I'd not want to have that life back as much as I do. I apologize if I've been the cause of more trouble for you, cousin. God alone knows you have enough with the rest of our mad family. How you've kept your sanity all these years I'll never know. But isn't that all the more reason why you should give me this chance?"

Lord Graymar regarded him for a silent moment, a chill breeze causing his elegant greatcoat to flap about his slender figure. "Do you even remember Julia Linley from those days before you were cursed?"

Niclas hadn't been expecting that. The question brought him up short.

"No," he replied slowly, though he couldn't be entirely certain that he spoke the truth, for his mind was so muddled, and his memory had failed him more than once in the past three years. "Did I know her? Were we introduced?"

"I don't believe you ever were," the earl said. "She wasn't of any particular consequence in those days, save for her family's name. But you were quite the opposite, Niclas. You were one of the most admired gentlemen of the ton, and justly famed for your intellect and wit, to say nothing of your elegance in dress and manner. It's extremely likely that Miss Linley will remember you as . . . well, as you were then. If I were to ask her now to consider your escort in place of mine, she would surely expect that you would at least give the appearance of a gentleman, if not behave like one. Were you to present yourself to her in your present state, you'd terrify the poor woman."

Niclas looked down at himself. His clothes were muddy and torn, but looked respectable, he thought. And his appearance certainly hadn't frightened away the various fellows who'd attempted to rob him in the past several days.

"It's not as bad as that, is it?" he asked. "I shall have Abercraf give me a proper shave and trim before I go to meet her."

"Cfender," Malachi said gently, opening his palm to reintroduce the flame, which flickered violently in the night's breeze. "Forgive me for saying so, but you look very much like a man who hasn't slept in three years."

Niclas's gaze riveted to his cousin's, illumined in the light of the flame.

"As that is precisely what I am, I doubt that can be of any surprise."

The earl's expression was sympathetic. "That's true, but I don't believe the explanation will go far with anyone outside the family. And that includes Miss Linley. You will have to do more than simply take a bath and change your clothes."

"A nap would help, I'm certain," Niclas snapped, "but I doubt it would be possible." He began to pace again. "It's been three years since I was able to lay my head on a pillow and close my eyes and escape into slumber. Three years without rest or respite or peace." Turning, he met his cousin's unhappy gaze. "I wander the streets without marking time," he said angrily, flinging out a hand, "and take your wretched potions and try to exhaust myself with fights and drink. But nothing helps. My mind is sick with weariness, and the powers that I once held in complete control now burst out unleashed. Every emotion felt by common mortals is flung at me like a knife, and when I'm in a crowd it's as if they're all shouting at once. I'm going mad," he said, then forcibly stopped and shut his eyes tightly, struggling to regain his precarious balance. "I'm going mad, day by day," he said more slowly, "and you don't seem to give a damn. You won't even give me this last chance to redeem myself."

Almost before the final words were out of his mouth, Niclas was cringing at the bitterness and childishness of his tone, at the pained expression on his cousin's face, and was wishing he could wash the words away. But bitterness and anger, he had learned, came part and parcel with the curse that had been laid upon him.

"I'm sorry," he said before Malachi could speak, turning away toward the river again. He thought briefly of flinging himself in, and wondered whether his cousin wouldn't find the splash not only entertaining but a great relief. "I have no right to speak to you in such a manner. There is no one to blame but myself for all that's happened. I'm sorry, Malachi."

The light from the flame went out. There was a moment of silence, and then he heard his cousin's slow footsteps. Niclas appreciated the warning, for Malachi had the power to walk in complete silence when he wished. The comforting hand upon his shoulder, however, came as a surprise.

"You were not entirely at fault," the earl said. "Drew played a part, and his faithless wife, as well. You, at least, meant to be of help."

"It doesn't matter." Niclas shook his head. "Drew still died because of me."

"He killed himself because the wife he loved was unfaithful," Malachi countered, giving him a shake. "That was no fault of yours."

"I was the one who told him," Niclas retorted angrily. "I knew what her thoughts were and broke every rule of our kind by telling him. To this moment I don't know why I thought that he would receive the news with anything but despair. Drew loved her so."

"And that was why you told him," said Malachi. "You feel the emotions of others, but you can't predict how they'll behave. The love that Drew felt for Lucilla was so powerful that it drowned out all other emotions. You had no idea that he would kill himself, rather than simply take his wife in hand and put an end to her affairs, as he should have done. She loved him, too, did she not?"

Niclas nodded. "The affairs were nothing to Lucilla. Merely a way to pass the hours while Drew was fixed on Parliament. She would have stopped if he'd shown the least vexation. I tried to tell him that, but he wouldn't listen beyond the facts of her betrayal. He didn't realize that there was so much more to the problem."

Malachi sighed. "Mere mortals often find it difficult to understand the complexities of such matters. You mustn't blame yourself too harshly. It might very well have turned out as it did, regardless."

"And it might not. The curse is proof of my wrongdoing. The guardians never lay them upon our kind without good cause. But *this* curse—to never know slumber or be at complete rest! Death would have been kinder."

"Death is not a curse, but a release," Malachi reminded him gently. "But I understand very well what you mean by the words. I, too, was surprised at the manner in which your punishment was laid upon you, and the difficulty we've had in finding the way in which the debt might be paid. I suppose . . ."

Niclas lifted his head.

"I'll do whatever you ask, Malachi. Give me this chance, I beg it of you."

Lord Graymar gazed at him thoughtfully, his blue eyes glittering in the darkness as if lit by some inner fire.

"You would have to take protection, in whatever form I determine is best. No arguments."

Niclas's heart began pounding loudly in his ears. He straightened.

"Of course."

"And you'll require a mount," Malachi went on. "I mean no insult to your very fine cattle, but I want you to take Enoch."

Niclas blinked at that. Enoch was descended from a long line of fabled and magical steeds which only those who were *dewin* rode. The beasts did not suffer the touch of those who possessed lesser magic.

"No one but you has ever ridden him," Niclas said. "He'd kill me before letting me sit astride him."

"He will not do it for your sake, but for mine," Malachi informed him. "And you will be exceedingly glad to have him on your journey, if you indeed undertake it."

"I mean to do so," said Niclas.

"Aye, and that you do," said the earl. "But you must meet the last requirement first, and that will be a task almost as difficult as facing down our uncle Ffinian."

"What is it?"

"You must convince Lady Eunice that you are a better choice than I am to escort her niece to Wales and rescue her sister from our uncle's clutches."

Niclas frowned darkly. "Lady Eunice," he repeated. "She'll be stubborn, but Linleys are famous for that—"

"Lady Eunice sets the standard for stubbornness," Malachi murmured. "She glories in her reputation."

Niclas ignored him. "I haven't seen her in years," he said. "But there was a time when she used to gaze upon me with a great deal of favor."

"Of course she did," his cousin said. "You were one of the wealthiest and most marriageable men in England, and she is the head of a family with numerous females to launch. The trouble now is that she wouldn't consider you a suitable match even for that youngest one, the unfortunate, spotted girl with the prominent teeth and unpleasant—"

"Aye, it will be difficult convincing her," Niclas said, "but not impossible. I must simply prove to her that I'm not mad, and—"

"But the girl is well mannered, for all that," said the earl, gazing up at the sky. "I've danced with her, and I've seen the potential she possesses, not unlike our own young cousins who will be having their come-outs this season. Rhosyn and Cordelia. Can you believe they're old enough?" He shook his head. "It seems like just the other day that they were teething. Do you remember how all the books used to fly off the shelves at Glain Tarran whenever Cordelia began to cry? Gad, what a horrid mess. But she only affected the books, curiously. I do hope she's learned to control herself." Frowning, he murmured, "I'd better not allow her into any libraries."

Niclas, lost in thought, made no reply, and Lord Graymar was obliged to clear his throat loudly to gain his attention.

"Have you settled on whether you're willing to approach Lady Eunice?" he asked.

"Aye, I have," Niclas said, "and I accept your terms in full. I'll find a way to make her ladyship listen to me."

Even in the darkness he could see Malachi smile.

"It will be exceedingly interesting to see you make the attempt, at least," said the earl. "And even more interesting to discover what Miss Linley's response is. Go home and make yourself presentable first, and make certain to send me word once your meeting with Lady Eunice has concluded. I shall want to hear every word of what has taken place."

Two

"Niclas Seymour," Julia repeated, slowly setting down the quill with which she'd been writing. She stared at her aunt in disbelief. "Niclas Seymour is in the sitting room. Mister *Niclas* Seymour—*not* Lord Graymar?"

"I was as surprised by it as you are, my dear," Lady Eunice replied, sniffing disdainfully. She was standing near one of the room's tall windows, twisting a silk handkerchief in both hands as if it were Niclas Seymour's neck. "The fellow hasn't been seen in respectable company for years, yet he has the cheek to appear at our door and demand an audience. I can't imagine what he wants. And," she added in a more meaningful tone, "Puckett informs me that he looks as rumpled and unkempt as a common dockworker. Of course he had to allow him entrance—he is Earl Graymar's cousin, after all, and a Seymour." She threw her hands up. "It would be just as impossible to refuse the Prince Regent."

Lady Eunice began to move in an agitated circle, tormenting the handkerchief with new energy. "I can only pray that no one of consequence saw him entering. Lady Evanstone, of course, will surely hear of it from one of her servants. That can't be helped. And you know what a gossip that woman is." Lady Eunice fell still and let out a loud, taut, telling breath. "The entire ton will have heard the gossip before nightfall. We'll hear little else at the Dubrow ball tonight. It will be utterly horrid."

"Not at all, Aunt," Julia said with as much calm as she could muster, which, given the increased pace of her heartbeat, wasn't a great deal. "His visit should only increase our consequence. We shall be the center of attention, and haven't you always told me that such is the most desirable position to achieve in society?"

Her hands, Julia saw as she began to put away her writing things, were actually trembling, and when she drew in a breath it seemed far too brief and insufficient to keep her from losing all sensibility.

Julia gave herself a firm mental shake and strove to collect her scattered thoughts.

It was ridiculous to react in such a foolish manner. Niclas Seymour had never paid the least attention to her, had never even been formally introduced to her, and probably had no memory of her at all. The fact that she could still react like a young girl in the throes of her first serious crush, simply at the sound of his name, was painfully embarrassing.

"But not in this manner, Julia," Lady Eunice replied unhappily. "Niclas Seymour is reported to be half-mad, an oddity who wanders the worst streets in London at all hours. What could he possibly want to speak to us about? Oh, dear"—she set a hand to her forehead—"is he here to ask for aid? But no," she added before Julia could say a word, "he would have gone to Lord Graymar first, and the earl would scarce turn one of his closest relatives aside."

"I'm sure he would not," Julia agreed, standing and pushing back the chair at the writing desk. "Lord Graymar isn't the sort of man who'd do such a thing. But apart from that, I fear you're forgetting that Mister Seymour remains quite wealthy, despite his odd behavior in recent years. He inherited a large portion of the Seymour fortune and has no reputation as a gambler or wastrel."

"I believe that's so," her aunt agreed thoughtfully. "I've always thought it a shame that so promising a gentleman as he once was became so ineligible a match. But perhaps it's just as well now that he never took a wife. It would be a dreadful thing to be wed to such a creature, regardless how wealthy or wellborn. But then, why on earth has the man come?"

Julia ran her shaking hands over her hair, praying that she looked well enough to see him and wishing that she had dressed in something more becoming. But how could she possibly have divined that he would come? Would he recognize her? No, she chided silently, it was foolish to hope for such a miracle. She was so changed from what she had once been.

"I'm sure Mister Seymour must be here to discuss my upcoming journey to Wales," she said with a calmness that she was far from feeling. Would he think her attractive? Even pretty? "Perhaps—" she said, smoothing down the front of her dress, "perhaps he has a great fondness for his uncle, Baron Tylluan, and desires to attempt discouraging me from disentangling Aunt Alice from the baron's attentions."

She was going to see him in a few moments, she thought with inner panic. She was going to be in the same room with Niclas Seymour—and speak to him face-to-face. God help her. She would probably make a terrible fool of herself.

"Yes," Lady Eunice said, nodding. "Yes, that's it. You're perfectly right, Julia. I'm sure there's nothing more to it. Well, if he's come as Baron Tylluan's second, we must simply be firm with him," she stated emphatically. "Your journey with Lord Graymar has been planned down to every detail, and nothing must happen to alter it."

Julia patted her aunt's hands. "Nothing will happen. Aunt Alice will be made safe from Baron Tylluan's demands, and all will be well. Mister Seymour doesn't possess the power or influence to change the decisions that have been made. I'm certain he'll understand once everything has been explained to him."

The words seemed reasonable enough when she said them, but Julia wasn't sure if they were perfectly true once she and Lady Eunice had been announced into the room where Niclas Seymour was pacing back and forth before the fire. He looked, she thought, like a caged animal. And her aunt had been correct in relating the butler's assessment of the man; he appeared very much to have the same grooming as a common laborer, albeit one dressed in expensive—if rather dated—clothing.

But some kind of effort had clearly been made, probably by his valet, to make Niclas Seymour resemble the proper gentleman he had once been. His black hair had been ruthlessly brushed and tied back at the nape of his neck, but it had been left so long without a proper trim that the thick tail fell well below his shoulders. His handsome face was clean-shaven, but the skin on his cheeks and chin was so pale that he must have only recently become unbearded. The visage that had once been the picture of physical health was now thin and drawn, and his blue eyes were rimmed with red. The clothing he wore, almost entirely black and terribly outdated, only made matters worse, for the dour color emphasized the paleness of his skin. He was so different from the Corinthian Julia remembered that if she'd seen him on the street, her eyes might not have known him.

But her heart would. And did.

There was a sharp pain in her chest, and Julia knew a shocking, and rather frightening, urge to weep. She had thought her feelings for him long dead, but the simple fact of him, here before her, even in such a state, gave proof of that lie.

She knew firsthand just how elegant Niclas Seymour could be. It had been eight years since her first of seven failed seasons, and though he'd never noticed Julia, she had most assuredly noticed him. In those days, the earl of Graymar's cousin had been one of the most sought-after bachelors in London.

Handsome and dashing, with shining black hair and deep blue eyes, Niclas Seymour had been the stuff of a young girl's dreams. His manners had been all that were perfect, and nothing could be faulted in his dress or conversation. He was so self-assured and admired that he'd been the focus of every gathering, and women flocked to him.

Julia, like all those hopeless others, had been secretly in love with him, though she'd been far too shy and awkward to do anything about it. She'd still been very young at the age of seventeen, and it had been a terrible mistake for her parents to force her into a Season. Julia had understood their reasoning, of course; with four daughters to launch, getting the first and oldest married off as soon as possible was a necessity.

But Julia had been far from ready for either society or men. Her body and mind had yet been immature, and she'd been cursed with spots. None of the eligible bachelors in London had taken a second—or even first—glance at her, and Julia had been wretched through every ball, dance, assembly, and dinner that she'd dutifully attended. Wretched, save for her one furtive pleasure: watching handsome Niclas Seymour as he smiled and danced, dreaming that it was she whom he was laughing and dancing with.

She had known him at a glance those many years ago, even if he was walking down a street, some distance away, with his back turned to her. The very sight of him had made her heart beat with embarrassing quickness.

But he was so changed, almost a different man. She could see nothing of his old, easy charm or self-assurance; indeed, when he stopped pacing and looked at them he appeared not to know how to proceed, although he surely had made hundreds of social calls in his life. The proper protocol should come as readily to him as it did to all of those who'd been raised in families like theirs.

"Mister Seymour," Lady Eunice said calmly when he made no attempt to either bow or acknowledge their arrival. "I don't believe you've ever been formally introduced to my niece Miss Linley, though I'm sure she will be familiar to you. You share many acquaintances in society. Julia, this is Mister Niclas Seymour, cousin to Earl Graymar, whom you know well."

It was perfectly clear by his expression that she wasn't familiar to him at all. With her heart in her mouth, Julia curtsied and murmured, "Mister Seymour."

He said nothing, but stared at her in an openly confounded manner for a long, silent moment before at last making her a very awkward bow. Straightening, he took up staring again, first at Julia, then at Lady Eunice, then at Julia. Still he said nothing.

Julia and her aunt exchanged looks, then moved together a bit farther into the room.

"You are very kind to visit," her ladyship said politely, if not with actual pleasure. "Won't you please make yourself comfortable while I ring for tea?"

"I'll stand," he said stiffly, adding, as an afterthought, "Thank you. You ladies please . . . sit and be comfortable." He waved a hand to indicate the nearby chairs.

Julia and her aunt exchanged looks again. Their guest appeared to be confused about whose house he was in, and whose duty it was to invite anyone to sit.

Lady Eunice was renowned as a hostess in London, but she was also famous as a stickler for propriety. Julia divined what her aunt was going to say and, before her ladyship could utter a syllable that she would surely later regret, took her by the arm and guided Lady Eunice toward a favorite chair. "Yes, do sit and be comfortable, Aunt. I'll ring for tea. Excuse me a moment."

As she walked across the room to the bellpull, she could feel Niclas Seymour's gaze fixed upon her, and wondered whether he stared because he found her attractive or horrible. Or, perhaps, and far more likely, he was trying to recall when, and whether, they had ever met.

He continued to stare even after she had ordered the tea and returned to sit opposite her aunt. Still he seemed disinclined to say anything, but only gazed at Julia in a perplexed and disturbing manner.

Lady Eunice cleared her throat loudly, drawing his attention.

"We've had the pleasure of Lord Graymar's company several times in the past month. He has agreed to help us with a certain family difficulty. I believe you must be aware what it is I speak of."

"I am," he replied, casting another troubled glance at Julia. "Miss Linley's proposed journey to Wales is precisely what I came to speak to you about. I—" He broke off and briefly set a hand to his head, shutting his eyes as if he had an ache. "I understand your feelings, Lady Eunice, but I assure you that your apprehensions are misplaced. I'm not here to talk you out of the journey or the attempt to rein in my uncle—God alone knows he needs it from time to time. I've come to suggest myself as a replacement." He appeared to cringe slightly. "What I mean to say is," he said, dropping his hand and looking directly at her ladyship, "I should like to take Lord Graymar's place in escorting your niece to Wales."

Niclas knew that he would never, in his life, forget the expressions on the faces of the ladies before him. The elder one both looked and felt shocked and horrified, but the younger—her eyes widened with surprise and various other emotions, yet he could feel nothing.

The uncomfortable realization rushed over him again as he helplessly stared at her. *He couldn't feel her.* Nothing.

Not even a small measure. None of her thoughts or feelings were revealed to him at all, and that was impossible. *Impossible*.

With exceptions.

Niclas felt the emotions of those he was near unless they were in some way related by magic. All who were descended of those families who had so long ago been banished from their original world were immune to such minor gifts as he possessed. And that meant that Julia Linley either possessed magic, or . . . or there had to be some other cause that he wasn't aware of. And Malachi would have warned him if she was one of them.

Wouldn't he?

It would help if Niclas could recall having met Julia Linley before. Considering their families and the society they moved in, it was more than likely that their paths had crossed numerous times. Yet he couldn't believe that he would ever forget meeting a woman as beautiful as she was. That would be just as impossible as the fact that he couldn't feel her emotions.

Julia Linley was far too striking for a man to forget, regardless of how many years might pass. Her hair was a soft mixture of gold and brown, and had been arranged in such a manner that long, delicate tendrils curled attractively about her elegant face, framing cool blue eyes that were presently gazing up at him as if striving to discover exactly what sort of creature he was. She was delicate, and very feminine, and disturbingly alluring.

No. Niclas would not have forgotten such a woman.

If his mind hadn't been on edge before he began his visit at Linley House, it certainly was now. And Lady Eunice's piercing emotions weren't helping any. He'd already stepped far wrong by commenting aloud on what he had sensed of her feelings. She thought him bordering on madness, and hid her fear very well with the politeness that had been bred in her. He had no doubt that Miss Linley felt the same. Not that Niclas blamed them; he was inching closer each day to that very destination.

Why couldn't he feel Julia Linley's emotions? If she and he were somehow related, even if very distantly, would performing a good deed for her still remove the blood curse? No special powers could be used in making recompense—on either side. If she possessed magic, even a small measure . . . Niclas tamped down the unease rising within and forced himself to focus on the task at hand. Later, he would have the luxury of pondering the matter, and of seeking Malachi's opinion.

He *had* to make a good impression. This was his last chance, and Niclas wasn't going to lose it. Ignoring their shocked expressions, he shut his eyes and strove to recall what it meant to be a gentleman of the ton. It had once been so easy for him. More than easy. He'd been admired, cosseted, sought after, praised. And he'd been so insufferably vain about his own perfection that he'd taken all of it in stride.

If only he could call back his old self for a few minutes. Just long enough to convince Lady Eunice and her distractingly lovely niece to grant his request. It had been so easy, once, to be Niclas Seymour. So incredibly easy . . .

"I understand," he began, considering each word carefully, "why the idea of such an exchange may be alarming to you, but if you'll only give me a few moments to explain, I believe I may succeed in recommending myself to you both."

Lady Eunice's feelings fairly shouted themselves at him, saying, clearly, "not in this lifetime or the next." Her features, however, were fixed into a frigidly polite expression.

Julia Linley, on the other hand, appeared to be genuinely curious. He wished he could sense whether her feelings were the same.

Clearing his throat, Niclas forged on.

"The trouble, as I understand it, is that my uncle, Baron Tylluan, has been threatening to force his widowed neighbor into marriage. The woman in question is, I believe, closely related to you, Lady Eunice. Is that not so?"

"My sister." Lady Eunice's voice was tight with repressed anger. "Alice. She was married to Sir Hueil Morgan until he died five years ago. Morgan's estate neighbors your uncle's."

Niclas knew that he had to proceed delicately. "My uncle is a scoundrel. There can be no denying the truth of that. Nothing can possibly excuse his determination to wed your sister by force. However, I have also heard that Lady Alice hasn't been entirely . . . averse to his attentions."

Julia Linley uttered a feminine laugh that sent a shiver of delight tingling along Niclas's spine.

"You are delicate, sir," she said, smiling up at him. "The truth is that she has been his mistress since six months after Sir Hueil died. She has never, however, wished to be made his wife, and upon this point she has been most clear."

"I see," said Niclas, distracted by the peculiarly strong fury emanating from Lady Eunice. Other emotions were at play, as well, and equally powerful. Envy, regret, and pain.

"Yes," Lady Eunice said, staring fixedly at the fire,

though he knew she was seeing something else in her mind's eye. "My sister has been so foolish as to become involved with Ffinian Seymour. It's not so difficult a thing to understand, disgusting as all who know of it must find the relationship. They're both widowed, after all, and neighbors. Such things happen," she added with bitter disapproval. "But my sister has always been careless of society's wiser dictates. If she'd had more sense, she never would have married that dreadful Hueil Morgan and ended up living in his godforsaken manor in such an uncivilized land with"—she lifted her head to spear him with a frigid gaze—"your wild relatives for neighbors."

"Aunt!" Julia reprimanded, her cheeks reddening further. "Mister Seymour has come to offer us his help, not to be insulted. Pray forgive us, sir," she said with a sincerity that Niclas found most charming. "It's merely the strain of the situation. We have been terribly worried about Lady Alice, as I'm sure you'll understand."

"Indeed, I do," he replied. "I am fully aware of my uncle's reputation for scandal and mayhem. He and his two sons, my cousins, have long been a prickly thorn in our family tree."

"Well," she conceded delicately, "we have heard rumors . . ."

"They are *not* rumors," Lady Eunice stated firmly, "and I'm sure that Mister Seymour would not pretend otherwise."

"No, I wouldn't," Niclas agreed, wondering if she was referring to the time when Ffinian's wild twins burned down a gaming hell, or the incident that started a tumultuous riot on the docks that lasted for nearly a full day before finally being quelled.

"Clearly, then," he said, "you understand what we're up against. My uncle is far from likely to heed any requests set before him. He'll certainly care nothing for what anyone outside the family thinks, and will give scant attention to what any of the Seymours has to say—including the earl."

"There's no need to explain such things to me, sir," Lady Eunice stated tightly. "I've known Ffinian Seymour longer than either you *or* the earl, indeed, well before either of you were born. I met him forty years past on the day my foolish sister wed that rakish Welsh lord of hers and took up residence in his estate, neighboring Castle Tylluan. I've had little pleasure in dealing with that man during my few visits to those wretched mountains. I know full well what he'll do and say to those who try to counter him, but that"—she poked a long, elegant finger at him—"is the least of our worries. If that horrid man should make my sister wed him by force, the outcry among the ton will ruin both our family names. Now," she went on, sitting back, "you just *think* a moment about what that will mean to your two young cousins who are about to have their first Season."

Niclas's brow furrowed at this unexpected news. Two of his cousins were coming to London for their come-outs? Malachi hadn't said anything of that. Or had he? Niclas had a vague memory of Earl Graymar mentioning a couple of their female cousins the night before. And it made sense, of course, that some relative or other would be coming, for Seymours, though generally kept safe in Wales, often traveled to London to feed social desires that couldn't be met in their more rural communities.

When he'd been himself, and not affected by the curse, in years past, Niclas had been recruited to introduce his younger relatives into London society. Female cousins had been accompanied to every important event, from Almack's to balls to a presentation at court, while the males had been given a bit of town bronze at certain establishments where women and gaming were readily found, or at sporting events where their appreciation of such Corinthian skills as boxing, fencing, or racing could be more fully developed. Now, of course, he could no longer be trusted with the care and guidance of younger, wilder relatives, for he was increasingly proving to be even less restrained than they were.

"You're perfectly in the right, my lady," Niclas said, slowly at first, then with growing confidence as he plotted his unknown course. "And that is precisely why I propose being the one to accompany Miss Linley to Wales in Lord Graymar's place. My cousin will not have mentioned it to you, for he is a gentleman by all accounts and wouldn't wish you to consider the grave difficulties that his absence in London, at this time, would cause. Even a brief absence," he added, considering how quickly Malachi would actually be able to deal with their uncle. "I'm sure you will agree, Lady Eunice, that it would be far better, and kinder to my young relatives, if the earl remained in town to oversee their come-outs while I take his place in dealing with our scurrilous uncle."

Lady Eunice and Miss Linley exchanged glances once more, as they had repeatedly done since they'd entered the room. Lady Eunice, he felt, was beginning to waver, and he could only assume by her expression that Julia Linley was, too.

Encouraged, Niclas pressed on.

"I realize, of course, that I make a poor substitute for someone of Lord Graymar's consequence . . ."

"Oh, no, sir, not at all," Miss Linley assured him. "But we did think that, perhaps, as the earl is the head of the Seymour family, he might assert a greater level of persuasion over Baron Tylluan."

"That is very likely," Niclas conceded readily, beginning to feel quite like his old self. Even his constant weariness seemed less pervasive as he took on the challenge of bringing the two women around to his perspective. "But I've had a great deal more experience than Lord Graymar in dealing with my uncle and his sons. They have always been my responsibility whenever they visit London, even since the—" He very nearly said "curse," but stopped just in time. "Even though I am no longer given to going out much in society."

Keeping an eye on his uncle and twin cousins, Kian and Dyfed, had been one of the few remaining tasks that Malachi had left with Niclas following the curse, and for two very good reasons. First, no matter how mad sleeplessness drove Niclas, he could not possibly become more crazed than Ffinian and his offspring, and second, Malachi possessed neither the patience nor the desire to deal with their relatives from Castle Tylluan. But these things, Niclas could not tell the ladies.

A scratch at the door announced the arrival of tea, and he felt just how relieved Lady Eunice was at having a brief break in their conversation, and saw the same on Miss Linley's face. For his part, Niclas declined refreshment and, as the women filled their plates and cups, took up pacing again.

He was pacing again, Julia saw over the brim of her delicate cup as she took a sip of hot tea. She wondered if he was going to survive the remainder of his visit, and what his reaction would be when her aunt kindly, but firmly, rejected his proposal.

Whatever he felt, he could certainly not lay the blame too heavily at his own feet. Seldom had Julia seen a man strive harder, or better, to achieve his goals.

Niclas Seymour had been almost himself again for a few moments. The confidence of his tone, the fineness of his intellect, and the careful phrasing of his arguments had made him seem once more the famously educated and quick-witted gentleman she had known. Or, rather, known of.

He had never been the kind of wellborn man who was given to foppishness or feigned foolishness, but had spent as much time in debate and discussion at various balls and parties as he had dancing. It had been considered shocking and even impolite, and yet his determination to continue with such dialogues only increased his desirability as a guest among London's hostesses. Even Lady Eunice had been well pleased to receive an affirmation of attendance from Mister Niclas Seymour when she was planning one of her dinners or musical evenings. She had even bragged a little, as other hostesses were also given to do, when he was to be present at one of her gatherings.

Now, she was horrified to receive a simple afternoon call from the man. But Julia could scarce fault her aunt for that, for he was truly changed, proof of which was his behavior in the past few minutes, swinging from odd to almost normal and back to odd like a clock's pendulum.

What had happened to alter him so greatly? she wondered. Still pacing, he absently ran a hand through his hair,
loosening the neat arrangement that his valet had so carefully created, so that several long strands fell loose to his
shoulders.

With a sigh, Julia lowered her teacup and tried not to
think of what was going through her aunt's mind at this
very moment. He would be fortunate to leave the house
unmolested; Lady Eunice would rather attack him with a
comb and brush herself than let anyone she knew see him
leaving Linley House with his hair looking like a pirate's.

Julia had thought of him so often in the past three
years and hoped that he was well, though the rumors
she'd heard had dimmed those hopes somewhat. It was
whispered that the death of his dear friend Andrew Payne
had been the starting point of Niclas Seymour's decline,
but Julia had always thought that dubious reasoning. The
death of a close friend would surely be a painful thing,
especially when that death had been self-inflicted, but
Niclas Seymour had been far too strong and intelligent a
man to let even a very sad event like that so completely
change him.

Julia took another sip of tea and continued to watch.
He was still the handsomest man she had ever set sight
upon, without exception; she supposed nothing would
ever be able to alter that. And he could still speak well
and logically. His manners had been almost perfect
throughout the visit, following his initial minor missteps.
If his clothing and grooming weren't entirely what they
should be, that was understandable in a man who had
been out of society for so long. Such trifling details could

not diminish a man who had stood out as a powerful and arresting figure even among his most distinguished peers.

What would it be like to take that journey with him? Julia's heart began to beat a little more quickly. She would be in his company for several days, be able to speak to him and be close to him. And she wasn't so plain and horrible now, she thought, straightening in her chair, nor was she as painfully shy. She would be able to smile at him at last, as she had wanted to do so many times before when they had crossed paths in parties and balls. She . . . she might even flirt, as all the finer and more beautiful ladies had done. And he would smile back, and . . . perhaps . . .

No. She was being foolish, she told herself firmly, setting her teacup aside. It was impossible. Her aunt would never agree to let an unstable man accompany her on a journey of such length; he would probably find it difficult convincing her to trust Julia in his company merely for a drive about the park on a sunny afternoon. Not that Julia needed her aunt's permission for such minor outings any longer, for she was five and twenty and so far on the shelf that her reputation no longer required safekeeping. It was even acceptable for her to be accompanied by a man like Lord Graymar, who wasn't a relative, on a journey hundreds of miles in distance, to Northern Wales.

Abruptly, Niclas Seymour stopped pacing and turned to face them once more. With an effort he schooled his features into the polite expression that he'd maintained earlier, and spoke in the same calm, logical tone.

"I understand, Lady Eunice, why you should feel some reluctance in allowing me the honor of escorting Miss Linley to Castle Tylluan, but I would ask you to consider the benefits. As I have already stated, Lord Graymar is greatly needed in London as the head of the Seymour family, and I have had far greater experience in successfully dealing with my uncle, the baron. But there is yet another reason, with even greater import, that you should consider."

"And what is that, Mister Seymour?" Lady Eunice asked primly.

"Merely that I am no danger to Miss Linley's reputation, as I fear my cousin, the earl, will be. The gossips will have a fine time spreading every possible rumor if Miss Linley and the earl of Graymar should journey together. But it's entirely likely that they'll see nothing exceptional should I be her escort."

"Why should that be, sir?" Julia asked with interest.

Turning his intense blue gaze upon her, he replied, "Because the earl is counted as one of the most marriageable men in England, while I am not. It would be impossible for so beautiful a young lady as you are to have an interest in a man like myself. You're far too lovely to waste a chance at marriage with a respectable man by having anything but business to attend to with me."

Her aunt actually chuckled with amusement.

"Nonsense, sir. Julia doesn't consider the issue in any of her dealings now. She is well beyond the age to marry. The suitability of her being escorted through the country by a wellborn gentleman—especially with a coachman and footman and maid in attendance—is not in question. It will be perfectly proper."

Niclas Seymour looked rather astonished. He turned his gaze upon Julia and surveyed her for a long, silent moment.

"That's ridiculous. She looks perfectly marriageable to me."

"She is five and twenty," Lady Eunice informed him. "Seven useless seasons have only proven how hopeless her case is. All of her younger sisters have taken husbands, but Julia has refused every offer put before her, though several were most flattering. She might have had an earl, you know, but he wasn't good enough for her. No, indeed. Not good enough for Miss Julia Linley."

"Aunt!" Julia protested indignantly, her cheeks as hot as fire. How could she say such things? To *him*? Niclas Seymour was the last person in the world she wanted to be so humiliatingly exposed to.

"Do you deny it?" Lady Eunice asked, oblivious to Julia's misery. "No, you can't, because it's true. And so you see, Mister Seymour, there's no need to concern yourself with my niece's reputation. It's quite safe, regardless who her escort is."

Julia expected his look of bewilderment to change to disdain or, worse, pity, but he only continued to gaze at her aunt as if Lady Eunice were quite mad. Then he turned and gazed thoughtfully at the fire. Julia watched him while her aunt sipped at her tea, and strove to find something more to say. But it wasn't necessary, for after a moment he turned back to face them.

"Then," he said quietly, "if that is how you truly feel, my lady, there is nothing left for me to do save throw myself on your kind mercies and ask that you consider allowing me the honor of escorting Miss Linley to Wales in place of my cousin."

Lady Eunice regarded him steadily.

"Mister Seymour," she said, "you have been out of society for several years, and this is the first time that I've spoken with you since a musical evening given long ago by

Lord and Lady Bixby. Do you recall the night I speak of?"

A flash of unease crossed his handsome features, Julia saw, but he mastered himself quickly and replied, "Yes, my lady. Very well."

"After so long an absence, and many rumors regarding your state of mind, you come to me now and request that we agree to accept you as escort for my niece in place of your cousin, a gentleman whom we both frequently see and speak with, whose temper and judgment we know and approve of, and who, without question, can be trusted to convey a gentle-born lady to her destination without harm or mischief. Do I summarize our circumstances correctly?"

"Yes," he said solemnly, "you do, indeed."

Lady Eunice slowly set her teacup aside.

"I believe, then, that you would not be in the least surprised if I were to decline your request."

"I would not," he said, his expression resigned.

"Aunt," Julia said, "couldn't we—"

Lady Eunice set a hand on her arm, silencing her.

"I may surprise you, yet, Mister Seymour," she said. "Lord Graymar has much to recommend him as an ideal escort, but Julia's purpose in undertaking this journey is not for simple pleasure. It is with the express goal of making my sister safe from your uncle, and this goal must be foremost in the decision we ultimately make. Considering your greater experience in dealing with Ffinian Seymour, I believe that you may, indeed, be a better choice. In addition, your behavior this morning has given proof that many of the rumors I have heard are false. However," she added quickly when it appeared that he would speak, "I wish to have greater assurance of your . . . behavior," she said delicately, "before making a final decision."

"I shall be glad to supply whatever proof you desire, my lady."

Lady Eunice stood, and Julia, unable to do anything less, stood as well.

"Lord and Lady Dubrow are having their annual ball this evening, which was an event that you used to attend with great regularity."

He began to look suspicious, but nodded and said, "Everyone did."

"Indeed," said Lady Eunice. "It is one of the great gatherings given each Season. Julia and I will, of course, be there. If you were to be in attendance as well, Mister Seymour, and prove that you can be trusted in society, I believe I will be far more inclined to grant your request."

If it was possible, his already pale complexion went further white. But he gathered himself with admirable speed.

"I regret to say, my lady, that I have not had the pleasure of an invitation to the Dubrow ball this Season."

"That," she said, "can hardly be wondered at, sir. Fortunately, Lady Dubrow is one of my dearest friends. Expect an invitation to arrive on your doorstep within the hour. Whether you accept or decline is up to you. If you decide to come, which I hope will be the case, then you may have my final decision before the evening is done. Does this suit you, Mister Seymour?"

"Very much, my lady." He bowed, first to her aunt, then to Julia. When he straightened, she thought she could see more color in his cheeks. "I hope that Miss Linley will reserve a dance for me?"

"Thank you, sir," Julia murmured, "but I no longer dance."

"Tonight, however," said her aunt, "you will. My niece will reserve the first waltz for you, Mister Seymour. I assume you know the steps?"

"I—"

"Good. We shall expect to see you then, sir. You will have my answer before the night is out."

Three

"This coat, sir?"

Niclas stopped fiddling with the buttons of his shirt and glanced at Abercraf, who was looking rather pained upon presenting the garment he held.

"Where in heaven's name did you find that?" Niclas murmured with wry amusement. He hadn't seen that old coat in years.

It had been elegant once, a marvelous creation of dark green velvet, paired with matching breeches and a vest of gold paisley silk. He had worn it often when attending special events. It had been his favorite, in those long-ago days when he'd found so much pleasure in going out and being with others.

"No, not that one," he told his butler, who also served as his occasional valet. "It's out of fashion now. Far out of fashion."

Like himself, he thought, turning back to gaze at his reflection in the mirror. He'd once been a desirable guest, but his final attempts at attending ton functions—all at

Malachi's insistence—had been disasters. The curse left him so continuously weary that controlling his ability to feel the emotions of others had become impossible, with the result that being in even small gatherings was nightmarishly chaotic. Niclas hadn't been able to tolerate more than a few hours in society, and then he had spent days afterward forcing the memories away. Finally, he'd stopped going altogether.

But tonight would be different. He would make certain of that. It *must* be different.

Tonight, he would have to be what he once was, or as close as possible, no matter how difficult or unpleasant. He had to settle matters with Miss Linley and Lady Eunice, and if he showed up looking like a man who'd been living in a cave for the past three years, that would be impossible.

"I suppose it must be the black that I wore last night. Is it terribly stained?"

"Yes," Abercraf said, his voice absent the displeasure Niclas felt emanating from him. "Terribly."

"We must find something else, then," Niclas told him. "I shall both feel and look a fool in the green velvet, but if that's all there is—"

A knock came at the bedroom door, and Abercraf left the dressing room to open it. He returned in less than half a minute, bearing a large package tied with a voluminous quantity of elegant ribbons. His mood, Niclas felt, had lightened considerably.

"It is from his lordship, the earl," said Abercraf, inspecting an attached note. "He instructs me to make certain that all wrinkles are absent before allowing you to don his gift. He will meet you at the Dubrow ball just before midnight."

The package was untied to reveal a stunningly crafted outfit, perfect in fashion and fit, ready—save for a few wrinkles that Abercraf deftly dealt with—for Niclas to wear. Best of all, it wasn't the unrelieved black and white that Malachi always wore, but rather a sapphire blue, with a silk vest shot through with silver. Malachi had remembered Niclas's old love of color.

"He's a devil," Niclas murmured, surveying his image in the mirror. "But for once I'm thankful for some of his more particular gifts."

Abercraf's eyes were filled with happy tears.

"You're perfectly presentable, sir. I'm certain no other gentleman could possibly outshine you."

Niclas thought his manservant a touch too optimistic, but he had to confess that his appearance was much improved from what it had been earlier in the day, when he'd foolishly assumed that a shave and combed hair had made him fit to be seen. How much he had forgotten of the effort required for a gentleman to achieve distinction.

But it was starting to come back to him.

For the first time in years he had given Abercraf free rein in the management of his grooming, with remarkable results. Niclas had been vigorously scrubbed from head to toe, then left for an hour soaking in a hot tub. Abercraf had then massaged him with a seemingly unending collection of oils and lotions, and, following this, he had spent a great deal of time utilizing clippers and scissors and blades. A shocking quantity of hair lay on the floor by the time his manservant was done, and Niclas had looked into the mirror and seen the self he'd known so long ago staring back at him.

He'd done something else that he'd long resisted, as well. He had forced Malachi's latest potion down his throat and reclined for a full hour, repeating a chant in the ancient language that his cousin had insisted would refresh his mind, body, and spirit. It had never seemed to do much good before, but tonight, perhaps because he wanted it so badly, Niclas rose feeling almost as rested as if he'd actually slept for a short while. Almost. But that would be enough.

"I'll do naught to shame you, Abercraf," he said, setting an assuring hand on the older man's shoulder. "I promise. After all, I was once used to attending such functions every night. They can't have changed as quickly as fashion has."

He was surprised to discover, upon being let out of his carriage, that he was actually looking forward to the evening. The final ton event he'd attended—dinner and an operatic performance at Lord and Lady Bixby's, where Lady Eunice had also been in attendance—had been endless and miserable. During dinner, he'd been seated next to Viscount Rosser, whose lustful thoughts had been fixed on Lady Ellison, sitting across from them, and not on his wife, who had been on Niclas's other side. The viscountess had been thinking quite forcibly about killing both her husband *and* Lady Ellison, a fact that hadn't shown on her lovely, smiling, perfectly serene face. Niclas had felt her distress and fury so keenly that it had been almost impossible to carry on polite conversation. He'd wanted to stand up, drag Viscount Rosser from the table by the scruff of his neck, and give him a good thrashing for being so foolish and unfaithful. Or to warn Lord Ellison of his wife's potential infidelity. Or even to advise the viscountess on the futility and unpleasant legalities surrounding murder.

But such revelations could only make matters worse. People outside the Seymour clan tended to be extremely upset—and rightly so, he knew—to think that someone else could divine their emotions. No one, apart from family members, had ever been thankful for his youthful utterances. Indeed, quite the opposite. They'd been frightened of Niclas. He became something of a monster in their eyes, at least until they convinced themselves that the whole thing was merely a foolish joke. Then they'd held him in contempt. Added to that was the constant fear of the family being found out. Society didn't take kindly to those possessed of unusual powers, and not a few Seymours in the past had found themselves dangling at the end of a rope or tied to a stake.

And so Niclas had spent his final evening in formal society biting his tongue and silently cursing Malachi for talking him into attending the function. When it was over, he decided to never again attend another gathering of the ton.

Now, he was about to break that vow. Niclas told himself that it was only because Lady Eunice had forced it upon him, that he had come because he had no other option, but he wasn't entirely certain that was the truth.

Julia Linley had intrigued him. Bothered him. And most certainly bewildered him. He'd felt nothing from her, no emotions or feelings, and the reason for it was a mystery that needed solving before their journey together.

Perhaps he'd been too distracted by being in the

company of a beautiful woman again, or perhaps Lady Eunice's fierce emotions had simply drowned out whatever her niece had been feeling. Neither of those factors had ever deadened Niclas's senses before, but, apart from them, there was no explanation.

The footman who took his invitation showed no surprise upon reading Niclas's name, but there was a moment's hesitation after that same invitation was passed to the butler. The pleasure that the man felt at seeing Niclas in attendance, though perfectly hidden behind a mask of correctness, warmed him considerably, and his mental approval of Niclas's attire was just as encouraging. Bowing deeply, the manservant murmured, "Welcome, Mister Seymour," then straightened to formally announce his arrival to those already gathered.

If the butler had been surprised, it was as nothing to the surprise on Lord and Lady Dubrow's faces when Niclas approached to make his formal bow. But delight followed their amazement, and he was warmly greeted.

This had been his life once, and he had loved it beyond measure. Being back, even for a few precious hours, was intoxicating. He moved slowly about the crowded ballroom, taking in the music and colors and faces. People were dancing; women in their beautiful gowns and men in their finest formalwear. Individuals turned to look at him, then turned away to murmur excitedly. He sensed a variety of emotions, from surprise to pleasure to curiosity. It was all simple and easy thus far, as it had once been long ago.

"You're causing a stir, *cfender.*"

Niclas turned to see Malachi standing beside him, perfectly attired and groomed, his handsome countenance relaxed and smiling.

"I'm glad you came, even if you were forced to it," he said. "Your friends will be glad, as well, though shocked. It's been far too long, Niclas."

"Only if no one is plotting a murder," Niclas told him, striving to keep his tone light. "Or worse. In which case I shall curse both Lady Eunice and myself for coming. Thank you for the clothes." He glanced down at himself. "Your taste is excellent, as ever."

"I would have bought an entire wardrobe just to see you in society again." Malachi examined him more closely. "Why, Niclas," he said with faint surprise, "you've had your hair trimmed. You look quite your old self. A veritable pink of the ton."

Niclas gave a laugh. "I was merely weary of two of us in the family looking like pirates. People might think I was copying your odd fashion, rather than simply wishing to be left alone."

Malachi nodded toward the far end of the room, where a group of women sat together on low couches. "Lady Eunice and Miss Linley are sitting there, among a fine gathering of spinsters and widows."

"Why?" Niclas asked, gazing across the room with bewilderment. "She's far too lovely to be sentenced to such a lack of merriment. Is it Lady Eunice's doing? I confess that my memories of her include a certain diligence of duty and all that is right, but she never seemed so cruel as to consign anyone to such an unhappy, and far too early, fate."

"I only wish it might have been so simple a thing as Lady Eunice," said the earl. "She may be stubborn, as Linleys so famously are, but she is also quite reasonable when presented with a logical argument. You discovered the truth of that this very afternoon. No"—Malachi sighed aloud—"I'm afraid Miss Linley is the one to blame. She has fallen into that most awful trap that women are prone to give way to. She has decided," he said, gazing at her from across the elegant room, "that she is too old to experience such pleasures as dancing or flirtation or love."

"Nonsense," Niclas muttered angrily. "That's ridiculous."

"And most trying, as well," said his cousin. "I've done my utmost—twice tonight alone—to charm her into dancing, but she refuses."

"No one refuses the earl of Graymar when he exerts himself," said Niclas.

"It is rather uncommon," his cousin agreed. "There was a time, you know, when she accepted me as a favored partner. But that was well over a year ago. Her obstinacy now is remarkable, especially given Lady Eunice's unhappy insistences that she oblige."

"And still she refused you?" Niclas asked.

Earl Graymar nodded. "Still. It's regretful, though. Miss Linley has bruised my tender sensibilities with her rejections."

Niclas snorted at that, but refrained from informing the earl that only those who possessed hearts had "tender sensibilities."

They were being stared at from all sides; Niclas could feel the beginnings of discomfort as the flood of emotions began to swell and blend. A few particularly unpleasant persons—Niclas had no idea who, exactly, since it was difficult in such a crowd—were feeling bitterness, jealousy, even violent hatred. But when he gazed out at the sea of faces glancing at him none showed anything more than polite curiosity and smiling welcome. That was how it always was: sadness masked by smiles, hatred by blankness.

"She'll dance with me," Niclas vowed. "I won't leave until she has."

Malachi's eyebrows rose. "Will you not, *cfender*? That is an odd thing to say. And what will you do if she refuses?"

Niclas nodded at a passing acquaintance who had nodded at him first.

"It won't matter. She'll dance with me, and not merely because her aunt desires it. There's another reason." He looked at his cousin. "I have to get close enough to assure myself that she's not an anomaly."

"An anomaly?" Malachi repeated blankly. "Miss Linley?"

They both turned to watch as the music came to an end and the dancers moved off the floor.

"I can't feel her," Niclas said quietly. "Or, rather, I couldn't feel her this morning, when I had my audience with her and Lady Eunice."

Malachi was, for once, stunned speechless. He stared at Niclas as if he suddenly didn't know him.

"There was nothing," Niclas went on, his gaze moving slowly about the room, seeking out particular faces from his past. Certain individuals would be easier for him to converse with than others, and would aid him in making a better impression on Lady Eunice. "No emotion at all. I guessed what her emotions were because of her outward manner, yet I could *feel* nothing."

The first waltz was announced, and new sets of partners started to materialize on the dance floor.

Malachi continued to look dumbfounded. "But that's impossible. She's not even remotely related to the Seymours."

Niclas looked at him sharply. "Are you certain, Malachi? Because if she is, it might alter my attempt to lift the curse. Can you be absolutely, completely certain she isn't of magic blood?"

"I have always known before. It's part of being *Dewin Mawr* to have a perception of our kind. But perhaps . . ."

"What?"

Malachi gave a shake of his blond head. "I shall have to think upon it."

"Aye, you think upon it," Niclas said. "And let me know what you discover. In the meantime, I'm going to claim the waltz that was promised to me, and see whether I was merely mistaken about Miss Linley earlier. By the way," he added before he left his cousin's side, nodding toward a beautiful woman standing not far away with another gentleman. "Lady Cosgrove has been lusting after you in a most fervent manner for the past several minutes. She must like pirates."

She *was* lovely, Niclas thought as he neared the group of ladies clustered at the far end of the room. Entirely lovely, and far too young to be relegated to the shelf. And yet there she sat, with her soft brown hair hidden beneath a horrid silk turban and her delightfully curved figure covered by an equally awful, out-of-fashion gown of pale blue. Not that blue didn't suit her; her eyes were blue, and looked perfectly well against her other features. But that particular garment looked as if it had come out of her great-aunt's closet, suitable for a very mature woman but not in the least for someone so young and attractive.

For the life of him, Niclas couldn't understand how such a beauty had, at the age of five and twenty, managed to escape marriage. If she'd been a man, he would have admired her ability to avoid the parson's mousetrap, but it was an oddity for an attractive, well-bred young woman to have staved off wedded bliss. Her family could easily have forced her to accept a husband. That they'd not done so said a good deal about either the level of her Linley obstinacy or her inability to lure the attention of a suitable match. Since the latter was impossible, he assumed it must be the former, and steeled himself accordingly for their coming confrontation.

She was aware of his approach, he saw. Indeed, both she and Lady Eunice, sitting beside her, had been watching his progress from the moment he'd left Malachi, as had the other women they were sitting with and nearly every other person in the room. But Niclas had no care for them, or for the various acquaintances who hailed him as he made his way. He looked steadily at Miss Linley, fixed his thoughts on her and what he wished to accomplish, and didn't let the various emotions flying at him from all directions distract his purpose.

Niclas came to a stop directly in front of Lady Eunice and made his most formal bow. It was less stiff than the one he'd made earlier in the day, and yet, he thought with a touch of aggravation, it was far from the fluid gesture that had once been second nature to him.

"My lady," he said in solemn greeting before making an identical bow to her niece. "Miss Linley. I hope I find you well this evening."

"Very well, indeed, Mister Seymour," her ladyship replied. "Your looks are much improved."

"Thank you," he said, and cast a glance at Miss Linley, taking brief note of the color that had risen in her cheeks. "I have come to collect the dance that was promised to me."

"I fear my niece is proving the truth of our Linley stubbornness this evening, sir," said her ladyship, and Niclas felt a curious amusement emanating from her. Clearly, she didn't believe him capable of overcoming Miss Linley's objections, and he understood very well the test that was being laid before him. "She refuses to dance. With anyone. Not even Lord Graymar was able to prevail upon her to change her mind."

"I fear my aunt makes me sound cruel, sir," Miss Linley said, and he could see from her expression that she was deeply embarrassed, "but, as I told you earlier, I no longer dance. I am thankful, however, for the compliment. It was most kind of you."

Behind Niclas, the music began to play. He reached for her gloved hand.

"I hope you'll continue to feel that way, Miss Linley, after we've danced."

Her eyes widened. "Mister Seymour—"

He pulled her to her feet, ignoring the gasps of a few of the matrons and spinsters surrounding her. Lady Eunice, on the other hand, uttered a soft, delighted laugh. Niclas set an arm about Miss Linley's waist to gently, but firmly, move her toward the dance floor.

"Mister Seymour, I fear you don't understand—"

"Certainly I do," he said. "You don't wish to dance. But we shall, nonetheless."

The floor was filled with couples already whirling in time to the music. The waltz had not been a popular dance three years ago, and Niclas had performed it perhaps a dozen times. He had no idea how long it might have been for Miss Linley, but he supposed the skill would come back to them quickly enough.

She struggled briefly as he took her in his arms, but said nothing. She didn't need to. Her expression told him almost as much as her emotions would, had he been able to feel them.

They moved stiffly at first, nearly bumping into several other couples. Julia Linley didn't make matters any easier, as she apparently had turned into a slender but unyielding tree. He all but carried her about the floor in time to the music. Fortunately, she was a petite, small-boned female, and exceedingly light.

She was as close to him now as she was ever likely to be, and yet he could still feel nothing emanating from her. Perhaps, he thought, he hadn't yet made her angry enough.

"I hate that turban." The words were out of his mouth before he could stop them.

She reacted just as any lady would, with full insult.

"I'm terribly sorry, sir," she replied in a short, tight tone. "If I'd had any idea that you felt so strongly, I would have made certain to wear something more appealing to your tastes."

What a foolish way to go about making a good impression. Niclas didn't know how to redeem himself. "What I meant to say," he began, making an attempt, "is that you shouldn't wear one at all. You haven't a speck of gray in your hair to hide."

That only served to make her angrier.

"Mister Seymour"—her tone was icy now—"I understand that you've not been in polite society for some time, but even that is no excuse for such boorish conversation."

He couldn't feel her. That was all there was to it. She was in his arms, she was clearly very angry, but the only emotions he could feel were those coming from the crowd of people surrounding them.

It was impossible, yet it was so. He glanced about until he saw Malachi standing on the edge of the dance floor, watching them. His cousin lifted an eyebrow in question. Niclas gave a minute shake of his head and saw Malachi's forehead furrow with uncharacteristic concern.

"You're quite right," he said, turning his thoughts back to Miss Linley. "I'm not much used to society any longer, and my manners are atrocious. I apologize."

She was silent for a long moment, as she gazed fixedly over his shoulder, but at last she said, "You are forgiven," then added, in a more reasoned tone, "I'm sure it is rather strange for you to be in company again. It was terribly wrong of my aunt to insist that you attend this evening. I'm sorry for the way she behaved this morning. It's her habit, I fear, to command everyone to her will."

She had rather remarkable features, he discovered as he inspected her face at this close distance. The fineness of her bones, the elegance of her cheeks and nose and high, arching brows bespoke her gentle birth . . . and gave him pause. There were those among his kind who possessed such delicate features. Like Malachi, they were generally said to have inherited elvish blood.

"There's no need to apologize, Miss Linley. I'm used to my cousin's dictatorial behavior. I believe it comes with being the head of families such as ours."

"I must confess," she replied, "that there are moments

when Lord Graymar quite reminds me of my aunt." She smiled. "I do not mean that unkindly."

He almost laughed. "I know you did not. But I promise that the earl shall never hear of the comparison from my lips." He hesitated a moment before asking, as casually as he could, "The Linleys are an old family, are they not?"

"Very old, I'm afraid," she said, with such an odd expression that he wished he could know what she was feeling. "My aunt would tell you that we are among the oldest families in Europe, with one of the purest bloodlines. She's fond of speaking about our family history."

"And you aren't?" he asked.

"No, not really," she said. "It can be rather exhausting to belong to such a family. There are so many things one must do, and many more that one mustn't, lest the family name be disgraced. But I needn't tell you any of that, for you know very well what I mean. The Seymour name is ancient, is it not?"

"Unfortunately, yes," he said. "I believe we must be kindred spirits in that regard, Miss Linley."

Again he caught a flash of that odd, sad expression before it was covered over with a smile.

"As both our families are so antiquated," he said, "I can't help but wonder if we're in any way related."

"I've never heard of any connection," she replied as he spun her into a turn.

"Perhaps there's some tie through another family, to which we're both related?" he asked. "Are there any Theriots in your family line? Or Llandrusts?"

Her brow furrowed in thought. "I don't believe so. Are you related to the Theriots, Mister Seymour?" she asked with unfeigned interest. She sounded excited by the possibility. "They're rather infamous, almost like Gypsies, are they not?"

Almost, he thought, and regretted having brought the subject up. That particular branch among the Families was given to gambling and thievery, and excelled at both. Why in heaven's name had he mentioned them, rather than one of the other, far more respectable family names? And why wasn't she insulted that he should even suggest a relationship, rather than appearing fascinated?

"Distantly," he replied, and decided that it would be best to let Malachi pursue the question of any relationship between them. "You dance beautifully, Miss Linley, for a lady who no longer dances."

He realized, as he said the merely polite words, that they were true. They were dancing. Together. Miss Linley was no longer rigid in his arms, and they were moving with ease, dancing as gracefully as any of the other couples on the floor.

And there was something even more astonishing—something that he had only just realized. Not only was he not feeling her emotions, but the emotions of all those around him had dimmed, as well, until they were nearly covered by the loudness of the music.

They had been conversing so easily because of this unexpected miracle, and because they'd been conversing so easily, he hadn't noticed it until the music had nearly come to an end. And then, before he could really turn the knowledge over in his mind, they had come to a stop and Miss Linley had stepped out of his arms.

Immediately, the swell of emotions began to fly at him as they had been doing before the dance started. Without thinking, he reached out to pull her back into his arms . . . and the din lessened again.

"God above," he muttered, taken aback by this new development. Julia Linley certainly was a surprising young woman.

"Mister Seymour?"

Niclas let her go . . . then took her back into his arms again, then let her go. Each had the same result as before.

"I believe," she said, putting out a hand to stop him as he tried to take her into his arms again, "that the music has ended, Mister Seymour."

Niclas came to his senses, to discover that they were standing alone on the dance floor, surrounding by many interested onlookers. He didn't need to see their expressions more closely to feel how amused, and bewildered, they were. A few were gloating because Niclas was making such a fool of himself. Some, probably women, were glad to see Miss Linley embarrassed. A few kindhearted souls felt sympathy.

"Forgive me," he began, his heart sinking. This certainly wasn't the way to convince Lady Eunice that he should be trusted with the care of her niece. "I—"

She smiled and set her hand upon his arm, and, somehow, she had them walking off the floor in so natural a manner that their onlookers rapidly lost interest.

"It's quite all right, sir," she assured him. "I would have enjoyed another dance, as well, but I can't think they'll play another waltz for some time. Ah, you see?" she said as the musicians struck up the tune for a reel.

The press of emotions wasn't as muted as before, but she only had her hand upon his arm, and it was gloved. He wondered how closely they would have to touch or embrace in order to make all foreign emotions disappear completely.

The visions that filled his vulnerable brain were both vivid and much too stimulating. Niclas forcibly pushed them aside and said, "Miss Linley, may I ask you to do me a great favor?"

"Certainly, Mister Seymour. I should be pleased, if what you ask is within my power to do. I must warn you beforehand, however, that, despite my own Linley stubbornness, I do not possess the will to overcome Lady Eunice. She is stubborn beyond even what Linleys are famous for."

He laughed. "I've been acquainted with Lady Eunice for many years, and you're quite right. Only she can, and will, make up her mind. But I hope to sway her in my favor tonight by doing well."

Miss Linley nodded and murmured in the affirmative, and Niclas slowed their pace.

"The trouble is," he went on, "that I've been out of society for so many years that my manners, as you've seen firsthand, are somewhat stiff. I wonder if you might help me by granting me your company for a little while longer. I must necessarily greet several acquaintances and don't wish to make another misstep that might decide Lady Eunice against me."

She hesitated, and Niclas pressed, saying, "I would be deeply grateful, Miss Linley."

They were walking so slowly now, avoiding a return to Lady Eunice, that they had nearly stopped.

"Mister Seymour," she said with all seriousness, looking up at him. "Why do you want so much to go to Wales in place of his lordship?"

Niclas gazed into her lovely face and wondered, again, how he could possibly have avoided knowing such a beautiful woman before now.

"I cannot tell you, Miss Linley. Not now, leastwise, and I apologize for that. But I hope that I shall be able to do so before our journey is entirely done. If I have the honor of escorting you."

She smiled gently, in such a manner that Niclas suddenly felt short of breath.

"I should be pleased to stroll about the room with you, sir. I'm quite sure my aunt won't mind for, as she told you this morning, you and I share many acquaintances."

Niclas didn't smile often these days; it felt so strange to do it so easily now with her.

"Then, if you truly don't believe Lady Eunice would miss you for a little while longer, why don't we go and discover who they are?"

She made it so easy, Niclas thought later as they walked about the room. As long as her hand was upon his arm, he was able to force the emotions of others out of his mind and focus on his own thoughts. Just as he had been able to do before the curse had robbed him of peace.

Apart from that, Julia Linley was extremely pleasant company. She was intelligent and witty and possessed the kind of refined sense of humor that Niclas especially appreciated. And they discovered, as they moved from group to group, that they did, indeed, have many acquaintances in common.

After twenty minutes of polite conversation, Niclas returned Miss Linley to Lady Eunice's side. Bowing low, he apologized for their delay in returning, thanked her ladyship for allowing him the company of her niece for such a pleasant length of time, and asked if he might make amends by bringing them refreshments.

Lady Eunice eyed Niclas up and down, her expression very solemn.

"Thank you, Mister Seymour, but I believe you'll be far too busy for such minor activities as fetching drinks. How quickly can you be ready to leave for Wales? I should like the journey to begin no later than three days from tonight."

Fifteen minutes later Niclas was ready to thank his hosts and make his good-byes. First, he found Malachi, and pulled him outside to a quiet balcony.

"What the devil were you about on the dance floor?" the earl asked just as soon as they were safe from being overheard. "I was about to come and rescue you before Miss Linley took you in hand."

"Have you thought any further about why I can't feel her?"

Lord Graymar shook his head slightly. "I haven't really had the chance. I've been dancing, too, you know, and—"

"I'll be leaving for Wales in three days," Niclas interrupted impatiently. "I need to know before then whether we're related in any way, or whether she possesses some magic that we aren't related to or aware of. Can you find out for me?"

Lord Graymar's handsome face lit in a sudden smile.

"You did it, then. You convinced Lady Eunice to take a chance on you. Well done, *cfender*." He took Niclas's hand and shook it. "Now we must only hope it does the trick in clearing up your trouble."

"Malachi, this is vitally important to me. Can you find out about Miss Linley?" Niclas repeated.

"I shall do my best," his cousin promised. "But what's happened to create such an urgency?"

Niclas gave a slight shake of his head, still reeling from the discovery he'd made.

"I can't feel her at all—you already know that—but there's more." He lowered his voice slightly, and drew nearer to the earl. "When I danced with her, held her, my senses were all dimmed. I still felt the emotions of those around me, but it was as it used to be, and I was able to keep it all within my control."

Even in the darkness, Niclas could see his cousin's eyes widen with surprise.

"Are you certain? Perhaps you were merely confused by the music, or your weariness?"

"Entirely certain," said Niclas. "It all came shouting back at me the moment I let her go—then dimmed again when I took her back in my arms. Even her hand upon my arm had an effect, though much less so. Malachi," he said, gripping his cousin's arm, "you've got to find out why. No one among our relations, not even you, possesses that kind of power."

"No," the earl said slowly. "We don't. Certainly not when a blood curse is involved. I can't promise you that I'll have the answer before you leave for Wales, but I'll try."

Four

"This is ridiculous." Lady Eunice sniffed loudly and looked down her long, straight nose at the missive she held. "Of course you must stop for tea each afternoon." Frowning, she thrust the note back at her butler. "I'm surprised that any well-born gentleman would even consider forgoing so necessary a respite merely for the sake of gaining a few additional miles," Lady Eunice went on, turning to Julia, who sat across from her, pouring tea. "You will arrive in Wales in perfectly good time without making such sacrifices." She accepted the cup Julia held out to her. "Bring me paper, pen, and ink at once, Puckett, and tell Mister Seymour's boy to wait for a reply. I shall have it ready for him shortly."

Puckett bowed and quit the room.

"I'm sure Mister Seymour is merely anxious to make good time, Aunt," Julia said gently, setting the teapot down with care. "And I do think we should try to be sensitive to his feelings on the matter. He's already been so kind as to give way on so many other of our demands."

"Kindness has nothing to do with it," Lady Eunice said insistently, using a pair of delicate silver tongs to place a sugared tartlet on her plate. "Niclas Seymour may have the great calamity to be born of an unfortunate family, but he understands full well what society requires of him. If he didn't, your parents and I should never let you go for so much as a drive in the park in his company. Now," she poured a teaspoon of sugar into her cup, "you set your mind to the task ahead and let me take care of the arrangements. I promised your parents that all would be well, and that no reproach should come of the venture. Ah, here's Puckett. Very good."

All was silent while Lady Eunice wrote a reply to Niclas Seymour, save for Julia's absent stirring of her tea.

Her thoughts began to wander, in the quietness, as they had continuously done since the Dubrow ball. It seemed impossible to stop thinking of him, remembering his beautiful, expressive eyes and his wonderful face, the power of his arms as he'd gracefully moved her about the dance floor, the warm and subtle scent of the cologne he had worn. She had spent years wondering what it would be like to dance with him. Now she knew, and the reality made all her imaginings insipid by comparison.

"There," Lady Eunice said with satisfaction, drawing Julia out of her reverie. "This will suffice. He'll understand me perfectly." She folded the brief message and gave it into her butler's care. "Have it taken at once, Puckett. I shall expect a reply from Mister Seymour within the hour."

Julia sighed and tried to imagine how Niclas Seymour would receive yet another message from Lady Eunice. There had been so many over the past two days, since the

Dubrow ball, back and forth. He could scarce give answer to one of her aunt's demands before receiving another. She wondered if he wasn't now regretting his offer to accompany her to Wales, and wouldn't blame him in the least if he was.

For her own part, Julia could scarce wait to be away from London and her family's control. She had always believed that by the time she reached so advanced an age as five and twenty she would be allowed some small measure of freedom, but it wasn't so. Marriage might have afforded her greater independence, at least so far as a husband would allow, but spinsterhood, she had discovered, was a benign prison. Now, instead of pleasing a husband, her duty was to serve her family, and they were proving to be a demanding master. Julia was beginning to understand why her Aunt Alice had decided to remain in Wales following her husband's death. She was safe there from the intrusion of Linleys. Or had been until now.

Poor Aunt Alice, Julia thought. She had no expectation that family duty was about to be thrust on her, too.

"I've instructed Jane to pack your warmest garments," Lady Eunice said. "The weather is always uncertain in that heathen country—"

"It's beautiful there," Julia murmured, turning her teacup about in its saucer.

"—and you'll need to be prepared for any eventuality. How Alice has survived in that uncivilized wilderness all these years I simply can't imagine."

Julia smiled wistfully. "I should love to live in such a place. It's so peaceful."

"Don't be foolish," Lady Eunice chided. "You've no

time for jests. Now, you know what you must do, Julia. Your aunt will resist obedience, as she has ever done, but you must be quite firm."

"Yes, Aunt," Julia murmured obediently.

"I would have undertaken the task myself," Lady Eunice said, "but my sister has never been given to listening to me. Or to anyone in the family, for that matter. She's obstinate beyond all measure. Even as a child it was so."

"She's a Linley," Julia reminded.

Lady Eunice gave a shake of her head. "No, it's more than that. Linleys may be stubborn, but they are always loyal to family. Alice," she said tautly, "set all loyalty aside when she wed Hueil Morgan. But that faithless act will be as nothing should she be persuaded into taking Ffinian Seymour for a husband. It *must* be stopped, Julia. Set your mind to it—" she looked very directly at her niece "—and don't disappoint the family. No matter what is said or done, you must not fail us."

"I won't," Julia promised, slowly pushing her cup away. "And even if I should, Mister Seymour is clearly determined not to. We both know he won't leave Castle Tylluan until his uncle has agreed to leave Aunt Alice in peace. That's why you decided to let him accompany me."

"Precisely so," Lady Eunice agreed.

"Then all will be well, and there is nothing to worry over," said Julia. "And now, if you don't mind, Aunt, I believe I'll go lie down for awhile. I fear I'm still rather weary from Lady Beatrice's ball last night."

"Of course," Lady Eunice said more kindly as Julia stood. "It's an excellent thought. You must rest before tomorrow's journey begins. I'll have Jane wake you in an hour or so. We're promised for your sister's card party tonight."

"Oh, really, Aunt, must I go?" Julia protested. "I shall want an early night in order to leave on schedule in the morning. Mister Seymour insisted upon a timely departure. Surely Martha will have enough without me?"

"She was quite specific about your attendance," Lady Eunice said, "and I want your company, as well. You may sleep as long as you wish in the coach on the morrow. Jane certainly won't mind."

"But—"

"There is nothing to discuss," her aunt said dismissively. "Your sister is expecting you, and it's the least you can do for her. Martha serves a husband, and you do not. It would be unspeakably selfish for you to withhold from aiding her in that task. If that seems a cruel thing to say, and I grant you it might, you must take comfort in the knowledge that your family needs you." Lady Eunice helped herself to another tart. "That should more than suffice."

Julia nodded and silently left the room, knowing full well that her aunt only spoke the truth. She had failed to marry, yet her family still held her in esteem. At least so far as she was useful and fulfilled her duties as daughter, sister, and niece. And for that, she was thankful. She could have far more easily been sent to live in the country, in exile.

Yes, she was thankful. And she meant to be as dutiful and helpful as she possibly could. In the morning, she would begin the journey for Wales, and for Aunt Alice, in order to do her family's bidding.

"Gad," Niclas muttered, tossing the note on the desk. "How many does that make, Abercraf?"

"Today, both days, or this hour, sir?" the manservant asked calmly.

Niclas glared at him. "Collectively."

Abercraf was thoughtful, then replied, "Including the first one that came before you arrived home following the Dubrow ball, this makes thirty-four."

"Thirty-four!" came a surprised voice from the open study door, which had previously been tightly shut, for Abercraf, though occasionally sardonic, was never lax in his duties. But closed, or even locked, doors were not a problem for the earl of Graymar, who now stood in the room looking very pleased. He went where he wished regardless of such trifles. "I'm terribly glad that you took my place on this journey. I've forgotten how insistent Lady Eunice can be in the small details." He strolled forward, tugging off his gloves and placing them in Abercraf's ready hands. "I've come as promised. How do your arrangements proceed?"

"Slowly," Niclas said, briefly rubbing his eyes with both hands. Rising, he moved around his desk and toward a high table set with various glasses and crystal decanters.

"You may go, Abercraf. I'll pour his lordship a drink." He nodded toward one of the plain wooden chairs set in front of his desk as the manservant bowed himself out of the room. "Make yourself comfortable, cousin."

Lord Graymar eyed the chairs with a pained expression. "I understand why you have such Spartan furnishings, as they're easier on your sensitive nerves, but can't you keep at least one chair suitable for those of us who desire a bit more comfort?"

"No," Niclas replied shortly, turning to set a glass in his cousin's hand. "No colors, no patterns, no flowers or decorations. They drain whatever energy I have left when I come home."

"That's because you aren't taking your potion on a regular basis," said the earl, reaching into his coat to pull out a small stoppered bottle. "I've made an improved mixture to accompany you on your journey. I believe you'll find this more efficacious in repairing your energy and mental strength."

Niclas eyed the bottle doubtfully. "The last one worked better than I expected," he confessed, "but you know that the relief is almost too temporary to be of any great help."

"This one may do better," Malachi said. "Try it this evening when you give your body the rest it requires, as I'm sure you will do," he gazed at Niclas very directly, "and I'm certain you'll notice a difference."

"Thank you," said Niclas, moving back to sit in the large chair behind his massive desk. "Before we begin speaking of the protections you've brought, tell me what you've discovered regarding Miss Linley."

The earl of Graymar gingerly, and uncomfortably, perched upon one of the hard, unadorned chairs available.

"Unfortunately, there is very little to tell, save that we are not in any way related to the Linleys. Not distantly, slightly, or minutely."

"Could there be a crossing somewhere?" Niclas asked. "It seems impossible that none of the families in our union have never crossed with a family related to the

Linleys. Within so many hundreds of years, surely a match has occurred."

"Not that I can discover," Lord Graymar said. "And there's no other connection, either. I'm sorry, *cfender*, but I don't know why she possesses such mysterious powers. Did she appear to know she was affecting your senses?"

Niclas gave a shake of his head. "No," he said. "We even spoke briefly of the Theriots, and she merely appeared curious to know that the lauded Seymours are related to so infamous a family. If she knew anything of magic, I can't believe she would have evinced ignorance of matters that are elemental to us."

"It is unlikely," Malachi agreed. "Related or unrelated, we recognize our own kind. And there is this to consider as well. Unlike you, I have known Miss Linley since her first Season, and have danced with her any number of times, yet she has never had the least affect on my powers. Nor have I ever divined even a small measure of magic abiding in her, and that, as we have already touched upon, is one of my gifts."

"Then how is it that she has such a striking affect on me?" Niclas asked.

"I do not know," replied the earl, "but for that very reason, I've brought this."

He placed a small, red velvet pouch on the desk. Its shining golden pull-cords drooped to touch the dark, polished wood.

"What is it?" Niclas asked in a low voice.

"Only a quieting powder," Malachi replied. "Nothing more. Until we know whether Miss Linley is one of us or not, it will be safest to proceed as if she is not. You know that we cannot have an outsider discover too much about our kind. But if it should become necessary for you to reveal yourself to Miss Linley, or if Ffinian or our cousins should exhibit their usual lack of restraint in her presence, this will quickly correct the problem."

"A quieting powder," Niclas murmured, gazing at the elegant bag. "I believe what you mean to say is a forgetting powder. Isn't that what it truly is, cousin?"

"Call it what you wish," the earl replied with ease. "A quieting powder, a confounding powder"—he fingered one of the shining cords—"a forgetting powder. They all mean the same thing, in principle. I shouldn't think you'd want to quibble over the precise word. The outcome is what matters, not the means."

"But must it be a powder that erases her memory?" Niclas asked. "I have trouble envisioning Miss Linley sitting by without comment while I toss pink powder in her face. Or green or purple or yellow, or whatever it may be this time. Can you not merely resolve the matter as you usually do, once we've returned?"

"We cannot take the chance that she won't speak to someone during the journey. And never fear," the earl said, "she won't remember you tossing it at her afterward. And it's blue. I mixed it specially to match the color of her eyes."

Niclas stared at him. "Sometimes," he said slowly, "you truly terrify me." He picked the velvet bag up and tucked it safely into an inner coat pocket. "Is there anything else?"

"There's Enoch, of course, as we've already agreed. I'll bring him in the morning, ready for the journey. He's made the trip any number of times and could almost find his way blind. There's no need for me to remind you of his stamina and intelligence."

"Of course not. I'm honored to have the use of him. I only hope he'll accept me as a rider."

"For my peace of mind," said the earl, "he will. Niclas," he said, gazing at a collection of small white rocks that resided on a nearby shelf, "why have you not yet packed some of the stones?"

Niclas followed his cousin's gaze, and frowned. "I never carry them. It's too dangerous. Only imagine what an outsider would think if one should fall into his—or her—hands."

Malachi stood and strode to the shelf, scooping up three particularly small stones among the collection. "Nonetheless, you'll want to be sure to take these." He placed them on the desk in front of Niclas. "They're very handy on a journey. And they're far more useful than dangerous. I always have one in my pocket."

Niclas smirked and pushed the stones away. "Of course you do," he said. "I can imagine how easily the earl of Graymar explains having odd little rocks in his pocket. Especially when those same rocks do strange things that make more normal beings faint dead away. Please, Malachi, spare me your jests. I have too many trying matters on my mind at present."

"I'm not jesting," Malachi told him, and with his other hand rooted about in his coat pocket. After a moment he pulled out a smooth white stone. "There. This is the old one—given me by my father. You remember it. I have it with me always, in all company, even before the king."

Niclas gazed at the small object held out before him

with suspicion. Though it was daylight, he could see a faint glow against his cousin's palm.

"I don't believe you," he muttered. "You're not that foolish."

"Aye, that foolish at least, and probably far more," Malachi said. "Take them." He nodded at the stones upon the desk. "You'll be glad of their company before your journey is done."

Knowing he'd have no peace on the matter, Niclas sighed and reached to pick them up.

"Very well," he said. "I don't want you lying awake nights worrying about whether I've got pestilential stones, so I'll take them. But they are not considered protection, as per our agreement, so they'll be packed in the bottom of my trunk. Now, is there anything else?"

Lord Graymar sat again, serious now. "Aye," he said, his tone somber. "The most important protection that you must bear on this journey." He reached into his elegant black coat once more and slowly began to pull a strand of something golden out into the lamplight. "You will take this with you. There can be no argument. You *must* have it."

Niclas stared at the necklace in his cousin's hand, blinking twice before he comprehended—with a shock— what he was looking at.

Tarian, it was called. The Shield.

It was an ancient Celtic pendant, among the most powerful objects possessed by the Seymours. And as stunning as it was powerful, with a large, glowing stone set in the midst of an intricately woven medallion of gold. The stone was unique—to his knowledge there wasn't another like it—and mesmerizing to behold. It was principally amber in color, but upon close inspection the beholder could also see deep greens, reds, oranges and even a touch of purple glittering in its depths. Sometimes, beneath certain lights, the palette appeared to come to life, dancing and glowing like a merry fire composed of bright, many-colored jewels.

"Are you serious?" he murmured, then, realizing that Malachi would never make jest of so important an object, added, "Why?"

The answer was brief and sobering.

"Cadmaran left Castle Llew yesterday."

"Cadmaran?" Niclas murmured, feeling his heart turn over in his chest. "Is he heading toward London?"

Malachi nodded. "I can't be certain which roads he'll take, but if you should meet him, God forbid . . ."

"God forbid," Niclas agreed fervently. "Especially with Miss Linley in company. Malachi, you know very well that I'm a lesser wizard. The gifts I possess are useless against sorcerers such as you and the earl of Llew are. How can I protect Miss Linley if we should cross his path? My own life would be as nothing to lose, but my hope in undertaking this journey is to lift the curse, not cause greater harm. Especially not to her."

"That is the very reason why you must take the Tarian," said Lord Graymar. "I'd not let it out of Mervaille for any but the gravest need. If you should meet Cadmaran, it will be her only protection."

Niclas stared at the necklace as it swung gently in his cousin's grasp, its colorful stone glowing brightly in the room's simple light. He had seen it before, though not often, but had never actually touched it.

"I would almost rather lose the powder or one of the stones to a complete stranger than take something so incredible with me. If he should discover it, Malachi . . . if he should see her wearing it and find a way to take it . . ."

"It cannot be taken from the one who wears it, unless that one is dead," said the earl grimly. "It can only be willingly given. But if Earl Llew should meet you and find a way to use his powers on Miss Linley, and she is not protected by the necklace—"

"I'll take it." Niclas reached out and pulled the delicate gold chain from his cousin's hand. It was light, almost weightless, and yet he could feel a cool tingling in his fingers, evidence of the object's hidden powers.

"Miss Linley may or may not be related to us in some unknown manner, and therefore have some measure of immunity to the likes of Cadmaran," he said, "but that's not a chance I'm willing to take." Niclas lifted the necklace high and gazed into the stone. The light within flickered like an ember ready to burst into flame. He had to force himself to breathe slowly.

"What have I gotten myself into?" he murmured. He looked beyond the mesmerizing golden glow to his cousin's solemn face. "Is it going to work, Malachi? Will it be enough?"

"I've already told you that doing this thing for the Linleys is unlikely to be sufficient to lift the curse," Lord Graymar said. "But what it may be, if Cadmaran becomes involved, is far more dangerous than you or I or either of the Linley ladies could have imagined. Take no chances, *cfender*," he said sternly, "but every care."

"That I will," Niclas vowed, very carefully lowering

the golden necklace to the desktop. "I'll have Enoch and the Tarian, and the servants who are going with me are either of our kind or sympathetic to us. They'll be ready for the earl of Llew and his men, should they come upon us, and won't be shaken by the thought of his magical powers, great as they are. And," he added, "I have one other advantage that will prove helpful."

"What is that?" Lord Graymar asked.

Niclas smiled and replied, "Cadmaran will never be able to catch me sleeping."

Five

"Is Coventry much farther, miss?" Jane asked plaintively. "Will he let us stop soon?"

Julia smiled at her maid encouragingly. "We should arrive before too many more hours. Try to rest, Jane. I know it's been a long day."

Jane looked chagrined. Proper servants never complained. In fact, proper servants seldom spoke to their employers without being addressed by them first.

"I'm sorry, miss. Please don't tell her ladyship I've been so forward. It's just that my legs are aching something terrible, and except for when the horses have been changed—which you will agree, miss, has been scarce long enough for a swallow of tea, let alone a proper stretch—we've only had that one chance to step out of the coach today."

"And that was hours ago, and quite brief," Julia said sympathetically. "If we hadn't eaten as quickly as we did I almost think Mr. Seymour would have left without us."

"He does seem to be in such a hurry, doesn't he?" Jane sighed and rubbed her legs. "But it *was* thoughtful of him to have such a fine meal waiting for us at the inn, wasn't it, miss?"

"Most thoughtful," Julia agreed. "Mister Seymour has given consideration to our ease in every degree—save in the stretching of our legs. His coach is superbly comfortable, far nicer than my aunt's." She patted one gloved hand on the padded leather seat on which she sat. "And his servants are devoted to our care. The weather," she said, glancing out at the blue sky and white clouds overhead, "is quite fine, and if the arrangements made for us earlier are any indication of Mr. Seymour's consideration, we may look forward to spending the night in a comfortable inn. We really have very little to complain of, Jane."

"Yes, miss, I know that's true," Jane admitted, sounding both guilty and contrite even as she continued to rub her legs. "It's very wrong of me to complain, for Mister Seymour has been such a gentleman. And he even helped me out of the carriage when we stopped for our afternoon repast, which was so kind when his footman was there to do it. But my legs, miss—" She winced, and rubbed harder along the tops. "I'm having the most awful cramps. I don't mean to—"

Julia was already opening the nearest window. A cool, welcome breeze caressed her face.

"Mr. Seymour!" she called. "May I have a word with you?"

He was riding near the carriage and came up beside her at once, expertly guiding the magnificent horse he rode so that he could lean down to address her.

"Yes, Miss Linley?"

"I'm sorry to trouble you, but could we possibly stop for a few moments at the next inn? My maid and I should like to stretch our legs."

He frowned. "We've some miles to go before we reach Coventry. I'm afraid another stop may see us arrive after dark."

Julia smiled up at him with all the charm she possessed. "I don't mind in the least, sir. We feel quite safe in your company. Is there a convenient place to stop soon?"

The expression on his handsome countenance informed her that there was nothing in the least convenient in stopping before Coventry, but his voice was polite when he spoke.

"There's a village a few minutes farther with a respectable inn. I'll send my man ahead to reserve a private room and order refreshments."

"There's no need for you to go to any special trouble," Julia assured him. "We'll be content with a cup of tea in the common room and a few minutes to walk about. It's such a lovely day, and there's not any particular hurry to reach Coventry, is there?"

For a fleeting moment, he looked troubled, almost panicked, though she knew that was impossible. He wasn't the kind of man given to panic, regardless how long he'd been out of society. Whatever his emotions were, they passed quickly, and he schooled his features once more. "Not the common room," he said firmly, in a tone that she recognized as similar to one her aunt and parents often used, allowing no argument. "I'm afraid that's out of the question. Will half an hour's stop suffice? I hesitate to stay longer."

"Thank you, Mister Seymour, it will more than suffice."

• • •

The day had gone better than he'd hoped, Niclas thought, turning his attention away from Miss Linley's lovely countenance and back to the road ahead. Both Lady Eunice and Miss Linley had greeted him with smiles this morn, despite the early hour that he'd set for their departure, and thus far there'd been no sign of Cadmaran or his minions. Perhaps a brief stop wouldn't be amiss. They'd made excellent progress on the road, and even with a delay they should reach Coventry in good time.

Still, he'd not rest easy until he had Miss Linley safe at the inn where their arrangements for the evening had been made. The Tarian was heavy in his pocket—a constant reminder that Cadmaran might potentially appear along the road at any time. He had carefully placed the necklace in a velvet pouch that hung about his neck beneath his shirt, but the dratted thing kept showing up in his outer coat pocket, regardless of the number of times he replaced it in the pouch. It was Malachi's meddling, as usual, and Niclas was sure his cousin had a good, if ridiculous, reason for it. But having the Tarian in so vulnerable a hiding place only served to stretch Niclas's nerves on end. If it should fall out or be dislodged by the movement of his hand . . . His throat tightened at the thought.

Aye, he'd be far easier once they reached Coventry, and easier still when they'd crossed over into Wales. The roads wouldn't be quite so amenable to fast traveling once they passed the northern border, especially when they reached the hills, but there were protections in Wales that Niclas preferred to easy travel. He was nothing compared to Earl Graymar in the way of power, but all Seymours found welcome in the land that had been adopted by their ancestors so long ago.

"Ioan."

The footman stopped chatting with Abercraf, whom he was riding beside, and gave Niclas his attention.

"Aye, sir?"

"There's a village not much farther along, with but one small inn. The Hound and Hare, I believe it's called. Ride ahead and make arrangements with the keeper for a private room and light refreshments for Miss Linley and her maid. We'll stop for half an hour, but I don't wish to waste time waiting for any preparations."

"Shall I go as well, sir?" Abercraf asked. "I should be happy to make sure of the arrangements."

Niclas gave a nod of assent. Abercraf would have things well in hand at the inn by the time they arrived. If the keeper didn't hurry with his requests, the manservant would simply take charge of the kitchen himself.

"Yes, go with Ioan. We'll be enough here with Gwillem and Evar." He glanced up at the coachman and stableboy riding atop the coach. "And Frank and Huw."

Malachi had put the proper fear of Cadmaran into him the previous day, Niclas thought as the two men rode off, with the result that he'd brought two more footmen than they needed for mere comfort.

But despite the shadow of not knowing where Cadmaran might be, and the difficulties of the task ahead, it was good to be out of London. The day, as Miss Linley had said, was indeed fine, and all their company in good spirits. Even Abercraf was smiling and laughing—a thoroughly unusual occurrence. And Miss Linley's smiles had been so charming and pleasant that they threatened to make

Niclas's heart turn over in his chest each time he looked at her.

Her pleasant mood was understandable, of course. He'd be smiling like that if he were leaving an overbearing relative like Lady Eunice for a few days.

Adding to the journey's pleasure was Enoch. The noble beast was a wonder, scarcely requiring any guidance, for he seemed to know what his rider desired without signal.

Abercraf had everything ready by the time they reached the Hound and Hare, and was waiting at the inn's door as the coach pulled up to help the ladies alight. Ioan held Enoch's head while Niclas dismounted, and then led the proud beast away.

"I hope this humble inn will please you, Miss Linley," Niclas said, holding out a hand once she'd achieved the ground to escort her indoors. "It's a simple place but quite hospitable, if memory serves. I believe that you and your maid will be comfortable during our brief visit."

She gave him another of those dazzling smiles, and his heart emitted the now expected loud thump in response.

"It appears to be perfect, sir. I'm so thankful that you've agreed to stop. I confess I'm terribly thirsty."

He found himself smiling, too, into her upturned face. "You'll be glad for a cup of tea, then," he said, thinking once more how odd it was to have to discern her emotions from her facial expressions.

But that was dangerous, to assume that her expression told the truth of what her feelings might be. If he knew anything for a fact, it was that human beings constantly concealed their true emotions with smiles, scowls, or completely blank faces. They were masters of deception, and Niclas didn't blame his fellow beings a moment for it; he employed the same devices on a regular basis.

"My lord?" Abercraf called.

Both Niclas and Julia turned to find the manservant supporting Jane, whose current expression revealed precisely her emotions. Niclas felt her pain almost as keenly as she did, and hurried back to take her other arm.

"I'm terribly sorry," he said without thinking. "If I'd known just how painful your condition was . . . I should have felt it sooner, but Miss Linley was in the way, and I can't—"

He felt Abercraf's alarm before the manservant said, "Sir!"

Niclas ignored him and turned his attention to Julia, hovering nearby.

"You should have said something," he remonstrated. "We could have stopped much sooner."

"But you didn't seem inclined to stop," she said defensively. "We rushed so quickly through the horse changes and our brief meal that I assumed—"

"I do apologize," Niclas said abruptly, aware that she was perfectly in the right but distracted by both Jane's and Abercraf's strong emotions. It was difficult to manage so much silent shouting all at once. "You've nothing to fear," he said to Jane, "I'm not in the least angry, I give you my word." To Abercraf he added, "And you needn't worry so much. I only want to—"

"Sir!" Abercraf said again, much more loudly, gaining Niclas's full attention at last. "Miss Jane needs a slow walk to relieve her distress. Perhaps it would be best if you'd allow me to accompany her through the inn's garden, while you take Miss Linley indoors. We'll return shortly, well in time for Miss Jane to enjoy a cup of tea."

"Oh, no, I do think I should come with Jane," Julia said quickly.

"I'm fine, miss," Jane assured her, her face bright with embarrassment. "Please go with Mister Seymour and have your tea. Mister Abercraf will see me back safe, I'm sure. I only need a little walk."

Niclas reluctantly released the maid, knowing how distressed she was by his touch. The emotion almost overpowered the pain she felt.

"Perhaps that would be best, Miss Linley," he said, the sting of guilt making his voice tight. Regaining his composure, he offered her his arm. "Abercraf has matters well in hand, and the innkeeper is growing anxious." He nodded toward the inn's open door, where a tall, thin man stood rubbing his hands on a white apron. "We'd best go and relieve his mind."

The inn, Julia found to her delight, was both clean and well ordered. The innkeeper bowed them inside and she found herself in a large, cheerful room where several men sat near a fire, drinking and conversing. Some of them turned to look at Julia as she entered, their expressions changing from one of curiosity to interest. A few even smiled, and she heard Niclas Seymour draw in a sharp breath. The arm upon which she rested her hand swung suddenly and protectively about her waist, and he muttered something indistinguishable but clearly irate.

"This way, please," the innkeeper said, gesturing toward a set of open doors revealing an inviting private parlor where a hearty tea had been laid out for their pleasure.

Julia took a step toward the doors, but stopped when she sensed that Niclas Seymour wasn't behind her. Turning, she saw that he stood where he was, his gaze fixed toward the inn's far corner. Following the direction of his gaze, she saw what, or rather, who, he was looking at: a fair-headed young man sitting at a table alone, his head bowed, a tankard of ale at his elbow.

"What's the matter?" she murmured, turning back. His brows were knit together, as if the sight of the young man worried him. "Do you know him?"

"No," he said, his gaze yet fixed upon the lad. "No. I hope he'll . . ." He shut his eyes tightly and seemed to struggle, but the next moment was himself again. "Forgive me. My mind was wandering. Perhaps I needed this stop more than Jane did. Shall we go in?"

He accompanied her to the open doors this time, but she saw him glance back at the young man in the corner before they entered the parlor.

"How lovely," she said as she surveyed the pleasant room. Setting her gloves on the table beside her hat, she motioned to the delights set before them. "I realize that you would most likely prefer something else—gentlemen aren't usually given to drinking tea—but will you let me pour you a cup, Mister Seymour?"

He began to remove his own gloves. "Thank you, Miss Linley. That would be welcome."

The words were polite and expected, but he sounded as if he'd far rather go back to the inn's main room and join his servants, who by now were most likely enjoying a tankard of ale. But he'd not leave her alone in a strange place until Jane arrived, Julia knew, and as there was far too much food laid out for two mere women to consume, it only made sense for him to enjoy a part. Besides, she thought as he took his seat opposite her and received the cup she'd poured for him, tea would refresh him far better than ale. Not that she would have minded him drinking anything he liked, but he looked so weary and distracted that anything much stronger than tea might do him in altogether.

"Everything looks so delicious," she said appreciatively as she took up a plate to fill for him. "Abercraf is quite a wonder, isn't he?"

"Yes," he replied quietly. "A miracle, at times."

"There's a nice meat pie here—I imagine it's a specialty of the house for the keeper to have it on hand so readily—and a variety of cheeses. Cold chicken, bread, some lovely mince tarts . . . . it's enough for another full meal. What can I give you? Would you like a little of all?"

He assented with a nod and Julia gave him enough for two men. He began to eat with gusto, which didn't surprise her; he'd scarcely taken two bites when they'd stopped to eat earlier in the day. Niclas Seymour, she thought, seemed to be a man in need of a little managing. Abercraf clearly had his hands full.

"Were you born in Wales, Mister Seymour?" she asked conversationally, filling her own plate far more delicately. "Most of your family harks from there, do they not?"

"Yes, I was born in Pembrokeshire," he replied, taking a long swallow of tea and holding out the cup for her to refill. It looked impossibly tiny in his large hand. "At Glain Tarran, the ancestral estate of my family. Many Seymours are born there."

"Indeed?" she asked. "That's a fine, old custom to keep, I think. Linleys are the same, though Linley Manor in Devonshire is nothing to compare to so fine an estate as

Glain Tarran. I understand it's beautiful in every aspect."

His expression softened slightly. "It is. I'm prejudiced, of course, but I do think Glain Tarran the most beautiful spot on earth. I long to see it again."

"Has it been a great while since you've done so, then?" she asked.

He was silent for a moment, not looking at her, before replying, simply, "Yes."

"I should like to see Glain Tarran," she said, as lightly as possible. "I've heard so much about it. Some people even say that spirits and magical beings live there"—she smiled—"but that's foolish."

He smiled weakly in return. "Yes, quite foolish."

"Do you have a home in Wales, Mister Seymour? Your own home, I mean?"

"I do," he said with sudden and open affection in his tone. He sat back a bit farther in his chair, and his handsome features relaxed. "Tawel Lle. It was my boyhood home, and as dear to me, perhaps dearer, than Glain Tarran, though Glain Tarran holds a central place in the hearts of all Seymours."

"I can well imagine," she murmured, and felt a stab of the old infatuation in her heart. When he smiled he looked so much like his former self, so handsome and gentlemanly. "I know a little Welsh from the time I've spent at Glen Aur, my aunt Alice's estate, but I fear I don't know what 'Tawel Lle' means."

"Roughly, it means 'a quiet place,'" he said, looking a little embarrassed. "I inherited the estate when I wasn't yet out of university. It's not a large property, but the house is good—beautiful—and very comfortable. When I'm in London, I dream of being there, and when I'm there, I think of the day when I'll never again have to leave."

"Is it in Pembrokeshire?"

"No, in Brecknockshire, near the Brecons. It's not too far from Trecastle."

"The Brecons?" she asked. "How lovely it must be. Will you have more tea, Mister Seymour? These are such small cups that I fear you're hardly having a swallow with each filling."

"No, thank you." He pushed the empty cup aside. "Tawel Lle is in a valley, and, yes, it is quite lovely. A river runs nearby, excellent for fishing. And swimming, as well, when weather permits. There are many slow, deep areas."

"You can swim?" she asked, much impressed.

He nodded. "All Seymours swim. It's necessary for us to . . ." He stopped, looked away briefly, then continued in a more measured tone. "The mountains surrounding Tawel Lle are ideal for walking. I spent much of my childhood exploring them. I've often wondered at people saying there's not much to admire in the region, that the mountains are grand but plain. I've seen a good part of Europe in past travels, from the Alps to the Black Forest, but I've never yet seen anything to compare to the mountains surrounding Tawel Lle."

"You love Wales so much, then?"

"Far more than London, certainly," he replied, looking fully into her face for perhaps the first time since they'd entered the private room. "Oh, well, they're very different, aren't they? London is for society and family business. Tawel Lle is for pleasure, and for living."

Julia knew exactly what he meant. She hated living in London, too, but unfortunately had no private sanctuary to escape to.

"But the family name," she went on. "Seymour—it's not of Welsh origin, is it?"

He wasn't looking at her any longer. In fact, he was staring at the wall, a pensive expression in his blue eyes. "That foolish lad," he murmured. "His head is going to burst if he doesn't calm himself."

"Pardon me?" Julia asked, bewildered. She turned to look at the wall, too, and could only see a rather unskilled landscape painting hanging at a crooked angle. "Do you mean the young man who was sitting in the corner earlier? In the main room?"

"He's upset," Niclas Seymour said, his gaze narrowing with concentration. "He's filled with a terrible grief. The kind that drives all common sense away."

Julia slowly turned back to look at him. She couldn't decide whether to be amused or alarmed. Was he jesting? He appeared to be perfectly serious, but some people had odd senses of humor. Or perhaps he was far wearier than she'd imagined. Or . . . well, he certainly wasn't mad. He might have grown rather odd in the past few years since leaving society, but surely he hadn't become so altered that he imagined things.

She hoped.

"Mister Seymour?" He made no response. She spoke a little louder. "Mister Seymour?"

Startled out of his absorption, he turned back to her, staring as if he didn't know who she was or where they were. When realization struck, it was accompanied by dismay.

"By the rood, I am sorry, Miss Linley. Please forgive me. How thoughtless. Careless." He appeared not to know how to explain himself. "I'm not fit for society any longer, I vow."

"Please, sir, don't be troubled," she pleaded. "It's of no consequence. The young man did appear to be unhappy, from what I observed of him, and you were always a kind gentleman. I'm ashamed that I've not spared the poor fellow a second thought, when you've clearly had him in mind."

"Yes," he murmured. "He's definitely . . . in my thoughts. I'm sorry—what were we speaking of?"

"Your family name," she said. "I wondered if it was of Welsh origin."

"No," he said shortly, glancing once more at the wall before returning his attention to the plate he held. "The Seymours are of foreign descent. Wales has long been our adopted country, however, and so many generations have been born there that our distant origins have been nearly forgotten."

Julia's interest was piqued. "My aunt told me that yours is among the oldest families in England. If you are able to recall your lineage from before that, I confess it is something to be admired. From what country, then," she asked, refilling her cup, "do the Seymours originally hail? France? Or Normandy? Did one of your ancient fathers arrive with William so long ago?"

"I only wish they had." He set his plate aside and took up a napkin to wipe his lips. "My ancestors were exiles and wanderers, and cursed. There was no welcome for them until . . ." He sat up suddenly and turned to look at the closed doors. "Damn that lad," he said angrily, pushing to his feet. "He can't mean to be so foolish."

"Mister Seymour?"

"Please excuse me." He scarcely looked back as he headed for the door. "There's something I must tend to at once. Forgive me."

He opened one of the doors only to find Abercraf and Jane standing there, ready to enter.

"Oh, here you are," he said with relief. "Excellent. Be so good as to bear Miss Linley company while I—"

"Sir!" It was Huw, hovering in the background. "Forgive me, but one of the horses has lost a shoe. Frank Coachman begs that you come at once and tell him what you wish."

Niclas's distracted gaze moved from the couple before him to his stableboy to the young man still sitting in the far corner. "I can't come now . . . in a moment. Jane, I do hope you're feeling better. Come in and be comfortable. Abercraf, see that she has a proper tea. Excuse me, please."

"But sir, Frank says he must know right away whether you want to wait for the horse to be shoed or a new horse in its place . . ."

Noise and confusion, just as if every person in the entire inn, save Miss Linley, were shouting at him. Niclas had tried to explain it to Malachi, but it was truly impossible to describe. The innkeeper stood off to one side, alarmed, perhaps because of the situation with the horse or Huw's raised voice. Jane was both alarmed and afraid, Abercraf was concerned, the vast majority of patrons in the main room were filled with curiosity, and Huw was increasingly exasperated. Above all, the young man in the corner, who wasn't paying attention to any of them, sat head in hands, his tormented grief becoming almost unbearable.

Niclas had to force himself to focus on Huw's animated face—what else could he do when the lad was standing right in front of him?—and listen to what he was saying.

A horse had thrown a shoe. A decision had to be made. Frank wanted him. Now.

"I—"

Grief and pain made it impossible to think. He had a strong urge to bash the depressed young man on the head and make it stop before either of them did something unforgivable. And what was that coming from Abercraf now? It felt unmistakably like lust. For Jane.

God help him, that was just what he needed.

"Sir? What shall I tell him?"

Tell him? Niclas tried to think of what he wanted to do. The innkeeper's alarm was growing stronger. Not surprising given that one of his customers was standing like a complete fool, unable to speak to his own servants.

And then, suddenly, it was gone. All of it. Gone.

The tumult in his brain silenced, leaving only the sweet peace of sound in his ears. Normal sound, such as any man felt in a crowd.

"Tell the coachman that Mister Seymour will be with him in a moment."

It was Miss Linley. She was standing there beside him, touching his hand. Miss Julia Linley, whose emotions he still couldn't feel, had made it all go away merely by touching his bare hand with hers.

Niclas stared down at where her ungloved fingers rested

lightly upon his hand, and what he could feel—all he could feel—was peace flowing from her simple touch. He could actually feel it, though it was a physical sensation, not emotional.

"Will that be all right?"

She had been speaking to him, and he hadn't even heard her. Now he knew how closely they had to touch for her to give him complete peace—flesh upon flesh. Even in this simple manner.

"What?" he said stupidly, lifting his head to look into her eyes.

"I'll speak with the young man," she said. "You go and tend to the coach."

Now he could feel something—his own alarm.

"Speak to him? You? To a strange man? No, that isn't a good—"

"Please don't worry," she said reassuringly, patting his hand. Each release and touch was a striking contrast, from peace to clamor, silence to noise. His head was spinning with the fact of it, yet he couldn't fathom what it meant. This was magic, a gift, something akin to what he'd been born with. Surely it was proof that she was one of his kind.

But suddenly her hand was gone altogether, leaving him in chaos, and with a brilliant smile she turned and began to walk toward the grief-stricken lad.

Niclas reached out and grasped her by the elbow. Covered by the cloth of her dress, he found only that much dimmed relief that he'd known at the ball. And that was hardly enough to halt the surge of interest, admiration, and outright lust that he felt emanating from the male patrons at the inn, many of whom had fixed their gazes on Miss Linley's attractive person.

"Miss Linley, I must insist that you return to the parlor and finish your tea."

She kept smiling, but showed no inclination to obey.

"I shall be fine, I promise you, Mister Seymour. I know you don't wish to delay our departure, and to that end it makes more sense for you to attend to the matter of the horse."

"The horse will wait," he said sternly. "I can't have you speaking to strange men. Lady Eunice would have my head on a platter, to say nothing of my cousin, Earl Graymar, and I'd not blame either of them for it."

"They need not know," she said, then innocently touched his hand once more, plunging him into that delightful peace. "Trust me in this, please. I'm confident that I can handle the matter perfectly well. I have a gift with words—it's true, I assure you. And speaking to so young a gentleman can be of no consequence to my standing in society." She smiled that certain smile once more; the one that made his heart turn over. "I've already no chance of marrying, so there's no fear my reputation will be ruined by such small scandal. Go and reassure the coachman. I'm sure he's concerned about how best to proceed."

Yes, Niclas thought dimly as he—and the rest of those present in the inn—watched her walk away. Frank was worried, if Huw's anxiety was anything to go by.

He should go after her, he told himself, striving to push his own thoughts past the increased volume of emotions flooding at him. He should drag her back to the private parlor by force and have the innkeeper lock her in. But he couldn't. She had asked him to give her a measure of trust, and he couldn't find it in himself to deny the simple request, regardless of what his duty as a gentleman might be. He only prayed that Lady Eunice never heard of it.

Niclas turned back to Huw, whose worried expression perfectly matched his emotions.

"Take me to Frank," he said, "and we'll get this matter of the horse settled."

The decision was quickly made, though he understood Frank's dilemma in making it on his own. The horse was too good to leave behind, but waiting for the local village smithy to shoe it was out of the question. Ioan would remain behind while the rest went ahead to Coventry with the help of a rented horse, and would follow as soon as possible. Within ten minutes the arrangements had been made and Niclas anxiously made his way back into the inn.

And immediately grew angry. Far too many of the patrons were indulging themselves in strong admiration of Miss Linley, and worse. If their wives and ladyfriends could divine their feelings as Niclas could, those same men would shortly find their ears soundly and rightfully boxed.

But that, Niclas told himself, was a bit like the pot calling the kettle black. He admired Miss Linley, too, and far more than he should.

She was sitting with the young man in the corner near the fire, the gold in her brown hair shining and her lovely, smiling face lit by the flames as she spoke to him. The lad's grief, Niclas felt, was yet present, but surprisingly lessened. Julia Linley, it seemed, had not only told the truth about having a gift with words, but was a fast worker.

"Miss Linley," he said when he reached her side. He nodded at the young man—Niclas could see now that he was really closer to being a youth—who had looked up at his approach. Wonderment and a touch of apprehension mixed with the boy's pain, and Niclas strove to soften what he knew were his sometimes harsh features.

"Mister Seymour, I'm so glad you've come," she said, smiling up at him with real welcome. "Is the carriage waiting? I'm sure Jane will be ready to go by now. This kind young man has been bearing me company until your return. Mister Alexander Larter, this is Mister Niclas Seymour, of whom I was telling you. Mister Larter has a farm nearby," she chattered on pleasantly, "which he has just inherited. It's quite a large farm, and a great deal of work for him to manage alone."

"I see," Niclas said with a nod, taking the boy's hand in greeting as he politely stood. "You've no family to help you, then? No brothers or sisters? Your parents are both gone?"

The boy nodded and looked as if he might start to weep—again, Niclas noted, for it was clear by his reddened eyes that he'd been doing a good deal of it already.

"My mother died last year. I've just buried my father two days past." The last few words came out in a whisper.

So that was it, the source of his pain. But there was something more, too. Niclas could feel it.

"I'm terribly sorry for your loss," he murmured, taking the boy's arm and pulling him back down into his chair even as he, himself, sat, placing himself between Julia and the lad. "I perceive that your father's death has meant some trouble with your farm?"

"It's my trouble, sir," the boy said miserably. "I shouldn't be speaking of it, especially not to such a fine lady and gentleman. It's not right that you should even take notice of me."

He looked to be about seventeen. So incredibly young. Niclas had lost his own father when he'd been only a year older, and remembered very well how alone and bewildered he'd felt.

But the boy was calmer now; he was still filled with despair, aye, but not thinking of a way to end that despair.

Niclas tried to concentrate on this one person's feelings and not the myriad others tiding toward him. None of them was so important as this, or so desperate. He saw Julia's bare hands folded politely on the tabletop and longed to touch them and find peace.

Alexander Larter. Focus. He could help this boy. He could help to soothe the despair. If he could only focus.

And then he could. Julia had reached out to touch his hand in order to gain his attention, and before she could pull away he'd clapped his other hand over it, trapping her.

Her eyes widened a little, but she didn't try to pull away. Clearing her throat, she said, in the same light tone she'd used before, "Mister Larter has discovered that his father left his estate in debt. And he has no close relatives to turn to for help and advice. He's just this morning had to send away the couple who worked on the farm—an elderly couple who were very like family to him."

Julia Linley was a miracle, he decided, deeply enjoying the quiet that her touch gifted him with. She possessed the best magic he'd ever come across in his life—and considering his life, that was saying a great deal.

"It's a terrible shame, is it not, Mister Seymour?"

"Yes," he said, gazing into her lovely face and thinking of how pleasant it was to look at a beautiful woman and be able to concentrate solely on her without the usual distractions. "It is."

Her hand pressed slightly within his grasp, recalling him to his senses.

"Yes," he said more firmly, turning again to Alexander Larter, who had once more covered his face with his hands. "It is. Now I want you to tell me everything, Mister Larter. I have a problem at the moment, too, and I believe I may have a solution that will benefit both of us."

He truly was a kind man, Julia thought half an hour later as Niclas Seymour handed her into his carriage. He had managed the situation perfectly, making Alexander Larter believe that he would be doing him a great favor by accepting both his monetary assistance and the help of a few fine fellows who were in want of work in exchange for a roof over their heads and food in their bellies. She knew very well, of course, that Niclas Seymour would secretly be paying their wages. And he had insisted that the elderly couple return to Mister Larter's farm at his expense, as well, for all those fine young fellows would require a great deal of food and care, and someone must be there to provide it for them.

It had all been managed so quickly and easily that she was certain he must have done it many times before.

Her only question, which she kept to herself as she folded her skirts about her legs, was whether he always did so holding someone's hand as tightly as he'd held hers.

"We should be in Coventry before dark," he said before shutting the door. "Are you quite comfortable now, Jane? The pain is gone, is it not?"

"Oh, yes, thank you, sir," Jane replied, leaning forward to look him in the face. "I do apologize for the delay."

He smiled at her warmly. "Except for your discomfort, I'm glad of it," he said. "I would have spared you that, if I could, but I cannot be sorry now for stopping." He looked at Julia and held her gaze. "It was," he said, "quite an unexpected pleasure."

Six

"Is everything ready?"

"Quite ready, sir."

"Then I suppose we should go down."

"Yes, sir. I believe Miss Linley is waiting."

Niclas surveyed his image in the mirror, thinking back to the last moment when he'd spent so much time and care on his appearance. It had only been three nights past, before the Dubrow ball. It seemed like much, much longer.

He wished he possessed more modern clothes. Except for the one fine outfit that Malachi had sent him—which definitely was not suitable outside a formal setting—his wardrobe was years out of date. But that was his just due for growing so careless of what anyone thought of him. Now, when he cared too much, he had nothing at hand to impress the lone person whose good opinion he craved.

God help him, he was nigh on infatuated with the woman. Which was terrible. Unwise. Completely wrong in every way. But unavoidable. He might have been born into an odd family, but his heart was perfectly normal, and just as vulnerable and unruly as any other man's.

But it was harder for him, because even above her beauty and intellect and wit, which were sufficiently dazzling, was her ability to give him peace—something that no one had ever been able to give him before. Certainly no woman: other women filled his mind with their emotions, and his female relatives made him insane with their antics.

Julia Linley did neither. She was as clean and sweet to him as fresh air might be to a coal miner coming out into the new morning after hours of being entombed in darkness and dust. Even now he felt the anticipation of being with her again, of being in the company of a beautiful woman without having all her emotions distracting his thoughts. Just as other men did. She made him feel so . . . normal.

The question he still couldn't answer was, Why? How could she only be a Linley and yet possess powers akin to magical families? She would know—she must know—what her powers were. Yet she gave no sign of such understanding.

And there was something more. She had said this afternoon that she had a gift with words, and he had assumed that she'd meant in a natural, human sense. But now, thinking upon it, he wasn't so sure. Among his kind were those who had been born with the gift of persuasion; it was rare, granted, and usually only fell once in a generation, yet it wasn't impossible that she should possess such a power.

He'd seen her wielding it with Alexander Larter that very afternoon. She'd held the lad completely within her sway, drawing him out of despair and into hope. By the time they'd left the inn, young Larter had actually been smiling and making plans for his future. Niclas knew full well that the boy's transformation had very little to do with the small aid he was providing, and a great deal to do with Miss Linley's enticing speeches.

They had left the young man full of hope, while Niclas had been plunged into even greater bewilderment. Was he on a fool's errand? And what, precisely, was he getting himself into by becoming involved with someone who possessed unknown magic?

He was going to uncover the mystery of Miss Julia Linley now, before their journey continued, so that he would at least know what he was dealing with, and to that purpose, he had a plan. Not a very good plan, but a plan, nonetheless. He was simply going to ask her straight out whether she was of his kind. If she feigned shock, he'd know. If she *was* shocked . . . well, he had a plan for that, too. Thanks to Malachi and his forgetting powder.

"Do you have it, then?"

"Yes, sir. I have it here. Are you quite certain you wish to take it with you?"

Niclas looked at Abercraf's reflection in the mirror. He felt just how anxious the older man was, and was in complete sympathy with him. It was always a tricky business using one of Malachi's powders or potions in public places. Discovery by others at the inn would be disastrous; Niclas would probably have to toss powder at every single occupant in order to make certain no one could remember. Gad, what a thought.

"What I would like to do is throw it down a high cliff, or into a well, or out to the middle of a very large lake—but that would never serve."

"No," Abercraf agreed. "Someone would find it, I fear."

"*They* would find it," Niclas said. "Faeries. Or, worse, brownies. And then they'd tell Malachi, and I don't even want to think of what would happen after that."

"He is the *Dewin Mawr,* sir. The great sorcerer. They've no choice but to do his bidding. For my own part, I shall rest much easier once we've crossed into Wales, knowing they're keeping their eyes on us."

"They're not all to be trusted, Abercraf," Niclas warned. "Bear that in mind. Now, the powder."

"Here it is, sir."

Abercraf handed Niclas the velvet pouch, and they both gazed at it soberly.

"How much should I use?" Niclas asked. He had very little experience with Malachi's mixtures, excepting the potions he'd drunk since the curse, and no experience at all with forgetting powders. "How much will she forget? I don't want to erase her entire memory." He looked up at Abercraf, who only shook his head. "Why didn't I ask him for specifics? Oh, gad," he said as realization dawned. "I can't use it without knowing what the effects will be. The wrong dose and she might forget everything she knows—even her name." He held the bag back toward the manservant. "I can't take it. Put it away where it will be entirely safe."

Abercraf obediently took the bag, but held it back out to his employer. "I do apologize, sir, but I can't think there's any other choice open to you. If Miss Linley is, indeed, of magic blood, then all will be well and good. But if she is not, it will be even more necessary that she be made to forget. And consider, too, sir, that if she shouldn't be what you believe, she might very well become alarmed by the revelations you must necessarily make. We wouldn't want her fainting. Or worse."

"Aye, she might scream," Niclas said consideringly, then came to his senses. "No she wouldn't. Miss Linley is a calm and sensible young woman. Did you see her at the inn this afternoon? She didn't so much as turn a hair in dealing with young Mister Larter. No, our trouble with Miss Linley would be alarm and confusion, possibly trying to run away, but not fainting or screaming." He absently rubbed his forehead. "I don't think so, at least. Oh, very well, give the accursed powder back to me, then." He stuffed the pouch into a convenient pocket. "I shall both look and feel a fool trying to get it out without her seeing, should I need it, and only a complete boor would throw something into a lady's face. Especially a forgetting powder."

"I'll strive to remain in the room as much as possible," Abercraf said, reaching to straighten the folds of Niclas's cravat. "I would advise only a pinch to start. A small pinch."

"Yes, that seems best," Niclas agreed. "I suppose I can make additions if she appears to remember too much."

"And sir," Abercraf added more delicately, "there is one more subject that, though I am loath to mention it, I believe you must discuss with Miss Linley."

Niclas already knew what his manservant was referring to; he'd been trying very hard not to think about it since they'd left the Hound and Hare.

"I should never mention such a thing without very good cause, sir," Abercraf went on, "but you were holding her hand, in public view, for a great length of time and, although your reasons might be perfectly sensible to those of us who understand extraordinary powers, the common world views such matters with certain . . . expectations."

"God help me, I know."

Abercraf had understated the matter. For a gentleman of birth to be so familiar, in public, with a lady of birth was, in the eyes of the ton, the closest thing to an outright declaration of betrothal. Except far worse, for a betrothed couple possessed of even the slightest amount of good breeding wouldn't be so vulgar as to hold hands in a public place.

"I don't know what came over me to lose every shred of common sense in such a dismal manner. Not even the weariness can account for such a foolish lapse. I suppose she'll be expecting a proposal of marriage now."

For a fleeting moment Niclas tried to imagine what marriage to Miss Linley would be like, and was surprised to find the idea rather appealing. Unfortunately, unless he was able to lift the curse, marriage to anyone was impossible. He'd managed to maintain his sanity during three years of sleeplessness, but he could not forever stave off a slide into madness. Only a cruel or unspeakably selfish man would bind a woman to himself, knowing what kind of suffering she had to look forward to.

"Not if you can explain, sir," Abercraf said encouragingly. "Society may feel differently, but if Miss Linley is possessed of magic then she'll understand, and forbear."

"Yes," Niclas said, tamping down a sense of unease. "And if she doesn't possess magic, then what? Never mind." He cut the other man off impatiently. "Let's not delay the matter. Miss Linley must be wondering whether I've forgotten her entirely."

"Hurry, Jane," Julia pleaded. "Mister Seymour will think I've forgotten him. He must have been waiting for well over a quarter of an hour."

"I don't believe he's left his room yet, miss," Jane said calmly, deftly looping a few last strands of hair into a curl. "You have enough time to finish dressing."

Julia gazed at her reflection and felt, not for the first time that night, a stab of panic.

"I'm overdressed," she told Jane. "This is a very nice inn, but it is an inn, nonetheless. And Mister Seymour and I are not sitting down to a formal dinner. I'm terribly overdressed."

Jane smiled. "You look beautiful. Mister Seymour will be pleased."

Julia's face flamed red. "Mister Seymour doesn't care anything about my appearance."

"Every man admires a beautiful young lady, which is what you are, miss. And Mister Seymour has already admired you, if you will pardon me saying so, for I know it's not my place. But it's true, for all that. And he did hold your hand today. Her ladyship would have died on the spot to see it, but I thought it most romantic."

"Oh, dear," Julia murmured, and felt her stomach twist with nerves. "It did seem that way, but I promise you it was nothing of the kind. He seemed to need a measure of . . . support . . . and holding my hand appeared to help. I'm not entirely certain that he even knew what he was doing."

"I'm sure no one looking at the two of you would have thought wrong of it, miss," Jane said, fussing with the elegant lace on Julia's collar, "but I confess it did surprise me. I think he must be sweet on you, for no gentleman would do such a thing otherwise."

Julia's heart might wish that it was so, but her mind, as rational as ever, told her otherwise. He was drawn to her, she sensed, but not for any romantic reason. When she'd instinctively touched his hand this afternoon, he'd grabbed hold of her as though that connection had been utterly vital to him. And he had kept holding on to her until their conversation with Alexander Larter had come to a successful end. He hadn't even seemed to realize how inappropriate their situation was until Mister Larter had at last agreed to Niclas Seymour's terms. Then, when they meant to shake on the bargain, he'd stared down at their joined hands with something akin to horror, and had released her so quickly and with such stammering apologies that she'd felt as if she'd somehow been at fault.

Had she been? That was the question burning in her mind. Had she so desired his attention—even that simple touch—that she'd not pulled away or drawn his notice to the impropriety of even such innocent contact?

"Oh, lord," she murmured again. "I hope he won't be so foolish as to propose marriage. Not because of that."

"I'm sure he won't, miss," Jane said, "but if he should, I hope you won't mind me saying that I think it would be a lovely match. He's quite the handsomest gentleman, and so kind and considerate. He was so thoughtful about my suffering earlier today, and Mister Abercraf tells me that Mister Seymour is a very fine employer. I'm sure he'd make a fine husband, as well."

"Jane," Julia said reprovingly.

"Oh, I know I shouldn't speak so freely, miss," Jane admitted. "But you would make such a handsome couple—"

"*Jane.*"

Jane sighed and finished fussing with the lace. "Very well. I know my place, and won't say another word. But if he should ask, I do think you should at least consider it. Her ladyship and your dear parents would see you dead first, most like, but even that would be worth having a gentleman like Mister Seymour for a husband."

Julia didn't need anyone to tell her that; she'd known it since her first season in London. But the idea of Niclas Seymour wanting to marry someone like her was ridiculous. And that wasn't why he'd clung to her hand so firmly. She had no answers for that yet, but she knew that whatever his reason had been, love and desire had nothing to do with it.

"Do you find the soup to your liking, Miss Linley?"

"Very much." She glanced at him and smiled fleetingly, then turned her attention back to the bowl set before her. "The food is wonderful. And the inn is exceedingly fine. Thank you for being so thoughtful in our arrangements."

"There's no need to thank me," he said, wishing that both she and her maid would stop being so grateful. It was his duty as a gentleman to provide for guests, especially for a lady.

"I know," she said, as if reading his thoughts. "But I do, regardless."

Something was wrong, he thought, giving his own attention back to his soup. She was too quiet, too reserved, as if they were suddenly strangers. But that was impossible, considering the afternoon they'd spent together. They had shared an understanding, had helped that boy together. They couldn't go back to pretending that they were merely acquaintances journeying to Wales with a common purpose.

Or could they? She certainly seemed to be trying.

He wished that he could read her emotions for a few moments. It occurred to him how soft he was compared to other men; he had become far too dependent on feeling emotions in his dealings with women. He'd never really had to exert himself to understand the female mind.

Until now.

He didn't know quite how to proceed. Glancing at her, he saw that her expression was polite, void of any anger or coldness, but he knew that was the mask all those who were well bred put on to cover every emotion under the sun.

It had to be the hand holding. Either she was expecting him to propose or she was concerned that he would. If she was of his kind and already understood why he'd held her hand, then it was probably the latter—which, he admitted, wasn't a very cheerful thought.

"Miss Linley," he began, then stopped when Abercraf appeared to remove their now empty bowls. They sat in silence as the manservant expertly carved slices of beef and arranged them on plates, then set them on the table. Moving back and forth from the sideboard, he brought other various offerings for their consideration. Roasted potatoes, overcooked carrots, a fine Yorkshire pudding, and a slightly lumpy gravy to pour over it all. When their plates and glasses were filled, he bowed out of the room, leaving them alone once more.

Neither of them ate, but sat gazing at their plates.

Drawing in a breath for courage, Niclas tried again.

"Miss Linley—"

"Mister Seymour," she said, her voice shaking slightly. "I know what you wish to discuss, and hope that you will believe me when I say it's not in the least necessary. The circumstances that we found ourselves in this afternoon were most unusual and not entirely without strain. Mister Larter's situation was worrisome and both you and I were fixed upon solving his troubles. If you found some comfort and help by holding my hand, then neither I nor anyone else can argue with the rightness of it. There was nothing wrong or insulting in your behavior, and therefore no need for you to make amends or even to apologize. Please, I beg, let us put it aside and speak of other matters."

Resolutely, she picked up her knife and fork and gave her attention to her meal.

Niclas sat in stunned silence, simply staring at her.

She looked amazingly beautiful tonight, dressed in an elegant rose-colored gown that would have been well suited even for a ball. Upon seeing her, he'd felt the shabby condition of his own clothes even more keenly. And her shining brown hair, thankfully, hadn't been stuffed up into one of those awful turbans, but curled softly down about her cheeks, framing her elegant, elfin features in a most attractive manner. His gaze moved to her bare hands, busy now as she ate. They were small and delicate, utterly feminine, as she was, and yet they held so much power. There was no need for him to touch her now, for he was at peace with her, and Abercraf, serving them tonight in place of the inn's servants, knew how to keep his emotions calm and quiet so as not to distract his employer. Despite that, Niclas felt an alarming urge to touch her anyhow.

"I'm sorry," he said suddenly, surprised to hear his own voice. "I know you don't wish to speak of it, but there's something I must know."

She finally looked at him, fully in his face, and held his gaze. Slowly, the knife and fork were lowered back to the plate. Taking up her napkin, she dabbed lightly at her lips.

"Yes, Mister Seymour?"

He didn't know how to say it, how to ask the question without sounding like a complete fool. He was famous for his ability with words, but he'd never before had to speak on his own behalf. Sliding a hand into his pocket, striving to make certain she didn't see what he did, he curled his fingers over the velvet pouch. Something cold pressed against the back of his hand—the Tarian, which he'd earlier left safe in Abercraf's care. Drat the thing. Why couldn't it stay where he put it?

"I need to know," he said slowly, "about your gift."

She blinked. "My gift?"

Niclas drew in another steadying breath.

"Or gifts. There's no need for you to keep it from me, for surely you know that I'm of your kind."

It was difficult to read her expression; she didn't appear to be alarmed, but she didn't appear to understand him, either.

"My kind, Mister Seymour? In what way?"

In for a penny, he thought, in for a pound.

"In the way of magic. I was born with the power of perception. Of feeling the emotions of others," he clarified at her blank look. "Except for those who are kin to me. But you must know that already. Our powers and gifts don't affect our own kind. Generally. There are exceptions, of course."

"I see," she said, considering this for a moment before asking, "And you can't feel me? I mean, my emotions?"

He nodded. "But there's more to it. When we danced at the Dubrow ball, your nearness dimmed what I was feeling from those around us. And this afternoon, when I touched your bare hand, all outside emotions stopped for me completely. I was able to concentrate on Mister Larter's problems without being distracted by what those around us were feeling."

Her eyebrows rose. "Because you held my hand?" She looked at her hands with some wonderment. "*My* hand?"

"You find that odd?" Niclas asked, beginning to feel distinctly uneasy.

"I confess, sir, that I find the whole thing odd," she said, though she didn't appear to be in the least distressed by it. "I didn't know that I possessed any kind of . . . gift, did you call it? Are you quite sure that it was touching my hand that caused this wonder?"

"Yes." He looked closely at her. There wasn't any sign of guile; she appeared to be truly baffled. "Is this a surprise to you, Miss Linley? Did you have no inkling that you possess such powers?"

"Why, no, I haven't." She looked at her hands again, as if she weren't certain what they were. "I've never done anything unusual before. Not with my hands, at least."

"But you are aware of your other gift. The gift of persuasion? You mentioned it to me this afternoon."

She uttered a laugh. "I suppose that I am rather gifted in being able to persuade others to my way of thinking, sir, but I don't believe that could be considered anything extraordinary. It's a talent honed by managing my family through many failed Seasons."

Niclas sat back.

"But you used it on Mister Larter. I saw you with my own eyes. You persuaded him not to commit suicide."

"If I did, which I pray is so, it wasn't because of any special powers. I simply listened to him and then discussed the situation in a calm and reasonable manner. And, in all truth, sir, you had as much, if not more, to do with his change of heart than I did."

"But you *must* possess some kind of magic, whether you're aware of it or not," he insisted. "I stopped feeling all those emotions the moment I touched your bare hand. And I cannot feel you at all, which is very strong proof that you have magic in your blood. Even if just a little."

"I believe you must be right," she said, giving a little shake of her head, "for I'm sure you know of such things. But I certainly have no knowledge of it. I've never done anything magical before, and my family—well, you've met my Aunt Eunice. She's extremely practical, is she not? That's what Linleys are. Practical. Not magical."

Niclas stared at her.

Oh, gad. This was the worst of all possible outcomes. Julia Linley was a mystery even to herself. How on earth would he or Malachi or anyone be able to solve it if she, too, didn't know who or what she was?

But now she did know about him and all the Seymours,

and, though she clearly wasn't bothered by the discovery (a fact he was going to ponder later), he would have to make sure that such knowledge was erased. Carefully, hand still in pocket, he began to widen the loosely tied opening of the velvet pouch.

"Are you quite certain, Miss Linley?" he asked. "Can you think of no family member in recent—or even past—history who has, or had, a reputation for being . . . different? Some crazy uncle or odd aunt? A great-great-great-grandparent who's still spoken of as being a black sheep?"

But she wasn't listening to him. She had lowered her head slightly, her expression thoughtful.

"You said that you can't feel my emotions," she murmured. "Then that must be why . . . all those years—" Her brow furrowed and then, slowly, a smile grew on her lips. "Yes, of course. I'm sure that must explain it."

"Pardon me? Explain what?" he asked distractedly, concentrating on getting his too large hand inside the too small pouch without letting her see what he was doing. He forced his expression into a polite mask, while inwardly he was cursing the earl of Graymar for not putting the dratted powder into a more convenient container.

"Why you don't remember me," she said happily. "And why you never once looked my way during all those seasons."

Niclas wasn't paying attention. His fingers at last made contact with the cool, grainy powder. A tingling sensation coursed over his fingertips and spread up into his hand, heightening his anxiety.

"You danced with every other girl," she went on, looking at him so directly that he had no choice but to give her his attention. "Especially those who were usually ignored. But you never danced with me."

"What?" Niclas was caught off guard by her words. Never danced with her? When? He'd not even met her until a few days before. "I'm afraid I don't know what you—"

But he could say nothing more. A soft scratch fell on the door and in the next moment Abercraf entered, bearing a tray upon which several small bowls of condiments lay. He stopped briefly to survey the occupants of the room and, reading his employer's expression rightly, walked over to stand on Miss Linley's side of the table.

Niclas wished fervently that his manservant had chosen a better moment to appear, for he would have liked to know what Miss Linley meant by her last comment. Surely he'd never known her before their introduction some days earlier. He might have been distracted a great deal of the time during those years when he'd gone out in society, but he hadn't been blind. Never would he have forgotten having seen a woman as beautiful as Julia Linley.

"Miss?"

Abercraf lowered the tray, and Julia gave her attention to it.

"Miss?"

She blinked. And tried to focus.

Where was she?

"Are you all right?"

"Yes, I . . . forgive me." She looked about to find that she was sitting at a table set with what looked to be dinner. Niclas Seymour was sitting to her left, and his manservant was standing on her right. They were both peering at her anxiously.

"I'm terribly sorry," she said, feeling unaccountably foolish. Had they been eating? Conversing? She couldn't remember. The food on her plate appeared to be as yet untouched, but she couldn't even remember sitting down to it. Or being in the room. Or much of anything beyond arriving at the inn some hours earlier. Everything past that was a blur.

"Did I faint?" She set a hand to her head and shut her eyes, striving to make sense of her surroundings. "I must be more weary than I imagined. I'm so very sorry."

"Fetch a glass of sherry for Miss Linley," she heard Niclas Seymour command sharply. "At once."

"No, thank you," she protested, though Abercraf moved quickly to fulfill his employer's bidding. "I'm sure I'll be fine. I don't know what came over me. You must forgive me." She didn't think she'd ever felt more embarrassed, or baffled, in her life.

"Please stop apologizing, Miss Linley," Mister Seymour said. "There's no need. If anyone should apologize, it's I. The fault is mine entirely."

Dropping her hand, she opened her eyes and looked at him, just as Abercraf returned from the sideboard bearing a small glass of sherry.

"It isn't," she said. "You're very kind, sir, but I can scarce allow you to take the blame for my own human frailty. It's not as if you poisoned the food." She smiled, and was disconcerted to see him grow pale and rather alarmed.

"I'm fine now," she assured him quickly. "Just a little weary, that's all. Thank you," she added, accepting the glass that Abercraf insistently held out to her. She took a small sip to mollify him, then set the glass aside and straightened. "Well, let's put the unfortunate occurrence aside and enjoy our meal. It does look delicious."

"Are you sure you wish to do so?" he asked, concern yet stamped on his handsome features. "Would you perhaps prefer to return to your room and rest?"

"Yes, miss, that might be best," Abercraf agreed, still hovering over her. "You do look pale."

"Very well," she said slowly, still trying to put her muddled senses in order. "Perhaps you're right."

Niclas Seymour stood and helped her to her feet as Abercraf carefully pulled out her chair.

"Please allow me to escort you, Miss Linley." He offered her the steadying comfort of his strong arm, which she gladly accepted.

"I'll prepare a tray with dinner and bring it shortly," Abercraf promised as they moved to the door. "I do hope you'll feel better in the morning, miss."

Niclas Seymour half escorted, half carried her up the stairs, clamping his own hand over the one she held on his arm and walking so closely to her that she could feel his warmth.

It was a narrow staircase, and he was so much bigger than she that she was obliged to bump up against him every step or so, his firm grip making it impossible for her to move even a polite distance away. To her shame, she discovered that she didn't particularly want to.

His body was hard and masculine—Julia had never been so close to an unrelated man before, not even when dancing—and he made her feel safe and protected. An unaccountable flush of heat suffused her limbs, and she was thankful that the dimness of the stairs and hallway hid her face, which was probably as red as a beet.

What on earth was wrong with her?

"You must instruct Jane to prepare your bed right away," he said. "A good night's sleep is what you need. Are you quite certain you feel all right? Does your head ache? Your eyes?"

"I'm fine," she assured him. "Please don't worry over me."

They stopped at her door, and with gentle care he turned her to face him.

"Miss Linley, please tell me. What's the last thing you remember?"

"About dinner, do you mean?"

"No, I mean . . . do you know where you are?"

He had such wonderful features, she thought, gazing up into his blue eyes. And he looked so terribly tired and worried. She longed to reach up and touch his cheek, to soothe his fears away.

Instead she smiled and nodded. "We're at the White Horse in Coventry. We left London this morning, and tomorrow we should be in Wales. The day after that we hope to achieve my aunt's estate."

He released a taut breath. "Thank a merciful God for that."

"Please don't worry, Mister Seymour. I'm fine. But I do thank you for your concern. And I apologize again for ruining your dinner."

He gazed into her face, his expression inscrutable.

"You didn't ruin my dinner, Miss Linley. Not in the least. I'll bid you good night. Abercraf will be here soon with a tray. Sleep well. And have no worries over our journey on the morrow. We'll go in easier stages and have longer stops so that both you and Jane will be quite comfortable."

"But I don't wish to delay our journey," she told him. "Achieving Wales and my aunt's estate is of the greatest importance. Jane and I will hold up much better tomorrow, now that we've had our first day on the road."

"We'll reach Wales in good time," he said in reassuring tones. "As long as the weather doesn't turn, we shall make excellent speed on good roads and find ourselves safe in Wales long before nightfall. So you must be easy on that account above all things. I do hope you'll sleep soundly, Miss Linley."

He was so close to her that she almost thought he might lean down to kiss her cheek—or perhaps even her lips.

"Good night, Mister Seymour," she said nervously, embarrassed at the wobbly sound of her own voice. "I shall sleep very well, and wish you the same."

She moved to open her door, but he stopped her before she could do so, grasping both her hands and raising them to his lips. He kissed the tops of her fingers, lightly, and then released her and stepped back.

"Good night," he murmured.

Niclas stood where he was until she went into her room, and even after she had closed her door he remained, listening to the faint sound of the women's voices as she and Jane spoke. Soon, he thought, she would begin preparations for bed. Jane would help her to remove her clothes, and then she would brush out her mistress's long hair, and, finally, Julia Linley would lie down upon a soft mattress, a soft pillow, and close her eyes and drift into a deep and blessed sleep.

He hoped it would be pleasant and dreamless; a dark, peaceful slumber to refresh body and soul.

Abercraf's footsteps called him to his senses, and Niclas looked up as the other man appeared, bearing the promised tray. He looked at his employer inquiringly.

"I'm going out," Niclas said. "I'll use one of the other horses, for I doubt Enoch will want to be called upon to suffer my foolishness."

"But sir, it may seem very odd to the innkeeper and the other guests for you to leave the inn at this late hour. And you've had a long day. Do you not think it might be best for you to lie down even for a few hours?"

"Not tonight," Niclas said. "Don't worry about my cape and hat. I'll fetch them before I go out."

"But sir," Abercraf protested again as Niclas began to walk toward the stairs. "I feel quite certain that Lord Graymar would wish you to take your potion and—"

"Not tonight, Abercraf," Niclas repeated as he began to make his descent. "Don't wait up for me. I'll be back in time for you to make me presentable for breakfast."

Seven

It rained the next day. All day. In truth, it poured. Relentlessly.

The roads had turned to mud, making progress slow at best and impossible at worst. Niclas had lost count of the number of times that he and the footmen had had to dismount and push or pull the coach out of a rut.

He was soaked to the bone, along with the coachman, stableboy, and footmen. Abercraf, wiser than they, had pleaded his delicate health and joined the ladies inside the relative comfort of the coach.

"Delicate health," Niclas grumbled, glaring at the curtained coach door, where he envisioned Abercraf warm and dry, enjoying the pleasant company of the two women. "He's never been sick a day in his life, the damned liar."

It was most unusual for an unrelated man, to say nothing of a servant, to ride in an enclosed carriage with a female of high birth, but Abercraf had looked so pathetic, and Miss Linley and her maid had pleaded so on his behalf, that Niclas had allowed it—on the strict promise that Lady Eunice was never to find out. Besides, Niclas had reasoned that morning when they'd first set out, the rain would let up soon, and then Abercraf would be back on his horse.

But that had been eight hours ago, and with the increasing darkness Niclas finally had to admit defeat. The rain wasn't going to stop, Abercraf wasn't going to get on a horse that day, and they weren't going to reach Wales that night. If they simply achieved Shrewsbury without damage to the coach, he'd be the happiest man on God's earth. Already he was dreaming of a hot bath, dry clothes, a warm fire, and a good, hot meal. Such luxuries could never replace the benefits of slumber, but they would help to take the edge off his weariness—which had been made worse by both today's endless rain and the long night of riding that he'd undertaken in an effort to empty his mind of memories.

He was filled with self-loathing for what he'd done to Julia Linley the night before. He couldn't forgive himself. She'd been so trusting, had spoken to him so freely. She hadn't even evinced any of the alarm or disgust that he'd expected when she'd learned about the Seymours and their odd ways. And about him. Then Abercraf had distracted her and Niclas had thrown a pinch of powder at her. It had sparkled and fizzed like all of Malachi's mixtures did . . . and then, even before she could so much as blink, she had frozen, as still as a statue, staring at nothing, utterly silent.

He'd been terrified that the pinch had been too much, and even more terrified that it had been too little. If she turned to him of a sudden and asked him what on earth he'd done, he'd have no answer. But long seconds passed and she stayed as she was, immobile, silent.

"Julia." He'd heard himself saying her name, but had scarcely recognized his own voice.

She didn't respond. It took Abercraf's firmer tone to bring her back. And then she'd been so innocent and completely unsuspecting of what had been done to her that Niclas had absolutely hated himself.

The fierceness of the emotion still surprised him. He cared for Julia Linley—regardless of how foolish it was. He wanted desperately to keep her safe. Yet the very person she needed protection from was him.

A clap of thunder overhead heralded a fresh, heavy downpour, and Niclas closed his eyes with resignation as new streams of water poured over him. It wasn't unlike standing under a waterfall. He had probably never been, or would be, so well washed in his life. Over the sound of the rain he heard a now familiar thud, and with a sigh looked to see that the coach had once again come to a halt at a somewhat tilted angle.

Another rut. God help them.

He pulled the ever-patient Enoch to a stop and slowly dismounted, and saw Ioan, Gwillem, and Evar doing the same. They didn't say a word as they took their places around the heavy coach and, waiting for Frank the coachman's word, pushed. Niclas wasn't always glad to be a wizard, even a lesser one, but one thing he had often been thankful for was the ability to tap into supernatural strength when necessary. He did so now, just as he had at all the previous ruts that had snagged a coach wheel, and with relatively easy effort the four men pushed the coach free. If it wasn't such a wet, muddy task, Niclas wouldn't have minded it so much.

"Thank God that's done," Niclas muttered, trudging through the mud to reach one of the coach's windows. Miss Linley was already rolling it down.

"Oh, dear, I'm so sorry. I do wish you'd let us step out to make the load lighter."

With water pouring over the brim of his hat like a small river, Niclas felt rather silly saying, "Not in this weather, Miss Linley." He'd said the same thing after each of the last ten such stops, and imagined she was growing as weary of it as he was. Polite society demanded such niceties, but Niclas was just about ready to condemn all niceties to eternal damnation. What he really wanted to say to her was more along the lines of, "I don't mind you ladies staying in the coach, but kick that blasted manservant of mine out here where he belongs, suffering with the rest of us."

Instead, his upbringing reared its prominent head and caused him to add, "We should reach Shrewsbury soon. We'll stop there for the night."

Even through the veil of water pouring down he could see her pretty features fill with worry and regret.

"We won't be able to reach Wales, then? I'm sure it can't be helped, considering the weather, but I know it isn't what you had planned. Please don't worry over the matter, Mister Seymour. It will be wonderful to be out of the rain."

"Yes," he replied with complete honesty. "It will. I hope you're comfortable?" Another clap of thunder obliged him to shout the rest. "I apologize that we've not been able to stop for you to stretch your legs today."

"Oh, no, we're fine," she shouted in return, and even so he could scarcely hear her. The wind had begun to gust, as well. "Mister Abercraf has shown Jane a simple exercise to perform whenever she feels a cramp coming on. It's been most effective." She smiled. "And he's been keeping us so well entertained that we've not even noticed the hours passing by."

Peering into the dimness of the coach, Niclas could just make out Abercraf's smiling face.

"I can well imagine that he has," he said irately, then gave Julia a slight nod—which sent even more water pouring off the brim of his hat—and strode back to where Enoch stood waiting.

"Ioan!" he called as they set out once more.

"Yes, sir?"

"Ride ahead to Shrewsbury and find an inn to lodge us tonight. With this weather every traveler on the road has probably sought refuge there. Do your best to find a reputable house and make arrangements for our arrival. I want a hot bath, and I'm sure Miss Linley will want one, too."

Ioan nodded and rode off into the downpour, his tall figure quickly lost in the day's gray darkness.

It was another hour, and two more ruts, before they at last achieved Shrewsbury. Ioan met them on the road outside the town with dismal news: there were no proper rooms to be found anywhere. Only one inn, the Blue Hind, was a potential place of refuge. The innkeeper there had offered them the use of his common room for the night. They would have to sit with those other unfortunates who couldn't find lodging in the town, but at least they'd be warm, dry, and well fed.

"We shall see whether the keeper can be called upon to provide something more with a little encouragement," Niclas said, "at least for Miss Linley and her maid." Almost any innkeeper, he'd discovered in his travels, could suddenly find an available room if generously persuaded to look again.

The Blue Hind was a large, well-maintained coaching inn. It wasn't the sort of place Niclas was used to stopping at, especially not in Shrewsbury, which boasted several finer establishments for wealthier patrons, but he had no doubt it would be comfortable enough for their brief stay.

As they entered the courtyard Niclas felt a sudden stab of something akin to unease. He tried to push the sensation aside, but the warning was too strong. As the coach and the others rode in, he pulled Enoch to a halt and paused to take a good, long look at the inn, trying to put a name on what he was feeling.

Surely it was merely the strangeness of the place and the long weariness of the day that gave him such a sense of foreboding. He could see nothing wrong with the place, at least not from outside.

But he was more tired than usual and wet. His mind often played tricks on him when he'd forgone such rest as he was capable of. Giving himself a firm mental shake, Niclas spurred Enoch onward, following the coach to where it had come to a stop.

By the number of horses and carriages standing in the yard waiting to be stabled, and from the loud, boisterous noises emanating from the inn, it was clear that the establishment was not only crowded, but overflowing with humanity. The prospect of securing a room was daunting, but not impossible. Niclas would have to call upon every ounce of persuasion he possessed—or perhaps even let Miss Linley have a go at the innkeeper. He doubted any man could deny whatever she requested of him.

Dismounting, he gave Enoch's reins into Ioan's waiting hands, then moved across the courtyard to open the coach door.

"I'm sorry that you must come out in the rain," he shouted over the din coming from the inn's entryway. "I'm afraid there's no other choice. Cover yourselves as best you can."

Miss Linley already had the hood of her cloak over her head. Setting her hand in his, she let him gently pull her forward.

"As my dear aunt would say, Mister Seymour, 'A little rain won't hurt us.' "

"I wish it was just a little," he said as she stepped into the downpour. Sheltering her with his cape, he hurried Julia toward the now open door, where the innkeeper stood to welcome the latest arrivals.

But just before they reached him—only a few steps away—Niclas came to a sudden halt.

Something *was* wrong.

Terribly, horribly wrong.

He could feel it as if it were a wall standing before him, warning him to turn back, to get as far away as possible. Closing his eyes, Niclas stuggled to make sense of it. This wasn't merely emotion he felt, but something far more . . . What?

Rain poured down with furious noise, thunder sounded in the distance, and Miss Linley, getting soaked, asked with concern, "Mister Seymour? Are you all right?" Behind him

Abercraf and Jane murmured with veiled indignation—
they couldn't go inside until their employers did, but they
didn't at all like having to stand behind them in the rain.

Niclas opened his eyes to see the innkeeper staring at
him with a look of apprehension. What kind of man
would stop in that kind of rain, forcing both a high-born
lady and everyone else to stand there, too? If Niclas had
hoped to have any influence over the fellow at all, it was
rapidly dissipating.

He had to make a choice, stay or go, else lose any
chance they had of finding a refuge for the night.

Every instinct told him to turn around and leave, but
reality—and the rain—won out. Niclas stepped forward.

The innkeeper was a pleasant fellow and eager to
please an obviously wealthy patron. Unfortunately, he assured Niclas as they made their way into the warmth,
crowds, and noise of the inn, finding a room even for the
young lady and her maid would be quite impossible. They
would simply have to make do with the common room.

"We'll discuss the matter in a moment," Niclas said,
shepherding Julia protectively to the nearest quiet spot.
"For the time being, be so good as to procure a private
parlor for Miss Linley to rest in."

"There are none left, sir," the innkeeper said. "What
with the rain, and all the coaches unable to—"

"I want a private room for Miss Linley," Niclas said in
a quiet but firm tone that didn't allow for argument. He
turned to stare very directly at the man. "It must be clean
and comfortable and quiet. I don't care if it's one of the
maids' rooms or even your wife's room, just so long as
Miss Linley may warm herself and take some manner of
refreshment."

The innkeeper paled. "Yes, Mister Seymour. I think I may be able to find something suitable. Only give me a moment, please." Bowing, he hurried away into the noisy common room.

A few moments later he returned, bowing again.

"We are most fortunate, sir," he said, breathing rapidly, his pleasant face flushed with success. "Another patron, a very fine gentleman, has kindly given up the private parlor he and his company had reserved. They've already moved into the common room and one of my girls is clearing their meal away. It will be ready to receive Miss Linley and her maid shortly. Shall you wish to join Miss Linley there for dinner, Mister Seymour? My cook has some fine chickens roasting on the fire."

It was all quickly settled. Niclas followed the innkeeper to the parlor, inspected it, and when he was satisfied, he saw that Miss Linley and Jane were comfortably settled before a fire with a promised light tea on the way. Dinner was to be served in an hour, giving both Miss Linley and her maid and Niclas and his men time to warm and dry themselves as best they could. Until then, Niclas intended to secure a room for Miss Linley to sleep in for the night, no matter how much it cost him, and then find the gentleman who'd vacated the parlor and properly thank him.

But first, he wanted dry clothes, and the innkeeper had kindly offered—for a small fee—the temporary use of his own private room in order to change.

It was wonderful to strip off his soaking garments and be warm and dry. Abercraf shook the folds out of a freshly unpacked coat and held it out for Niclas to slip his arms into.

"Thank a merciful God," he murmured, feeling comfortable for the first time in hours. His bones were yet cold, but they would warm soon enough before the common room's great fire, and after a pint or two of ale.

Since the day had been almost entirely miserable, Niclas felt that he and his men deserved a pleasant night. If they must spend it in the common room, then they would make the best of it. The noise from those currently assembled there sounded inviting enough, and he had no doubt they'd find amiable companions to pass the long night with. His mind would be under chaotic assault, but being in the company of a group of merry, half-drunk or even completely drunk men was a much easier thing to do than spending an hour in the presence of sober, scheming, conniving members of high society.

"Do you want this, sir?"

Abercraf had gone through the pockets of Niclas's wet jacket and pulled the Tarian out into the light.

For once, Niclas was glad to see it. That strong sense of danger was with him still, and even if it proved to be nothing more than the product of his weary mind, he wanted to be prepared.

"I'll feel better having it with me than packed away anywhere at this inn."

"Yes, sir." Abercraf stepped back to survey his employer's appearance, clearly satisfied with what he saw. "Shall I send the men in to change, sir?"

"Yes," Niclas said, shoving the Tarian into a safe pocket. "Tell them to be quick, lest the innkeeper lose charity with us. I'll go thank the gentleman who gave us the use of the parlor and make arrangements for you and the men to dine in the common room."

The inn was a riotous mixture of sound and noise as Niclas stepped out of the innkeeper's private enclosure and into the inn proper. Even more customers had arrived to seek refuge from the pouring rain; noblemen and ladies as well as common folk who'd been traveling on the public coaches. There was so much smoke in the air from both pipe and fire that his eyes burned, and he strode toward the open courtyard doors to draw in a breath of the fresh, damp air.

He stood there a long moment, staring out at the rain and letting the fitful breeze push at him. It was so pleasant and peaceful; the calm before the storm that awaited him inside.

And then, suddenly, he shook off his agreeable lethargy and attended to the warning bells that had begun to clang ever louder.

"Julia," he murmured, stiffening.

Turning, he pushed his way into the depths of the inn, toward the private parlor where he'd left her, shoving everyone in his way aside.

But he knew, even as he reached the door, that he was too late. The suspicion that had been growing in him since they'd arrived at the Blue Hind was real; he'd simply not wanted to accept it.

Niclas didn't even bother knocking, but thrust the door open.

And he was there, just as Niclas had known he would be, standing near a chair where Julia sat, but filling the room with his presence and power.

Morcar Cadmaran. The earl of Llew.

He was a tall man, powerfully built, intimidating. As dark as the earl of Graymar was light and fair, Cadmaran's hair and eyes were a deep and unfathomable black, so incredibly black that there wasn't a shade dark enough to describe them.

Niclas had only spoken to him twice in his life; once when they were both boys, and once as men. Both times he'd come away more than a little thankful that the only member of the Seymour family who had to constantly worry about that kind of evil was Malachi.

The earl of Llew. He wasn't the most powerful sorcerer in England—the earl of Graymar held that title—but he wanted to be.

"Julia," Niclas said breathlessly, moving toward her. She didn't move, didn't respond to the fact that he'd been so reckless as to call her by her Christian name. She was staring at Cadmaran, her expression completely blank. Jane, her maid, was doing the same on the other side of the room.

The door, which Niclas had left open, slowly swung shut of its own accord. A soft clicking sound gave evidence to the lock being engaged.

"I've been wondering when you'd make an appearance," Lord Llew said, turning from Julia to face Niclas. "I very nearly sent the innkeeper to fetch you, but it seems that your once famously facile brain began working at last. It appears that the rumors about the curse addling your wits are at least partly true."

Drawing up to his full height, he was even more imposing, and Niclas scowled to find himself looking up at the man. A tall man himself, he wasn't used to being in such a position.

But Cadmaran was more than simply abnormal in height. He was an arresting figure in every way, strikingly handsome, irresistibly charming, inhumanly compelling. Niclas wasn't afraid for himself, but for all those who were traveling with him and under his care. Niclas was a wizard, but, like other dark-haired Seymours, the powers that he had been born with were more intellectual than physical, excepting his strength and the ability to move very quickly. Apart from these, he possessed none of the magic that could help him overcome a sorcerer of Cadmaran's might.

"They've done nothing to you," Niclas said. "They're not Seymours. Nor are they from any of the Families, and you know what the rules we abide by say about using magic on humans who've brought us no harm. Release them."

Lord Llew laughed in a low, amused manner. "You wish to lecture me on rules?" he asked with a touch of sarcasm. "A cursed Seymour—pardon me, a *blood*-cursed Seymour—advising me on how to behave. How droll. You must forgive me, sir, if I decline to take your advice. As to Miss Linley and her maid not being one of us, of a certainty they're not. I knew that when I sensed a Seymour traveling in company with mere mortals while you were yet five miles away. Of course, it wasn't until your footman arrived, begging for rooms, that I knew precisely which Seymour you were. Then my curiosity got the better of me and I arranged for you to come to the Blue Hind." Glancing at Julia and Jane, he added, with a smile, "I'm glad now that I took the trouble."

Niclas frowned. "You arranged for us to come?" he asked with disbelief. "Ioan would never—"

"No, he's immune," Cadmaran assured him, "just as you are, regardless the weakness of his magical heritage. But the innkeeper isn't. I convinced him, as soon as I knew who you were, to offer the footman a place in the common room for you and your companions, despite his having to turn out several patrons who had already arrived. There simply wasn't room for all of you, but I was curious, just as I told you, to know what Graymar's dearest cousin was doing on the road to Shrewsbury, and in company with two mortals who were not among our sympathetics. Your servant was delighted to find any manner of refuge for his lord."

"I'm not his lord."

The earl of Llew looked at him curiously. "What?"

"I don't allow my servants to call me their lord," Niclas stated. "I am not titled, and have never agreed with the ancient custom that mere mortals should address our kind in such a manner. I'm simply their employer."

A small, disdainful smile crept over Cadmaran's lips. "Ah, I see. You are one of those odd Seymours who have little regard for their heritage and refuse to accept that all lesser beings should be properly servile to our kind. Lord Graymar doesn't share your sympathies, I would guess. But, then," he added, his gaze measuring Niclas with slow care and clearly finding him wanting, "you're a dark-haired Seymour, and nothing like the so great, so highly lauded Malachi." He lifted an eyebrow. "Are you?"

Niclas understood him very well, and could scarce deny that Lord Llew had the right of it. But falling into the earl's trap and discussing Malachi would be the gravest mistake Niclas could make at the moment. Cadmaran had only one use for such talk: to try and ferret out any information regarding the earl of Graymar. Indeed, Niclas had no doubt that this was precisely the reason that he found himself facing Cadmaran at the moment—he wanted news of Malachi. Niclas wasn't going to give it to him.

"I suppose the rain was your doing, as well?" Niclas asked.

"Hardly," the earl of Llew replied with a laugh. Moving across the room to the table, he picked up a small glass of wine. "I am not that powerful. Yet. Please, sit and be comfortable. Will you have some wine? Miss Linley was just telling me all about your journey to Wales."

"I imagine she was," Niclas said, and strode to where she sat. Kneeling, he took her hands in his and gazed closely into her face, into her eyes.

"Julia," he murmured, "are you all right? Do you know who I am?"

She looked at him, yet her eyes appeared to be unseeing.

"Yes, Mister Seymour," she said tonelessly, "I know you. I'm very well, thank you."

"You're under a spell," he told her, speaking firmly. "It's very powerful, but it *can* be broken if you'll only fight hard against it. Julia? Do you understand me?"

"You're wasting your time," he heard Cadmaran say from where he now sat. "She has no magic in her blood. She has no immunity, as another might."

She does have magic, Niclas thought. I know it. I've felt it. Surely she had enough—even a little—to fight Cadmaran's charm.

If he could find some way to get her out of the room, even for a moment, or away from Cadmaran, he could slip the Tarian over her neck and she'd be as immune to magic as the most pure-blooded Seymour.

"Julia," he whispered, squeezing her hands hard. "You wish to go to your room, do you not? I'm sure it's ready for you now. You wish to go and change before dinner."

She blinked slowly, and for a brief moment her eyes began to focus.

"Dinner?" she asked. "Mister Seymour?"

"Miss Linley will be having dinner with me," Earl Llew said mildly. "Is that not so, Miss Linley?"

She blinked again, and Niclas could see her struggling.

"Is that not so, Miss Linley?" Cadmaran stated more firmly.

She slid away, back into a trance.

"Yes, my lord," she answered dully.

"You must join us, Mister Seymour," Cadmaran added easily, a touch of amusement in his tone. "I should like to hear all about Ffinian and his plan to wed Lady Alice. They're neighbors of mine, in a way. Castle Llew isn't more than twenty-five miles south of Lady Alice's estate. But you know that, of course. We do tend to keep track of one another, don't we? Each of the Families. We always know what the other is doing."

"How I wish that were so," Niclas muttered in a low voice, but the earl of Llew heard him despite that, and laughed.

"How odd you Seymours are," he said, "in all your variety. None of my people are so lacking in power as some of you are. It's a wonder Malachi keeps any of you lesser ones in the lineage." He paused before adding, softly, "I wouldn't."

"What do you propose he do with us?" Niclas asked, not looking at him, his gaze held fast on Julia's lovely, empty eyes. "Drown us at birth?"

Cadmaran laughed once more, but this time the amusement in his voice was full and real.

"Something like that," he finally said, still chuckling.

Releasing a taut breath, Niclas stood and looked at
Jane, who hadn't said so much as a word since he'd entered the room. She was the sort of open, unaffected person whose emotions he felt in an especially keen manner.
When she'd been in pain the day before, he had felt that
pain as if it had been his own. But he couldn't feel any of
her emotions now. It was as if she'd turned to stone, and
had neither thought nor spirit left in her.

"I'm sorry, Jane," he murmured, gazing at the little
maid with sadness. He could only imagine how frightened she'd been of Cadmaran upon first sight of him.
How he wished he'd been here in that moment; perhaps
he might have been able to protect them from Lord
Llew's powers.

But it did no good to think of what he might have done
half an hour ago—he had to think of something *now*.

He finally turned to face Cadmaran, who was sitting in
a comfortable chair near the fire, the half-filled glass of
wine grasped lightly in his long, well-manicured fingers.

Like Malachi, the earl of Llew presented a picture of
the perfect gentleman of the ton. He was immaculately
tailored, shaven, and groomed, and his cravat was a thing
of perfection. He was also, like Malachi, a wealthy noble-
man, and the head of a family claiming an ancient, fabled
lineage.

Unlike Malachi, however, Morcar Cadmaran loved to
flaunt his wealth and power and ancestry. Especially his
power, which was exactly the sort of behavior that bred
the most danger for all magical families.

"What do you want of me?" Niclas asked.

Cadmaran smiled. "I want to speak to Earl Graymar.
Face-to-face."

"Then you must ask him for a meeting yourself," Niclas said. "I don't hold sway over my cousin."

"The coward won't meet me," Lord Llew replied curtly, the smile dying away. "I've made dozens of requests—even going so far as to swallow my pride and make them politely. But he refuses."

"Is it so urgent?" Niclas asked, baffled. "What could possibly be so important that you must speak to him in person? You've generally used emissaries in the past."

Cadmaran stood, setting the glass aside. His movements were graceful, easily controlled, and Niclas felt a new appreciation for just how powerful the man was. Not just magically, but in physical strength.

"Aye, it's important to me. So much so that a mere emissary won't suffice. I must gain Graymar's agreement or challenge him, but I can do neither unless we speak."

The earl of Llew towered over him, intimidating, but Niclas held his place, forcing himself to remain calm and think carefully. He was safe enough. Cadmaran could easily harm or even kill him—it would require nothing more than the lifting of a hand for so powerful a wizard to send Niclas flying into the nearest wall, something Niclas had seen the earl of Llew do to a mere mortal when they were boys. But to attack an unchallenged magical being would be a grave infraction of their laws, with serious consequences. Far worse than holding two mere mortals captive.

And that, Niclas understood, was precisely why it was so necessary for Lord Llew to meet Malachi face-to-face. If Cadmaran challenged him during a personal confrontation, they would be able to meet as equals. But if he breached the laws that had been laid down for families

like theirs centuries ago, Malachi's powers would be
twofold, and, though he didn't know the other man well,
Niclas doubted that the earl of Llew was clever enough to
best the earl of Graymar by relying on intellect alone. He
wasn't a stupid man, but neither was he particularly cun-
ning, and he would be hard-pressed to find victory in such
a match even with all his supernatural powers at hand, let
alone without.

"The earl's agreement," Niclas repeated, gazing
steadily into Cadmaran's telling expression. "You'd not
need Malachi's agreement for anything, save . . ." The
reason suddenly occurred to him, and he stiffened. "Not
Ceridwen?"

"Aye, just so," Cadmaran said tightly. "I want what was
promised to me. My wife."

The significance of his meaning sent a shiver coursing
through Niclas's bones. He had thought this matter long
dealt and done with. Malachi had let him, and everyone
else involved, believe that. Why on earth hadn't he warned
him that Cadmaran hadn't given up on his demands?

"It was agreed by the elders when you couldn't find a
wife among the Cadmarans that a suitable match would
be found from among the Families, according to your request," Niclas said slowly, choosing his words with care.
"But Ceridwen—"

"Is the wife I want," Cadmaran said, his black eyes
flashing with ill-controlled anger. "And the wife I'll have.
The Seymours have always striven to take what rightfully
belongs to the Cadmarans, from the very beginning. You
know what I speak of. But not this time. I *will* have Ceridwen to wife."

It wasn't uncommon for powerful wizards to appear to grow larger when they were extremely angry, but Niclas knew the phenomenon was more a trick of the imagination than reality. Even so, he had to force himself to stay where he was when Cadmaran, his appearance even more menacing, took a step toward him.

"Not according to the elders," Niclas replied in calm, even tones. "They all agreed—with the exception of those that are Cadmarans—that such a match would be . . ." He strove to think of the gentlest, least rage-inspiring word. "Unwise."

"They were *afraid*," Cadmaran retorted, and around the room small objects shook and rattled. A picture frame on the mantel fell over with a soft clattering and a hanging oil lamp swayed gently back and forth on its heavy golden chain. "Afraid of what such a marriage would bring. Of the children that Ceridwen and I would produce, of the powers they would possess. They have no vision or understanding. Foolish cowards."

Far from it, Niclas thought. They had been wise beyond reason to refuse the match, and had shown their courage by standing against Cadmaran's wishes.

Among those few magical families who yet remained, the Cadmarans were the only ones to almost exclusively wed other magical beings, including a regrettable habit of marrying those who were closely related. It had caused terrible problems: Cadmarans enjoyed markedly fewer births than the other families, and among those that were successful they sometimes produced strange children who didn't particularly resemble, or act like, human beings. But the unions had also gifted the small clan with extraordinary powers. Dark powers, aye, that had pulled them even farther away from the other families, but the Cadmarans had embraced them with fervor.

But even that wasn't enough for Morcar Cadmaran. Ceridwen was the most favored enchantress born among the families in a generation; her birth and accomplishments had been foretold over a hundred years before her arrival. She was a rare, mystical, and exceedingly beautiful sorceress, and if she were to wed a wizard as powerful as the earl of Llew their union would produce offspring possessed of unimaginable powers.

But Seymours, unlike Cadmarans, had for centuries sought union with sympathetic non-magic mortals, for such marriages had renewed and even strengthened their powers without drawing them down into evil. And Ceridwen, clearly unbeknownst to the earl of Llew, had already fallen deeply in love with just such a sympathetic man, and had received Malachi's blessing for marriage. Even if Malachi drew the blessing back—which he could not now do, having given it with his word of honor—Ceridwen would never agree to leave her beloved Colonel Spar and accept Cadmaran in his place. And Colonel Spar, whom Niclas had met several times in London at Malachi's insistence, wasn't the kind of man to let the woman he loved go for any reason. Nor would he care about Cadmaran's incredible powers. Niclas had felt the colonel's emotions and knew just what kind of sacrifice he was willing to make for Ceridwen's sake. They were well matched in that regard.

"What do you propose, then?" Niclas asked, glancing to where Julia sat so still and silent. "Are you going to hold Miss Linley and her maid captive until the Families agree to give you my cousin as a wife? Will you hold me captive?"

"Not captive," Cadmaran said, calming now. "Miss Linley and her servant will be my guests. You will be my emissary. You once had a talent for making others see your way, did you not? I've heard rumors that before the curse you had the happy chore of rescuing several of your cousins from society's censure. Convincing Earl Graymar and the others to let me have Ceridwen—as they ought to have done before—should prove to be a simple task for you to accomplish. Really," he said more affably, "it was providential that I came across you on the road. One might almost think that Lord Graymar had sent you into my path on purpose."

Eight

"Stop panicking, Abercraf," Niclas said sternly as he shoved a spare shirt into one of the saddlebags on his bed. "I can't think with all your fears screaming at me. Hand me that small bag there, will you, Gwillem?"

"Please, sir," Abercraf pleaded, utterly useless at the moment save for wringing his hands. "Send for Lord Graymar. He can be here in a few moments' time if you'll but ask him to come."

They were gathered in the room to which Cadmaran had sent Niclas following their conversation in the private parlor. Julia and Jane had remained with Lord Llew, supposedly to have dinner, while three of his burlier servants had escorted Niclas and all his men to this chamber and locked them in. Niclas was to be allowed to leave within the hour—alone—in order to ride back to London and fetch Malachi. Julia, Jane, and all his men would remain behind as the earl of Llew's "guests."

"He can't be called simply because I want him," Niclas said, mashing the contents of the saddlebag even farther inside so that he could pull the ties. "The *Dewin Mawr* only comes when another Seymour is either seriously injured or in danger of imminent death. If we could all make him appear at the snap of our fingers, Lord Graymar would never have a moment's peace."

"But you *are* in danger, sir," Abercraf said, his voice shaking with emotion. "Lord Llew will kill you if he divines your plan. Please, I beg you, send for Earl Graymar. No one else can wrest Miss Linley and Jane safely away from a wizard so powerful as Cadmaran."

"I'm going to get them both away from him," Niclas told him firmly. "Tonight. Now. And you're all going to help me, because it will be impossible otherwise. Even so, it might be impossible, but we're going to try." He glanced at Frank, who was trying very hard not to let Niclas feel his trepidation. "The horses, Frank. Will you be able to get them ready that quickly? And the carriage?"

"Aye, sir." Frank gave a determined nod. "They'll be ready. Have no worries on that account."

"Gwillem, Evar, Ioan, you know the paths you'll be taking?" He had to ask them, as they possessed enough magic in their blood to be immune to his gift.

They nodded, and Evar asked, "How will you find your way into Wales, sir? It's raining like the very devil, and there's no light at all to guide you."

"God is merciful," Niclas told him, "and even if I don't deserve a moment of heavenly grace, Miss Linley surely does. I'll cross the border one way or another. Have no doubt of that."

"There's no horse can catch Lord Graymar's Enoch, sir," Frank said. "Cadmaran couldn't catch him if he flew."

"Thank God for it," Niclas muttered, thinking of Malachi's singular ability to travel long distances with incredible speed. He wondered if the earl of Llew possessed a gift equal to that.

He tied the saddlebag with swift, hard movements and handed it to Huw, who stood in the midst of the others, trembling with a mixture of fear and anticipation. Niclas gripped the lad's shoulder reassuringly. "This is going to work. Cadmaran's a powerful wizard, but he's not particularly clever. If he was, he never would have left us all alone here, assuming that we're powerless to fight. He's vain, and that gives us a tremendous advantage. Wits have outdone him before and wits will outdo him now. We must remember that. Now, every man to his post. Abercraf, don't worry so," he said once more, turning to the older man. "You'll have Jane to take care of and once she's out of Cadmaran's spell she's going to require a great deal of reassuring."

Abercraf drew in a steadying breath, striving to stand a bit taller. "I shall use the powder on her if I must, sir. I have it in a safe place here." He patted a hidden inner pocket. "And Frank has the measure you gave him." He looked to the coachman, who nodded, before turning back to Niclas. "Do you have enough left for the guards? Are you quite sure it will have an effect on them?"

Niclas took up his greatcoat and swung it about his shoulders.

"The earl of Llew refuses to hire anyone possessed of a magic lineage to serve him. When his guards arrived to escort me here I felt their emotions at once. They'll not be immune to magic. Indeed, I have every belief that Cadmaran only manages to keep such faithful servants through the use of his powers. He despises all those who are non-magic. I can't believe his men would remain with him of their own free will.

"Now, this is very important," he said, and they gathered closer. "You must all leave the courtyard at once, for he'll be quick to react once he senses someone of magical blood departing. With luck, he'll set out in pursuit himself with several of his men, but I'll be content if he merely leaves Miss Linley and Jane in the care of his guards for a few moments. It won't take us long to get the women out of the inn, so long as Cadmaran's distracted. Frank, you must have both the coach and Enoch ready in the place we've agreed upon, for we'll have no time to waste once we're out of the Blue Hind. You know the course you're to take?"

"Toward Welshpool," Frank said with a nod. "And pray God Cadmaran doesn't follow us there."

"He won't go after the coach, for he'll have no sense of your whereabouts. It's those of us with magic blood he'll follow, not knowing which is me. If we all set out as closely together as possible, he'll have to make a decision quickly, and we must hope it's the wrong one."

"But what if he doubles back and chooses your direction?" Huw asked worriedly. "What if he doesn't go after any of the others? Or if he should break up his men, sending some in each direction?"

"It's a possibility," Niclas admitted, "but he's not particularly clever, just as I told you. He'll expect that I'll try to get Miss Linley safely back to London—to where Earl Graymar can protect us. By the time he discovers his mistake, however, Miss Linley and I will be in Wales, and he'll no longer be able to track magic blood.

"If Cadmaran should catch up to any of the rest of you," Niclas told them, "assert your lineage and claim Earl Graymar as your *Dewin Mawr*. He won't dare to harm you for fear of Lord Graymar's vengeance."

"What shall we tell Lord Graymar when we've arrived in London?" Gwillem asked.

"Tell him of Earl Llew's determination regarding our cousin Ceridwen. She must be made safe—perfectly safe. Tell him that I'll get Miss Linley to Castle Tylluan; he must have no fears on that score. It's Ceridwen he must set his thoughts to."

"But if Earl Llew should turn back and pursue you, sir . . . ?"

"Then tell Lord Graymar to come when he can," Niclas replied. "But *only* after Ceridwen is in a place where Cadmaran won't be able to find her. I wish I could say that Miss Linley's life, or my own, were of greater importance, but if Cadmaran should somehow succeed in securing Ceridwen, many more than two will be in grave danger. Take heart"—he held out his hand to grasp each of theirs in turn—"for all will be well. He's powerful, aye, and so we must take every care, but his love of that same power is what will give us success in this venture."

She was floating. Drifting. Dreaming.

It was dreadful.

Julia tried, for the hundredth time or more, to shake free of the heavy lethargy that engulfed all her senses, but each time she made even the slightest headway into sanity, she was pulled back down into darkness.

She was only dimly aware of what was taking place about her—sounds, voices, lights, colors—and felt that awareness only in brief moments. Otherwise she was in a dream world, asleep, unaware of anything unless drawn back to consciousness by a particularly intrusive event.

Niclas's voice had been one. She'd heard him telling her to fight against the dullness, against her sleeping prison, and Julia had obeyed. She'd tried so hard . . . so very hard to hold on to him, to come to him. And then she'd been pulled back by the harsh voice that held her captive. It had felt as if a strong hand had grabbed her by the hair and forcibly dragged her back, away from Niclas and all hope.

She was drifting. Sleeping, yet not asleep. The voices had been calm, even pleasant. Except for that harsh voice, which could never be welcome to Julia's ears.

But then, just as she was drifting back into unawareness again, everything changed. The voices were louder, more excited, though she couldn't make out what they were saying. But something was happening now. The harsh voice was gone, and there was a sound of scuffling, and then . . . then she heard Niclas's welcome voice saying her name.

"Julia."

He said it again, and she struggled to reply, just to focus her eyes and see his face. He was before her, so close that she could feel his warmth, and the warmth of his hands clasping her own cold ones, yet she couldn't see his face or form. There was only a whirling darkness in which the sound of his voice was her only anchor.

"Shock," she thought she heard, and "cold." But she wasn't certain.

And then, as if someone had poured a bucket of ice-cold water on her head, all the confusion came to an abrupt halt.

She was pitched headlong out of the endless, numbing whirlwind into stark, severe awareness.

It was painful. Her body didn't seem to remember how to work, or her lungs how to breathe. She felt like a fish tossed onto the ground, helpless and gasping.

"It's all right," a low voice murmured against her ear. "I have you. Don't be afraid. Everything's fine now. You're safe."

His arms were around her, holding tight. One large, strong hand rubbed gently over her back and shoulders, warming her.

"You've been under a powerful spell, and it will take a little time for you to feel quite right again, but I'll keep you safe until you do."

Julia drew in a shaking breath and blinked. Her eyes ached with dryness.

She was pressed to Niclas's firm chest, feeling quite small and delicate against his much larger frame. If he held her any more tightly, some of her bones would surely crack. As it was, the side of her face was firmly planted in the wool of his coat, and both the smell and weave seemed overpowering and irritating.

"I've put something about your neck," she heard him say, his voice low, soothing. "It's not merely a necklace, but a powerful enchantment that will protect you from being cast under such spells again. It has a name—we call it 'Tarian'—and it's very important to the Seymours for both its history and powers. As long as you wear it, you'll be safe from Cadmaran and all other magic. But you must give me your solemn vow, Julia, that you'll not remove it until I tell you to do so. That's of the greatest import. You mustn't remove the Tarian until I ask you to do so. Do you understand?"

"Yes," she managed. "I think so."

"It's all right if you don't. We'll speak of it later." She felt him pulling away, and sank her fingers into his coat with immediate desperation to hold him fast. "We must go," he said, gently pushing until she reluctantly gave way. "We have to get out of Shrewsbury as quickly as possible."

With care he grasped her chin and tilted her face upward. "Look at me, Julia. Can you see me? Do you know who I am and where you are?"

Colors that before had been a blur were now sharp and vivid—almost painfully so. Niclas's clear, blue eyes, gazing steadily into her own, appeared inhumanly bright.

"Yes," she murmured, licking her lips. "I know you, Niclas. Mister Seymour."

He smiled faintly. "After tonight, and what's to come, I believe we've moved past such formality, Miss Linley. Please call me Niclas, if you wish it. You may well want to call me something quite less appealing before this night is done. But we must hurry. I'll have to carry you." He stood, then bent and easily scooped her unresisting form up into his arms, holding her against his chest. Looking across the room, he said, "Have you got her, Abercraf? Is she all right?"

Julia turned her head to see the manservant kneeling before Jane, who was sitting ramrod straight in her chair, staring at nothing, her expression completely blank.

"She's not coming round, sir," Abercraf said worriedly. "I fear she's been deeply affected."

"She'll do better once she's out of this place and some miles down the road," Niclas told him. "You'll have to carry her, and quickly. We've no time to waste. Can you manage?"

"I can manage very well, sir," Abercraf replied with a touch of offense in his tone. "I'm not that old and she's not that heavy."

"What's happened to Jane?" Julia asked slowly, her tongue feeling thick and her mouth dry. "What happened to me?"

"I'll explain very soon," Niclas promised, gathering her a bit closer. "Trust me. Everything will be fine. But we must hurry."

"I'm ready, sir." Abercraf had hefted Jane's short, rather bulky form over one shoulder.

"That's an excellent idea," Niclas said, observing Abercraf's action. "I'm afraid you'll have to travel the same way, Miss Linley, for a short while, loath as I am to treat any lady in such a manner."

Julia felt herself being swung up in a swift arc, kept safe from falling by Niclas's able grasp, and coming to an uncomfortable landing on his shoulder.

"I beg your pardon," he said, securing her with one strong arm. "But there's nothing to be done for it. I must have at least one hand free."

Her mind wasn't working as it should be, so that as Julia surveyed the room from this new perspective she said, stupidly, "There are men lying on the floor."

And there were. Four of them, lying insensible about the room.

"They'll be fine in a little while," Niclas assured her, moving toward the door. Julia bumped slightly up and down against his hard shoulder. "Are you ready, Abercraf?"

"Aye, sir."

She could feel Niclas's body tense, and heard him draw in and release one swift breath.

"We're off, then," he said, and opened the door. "You and Jane first, Abercraf. Try not to breathe any of the powder. You won't have any immunity to it, and the last thing we need now is you forgetting what we're doing."

From her unfortunate vantage point, Julia wasn't entirely certain where they were going or what was happening, except that there was a great deal of noise and activity.

Niclas strode along at a rapid pace, greeted every few steps by someone trying to bar his way. He made a peculiar movement with his free hand, as if he were tossing something at everyone who approached, and Julia saw wisps of sparkling blue smoke leaving a trail behind them. There was something faintly familiar about the smell of it.

By the time they reached the kitchen the whole tavern was filled with smoke—and faces, at least those few that Julia could see, that looked curiously blank.

In the kitchen they were greeted by a chorus of female screams, and she heard Niclas saying, in pleasant tones, "It's all right, ladies. We're not here to steal the food. Stand aside, please." There was a puff of blue smoke off to Julia's right. "Thank you." Another puff off to her left. "And thank you." A final puff of smoke and all the screaming had faded to silence.

The next moment they were outside in the darkness, with rain pouring down on them. Julia twisted to look up and felt the cold splattering on her face. Her senses cleared

even more fully, and she suddenly knew where they were—
in Shrewsbury, at the Blue Hind.

They appeared to be in a small backyard on the opposite side of the inn, and were rapidly moving away from,
rather than toward, the courtyard.

"Don't we need the coach?" she asked loudly, over the
sound of the rain. Or at least a horse?"

"All in good time," Niclas replied, his pace quickening.
"But never fear, I don't mean to carry you over the border."

She heard the sound of a gate opening and saw two
sides of a low wall going past. The ground below had
turned to mud, and she realized that they had come to
some sort of road. Niclas's arms came about her legs and
hips in a much firmer grasp.

"Are you all right there, Abercraf? We'll have to run
for it, now."

Abercraf's voice sounded far more labored than his
employer's, but he replied gamely, "I'm ready, sir. Lead
the way. We'll stay with you."

"Hold tight, Julia," Niclas said over his shoulder. "This
is likely to be uncomfortable, but we'll reach our destination in a few minutes."

Julia shook her head to clear the water out of her eyes,
fisted both hands into the thick wool of his coat and said,
"Go on."

He did. He started running, not fast but at a good,
steady pace, first through a great deal of mud (some of
which kicked up into her face, but she didn't complain)
with the rain showering heavily over them, and then into a
thicket of trees, which provided a small measure of relief
from the downpour.

And he kept running, through the trees, weaving in and out, taking care in the darkness not to lose his footing. Every few seconds she could feel him casting a quick glance back, always holding her tightly to keep her from slipping off, to make sure that Abercraf was still behind them.

At last, finally, they came out of the trees and Niclas came to a stop. With care, he slid Julia from his shoulder and set her on the ground, holding her until she was steady on her feet.

There was no light to see his face, but she looked up toward the sound of his labored breathing.

"Are you all right?" she asked.

He laughed in the midst of two breaths. "Aye, I'm fine. Are you all right?"

"Perfectly," she said. "A bit muddy, and a bit confused," she confessed, scrubbing at her cheeks with the help of the rain to clean them. "But otherwise quite well."

"I'm terribly sorry," he said, the perfect gentleman of the ton, and reached his hands up to help, running his fingers blindly over her face until she politely pushed them away.

Julia mopped her wet hair out of her face and blinked up at him in the darkness. She couldn't quite see his features, but his form was there, towering over her.

"What on earth has happened?" she asked. "And where on earth are we? And *why* are we standing here in the rain?"

He had no chance to answer before Abercraf at last cleared the trees, breathing harshly and carrying Jane.

Niclas moved quickly to lift her from the manservant's

drooping shoulder, and Abercraf collapsed to his knees, gasping for breath.

"Good man," Niclas said admiringly. "It doesn't look like we've been followed."

"Jane!" Julia was at her side in a flash, touching her pale face in the darkness. "What's happened to her? Jane?" She patted her cheek lightly, but the maid didn't respond.

"She'll be fine in a few hours," Niclas said, cradling Jane with care. "Please don't worry. We'll have her out of this rain shortly and safely away in the coach."

"Where are they?" Abercraf managed between breaths, still on his knees.

"They're coming now." Niclas nodded toward the dark road. "I can feel them. Poor Huw is about to faint with anxiety."

A few seconds later they could hear the sounds of horse hooves in the mud, coming toward them at a rapid pace. Moments after that, shapes became clearer in the darkness: four horses, two with riders, two being led.

"Frank!" Niclas called out. "Here!"

The riders and horses slowed at once and headed directly toward them.

"Sir!"

"Were you followed? Did Cadmaran take the bait?"

Frank came to a stop and dismounted.

"Aye, sir. Just as soon as he realized that Miss Linley was gone and neither you nor the others were anywhere to be found. We had a tricky moment keeping him out of the inn long enough to give you time, but he was obliged to break up the fight Ioan had picked with his man without using magic, and Ioan did a grand job of making that difficult. I don't think we were followed. His lordship made certain that the coach was yet there—just as you thought he would, sir—and he and all his men mounted and flew away toward London."

"Excellent," Niclas said, his voice filled with relief.

"Hello, miss," Frank greeted Julia and touched the brim of his hat. "Are you all right? Miss Jane doesn't appear too well, does she?" He squinted through the darkness.

"Here, take her," Niclas said, carefully transferring the insensible maid into the coachman's arms. "Abercraf, let's get you up." He strode to where the older man had risen to his feet and accompanied him to one of the horses that Huw was holding. "Can you hold Jane, or shall Frank do it? It won't take long to reach the inn and the coach and then you'll be on your way."

"Be on their way?" Julia repeated anxiously, glancing from Niclas to where Frank held Jane. "But aren't we all going together?"

"No, we're not," Niclas said as he gave Abercraf a leg up into the saddle. "You and I are heading in another direction. I don't have the time to explain it all now, so I'm afraid you'll simply have to trust me that it's the safest thing for all concerned. Are you all right there, Abercraf?"

"Yes, sir. I'll hold Jane. Give her to me."

Julia moved quickly to kiss her maid's cold, wet cheek before she was lifted up to the manservant.

"Take every care with her," she said, looking up at Abercraf, unable to make out his features clearly in the darkness and rain.

"I will, miss," he vowed. "Please take care of Mister Seymour for me."

"I will." Reaching up, she quickly clasped his hand, wet

from the rain, and squeezed. "Be safe," she murmured, then stepped back to where Niclas stood.

"Do your best to get the coach away as quickly as you can, but leave it if there's any chance that Cadmaran or his men have returned. Go no farther than Welshpool tonight, then make your way to Tylluan as quickly as you can. God willing, we'll meet you there before the week is out."

"The baron will want to set out after you at once," Abercraf said, raising his voice above the sound of the rain.

"Make him wait," Niclas commanded sternly. "If we haven't arrived before week's end, then set him loose. Get Jane into Lady Alice's care as soon as possible. Don't make the poor girl stay in company with my wild relatives. Now, go!" He reached to slap the horse lightly on its rump.

The three horses cantered away at a brisk pace, swallowed rapidly by the darkness and downpour. Enoch, his reins firm in Niclas's grip, whinnied after them.

Julia turned to Niclas. "Why aren't we going with them?"

"We're going to somewhere safe. I hope. Do you remember what I told you earlier about the necklace, when we were still at the inn?"

Julia's hand crept up to her neck, and she felt, for the first time, the chain there. It lay beneath her dress, and she pulled to draw it out.

He stopped her. "No, not now. There's no time. I put it on you to bring you out of the spell—it's a powerful talisman."

"A . . . what?" she asked, confused.

"I'll explain later. Only promise me that you'll not take it off, for any reason, until either Lord Graymar or I ask you for it. Promise me."

It was an unreal moment, Julia thought. They were standing in the middle of a wrathful downpour, soaked to the skin, at God alone knew what time of night, on a muddy road just outside of Shrewsbury. Julia couldn't remember a large portion of what had taken place before they'd come to this spot, but now she was wearing some kind of talisman, and they were being pursued by some nameless danger. All in all, in her opinion, the whole situation could only be termed very strange.

"Please, Julia." He took hold of her shoulders and brought his face close to her own. "Give me your promise."

"Yes, of course," she said. "I promise."

"Good," he murmured with relief. "Now let's be on our way. I have a hat for you here." He turned to the saddle on Enoch's back and quickly untied one of the bags there. "I should have given it to you at once—I apologize for not doing so. And, here"—he quickly untied his multi-caped greatcoat—"put this on, as well, and we'll be on our way."

"But what about you?" she asked, slipping the heavy—and huge—greatcoat over her shoulders. "You've no hat or proper coat."

"I'm fine," he assured her. "Hold these for a moment, please." He pressed the reins into her hands and then easily swung up to the great beast. Just as easily, he lifted Julia up to sit before him, and settled her as best he could on the saddle.

"Are you comfortable?" he asked, tucking the folds of the coat about her.

She was wet and weary, but warmer in the coat and safe within the confines of his arms.

"I'm fine."

"Sleep if you wish. We'll not stop for some time. Now, Enoch." He leaned forward to pat the horse's neck once, firmly, as if to gain its full attention. "Find the way quickly. You know our destination. Go!"

Nine

*J*ulia fell asleep sometime after they crossed Wales' border. She had tried so hard not to, but exhaustion, the steady, sure rhythm of Enoch's stride, and the sheltering warmth of Niclas Seymour's body enfolding her against the cold rain all worked against her.

She didn't know how much time had passed when their halting woke her. Groggily she opened her eyes and took in their surroundings. It was still dark, but the rain had diminished to a heavy drizzle.

"Where are we?" she murmured as Niclas lowered her to the soggy ground.

"At the dwelling of friends," he said, dismounting to stand beside her. "I hope. It depends on how angry they are with Lord Graymar at the moment. We'll soon find out."

Julia rubbed her wet face and blinked. They appeared to be standing before a hillside in some kind of clearing, beyond which she could make out a scattering of tall trees. But there was nothing else.

"Where is the dwelling?"

"It's here, trust me. Among my people things like homes aren't always readily visible."

He raised his voice and spoke in Welsh, but, strangely, Julia understood what he was saying.

"Arianrhod! We beg your attendance!"

There was silence, and then Enoch whinnied and tossed his head. Niclas held his reins tightly and murmured for him to be still.

A mist appeared before them, swirling with light and color, and a woman's lilting voice said, also in Welsh, "Why do you come to us at this hour, Niclas Seymour?"

Before he could reply two wolves bounded out from the trees, running at them full tilt. Enoch whinnied again, though with greater alarm, and Julia took one full step back until she bumped up against Niclas's chest. His free arm lashed tightly about her waist, pulling her close.

"Tell your brothers to leave us be," he commanded harshly. "We come as friends."

The wolves came to a halt before them, teeth bared and growling.

"Friends, you say?" the voice asked. "And how are we to know the truth of that, Niclas Seymour? The lord of the Seymours has not seen fit to visit us these many months. We do not know what his intentions toward us are. Has he sent you to us?"

"No," Niclas said. "We come in need, asking for shelter and protection. This woman is not one of us, but Morcar Cadmaran wants her for his own purposes."

The swirling mist disappeared, leaving behind a beautiful young woman dressed in a simple but glittering tunic of green. Her feet were bare and her long brown hair was unbound, flowing to her hips. Even in the darkness she was fully visible, for she seemed to possess her own source of light, glowing like a heavenly apparition.

"You say that this woman is not one of us, and yet she bears great magic that we feel most keenly. If she is not of our kind, then of what people does she descend?" The lovely creature looked directly at Julia in a questioning manner.

"She's descended of mere mortals," Niclas replied, "but she bears a powerful talisman, given to her by the *Dewin Mawr* as protection against the lord of the Cadmarans. She wears the Tarian, which you will know."

With gentle fingers he reached to draw the necklace out from beneath the neckline of Julia's dress. She knew that she should object to the bold intimacy of his touch—society and Aunt Eunice would expect it of her—but Julia was beyond caring. Weariness and their most recent experiences had more than killed any sense of propriety. Apart from that, she was standing in a strange clearing in the dead of night, wet to the bone and smelling distinctly of horse, conversing with a woman made of mist and her two wolves. Any attempt at propriety on either her part or Niclas Seymour's would most likely send her into delirious laughter.

She had grown used to the curious warmth of the necklace lying between her breasts, but hadn't yet seen it. It glowed with an entrancing light as Niclas pulled it free.

Julia wasn't sure who made a louder gasp as the necklace came into full view—she or the brilliant creature standing before her. The wolves, standing at the creature's feet, instantly stopped their growling and teeth-baring and meekly paced a few steps away.

The necklace was beautiful beyond anything she had imagined. It didn't just glow; myriad colors burst from the crystal set in the midst of the gold, sending out rays like the sun.

If Julia hadn't believed in magic before—which she had—she certainly would now.

The lovely girl set one delicate hand upon her heart and bowed her head to Julia.

"You are welcome to enter, my lady, and remain for as long as you desire. Niclas Seymour may stay by your side. Come in and be comforted. The lord of the Cadmarans cannot pursue you here."

The creature began to swirl into mist again, disappearing just as she'd appeared, leaving the two wolves behind. But in the hillside there was now an opening—a wooden doorway that hadn't been there before.

"You will find a shelter and food for the horse hidden within the trees," the now disembodied voice continued. "The wolves will guard him until daylight. Enter the dwelling, my lady, and take rest without fear."

Rest sounded wonderful, but Julia looked doubtfully at the wolves. They stood where they were, looking back at her in a disarming manner that seemed almost . . . human.

"It's all right," Niclas murmured near her ear. "They won't hurt us. Let's get you inside."

With his arm about her waist, he led her forward, between the two watchful wolves, and opened the door.

Light and warmth beckoned, and Julia stepped inside to find that the dwelling in the hill was just like a small cottage. The floors and ceiling were made of wood, not earth, as she had supposed they would be, and a cheerful fire burned in a small fireplace—though heaven only knew where the smoke went to, for there'd been no evidence of it outside.

The dwelling was composed of a single room, with three long beds at the far end, a table and chairs at the front, and a hutch and pantry near the fire. Bread and cheese were set on the table, and something that smelled deliciously like beef soup bubbled in a large pot hanging near the fire.

"Is this real?" Julia asked. "Or am I imagining all of it?"

"It's real," Niclas said. "They—these people—require shelter and sustenance, just as we do. I can't attest to whether the food was ready before we arrived, but I assure you it's real enough."

"I've never smelled anything better in my life," Julia said with heartfelt honesty. "I hope I can stay awake long enough to eat."

"Sit by the fire until I get back, and then we'll address the matter of food and sleep. I'm only going to see that Enoch is settled. It won't take long. Julia," he said, turning her toward him, "tuck this away again." He touched the necklace with a light finger. "Don't let anyone else see it, unless it's absolutely necessary, as it was tonight."

She did as he said, and felt a sense of relief to have the astonishing talisman slide beneath her dress once more, safely hidden.

Niclas covered her shoulders with his hands and gave her a light, comforting squeeze. Looking up into his eyes, she could see that he was just as exhausted as she was.

"It's been a long night," she whispered, smiling. "I think our simple journey has turned into quite an adventure, Mister Seymour."

"Yes," he agreed, his thumbs stroking at the edge of her neckline. "I'm very sorry, Miss Linley, but I think it has."

He was so much taller than she that it seemed to take him forever to lower his head, for his lips to find hers.

From the moment she'd first set eyes on him so many years before, Julia had wondered what it might be like to be kissed by him. And she had spent no small measure of time dreaming of it, too. He'd been so far above her in every way that dreaming, she'd believed, would be as close as she'd ever come to the event actually happening.

But it *was* happening—Niclas Seymour's arms were about her, holding her close, and he was kissing her just as tenderly, just as beautifully as in her dreams. Plain, spotty, failed, on-the-shelf Julia Linley. It was even more astonishing than the Tarian or the mist maiden or the wolves or a dwelling set in the midst of a hill.

She stood on tiptoe to get even closer, and slid her hand up about his neck to hug his strength and warmth. The feeling was so wonderful that it was something akin to pain—like the pain of the love she'd always felt for him, and the pain of the fear that any moment he'd realize, through his exhaustion, who he was kissing and pull away.

But he didn't pull away. If anything, he clasped her more tightly and kissed her more fervently, so that the hat she wore fell to the floor. And even when he finally did bring the kiss to an end he didn't pull away, but continued to hold her close and press his cheek against her own. She could both feel and hear his harsh breathing against her ear, and was quite certain that he could feel and hear hers against his. She felt as if she'd just run a mile.

"Your aunt," he said at last, "is going to kill me. But I don't care. I've been wanting to kiss you since that day when I came to Linley House."

Julia laughed and closed her eyes with relief.

"It's been much longer for me," she said, so weary that she felt as if she might fall asleep leaning against him.

"That's something I want to ask you about," he said, pulling back at last to look at her. "But not now. Perhaps tomorrow. Go on and sit by the fire." His fingers plucked at the wet coat she wore. "You must be freezing in these wet things. We'll fix that shortly."

Turning, he left the little dwelling, shutting the door behind him. Julia meant to do as he said and sit down, but movement seemed impossible. She closed her eyes and stood where she was, listening for his return, half awake, half dreaming.

She didn't know how long it was before he came back, bringing the saddlebags with him. He set them on the table and suddenly produced dry clothes—her clothes, which Abercraf had thoughtfully packed.

"Can you change without aid?" he asked, helping her to shrug out of his heavy coat. "I'd ask Arianrhod—the young lady who greeted us—to attend you, but she's not quite herself yet."

"If you'll untie the back of my gown, I'll be fine," she told him, turning. "Just the top will suffice."

He did as she asked, though the strings were wet and difficult to untie. And then he went back outside, into the cold and damp, to guard the door until she had changed. It was heavenly to rid herself of her wet clothes and slip on the simple but dry undergarments and gown that Abercraf had packed. She silently blessed the thoughtfulness of the man, and felt a moment's gladness that Jane was in his capable care.

"Now you must change," she said when he'd returned. "The rain has stopped, hasn't it?" She moved toward the door; he stopped her, smiling wearily.

"Those are the only dry clothes you have, presently," he said. "There's no sense getting them damp. Come and sit by the fire. I'll bring you something to eat."

She·tried to argue, but he couldn't be swayed and she was far too weary to press the matter. Almost before she knew it she was lying down on one of the beds, her head cradled by a soft pillow and her stomach comfortably full.

"Sleep well," Niclas said as he covered her with yet another blanket. "Sleep peacefully."

It occurred to Julia, dimly, as her eyes inexorably drifted shut, that he needed to sleep, too. But the thought faded almost as quickly as it came, and she slid into an exhausted slumber.

The dreams she dreamt were like none she'd ever before experienced. They were vivid, filled with color and sound and emotion and power. She was pulled far back in time to ages past, into the lives of other beings, through valleys and over mountaintops to strange lands. She saw the faces of strangers, yet somehow, she knew who they were. She heard their voices—were they even human?—knew their feelings, and felt their movements.

And in the midst of some of these dreams she heard Niclas's voice, low and masculine and weary, speaking in soft, serious tones, answered by a woman. For a few brief moments, rising to wakefulness, Julia realized that he was sitting by the fire, conversing with the lovely creature who had greeted them. He sounded so very tired that she wondered how he could possibly stay awake.

It was morning before she woke again, though how she knew it, Julia wasn't sure. There weren't any windows in the dwelling.

Slowly she sat and pushed the covers aside, her body stiff from the long slumber, and glanced about. A freshly laid fire was burning in the fireplace, and a large teakettle had taken the place of the pot that had hung over it the night before.

There was no sign of Niclas, nor of anyone else, but she saw his coat lying across the bed next to her own, and proof that someone had lain upon the pillow, even though the bedding had been left undisturbed.

The dwelling's door opened, and Julia turned to see light spilling in upon the floor.

Two young men entered and stood, staring at her boldly. Two extremely handsome and unusual young men. They were identical in appearance, slender, elegant in form and frame with long, flowing brown hair and extremely fine features. Their garments appeared to have sprung from a much earlier era. They wore tan leggings and plain green tunics—those seemed almost medieval—but the white shirts beneath those tunics possessed voluminous and intricately embroidered sleeves, quite delicate and rather feminine.

But there was nothing either delicate or feminine about them; indeed, it was very much the opposite. They were fully masculine, and from the way they were looking at Julia, she was uncomfortably aware of being the immediate and sole object of that masculinity.

"She's awake, brother," the one on the right remarked, both his voice and expression filled with sensual admiration. He set the pail of water he'd carried into the dwelling on the table.

"Aye," said the other in equal manner, "she is." His arms were full of wood, and he walked to the fire and with agile grace tumbled them onto the pile already there.

Then they both turned and started toward her, smiling in a way that Julia found rather alarming.

"G-good morning," she stammered, scooting back on the bed and pulling the blankets up to her neck.

"Good morning," they said in unison.

"Is . . . is Niclas, I mean, is Mister Seymour up already?"

The brothers exchanged brief glances, then one said, "He is."

They kept moving toward her.

"I'm terribly sorry for taking . . . well, I suppose it was one of your beds last night. Unless it was your sister's. Which I do hope it was, although, of course, I should never have wished to deprive her of it." Julia realized, with an inward wince, that she was chattering inanely. But even knowing it, she couldn't stop. "It was very kind of you to let me . . . us . . . appropriate your beds for the . . ." She craned her neck to look behind them at the still open door. "Is your sister somewhere nearby? I should like to thank her, too."

"There's no need," one of them said, coming to sit beside her on one side of the bed. "We were glad to have you sleep here."

His eyes, Julia saw, were the color of gold. And they were mesmerizing. Julia found that she had to struggle to look away. But when she turned she nearly bumped into the other brother, who had come to sit on Julia's other side—very close to her.

"Yes, we're very glad to have you here," he murmured, his tone low and seductive. "Is there anything we can do to make you more comfortable?"

A shiver ran up Julia's spine and she tingled with goose bumps. It was almost as if he had lifted a hand to caress her cheek. Or unbutton her gown.

The other twin leaned nearer, drawing Julia's attention and causing her to move farther back.

"We could feed you," he said. "Or give you something to drink. Our desire is to meet your needs, my lady, whatever they may be. You've only to tell us what it is that you want, and we will obey."

The words were so simple and innocent. Why, then, did he make them sound so wickedly and wonderfully suggestive?

Julia's head bumped against the wall, but they still came at her, slowly, closer and closer, smiling those alluring, bewitching smiles.

"Thank you, but I'm perfectly fine," she assured them as firmly as she could, looking about for a way of escape. Unfortunately, Julia had never been in the position of having to fend off amorous gentlemen, and thus had never acquired the knack. "I should like . . ."

"Yes?" the one on her right murmured, at last lifting a hand to stroke a single finger lightly down her cheek. "What should you like?"

"To be left alone, I would imagine," came an angry voice from the still-open door. Niclas stood there, his hair damp and his face freshly shaven, a towel slung over his shoulder.

"Get away from her. *Now*." He moved into the dwelling.

The two younger men obeyed at once, hurriedly moving to the door, where they turned and stared at Niclas with wary eyes.

"She wears the Tarian," he told them. "I understand your desire to at least attempt your powers on her, but she's perfectly able to resist."

The brothers smiled, and one said, "She didn't seem to dislike us."

Julia glared at him. "I certainly didn't invite such behavior," she stated angrily. "I was about to say that I should like to speak to your sister. Nothing more."

"We'll not see Arianrhod again," Niclas said. "She won't return to the dwelling before dark, and we'll be on our way within the hour, God willing." To the young men, he said, "We'll feed and ready ourselves, thank you. Be so good as to leave us in peace."

They went obediently, if grudgingly, smiling at Julia until they were out the door.

"I'm sorry for that," Niclas said, tossing the towel onto the table. "Gwern and Gwydion have but one desire in life: to seduce as many maidens as they set sight on. Not that I suppose they can help themselves. It was born in them." He began to run both hands through his damp hair, combing it into place with his long fingers.

"What are they?" Julia asked. "Faeries?"

Niclas dropped his hands and looked at her.

"Faeries?" he repeated. "Do you believe in such things, Julia?"

She smiled. "I suppose I do now, knowing about you and your family. And about the other families like yours."

He gazed at her in silence.

"You're not going to throw more blue powder at me, are you?" she asked. "I do hope not, for I can't think it will do any good." She reached up to touch the place where the Tarian lay warm between her breasts. "I believe this necklace has greater powers even than you knew. It's not only made me impervious to present and future enchantments, but seems to have erased all past ones. I remember everything. Our conversation about your family, the blue powder that made me forget, and Cadmaran. I remember it all."

"I see," he said, and was quiet for a moment, considering her words. "In that case," he said at last, "they are indeed faeries. Tylwyth Teg, to be more precise. The fair people. Though Arionrhod and her brothers have been cursed for well over three hundred years, and so live in a kind of exile from others of their kind."

"Cursed?" Julia repeated.

"It's far too difficult to explain now," he said. "Suffice it to say that the brothers offended the wrong sorcerer, and that the tale involves the usual sordid elements." He waved a hand about. "Seduction, mayhem, deceit, thievery, treachery. Much like so many other tales in the history of my kind."

Julia nodded. "I think I dreamed of it last night," she said. "The history of your people, I mean. It seems that I even dreamed of Arianrhod and her brothers."

Niclas looked at her curiously. "That was probably because of the Tarian. It has very strange powers. But dreaming of such odd history seems more like a punishment than a help."

She smiled. "It was fascinating."

He didn't appear to believe her, but made no reply. Instead, he picked up the towel and headed for the fire.

"For now, let us put history behind us and see what Arionrhod has for us to eat. We must make haste. I want to get a good start before Cadmaran discovers our deception and comes looking for us."

Ten

They kept to the trees as much as they could; Niclas let Enoch choose his own path, for the horse knew their destination and how to get there as safely as possible.

Julia was silent for much of the morning, though it was a comfortable silence without anger. She leaned against him, fitted in the crook of his arm, small and warm and relaxed. She seemed not to care about the danger or discomfort of their situation, but gazed at the passing scenery with a quiet smile.

"It's so beautiful, isn't it?" she said at last. "I've always loved Wales. My aunt says it's wild and uncivilized, but I find it to be the most charming countryside in England."

"Parts of it are still wild and even severe," Niclas confessed. "But those are the places I find most beautiful. And those areas that are most civilized here grieve my heart. So much of the land has been spoiled by mining."

"Lady Eunice approves of that, of course."

"I rather thought she would."

Another comfortable silence followed, and Niclas thought again of how pleasant it was to be in Julia's company, enjoying the beauty of the morning and the surroundings, without knowing her feelings. She was happy and relaxed—he could tell that from her countenance and the way she rested against him. But there was nothing else. Just peace. And pleasure.

She remembered everything, she'd said. He didn't know quite what to make of that. He'd certainly not expected the Tarian to erase past magic, only to protect her when she wore it. More baffling was that Malachi hadn't known it.

Or had he?

"Tell me about your family," he said, pushing the disturbing idea from his mind. Malachi was a scoundrel, but surely he'd not have left out so important a detail on purpose.

She sighed. "There's not very much to say, I'm afraid. There's nothing remotely interesting about them. They're very—"

"Stubborn," Niclas supplied, and was delighted to hear her laugh.

"Oh, yes, they are that. We're famous for it, as you know. But we're also very respectable. And reliably consistent. And very dull." She sighed again.

"You're not dull," he said. "And from Lady Eunice's description, your aunt Lady Alice doesn't sound dull."

"No, she's not. Not at all," Julia replied meaningfully. "Aunt Alice is famous among Linleys as our great exception. She's discussed at length at every family gathering, always with many shakings of heads and dark frowns, and is pointed out to the children as an example of what not to be. Among all my relations, I can scarce think of one I admire more. Which is a good thing, I suppose, as I have frequently been informed by my parents and Aunt Eunice that I have the unfortunate tendency to be like Aunt Alice."

"Interesting and free-spirited, do you mean?"

"No," she said, shaking her head. "A great disappointment to the family. A disgrace."

Niclas was surprised at the anger that rose up in him at the words.

"You're no such thing," he said more heatedly than he'd intended.

She turned her head slightly to peer up at him, her blue eyes radiant with the sunlight that streamed through the trees.

"It is true, I'm afraid. I have done the unforgivable by not marrying."

"That can scarce be your fault," he told her. "If the men in England are such idiots as to let so beautiful a female pass through their nets untethered, then they're to blame. Not you."

She smiled faintly, then turned forward once more.

"I had offers. Three, actually. My sin was in not accepting any of them. I did try," she said, "and they were all very nice, sincere gentlemen—"

At this, Niclas sniffed loudly, disbelieving.

"—but I simply couldn't bring myself to make that final choice. It was foolish of me, I confess, for here I am, well on the shelf and likely to remain there."

He made another sound, this time of disagreement. "You make too much of it. You're hardly old enough to be out of the schoolroom, let alone on the shelf."

"I am five and twenty," she said, and he could hear a touch of embarrassment in her tone. "I am no longer so foolish as to dream of marriage. And, of course, I am a great burden to my family, as they are often given to reminding me. My days are filled with duty and responsibility, and always will be." She looked at him once more, smiling against the sorrow in her voice. "And that is why you find yourself stuck with me on this journey, Mister Seymour, and why my poor, dear aunt Alice must suffer my coming. Because I owe it to my family to make certain that she doesn't embarrass them any further."

Niclas brought Enoch to a slow halt with one hand, and lifted his other to cradle Julia's upturned face.

"You are not an embarrassment or a burden or a disappointment," he murmured, gazing into those blue eyes that had begun to fill with silent tears. "You are among the most beautiful women I've ever known, and any man would count it a gift beyond measure to call you his wife."

It was a reckless thing to say, he told himself as he lowered his mouth to hers. She would expect him to propose, most likely, just as any nobly bred female would do. And he wished he could. God help him, he wished he could be the man to name her as his.

She twisted in the saddle to meet him more fully, to fit herself to him. One soft, feminine arm slid about his neck and pulled him close, and Niclas answered readily, deepening the embrace.

He wasn't quite certain how long it lasted, but by the time he brought the kiss to an end they were both breathing rather harshly.

"I apologize," he managed after a moment. "I have kissed you twice now, and held your hand in public. I shall strive to behave myself better in future."

She looked embarrassed, too, and turned forward, her posture stiff and straight.

"Please don't apologize," she said, still rather breathless. "You must think me terribly forward. I should have slapped your face, but I'm afraid I didn't want to. I enjoyed both kisses too much. Oh, dear," she said with fresh alarm, setting both hands on her cheeks. "I shouldn't have said that, either. I must be more like my aunt Alice than I thought. She's famous for speaking her mind."

"An excellent trait in a female, I find," he assured her, reaching to clasp her hands in his and draw them down into her lap, where he carefully folded them one over the other. "I am entirely to blame in this matter, and that's all there is to it." He took up the reins again and set Enoch on his way. "For the record, however, that is the nicest thing any woman has said to me. Now, let's put the topic aside and speak of something else. Did I ever meet you in London?"

"W-what?" she stammered.

"You mentioned it the other night while we were dining at Coventry, just before I threw the powder at you and made you forget. You said that I had danced with every other girl during your Seasons in London, but not with you, and that I must not have remembered you because I can't feel your emotions. It's feasible, of course," he admitted, "for I do have the unfortunate tendency to depend upon my gift to take stock of those I'm in company with, but I find it impossible to believe that I could have forgotten

anyone so lovely. And now, upon seeing you, I certainly
would have moved heaven and earth to be introduced so
that we might dance. I might not be able to feel your emotions, but my eyes function perfectly well."

"You wouldn't have looked twice," she told him, "even
if we'd been introduced, which we never were. I was extremely plain. My looks have improved a great deal these
past three years, but by then you were already out of society. I never blamed you for not noticing me," she assured
him with all sincerity. "I simply wondered at it, for you
were always kind to dance with the girls who weren't taking very well. Except for me."

"Were we in company together very often?" he asked,
bewildered to have absolutely no memory of her. He
could remember seeing Lady Eunice quite often in his
former society days, and meeting several of her other relatives, including nieces whom he had dutifully partnered.
But not Julia.

"Oh, yes, several times," she said warmly. "I went to
every event we were invited to. My aunt and parents
forced me to go in the hopes that I'd miraculously find a
husband. My first three seasons were the worst. I don't
think a night went by without our attending some dinner
or party or ball. And you were at many of them. Especially the balls," she said, and sent a smile up at him.
"You were so handsome and fine. Every girl wanted to
dance with you."

Well, that was interesting to know, Niclas thought with
a little swelling of pride. He'd been handsome, had he?
And fine? Had she really thought so? He wished that he
had been able to feel her emotions back then, for it would
have been a welcome change. She would be surprised to

know that what he'd mainly felt from the girls he'd danced with had been greed and guile, not admiration.

"Did you?" he asked. "Want to dance with me?"

She laughed. "If I tell you how much, it will puff you up, I fear."

"I wish we had," he murmured. "I wish we'd been introduced. I can't think why Lady Eunice never did so. She managed to introduce me to plenty of other female relatives."

"She tried, several times," Julia said. "But it simply never happened. I don't know why. You either moved away before she could catch your attention or excused yourself just as she was about to introduce us. Lord Graymar danced with me, however, at various outings. I was extremely grateful to him. He was always very kind to me."

It was Niclas's turn to stiffen. "I imagine he was," he said, though silently he was thinking what a snake his dear cousin was to have kept Julia all to himself these many years. It had probably been some dratted charm of his that had kept Niclas from being introduced to her at all those gatherings.

"Tell me about the earl of Llew," she asked.

"What do you remember about him?"

"Only that he entered the private parlor and introduced himself. He was all that a proper gentleman should be, charming and polite."

"Charming, aye," Niclas muttered. "He is that."

"The rest is still something of a fog," she said. "The Tarian makes it clearer as time passes, but at this moment all I can recall is being in a kind of cold dream, hearing his voice, and then yours. You told me to fight—I remember that—and I did try, but it was as if all the spirit had been stolen out of me."

"It's perfectly understandable," Niclas said reassuringly. "Such a spell can be fought, but there are very few people who could manage it. It was wrong of me to encourage you to do so, for it might have resulted in greater harm. I'm not even certain I could have done it. Morcar Cadmaran is a powerful wizard, and he possesses the ability to charm his victims into complete submission. It would have been next to impossible to disobey anything he asked or commanded once you were held in his sway."

"Is Lord Graymar like him, then?"

"No one on earth is like Lord Graymar," Niclas responded dryly. "But yes, they're both extraordinary wizards and the heads of powerful families. Lord Graymar, however, is what we call our *Dewin Mawr*, and—"

"We?" she asked.

"Most of those who are of my kind," he said, not quite certain how much to share. It seemed only right to explain to her, at least in part, what she'd fallen into, and it was likely safe enough. Julia might remember everything now, but Malachi would remedy that before she returned to London, just as soon as she had removed the Tarian.

"There are ten families in Europe who possess magic," he began, "and perhaps two dozen more scattered throughout the world. We know of five in the United States and four in Canada, but little else of the others."

She was clearly surprised by this, and said, "To think that ordinary people live their lives day to day never knowing that some of their acquaintances possess unknown powers. It's quite strange, when you consider it."

"Very," he agreed. "And strange, as well, to be the one who has the powers."

"I can readily imagine," she said sympathetically. "But some of your kind are more powerful than others, like Lord Llew, is that not so?"

He nodded. "My people are generally referred to as being 'greater' or 'lesser,' regardless of whether one is male or female. I am a lesser, or common, wizard, which means I have one particular gift and other limited powers. Dark-haired Seymours are almost always lessers. Greater wizards and enchantresses are much rarer, and are called *dewin*. Among these are the mystics, seers, and healers, all vitally important to our people. And quite separate even from these are those very rare wizards or enchantresses who are called 'extraordinary.' Their powers are so wide and varied that it would take a great deal of time to explain them to you. My cousin Lord Graymar and Morcar Cadmaran are extraordinary wizards. Yet they are not equals. Lord Graymar is Cadmaran's superior, and thus is the *Dewin Mawr,* or great sorceror. That means he is not only the head of the Seymour clan, but of those who recognize him as the head of those magical families in Europe."

"But not everyone among your kind recognizes him as their . . . *dewin* . . ."

"*Mawr,*" he said, smiling. "*Dewin Mawr.* No, I'm afraid not. There are those who claim the earl of Llew as their recognized leader. Cadmarans, mainly."

"But why?" she asked. "Do they not wish to be united with the other magical families?"

"Cadmarans are different from all of us," Niclas said. "They chose a more dangerous path from the beginning days of our exile."

"Were they exiled, too?" she asked curiously. "Like the Seymours?"

"Aye, just the same," he replied. "Cadmarans want to protect and increase their powers, and are willing to go to great lengths toward those goals. Seymours strive only to control the powers we possess and keep them as secret and safe from the rest of the world as possible."

"It's odd to think of," she said softly, "that so noble and lauded a family should have to strive so hard to fit into society. It explains a great deal. And it makes clear the conversation you had with the earl of Llew in Shrewsbury. About his desire to wed your lady cousin and his determination to keep me as his 'guest' for that purpose."

"Your memory is definitely returning. But what you must remember most importantly about the lord of the Cadmarans is that he is a dangerous and powerful wizard, and that he wants you as leverage for gaining what he desires. The Tarian will be your only protection from him, but he can't take it from you unless you willingly remove it."

"Is he looking for us now, do you think?" she asked worriedly.

"I don't know," Niclas replied, lifting a hand to touch her cheek and cause her to look up at him. "But you mustn't give way to worry, Julia. If he or any of his men find us, we'll face that danger when it comes. Until then, we can only do our utmost to be as guarded and careful as possible."

She smiled up at him. "You're right, of course. I wish I were more practical, as you are."

His eyebrows rose. "You appear to be perfectly sane to me."

She laughed. "Practical," she repeated. "Sanity is beyond the measure of my family members, I've decided. I do try to be practical," she said more seriously, turning to face forward once more, "but it's not easy."

"I hate being practical," Niclas confessed, closing his eyes briefly as a fresh breeze caressed his face. The afternoon sunlight glittered on newly grown leaves in the trees around them, and the still damp ground smelled musty and fresh. It was altogether a lovely day, and he was very glad to be where he was and in the company of Julia, despite Cadmaran behind and the unpleasant task with Ffinian ahead. "If we didn't have our families forcing us to be dutiful," he murmured, "we could both consign practicality to the devil and do as we please." Then, realizing what the words sounded like, he added, quickly, "Not that we would, of course."

She laughed lightly. "Please don't worry, Mister Seymour. I understood what you meant and won't attach any other interpretation. I've always thought it a great shame that gentlemen must take so much care with their words, lest they find themselves trapped into wedlock. It seems unfair not to be able to say what you wish."

"A gentleman should be careful," Niclas said, "but I've been too long out of society to give myself that title, let alone recall precisely how I should behave. A gentleman would not have kissed you. Twice."

"I think you one of the finest gentlemen I've ever met," she said softly. "And I've already told you that you needn't consider the kisses. I liked them, and I have no intention of trapping any man into marriage, so you may rest easy on all counts."

Niclas felt a curious regret at the words and, more

intriguing, a rise of anger. Letting out a slow breath, he said, "Any man fortunate enough to have you as his wife would be blessed, indeed, Miss Linley. I would never cease to be thankful, if that man were me. But I cannot marry. At least not until . . . but I won't speak of that. And that is why I should not have kissed you. Twice."

He couldn't see her face, nor could he feel her emotions to know what her reaction to these words was. Most women would be insulted, even wounded, but her voice, when she spoke, revealed neither of these feelings.

"Why did you stop going out in society?" she asked. "The necklace . . . the Tarian," she amended, pressing her fingers over the cloth that covered the object. "It seems to make me feel things that perhaps I shouldn't."

Niclas's eyebrows rose. "Indeed?" He didn't know whether to be alarmed or not. Could she feel his emotions, now?

"I sense something within you," she said. "There's sadness, and a great weariness, as if you seek rest but cannot find it. And there's a . . . a darkness. Forgive me. I shouldn't speak of such things. I am sorry."

"Don't be," he said. "You're quite right in what you sense."

"I've heard the rumors," she said. "Things that my aunt and others have said."

"That I've been going mad? Or, worse, have already gone?"

"I never believed them," she assured him. "I'm glad now to know just how wrong they were."

"They might not be," Niclas said. "There are times when I wonder, myself."

"You aren't mad," she said firmly. "I don't know what

the trouble is, and I won't press you to tell me, but I do know that its source is not within your mind. It's . . . it seems to spring from another place."

"It affects my mind, however," he told her. "And the rest of me, as well, so the source isn't particularly important. I control it as best I can, but I'm not always successful."

"And so you no longer go out into society," she murmured, "and cannot wed. I understand everything now."

"Do you, Miss Linley?"

"Yes." She smiled up at him with gentle reassurance. "There's no need for you to say anything more. I only want you to know that I'm still not sorry for the kisses. The truth of the matter is that they were my first and second, and at the age of five and twenty, I'm glad to have had them."

Those were her first kisses? he thought, much shocked by this. What was wrong with all the men in England?

"That's a dangerous thing to say," he told her, "especially to a man whose weary mind isn't always inclined to listen to his better instincts. Don't you think that perhaps you should be a little afraid of me?"

"Never," she replied. "I know that you would not harm me, no matter the provocation. And I know, too, that you wouldn't have kissed me if you hadn't realized that I desired it, as well. I feel perfectly safe with you, Mister Seymour."

Niclas only wished he felt the same. After so much talk of kissing, he had a very strong urge to do it again.

Julia stretched a little in the saddle, and shifted slightly.

"Are you becoming uncomfortable?" he asked, slowing Enoch's pace. "We can rest for a little while. It's too early to stop for luncheon, but there's a stream close by and I'm sure Enoch would enjoy a brief respite and the chance to drink."

"I—" she began, but wasn't given the opportunity to say nay or yea.

A sudden and raucous yelling filled the trees, sounding like a chorus of fabled Irish banshees, and they were set upon by half a dozen or more men who sprang out at them with weapons at the ready.

"Yaaaaaah!" came a particularly loud shout, and a large, redheaded man flew at them from out of nowhere, snatching both Julia and Niclas from Enoch's saddle and knocking them to the wet, muddy ground.

With a mighty shove Niclas threw their attacker off, and at the same time twisted to soften Julia's fall. He landed on his back, and she landed directly on top of him, her shoulder digging into his stomach with all her slender weight behind it. Despite the fact that she was both small and delicate, it was enough of an impact to send his senses reeling and knock all the breath out of him.

"Niclas!" Julia's voice was in his ear. She was still lying atop him, though she'd turned to take his face in her gloved hands. "Niclas, open your eyes. Please, God."

He groaned and strove to do her bidding, as much to please her as himself. His back was on fire with pain, and his head felt as if it had landed on a rock, rather than soft muddy ground. One of his legs was yet tethered to Enoch's stirrup, but the noble beast hadn't bolted and dragged him away.

There was a great deal of scuffling and noise and fearful murmuring, until he heard the voice of their attacker saying, "I'll kill him! Damn you, Malachi, I think you broke my arm. I was only jesting. You didn't have to throw me so far."

The shock of recognition brought Niclas to his senses as nothing else could have done. His eyes flew open and he tried to push himself up.

"Not yet," Julia murmured, pushing him back. "You're bleeding. Give yourself a moment. It's not Cadmaran."

"No," he managed between gritted teeth. "It's not, by gad. It's one of my *accursed* cousins, and I'm disowning him for all eternity the moment I gain my feet. Help me up." She did, but he could scarce wait to stand before shouting angrily, *"Steffan!"*

A redhead popped up a few feet away, in the spot where Niclas had tossed him.

"Niclas?" a thoroughly shocked voice asked. "Can that be you, *cfender*?"

"Aye, it's me, you empty-headed fool! What do you mean by attacking this lady and me in so foul a manner? And don't tell me you never knew it wasn't me. You've vowed never to rob a relative, you lying thief."

Two of Steffan's men rushed to help their leader to his feet. They followed, brushing mud and leaves from his clothes as he strode forward.

"I swear I didn't know it was you, Niclas," he vowed, pushing long, copper-colored locks from his singularly handsome face. "I assumed it was Malachi. I felt his magic and sensed that the horse was Enoch." He came to a stop inches from where Niclas stood, his countenance smeared with dirt and set sternly with concentration. "Is he not here with you? That *is* Enoch, is it not? And there is a lady. Beautiful. Delicate." His sightless eyes turned toward Julia. "Ah, yes. Your lady, is she, Niclas?"

Niclas was in no mood for his wild cousin's jests. His back hurt like the very devil and blood was trickling from his forehead into his eyes. His entire body felt as if it had been thrown upon a pile of rocks. Reaching out, he grasped his cousin by the neckcloth and dragged him near.

"You'll watch your tongue, Steffan Seymour, or feel my fist. That lady is noble-born and bears the magic that has left you so confused. You and your men will treat her with the greatest respect. Do you understand me, *cfender?*"

Steffan cleared his throat and waved at his men to stand down.

"Completely," he assured Niclas. "Fully and utterly. I apologize with every regret, both for the insult and the attack. I meant it for a jest, I swear, but on Malachi, not you. Never you, Niclas." He lifted a hand to cover the one that Niclas held on his shirt. "I should never be so foolish as that."

Niclas let him go, still furiously angry.

"You make a habit of attacking the earl of Graymar as a jest, do you? No doubt Malachi takes pleasure in such sport and gives back as good as he gets, but I'll not suffer another such greeting."

"Of course not," Steffan agreed. "I know that perfectly well. I've never accosted you in like manner before, have I? Come, forgive me and give me your hand in greeting, and tell me why you're traveling so far from the road, riding the *Dewin Mawr*'s steed, with a lovely lady in your care. She bears the Tarian, does she not? I feel it more closely now. That's why I took you for Malachi, for I felt the magic of the Tarian and mistook it for his power, and recognized Enoch's presence. It was an honest mistake, *cfender,*" he said coaxingly. "Surely you'll forgive me for it."

Niclas didn't want to forgive the damned scoundrel, especially not while his back ached as it did, but he supposed the mistake had been understandable. Steffan couldn't have used his eyes to see who was riding Enoch, after all, and his men wouldn't dare to contradict him with the truth. They were standing about looking shame-faced, and as at least three of them were not of magical lineage, Niclas could feel their genuine embarrassment and no small amount of fear. With an effort, he forced his anger down.

"You might have harmed Miss Linley," Niclas said gruffly. "But as you did not, if she is willing to accept your apology, I'll do so, as well. Come and be introduced."

"With pleasure," Steffan replied happily, running his fingers through his long hair in a vain effort to straighten the tangled red locks. "There is nothing I love better than meeting a beautiful woman."

Eleven

Steffan Seymour was an amazing man to behold. Julia had never seen anyone of such high birth look so . . . wild and untamed. He possessed the same slender but masculine build as the earl of Graymar, and similarly refined features. But there the resemblance ended.

His hair was copper red, a wild, tangled mass that was so long it fell midway to his back. His clothes were common and ragged, the kind of outfit one might expect to find a highwayman wearing, but certainly not someone in the wealthy Seymour clan.

Most surprising of all, however, was the fact that although he was blind, he was able to move without any aid at all. His steps, as he accompanied Niclas toward where Julia stood, were certain and unfaltering, though his gaze wandered upward, unfocused. He walked right toward her just as if he could see her, and stopped before her with an expectant smile on his face.

Niclas, on the other hand, stood rigid with little-diminished anger.

"Miss Julia Linley," he said stiffly, "may I present to you my cousin Steffan Seymour. Steffan, Miss Julia Linley."

"Miss Linley," Steffan said with deft eloquence, bowing deeply before reaching for her hand. "A very great pleasure, indeed."

Julia was fascinated to see that he took her proffered hand with accuracy, though his eyes never once drifted to her face. He bowed again, kissing her fingers with courteous grace before releasing her and standing fully upright. Whatever his present circumstances might be, he'd obviously been raised to be a gentleman.

"The pleasure is mine, sir," she replied, nodding.

"No apology can possibly make amends for my—our"—he motioned to where his men stood—"most unfortunate manner of greeting you and my dear cousin, but I pray you'll accept our deepest and most sincere regrets. We should never have offered so grave an insult to so lovely a lady if we—I—had but realized who you were. Forgive us, kind Miss Linley. Forgive me, most of all."

She could scarce resist so splendid an apology, despite being wet and muddy from their attack.

"Of a certainty, sir," she assured him. "I understand full well how it must have seemed to you. I'm certain your cousin joins me in absolving you of any wrongdoing."

Niclas grumbled loudly, but said nothing to the contrary.

Steffan bowed low. "You are as noble in heart as you are beautiful in form. I thank you for such unwarranted and gracious kindness, Miss Linley. But what are you doing with my lordly cousin in such an unlikely place? Bearing the Tarian, no less?"

"We are on our way to Tylluan, to visit Uncle Ffinian," Niclas replied. "Miss Linley's aunt is his neighbor, and Ffinian is making a pest of himself. As usual."

"Uncle Ffinian, is it?" said Steffan. "And Kian and Dyfed, as well. God save you, *cfender,* but if he has to be reasoned with, 'tis far better you than me. And now," he said more loudly, straightening and addressing his men, "we must do whatever we can to make right our wrongs. A safe place, a warm fire, a fine meal, and a washing of clothes should make a good beginning. And a fine drink, as well," he added with a charming smile, turning to Niclas. "What do you say to that, *cfender?*"

"Do you have a safe place where we might accomplish all these things?"

"Very safe," was the reply. "Even Malachi would have difficulty finding us."

"What about Cadmaran? Would he find it difficult?"

"The earl of Llew?" Steffan said, sobering at once. "Aye, he would. But he's not anywhere hereabouts, is he? I've heard nothing of him for two days, since he crossed the border toward London."

"Excellent," said Niclas, and Julia shared his relief. "In that case, lead on, and take us to your safe spot. We accept your offer of hospitality, crude as it may be."

Steffan laughed. "Crude, you say? You shall see, cousin, and take back the insult. Come, men! Fetch the horses and let us be on our way to show our guests such hospitality as only we can offer."

An hour later, after following so many winding paths that Julia could never have found her way there again without help, they arrived at a sheltered camp hidden deep in a forest that abutted an abrupt rise of mountainous rock. Fissures in the rock revealed several caves, and in these Steffan and his men had created crude dwellings. It was to the largest of these, once they had all dismounted, that Steffan escorted Niclas and Julia.

"My humble home," he said, bowing grandly with one arm sweeping toward the entrance, which was covered by a dirty, tattered curtain of leather that had been nailed into the rock. "Welcome to you both."

They went in first, followed by Steffan, and were greeted by cold darkness, made even darker the moment the leather flap fell.

"Sit!" Steffan adjured happily, moving about without trouble, dragging what sounded like chairs across the dirt floor. "Make yourselves comfortable and I'll light a fire and get you something warming to drink. I've a very good wine and some excellent whisky—Miss Linley won't want that, of course, but I'm sure you'll have a glass or two, Niclas. My men have instructions to roast the rabbits that we came across earlier in the day, and we've a goodly supply of bread and cheese. We'll be quite merry and comfortable in a trice."

Julia expected Niclas to say something about the darkness, at least to remind his cousin that they, unlike he, required light in order to function, but he stayed silent. She felt him moving beside her, and then there came a soft glow of light between them.

She looked down and saw what it was—a small white rock lying on the palm of his hand, glowing like a candle. He spoke to it in Welsh and its light increased dramatically, gently illuminating the entire cave.

Julia glanced up at Niclas, now visible, and saw that he was looking rather disgruntled.

"That dratted Malachi," he murmured, more to himself than her. "He is *always* right. Blast him."

"What's that?" Steffan said from the middle of the cave, where he was building a small fire in a ring of rocks. "Malachi's been ordering you about again, has he? That's his habit with all of us. Very bossy fellow is our Lord Graymar."

"Aye, that he is," Niclas agreed, "but in this instance I'm glad of it. He filled my pockets with stones. I think you know which ones I mean. Don't you keep any lamps or candles in here for the sighted, Steffan?"

"Ah, that's what it is. You have one of *those* stones with you. I've never possessed one. Never needed it. Just as I don't need lamps or candles. But fire, now," he said with open affection, "is one of the great loves of my life. Next to water and air."

He struck a match and set it upon the small pile of wood he'd collected, then added a pinch of powder from a little stone bowl set nearby. The flames sparked and rapidly spread, quickly creating a fine fire that gave additional light to the small space. Steffan Seymour, still kneeling, held his hands over it in a caressing manner, closing his eyes and smiling and murmuring. Within moments he appeared to have forgotten that he had guests.

"He's speaking to the fire," Julia stated as calmly as she could, staring at the sight.

"To the spirits in the fire," Niclas corrected in an equally level manner. "It's a greeting, merely. It will be over in a moment. If he had something to speak to them about it would take forever, believe me. I don't know why it is, but they always want to take a long time with Steffan."

Though she knew it was rude, Julia couldn't tamp down her rampant curiosity and, still mildly, asked, "Your cousin converses with spirits?"

"Yes," Niclas replied with a sigh. "I know how it must seem to you, but it's quite normal to speak to other sorts of beings in my family."

"As you spoke with the faeries last night. Arionrhod and her brothers."

He nodded. "But Steffan is a greater wizard, a *dewin,* and possesses a far more powerful gift. He was born a mystic—and a redheaded one, which is very rare. You can see that he scarcely misses possessing the kind of physical sight we enjoy."

"Yes, indeed," she murmured. "It's marvelous. But surely he sees a little, for he seems to know exactly where everything—and everyone—is. When you introduced us it seemed as if he could see me perfectly well, even though his eyes weren't turned toward me."

"And so he could, in his way," Niclas said, "but I promise you it's not the kind of sight that you and I were born with. You must take every care with Steffan. He sees a great deal more than mere eyes can offer. Never let him fool you to think otherwise," he warned. "He's taken advantage of young ladies before by pretending to be harmless."

Julia had already had the same thought.

"He's very charming," she said, smiling when she saw Niclas frown at the remark. "I think that's true of your entire family. It's part of the magic you're born with." When he didn't appear to be mollified by this, she tried to turn his attention back to their original topic. "And this is because he was born with red hair? What an unusual family heritage."

"It is, I suppose," he said. "Seymours are generally of blond or brunet shades, and some are raven-haired, but once or twice in a generation a redheaded child will be born, and these are more powerfully magic than most of their more common relatives. My cousin Ceridwen has red hair."

That explained part of why the earl of Llew wanted her, Julia thought, but it only made Steffan Seymour a greater mystery. He was clearly powerful, yet he lived in these odd surroundings and spent his days as a highwayman. It was incredible that his family, especially Lord Graymar, would leave him to pursue his life in a cave.

Not that there was anything wrong with the cave, apart from having no actual door. It appeared to be comfortable enough for a lone man. There were four simple wooden chairs—none of which matched—a small table, a rather large side table across which a collection of crude pottery was strewn, bowls, pitchers, cups, and plates. Another table, not too far away, was adorned with a large kettle, some rags, silverware, and several wrapped items that were unidentifiable.

Steffan rose from his adoration of the fire at last. "Now, first things first," he said, smiling widely. "We must get you both clean. Miss Linley may remove her garments here in my dwelling, and you may go outside, cousin. There's a stream nearby for washing, and my men will be glad to do the deed while I make you both comfortable here with the fire and some drink. There are blankets aplenty to cover yourselves with until your clothes are dry."

Julia exchanged wary glances with Niclas, but before either of them could speak, Steffan said, "Not shy, are we? What, with a blind man before you? How foolish. Why, Niclas, *cfender,* how could you—"

"Steffan." Niclas cut him off. "Miss Linley is not a fool, and I know you would not make the mistake of taking me for one. You've one of Malachi's drying powders here, do you not?"

Steffan frowned, and said, reluctantly, "I might."

"Give it to me, then," Niclas said, "and I shall see to the washing and drying of Miss Linley's garments. She will stay here alone, and you and your men shall abide without the camp, guarding, until I call you back."

Steffan was scowling now. "Are you suggesting that I should ever—"

"And then," Niclas went on, "we shall enjoy the kind hospitality you've offered. *After* Miss Linley is fully dressed and perfectly comfortable."

"You're a cruel man," Steffan muttered unhappily, "but for Miss Linley's sake I shall make no argument, lest she think me a scoundrel."

"I shall not think so, I promise," Julia assured him. "I know you are a Seymour, sir."

Niclas said, "That's assurance of very little," but Steffan brightened and replied, "Aye, and that I am, miss. A gentleman by birth, regardless of what my cousin may say of me."

"I speak only the truth," Niclas told him.

Steffan laughed and moved to the sideboard. "The truth is as fluid as water among our folk. Here is a sip of wine for you, Miss Linley, to warm yourself after we've gone. You'll find blankets on the bed to wrap yourself in. They're not grand, but they're free of vermin, I vow. It's the one thing I ask of all creatures and spirits, to leave my slumber in peace, for it's terrible to be constantly waked with their play and nonsense."

They left her after that. Julia undressed and, having wrapped herself demurely in one of Steffan's blankets, set her things outside the leather flap. She heard Niclas on the other side, picking them up.

"This will only take a few moments," he said, and then walked away. A long silence followed, broken now and then by the sound of Enoch and the other horses in their fenced area near the caves.

Julia drank some of Steffan's wine and looked about the sparse dwelling, better lit now by three of the little white stones that Niclas had laid in various spots before he'd left. She touched one with a fingertip and was surprised to find that it wasn't the least bit warm.

"Julia?" It was Niclas.

"I'm here."

"I'll lay your clothes where you set them. There's no one here save me to see you retrieve them, and I'll keep my back turned. Tell me when you're dressed again and I'll go down to the stream to wash my own things."

Everything was wonderfully clean and perfectly dry; of all the magic Julia had encountered thus far on the journey, this was the most amazing. The fine cloth of her dress was neither damaged nor wrinkled. If possible, it looked as well as it had the first time she'd worn it some months before.

"If he weren't a gentleman," she murmured, running her hands over the material, "he'd make a wonderful laundress."

The men shortly returned to the camp and Julia could hear them talking and laughing, Niclas's voice markedly refined and measured against the jolly coarseness of the rest.

They were a merry party when Julia finally joined them a little while later. Steffan bowed grandly at her approach and introduced his men, all of whom seemed a little shy at having a woman in their midst. Niclas smiled and offered his arm to lead her to the fire they'd started in the center of the camp, and over which several rabbits were presently roasting, filling the air with a wonderful aroma.

A proper chair was brought for her to sit in and Steffan himself poured her a cup of wine.

"We've never had a lady visit with us before now, miss," he said, sitting beside her on one of several wooden stumps arranged about the fire. "It's a fine treat for us, i'faith."

"The pleasure is mine, Mister Seymour," Julia said truthfully. "My life has been rather dull before now. I shall recall my time here, and these past few days, with great fondness, I believe, once I've returned to London and resumed that placid life."

He laughed. "Aye, there's always something entertaining taking place among the Families. I never cease to be amused."

"I do," Niclas said from where he sat on Julia's other side, a cup of whisky in his hand. He looked handsome and relaxed sitting among his own kind, his clothes newly cleaned and dried, his face freshly shaved and his black hair combed, and yet terribly weary all the same.

"Ah, well, you've always had trouble seeing the humor in our singular lives," Steffan admonished affectionately. "I suppose, then, that we'd best talk about Cadmaran. Tell me everything, *cfender*, and then we'll make our plan for getting Miss Linley safely to Castle Tylluan."

Steffan's men gathered around to listen as Niclas and Julia told what they knew of the earl of Llew and his present determination to wed Ceridwen Seymour. They listened intently, and when the telling came to an end Steffan asked, "Do you think he's coming after you, then? Surely he would give up the idea of using Miss Linley as a hostage if regaining her would be so great a trouble."

"One would think so," Niclas agreed, "but Morcar Cadmaran is both stubborn and determined. Anger will drive him to be foolish and pursue us—I'm quite certain of it. The only thing I don't know is when he'll cross the border or what direction he'll take. I can't call on Malachi for aid, for he must keep Ceridwen safe. If I can get Miss Linley to Castle Tylluan, however, Kian might be able to keep the earl of Llew at bay."

"That's true enough," Steffan said thoughtfully. "His powers are stronger than yours and mine, but he's a far cry from being what either Malachi or Cadmaran are. Still, it might be enough. My men and I will come with you, of course, and lend our simple help."

"That would be most welcome, cousin," Niclas said. "I can ask no more than that."

"Can you not?" Steffan said with a laugh. "You needn't do so, much as you fear it. I shall ask it of myself."

Niclas reached out a hand to touch his cousin's knee, a brief but concerned gesture.

"No, Steffan. There's no need for you to do so."

"Do what?" Julia asked, looking from one man to the next.

"The reading of the bowl," Steffan replied, an easy smile on his lips. "Niclas doesn't want me wearing myself out, but the effort will be of great help, I vow. I want to do it, *cfender*."

Niclas looked deeply troubled. "I'll stay with you, Steffan. Will that be all right?"

"Oh, don't fuss over me like a nursemaid," Steffan chided, and Julia thought she heard a hint of nervousness behind his cheerfulness. "Stay if you like, and if it will ease your mind. I'm always glad for a bit of company. My men will remain to guard Miss Linley. She'll be safe in their care."

"But what is it?" Julia asked. "Can I not come, too?"

"Oh, no," Steffan said pleasantly. "I'm sure it would bore you terribly. Here, Simon, fill Miss Linley's cup. Roger, check those rabbits and see if they're done yet. No more of this dour talk. Let's feast and have a merry time! We've the rare company of a lovely lady to grace our camp, and my dear cousin, as well. Alun, take up your flute and give us a tune. We'll have a dance and a song and bless the hours before they're gone."

Twelve

$\mathcal{H}$aving been raised in a family like the Seymours, Niclas knew that he should have long since been inured to all manner of supernatural events. And he supposed he was, compared to more normal men. He didn't take exception, for instance, to those relatives who could move objects or converse with animals, and he had never had any trouble accepting the talents that other relatives possessed in making potions and powders or even in casting spells. But there were some exercises practiced by certain members of his family that always filled him with unease. Malachi's ability to journey long distances in but moments was one, and Steffan's gift for sending his spirit into mystical realms was another. Both were evidently quite exciting, at least according to Malachi and Steffan, but they were also dangerous. Steffan had been known to wander in other realms for days, leaving his physical body to lie as still and lifeless as a dead man's. Malachi had been obliged to go into that other realm twice in the past year alone to draw Steffan's unwilling spirit back.

On one of those occasions it had taken two full days before they had both been restored, for Malachi had encountered great difficulty in finding their cousin, and had had greater difficulty still in convincing him to come home. That was Niclas's fear now, as he watched Steffan preparing himself for the ceremony. What if he didn't come back in an hour or two? Niclas didn't possess the ability to go after him, and he couldn't call Malachi away from the task of keeping Ceridwen safe. If Steffan went into that other world and didn't return, what could he do to get him back?

"Almost ready," Steffan said, running his hands with care along the length of a deep blue blanket that he'd laid upon an area of ground that had been carefully swept free of rock and debris.

They were in a small clearing on the banks of the stream, very near the water. With Niclas's help, Steffan had prepared the site, laying out candles in specific spots and picking smooth stones from the stream to place in a small circle. Before this circle, facing the water, he had laid the blanket.

"Now," he said, kneeling in the middle of the rectangular cloth, "bring me the bowl."

Rising from the large rock he'd been sitting on, Niclas carefully lifted the elegant velvet sack that Steffan had brought and carried it to the blanket, setting it in his cousin's outstretched hands.

Steffan deftly untied the cord at one end of the bag and withdrew the single object contained within. Niclas had seen it several times in his life, but had never yet grown used to the sight. It had been crafted before the time of the Seymour exile, in that long-forgotten place that had once

been their home. They called it a bowl, because that was
what it resembled, but it was unlike any mere container that
a human might make. Its substance was unknown to them,
but similar to crystal—only much bluer and filled with far
more light. It had a radiance all its own, as if it possessed a
bit of starlight, and as Steffan drew it out of the sack the
bowl filled the clearing with multicolored rays of brilliant,
sparkling light.

"Ah, my lovely," Steffan murmured, cradling it in his
arms as if it were a delicate, adored child. With exacting
care he placed the bowl in the middle of the stone circle.
The moment the object touched earth it set forth an astonishing beam of light that went straight up into the darkening sky. Niclas thought that every village within ten miles
must see it and wonder.

"Take this away now, *cfender,*" Steffan said, tossing the
sack aside, "and fill the pitcher with water from the
stream. They will have blessed it for us by now."

"They" were the faeries who lived in the stream. Steffan had already spent a good half hour conversing with
those peculiar water spirits, paying no mind to Niclas,
who had patiently waited for their talk to come to an end.
Steffan had explained his need of their help, and they had
readily agreed to prepare the stream for his use. It was an
honor, of course, to participate in such a ceremony, and
the blessing of the water was a vitally important part.
With the help of the moonlight and that new light from
the bowl, Niclas was able to see a few curious, quite exquisite small faces peeking up at him from beneath various rocks within the stream as he knelt to fill the pitcher.
They looked like innocent children excited at the
prospect of a great treat, though Niclas knew full well

that they were the least trustworthy creatures on earth. Water faeries could be sweet and obliging one moment, and drown you the next if they took a sudden dislike. They were exceedingly temperamental, and Niclas did nothing to engage their attention.

Steffan took the pitcher, which was made of the purest silver, from Niclas's outstretched hand and, kneeling before the bowl, held it aloft.

"Be careful, Steffan," Niclas murmured, backing away toward his rock. "I'll be here if you need me. Don't take long."

"I shall be careful," his cousin promised. "Now be quiet and let me discover what I may regarding Morcar Cadmaran and his plans. I'll be back very soon."

Niclas sat and waited. Steffan held himself still for a long time, murmuring softly in the ancient tongue, until at last he poured the water into the bowl and set the pitcher aside.

Untouched, the water began to move, waving gently back and forth, glimmering with the same colorful brilliance as the bowl itself. Bubbles appeared in the swirls, and as each bubble broke it sent little sparks of light into the darkening twilight.

Silence descended on the clearing, as if every living thing watched and waited; even the stream seemed to soften its noise.

Slowly, Steffan leaned forward, bringing his face downward, until his nose nearly touched the water and the bubbles misted his face with little droplets. Even from a distance Niclas could see that his cousin's eyes were open, staring into the depths of the swirling colors as though he could actually see them.

Sitting forward, Niclas drew in a long breath, recognizing that moment when the change was about to occur. The water in the bowl swirled more violently, the colors became brighter and the bubbles burst more rapidly. Steffan leaned closer, drawn further into the bowl, and closer still as the water began to twirl like a violent whirlwind. Then, abruptly, it all went away, the color and lights and movement, fading to the bottom of the bowl as if it were draining right into the ground, though not a drop of water had spilled over. Just as quickly Steffan fell away, backward and to the side, as if he'd been struck by a mighty blow.

There he lay, perfectly still, his eyes yet open, staring at nothing. The water and bowl had become dull and gray, no color remaining, and the water's movement slowly ceased. Stillness and silence dropped over the clearing like a heavy, suffocating weight, and Niclas sat beneath it, forcing himself to breathe slowly and deeply, knowing that it would pass in but a moment.

And when that curtain lifted and both sound and movement began to return, he felt the stark aloneness that always accompanied such magic. Steffan had gone away in spirit, and had left behind his limp body for Niclas to look after. He had sat through this small wake before, and steeled himself for the tense hours to come.

It was dark now, though they'd left the camp while the sun was just setting. They had eaten and drunk and, true to Steffan's wishes, had danced and sung. Or, rather, Steffan and his men had taken turns dancing Julia into exhaustion, and Niclas, much pressed, had supplied a song. The Seymours had been in Wales a sufficient number of generations to have absorbed the unique gifts and customs of the people there, and most fortunate among these was the love of music and singing. Even Niclas found it possible to make a pleasant and passable noise when he made the effort.

The evening, like the day, was clear and cool, with no hint of the clouds that had plagued them so greatly the day before, lending even greater pleasure to the meal. By the time their feasting and merriment were done, they were all pleasantly relaxed and a little weary, and Julia bade them good night and retreated to Steffan's cave. Niclas went in after her briefly to assure her that she could lie down and sleep in safety, without fear of intrusion. He and Steffan would be gone for many hours, probably until morning, and Steffan's men would keep guard through the night.

And then Julia had done something that had both thrilled and baffled him: she had come very near, set both her hands upon his chest, and reached up on tiptoe to kiss him. Her lips had been soft and gentle, pressing lightly on his own in a brief, but certainly not hurried, caress. She'd said nothing afterward, but had smiled and wished him a good night. Stunned, Niclas had made a slight bow and then departed, almost too light-headed to consider what had occurred.

But his mind was clearer now, and he had all the time he needed to contemplate that brief, delightful kiss and what Julia had meant by it.

It was the third kiss they'd shared, but the first that she had initiated. And she had done it knowing that he would not offer her marriage. It was, he thought, the first time in his memory that a woman had kissed him without wanting something. Considering, however, that the only other women who'd shared such an intimacy with him were former mistresses, that was hardly surprising. They had been paid to kiss him, and had performed the duty with the hope of a generous bonus.

Julia had simply kissed him, without a word, without any pleading on his part, though God alone knew how much he had wanted it.

"Julia," he murmured aloud, and sighed. What was he going to do about her when their journey was done? Unless the curse was lifted, there was no hope of a future for them. And even if it was lifted, would she want to be united to a Seymour, forever tied to such a family and bearing children possessed of magical powers? She appeared to be a sympathetic, but even sympathetics didn't always desire to be wed to a supernatural mortal. It wasn't an easy life, by any means.

They couldn't go on kissing each other. It could do nothing but lead to pain. Either they would both become even more deeply involved and then face having to part ways, or she would end up bearing his child and be forced into wedlock with a man who was slowly journeying into madness. No matter how it ended, with the exception of a miracle happening and the curse being lifted, it was going to make them both miserable.

The bowl suddenly began to bubble, and color and light began seeping from the bottom up, swirling in the reverse direction it had taken when it had faded.

Niclas straightened and watched intently. This was very odd, for Steffan had been gone but a quarter of an hour—if that long. He had never spent so short a time in that realm where so many mysteries were unfolded, and Niclas hadn't expected this particular expedition to be any different. He had prepared himself to wait for at least two hours, and even throughout the night.

The bowl regained its color and light in full, and the bubbling grew more furious. Niclas knew what to expect and was on his feet even before Steffan's body began to twitch.

"I'm here, *cfender*," he said, coming down on his knees and sliding an arm beneath Steffan's shoulders. Just as he began to cough, Niclas lifted him up to a sitting position and supported his shaking form. He gasped for air and Niclas murmured soothingly, "Breathe slowly. All is well. You're safe."

But Steffan gasped again and flailed wildly, his eyelids fluttering as he fully regained consciousness.

"Where is she?" he demanded in a panicked tone. "Miss Linley!"

"Julia?" Niclas gripped his cousin by the shoulders and turned him about to face him. "What do you mean?"

"Has she come back? Is she here?"

"She's in your cave, fast asleep." Niclas gave him a shake. "Steffan, come to! What are you going on about? What did you see?"

Steffan drew in a harsh, shuddering breath and shook his head.

"It's the Tarian," he managed unsteadily, reaching up to grasp Niclas's coat by two fistfuls. "It brought her into the mystical realm. She was *in there*, Niclas, with me. The Tarian somehow got mixed up with the magic of the bowl and took her in."

Niclas's heart felt as if it had stopped. He stared at his cousin's fearful countenance for a long, silent moment before saying, "Did she come back out, Steffan? Is she back in her body? Did you manage to get her out?"

"I tried," Steffan said, shaking his head again. "But she knows nothing of magic and I didn't have enough power . . . God help me, Niclas, I couldn't get her out."

"No," Niclas said, pushing him aside and stumbling to his feet. "She's not in there. She's safe in the cave, asleep."

"She's not," Steffan said miserably. "I don't know how it happened, or why, but she's in the other realm."

"I don't believe you." He *couldn't* believe it. "I'm going to wake her up." He turned toward the caves. "I'll make her come back."

"You can't!" Steffan called after him. "Niclas!"

Niclas wasn't listening. His heart was pounding in his ears as his stride lengthened, and then he began to run through the trees, driven on by a panic that threatened to overwhelm him.

Steffan's men rose to their feet from their various spots around the camp as he reached the clearing, and stared at him in silence as he raced to Steffan's cave and threw the flap aside.

"Julia!" he shouted, breathing harshly. "Julia!"

She was lying on the pallet. He could see her clearly with the help of the little white rocks that he'd set out earlier, and with the light of the fire. She lay very still, covered by a single heavy blanket, one hand folded near her cheek, the other lying across her stomach. Beneath the neckline of her dress he could see the gold chain of the Tarian.

"Julia," he murmured, fear making his voice tremble a little. "Wake up."

He knelt beside her and laid a hand over the one that rested against her stomach. Her skin was chilled and slightly damp.

"Julia." He said her name over and over again, pleading with her to open her eyes and respond. When he could no longer speak without risk of giving way to despair, he stood and gathered her small body into his arms, sitting back down on the pallet and cradling her tightly against his chest.

"Come back," he whispered, though he knew it would be impossible, even with the help of the Tarian. She would need a guide, someone who could show her how to make the journey from the spirit world back to the physical one.

The flap opened and Steffan walked in, carrying the sack that bore the bowl. In his other hand he held the silver pitcher, and the blue rug was rolled up beneath his arm. He stood in the entryway, silent, waiting.

"It was supposed to protect her from magic," Niclas said helplessly, pressing his cheek against her cold forehead. How small and colorless she was. He had never felt so powerless in his life. "It wasn't supposed to draw her inside of it."

"The Tarian is a mystery, even to me," Steffan replied quietly. "Perhaps even to Malachi, a little. I didn't expect it to happen, either, and I'm sure he never thought anything like this could occur."

"You must go back," Niclas told him with sudden anger. "At once. You must go and show her the way and bring her back. She'll be afraid there, all alone. She must be terrified now that you've gone."

"I don't possess the power to bring a mere human back. I tried, but she hadn't the knowledge or power to help. There are some things that greater wizards simply can't do, even those of us who are mystics. Only an extraordinary wizard will be able to bring Miss Linley safely out."

"I'll go," Niclas said. "I'll find Julia and bring her back."

"You can't even get into the spirit realm," Steffan said. "We need—"

"An extraordinary wizard," Niclas said bitterly, closing his eyes. "That means calling Malachi and leaving Ceridwen unprotected. Or taking Julia to him." He gazed down into her pale face. "How long can her body live without her spirit? We can make London in two or three days if we ride without stopping. And without coming upon Cadmaran or any of his men."

"I don't know how long she has," Steffan said. "You know that I've spent many days in the spirit realm, but I was born for such mysteries. I can't say how long Miss Linley's body will wait for its spirit to return before giving way. I've never known a mere human to enter the mystical realm before, so I've no experience to turn to. She seemed—"

Niclas lifted his head. "What?"

"A little bewildered," Steffan said. "Not frightened, precisely. More curious. When I left her she understood that she might be there for some time."

"What did she say?"

Steffan smiled slightly. "She said that she knew you would find a way to get her out. I told her that she was right."

"Aye," Niclas said, gazing into her face. "I will get her out." Bending, he kissed her still lips. "I'll have you back safe, Julia. I vow it on my life. Don't be afraid." He looked at Steffan. "We'll leave for London immediately. I'm sorry, but I'll need you and your men to accompany me in case we happen upon Cadmaran."

Steffan moved toward him, setting everything aside and leaning to grasp one of Julia's hands.

"She's cold, and her heart beats very slowly. I cannot assure that she'll survive such a journey."

"There's no alternative," Niclas said. "We'll leave now."

He tried to stand, but Steffan held him back.

"There's another choice, Niclas. One that may serve us—Miss Linley—far better."

"What?"

"Kian," Steffan said, releasing a taut breath. "I think he might—"

"Kian?" Niclas repeated angrily. "Have you lost your senses?"

"Not in the least," Steffan assured him, rising to his full height. "Only think a moment. He's Malachi's heir and a powerful wizard, despite his youth. And he's been to the spirit realms before. Malachi bade me take him when he reached his majority, and he has accompanied me twice since. He'll know his way and how to find Miss Linley, and he possesses the power and knowledge to bring her back."

Niclas tried to clear his whirling head, to think on the matter more clearly. Kian Seymour was a wild, ill-behaved young man blessed with powers he could scarcely control and cursed by a willful, sometimes angry temper. He and his twin brother, Dyfed, gave Niclas no end of trouble during their yearly visits to town. When he thought of the

fights they'd gotten into, the riots they'd started, the build-
ings they'd set fire to, most of which had subsequently
burned to the ground, it made him want to consign them to
the netherworld. For the hundredth time.

But Steffan was right on two important points: Kian
had been declared Malachi's heir at his birth, by the Seer
of Llongolath, no less, and he was a powerful, if not yet
very controlled, extraordinary wizard.

"Do you really think he can do it? What if he should
fail? Julia might die."

Steffan's expression was completely sober and serious. "I cannot believe that will be the outcome. I'll go
back with Kian and lend him my aid. If we can't bring her
out together, then I'll return to her body to keep it alive
until Malachi can come. We won't lose her, *cfender*. Trust
me in this."

It took all his will to do so, but Niclas found that he
had little other choice. He would have to trust his mad
cousins to bring Julia back.

"What of Cadmaran?" he asked. "Can we reach Castle
Tylluan safely?"

"I didn't have time to seek any answers regarding him
while I was gone, but my senses tell me that he's not yet
crossed the border into Wales. Whether he will or not, I
cannot say, but we will be well ahead of him if we start
tonight. He'll not be able to catch us."

"Then tell your men to get Enoch saddled," Niclas
said. "We'll ride straight through until we reach the castle. I don't care what either weather or fortune may bring.
We'll achieve Tylluan before night falls on the morrow."

Thirteen

ut what are you, if you're not one of the *dewin*? What did you come for?"

"I don't know," Julia answered, weary of trying to explain the situation to her hosts. "I don't know how I came to be here. I was sleeping in a bed and—"

"Bed?" one asked, looking quizzically at the others. "What is that?"

"It's where a person sleeps," Julia explained, but they only looked more puzzled. "Rests," she said. "Don't you ever rest here?"

The beings surrounding her looked at one another and murmured wonderingly.

They had been very kind to Julia since coming across her some hours earlier, and had taken her to a safe place where she could wait for Steffan's return. They had assured her that he *would* return; he had told them so before he'd left the night before, and had asked them to take care of Julia until then. But she had wandered away from the spot where he'd left her—it was difficult not to wander

here—and it had taken them a great deal of searching to
find her. She'd been a little alarmed at first, for the creatures didn't look particularly . . . human. Rather, they appeared to be a cross between birds and cats—which was
astonishing, considering the natural enmity of those particular animals on earth, but the combination made for a
lovely being.

They were sleek and elegant, these creatures, covered
in gleaming fur, with luminous tilted cat-eyes and clawed
hands. But there the likeness to felines ended. Their
hind legs, on which they walked, were longer and heavier
than their forearms, but all four were similar to what
might be found on a hawk or eagle. Two large, beautiful
wings sprouted from their upper backs, and it appeared to
be their tendency to fly rather than walk, though they
could do both.

They could speak, though their mouths—also feline—
didn't move. And Julia wasn't at all sure whether it was
English they spoke or some unearthly language that she,
being here, was able to discern, as she was having a good
deal of difficulty making them understand common English words.

The first of these had been "sit," for she had wished to
find a place to do so. Her body—or spirit, or whatever it
was—had begun to feel weary after so many hours of
wandering, and she longed just to sit. But the creatures
appeared not to know what she meant. Further attempts
proved to be equally fruitless, for they didn't know what
"chair," "seat," or "couch" meant, either. Which made perfect sense, of course, for they rested upon their haunches
and had no need of anything other than the ground to rest
upon. With a sigh, Julia had resigned herself to staying

upright for the remainder of her time in . . . this place. Wherever it was. Whatever it was.

This certainly wasn't how she had envisioned heaven. Although she supposed it wasn't. Steffan had said something about a spirit realm, and had assured her that it was a safe place before he'd left again.

It had been such a shock to see him there. The entire event had been a shock. She had been wakened from a delightful slumber in Steffan's cave by the Tarian, which had begun to tingle and grow warm and very heavy. It had felt as if it might crush through her chest, but though she'd grasped the chain with both hands she'd been unable to pull the necklace away. The pressure had become so great that she'd been unable to breathe or call out for help, and then, suddenly, she'd started sinking. No, that wasn't quite right. It had been more like a draining, as if her soul were twirling right out of her body and into a hole in the cavern floor. Spinning, she had flown down, down, down through darkness, and then she'd lost her sense of direction. It seemed as if she had turned about and begun to spin upward again, only this time through light. She had never come to any kind of landing; she had simply stopped spinning and, opening her eyes, had found herself in a world not terribly unlike the one she'd just left, save for one marked difference—there was nowhere to sit.

There were fields of grass, streams, lakes, trees, and low rolling hills, but no rocks or stumps or fences. Everything was perfectly smooth and clean and bright. There wasn't a pebble in sight, or any patches of uncovered dirt. And very little variety to the landscape, or at least what she'd seen of it thus far. She had wandered a long time after

Steffan departed and had found that the land looked fairly much the same. The place that the creatures had brought her to was a little different, perhaps, for the trees formed a great circle and they stood in the midst of it.

"Steffan is one of the *dewin*," one of the creatures said. "They alone visit us. You must be one of them to have come. If you are not, then what are you?"

This particular question had been asked in various ways, but her answer (always the same) hadn't yet mollified them.

"I assure you I'm not a *dewin*," she said, speaking very slowly and clearly. "I possess no magic at all. I believe this happened because I'm wearing—I mean to say, my physical body, which I left in my own world, is wearing a necklace called Tarian. It's very powerful, and Steffan— the *dewin*—seemed to think it must have reacted to his coming and taken me along. I'm sorry I can't explain it more fully, for I don't quite understand it myself. This is all very strange to me, you see."

She looked down at her present form, which resembled her actual body as far as she could tell, save that she was wearing a long white tunic and appeared to be glowing. She could experience some sensations, such as touch, sight, and sound, but she had been in this mysterious place for at least a full day, perhaps longer—she couldn't be quite sure, as they evidently didn't have night here, either—and she hadn't yet felt hunger or thirst. Weariness, she suspected, was also supposed to be absent in this place, but that she most definitely felt. And it worried her.

But her worry must be as nothing to Niclas's. She had spent enough time with him even on this short journey to know that he'd be filled with fear for her. His concern for Jane and young Mister Larter—indeed, for anyone whose feelings he discerned—had told her a great deal about Niclas Seymour's kindness. She could only hope that Steffan had been able to allay his fears, as he had promised he would do before he'd left her here.

It had been such a surprise to find Steffan in the midst of her wanderings. She wasn't sure who was more shocked to see whom—although she had certainly known who was gladdest. She had never hugged anyone with such strength in her life, and certainly not any man she wasn't related to.

It was when he pulled away and looked down at her that she had first realized that he was actually seeing her, and had remarked, rather stupidly, "Why, Steffan, you can see."

"Can I?" he asked, looking about. "Is this what the physical world looks like to you? I think perhaps we may be seeing it differently, for I sense that our realm is far different from this, though I see it perfectly well in my own way. But Julia, what in heaven's name are *you* doing here? Niclas assured me you weren't of our kind."

And so it had gone, until Steffan had thought of the Tarian.

The Tarian had been the only explanation he'd been able to come up with for her presence. The trouble was, he didn't think the necklace would help her to get back. They had tried, goodness knows, with all their might, with disappointing results. She'd not been able to hold Steffan's hand long enough to stay with him when he made to depart, and in the end they'd decided that he must go back without her to alert Niclas and find a solution. Julia had agreed wholeheartedly, for she was certain that Niclas would think of a way to get her back.

"But if you are not one of the *dewin*," the same creature

asked yet again, "then what are you? We wish to know what manner of magic you possess."

"I don't possess any magic," she said wearily, wishing that Steffan would return. Or, better yet, that Niclas would suddenly appear. She longed to see him again, to feel his touch. It seemed as if an eternity had passed since she had kissed him in the cave. It had been bold, she knew, especially after they had discussed the matter of kissing in such detail only hours earlier. But she was five and twenty and had been in love with him for eight years. If she didn't kiss him now, during these last few days they would be together, she would very likely never have the chance. And, encouragingly enough, he hadn't seemed to mind. He'd been surprised, clearly, but not displeased. Not in the least.

"But what are you?" the creature pressed.

Julia sighed and tried to think of yet another way to explain it, but she was becoming so very tired.

"I'm—" she began, but a new voice interrupted.

"She is the lady of the Tarian, which the *Dewin Mawr* gave to her himself, and you are not to bother her with so many questions."

Julia opened her eyes to see a shining young man walking slowly into their midst; an extraordinarily handsome young man with white-blond hair, bright blue eyes, and elfin features that almost made her mistake him for Lord Graymar. But this man's hair was much, much longer than the earl's, falling well past his shoulders. He was tall and slender, as well, but younger; he scarce looked to have passed his twenty-first year. Like her, and Steffan, when she had seen him before, he was dressed in a tunic of gleaming white. The creatures, when they saw him, bowed low in recognition.

"Miss Linley?" he asked, holding out a hand and smiling. "I am Kian Seymour, one of Niclas's cousins."

"Oh," she murmured, allowing him to touch her fingers with a gracious kiss. "I know of you, sir. And of your brother. You—" But she stopped herself, and instead said, "Oh, dear."

His smile widened. "Yes, I imagine you've heard of Dyfed and me before, especially as I understand you spend much of your time in London. We've caused a great deal of trouble there, I fear." His countenance was so charmingly contrite that she couldn't help but like him. "Lord Graymar and our dear cousin Niclas have been quite put out with us. But now I have the opportunity to make some amends. I've come to bring you back."

"Oh, have you?" she said with relief. "I'm so thankful, sir. I confess I'm terribly weary and wish to leave."

"Yes, I know," he said, and his expression grew troubled. "And that is why we cannot delay. Steffan is coming to help. He'll be here shortly."

"I'm sorry to have been such trouble to you," she told the creatures, "and thankful for all your kindness."

They bowed low once more and one of them said, "It has been our pleasure, Lady of the Tarian, which was given to you by the *Dewin Mawr*. We are glad at last to know what you are. You will always be welcome here, should you wish to return."

"Thank you," she said, and curtsied. "You are very good."

"You found her!" Steffan came striding through the

trees, causing the gracious beings to bow yet again. "Are you well, Miss Linley?"

"Yes, thank you," she said, terribly glad to see him again. "I'm only a little weary."

"Yes, I can see that," he said, eyeing her critically. "And you've grown paler." He turned to his cousin. "There's not a moment to lose. And Niclas is waiting anxiously."

"I hope he hasn't been too worried," Julia said.

Kian Seymour grinned. "I've never seen him in such disarray, and you may believe me when I say that I've seen him extremely overset many a time. Having met you in a wakened state, however," he said, looking at her with masculine appreciation, "I can understand why this is different. Never thought I'd live to see the day when fusty old cousin Niclas got struck by Cupid's arrow, but here it is."

"Fusty?" Julia repeated, and opened her mouth to remonstrate, but Steffan stepped between them.

"There's no time for chatter. Miss Linley grows paler by the moment. Are you certain you can do this without me coming back, too, Kian?"

"If not," the younger man answered, "we shall simply have to try again with you on her other side. But I believe all will be well."

"You're not coming back?" Julia asked.

Steffan shook his head. "Not yet. I haven't discovered anything about Cadmaran's plans or whereabouts, and, as you may have learned from your time here, conversation with the guardians can take a good deal of time."

"The guardians?" she asked, looking at the noble creatures. "Is that what they are?"

"Aye, and seers, as well. They see many things in our

world that aren't visible to us, and guard many things, as well. But come," he said, and took her hand. "We must get you back to the physical realm at once. Stand here, in the very center of the trees. We will form a circle about you and lend our powers. Kian?"

Kian moved to stand directly in front of Julia, and reached to take both her hands firmly in his.

"You must hold on to me very tightly, Miss Linley," he told her. "Close your eyes and concentrate on our joined hands, and believe that I will not let you go."

Julia nodded and did as he said. She shut her eyes and held his hands so tightly that her fingers ached and she was certain that she'd leave marks in Kian Seymour's wrists. But he didn't complain, and spoke to her in reassuring tones.

"I'll count to ten, slowly. Don't be alarmed if you begin to feel yourself spinning. Just hold on to me and keep your eyes closed. We'll be back quickly, but you may not realize it for a day or so, for you will likely sleep for a time. When you awaken you'll find yourself at Castle Tylluan, which is where your body now awaits you, and Niclas will be waiting to greet you."

"And various wild Seymours, as well," Steffan put in, laughing.

Julia didn't open her eyes, but smiled.

"It sounds delightful."

"I'll start counting now," Kian said. "I have you safe. Don't be afraid."

"I trust you," she murmured as he said, "One."

It was like falling into an exhausted sleep, rather than spinning, though she felt that, too. As Kian counted each number slowly, carefully, Julia's thoughts faded away into darkness. She tried to keep listening to him, to remain aware of what was happening, but it was impossible. Her spirit self, which had felt very light in this realm, began to grow heavier, and her weariness turned into outright exhaustion. She couldn't fight the enticing pull of slumber, and, with Kian's voice growing dimmer and dimmer, she slid away into a deep and welcome sleep.

"Now, lad, stop your fretting. She'll come to in another day or so and will be as fit as my new mare. There's no sense in worrying yourself into the grave."

Niclas lifted his gaze from Julia's still, pale, sleeping form to look at his uncle, who was standing by the fire, holding a pipe in one hand and a cup of whisky in the other. Ffinian Seymour looked nothing like his fine, handsome sons: quite the opposite. He was short in stature, gray in color, and stooped in form. His wild, grizzled hair and beard grew out in all directions, untouched by comb, blade, or scissors for as long as Niclas could remember. And yet, for all his odd appearance, Ffinian had a gift for making women of all ages fall madly in love with him. Niclas had always found it a great, unexplainable mystery, and on top of that, his uncle was half-mad, just as his twin cousins were. What did women find in that to lure them?

"She's not a horse," Niclas told him, wearily rubbing his eyes.

"Well, I know that as well as any man," his uncle said with a laugh. "She's a woman, and a fine-looking one, i'faith. But there's no need to cast yourself into a gloom simply because the girl's taking a little nap. It's a waste of good time—time we might be using to make plans for dealing with my darling Alice."

"Uncle," Niclas said, "I've told you well over a dozen times now that we're not going to make any plans regarding Lady Alice, save these: you're going to leave her in peace and stop pressing her to wed you. That's how both she and the Linleys want it, and that's how it's going to be. There's nothing more to discuss."

"You're a stubborn lad," Ffinian muttered with impatience, "and ever have been. My sweet Alice is just there on the edge of saying yes to my proposal." He pointed the pipe he held toward an invisible spot somewhere in the middle of the room. "Just there on the edge. One little push and she's mine! But you, my own flesh and blood," he said, looking at Niclas with disdain, "won't even give your loving uncle a tiny little bit of help in his direst moment of need. If you didn't come to help, you would have done better to stay away altogether."

"I came expressly to rescue Lady Alice from your determination to wed her. We are at cross-purposes, uncle, but I promise you that I shall come out the winner in this contest."

"Bah!" Ffinian uttered, and took a long sip of whisky. "You have no love for your own family. No loyalty or consideration. Was it not one of your own cousins who just went into that other realm and bravely brought your good lady back to you? Eh? Was it not my own fine lad Kian?"

"Yes," Niclas said tautly. "And it was very good of him to do so. I am in Kian's debt. But one welcome deed cannot sway me from the task for which I came."

"And asked no thanks for it," Ffinian continued, "nor even a kind word. There was not a moment of hesitation when he saw how it was, but he went at once, the very moment you asked it of him."

"Yes, Uncle, I am fully aware of just how much I—"

"And yet here you are," said Ffinian, "determined to break the lad's heart by denying him the love and care of a stepmother, a fine lady to look after his brother and him while they're yet young enough to be shaped by her wise and guiding hand—" He stopped long enough to take another sip of whisky. "And to care for their father in his old age. It's a shocking thing to see from my own nephew. Your father never raised you to show such ingratitude."

Niclas turned his eyes to the ceiling and shook his head. If aggravation alone could lift the curse, then dealing with Uncle Ffinian would surely do the trick.

"And there you are yet again," Ffinian insisted, fully insulted, "making sounds at your own uncle. And faces! Your dear mother is rolling in her grave at this very moment."

"I am not making sounds at you," Niclas said, just as his cousin Dyfed entered the room.

"What's this, Father? Cousin Niclas is making sounds at you, is he?"

"*And* faces!" Ffinian declared, his tone filled with insult.

"I'm doing no such thing," Niclas insisted, but that only made Dyfed laugh.

"You held out three days, *cfender*. That's a true accomplishment. Earl Graymar lost his temper after only two hours the last time he visited us."

"He splintered one of the tables that time," another voice said from the doorway, and Niclas looked to see Kian standing there, lazily reclining against the frame. His arms

were folded across his chest as he took in the room's occupants, and his manner was, as usual, somewhat lordly and
bored. It was a posture that had always aggravated Niclas a
little, for it reminded him a good deal of the man whom
Kian was to inherit from: Malachi. The boy could at least
wait until he was the *Dewin Mawr* to appear so irritatingly
special. "We were obliged to use it for firewood."

"Aye," his father said sadly. "And it was one of the only
good large tables we had left." He shook his head. "It's a
terrible temper the earl has, i'faith, when he's been pressed.
And is that not a great pity, when he's so fine a lad in his
general ways?" He sighed. "But that's as it ever is with
Seymours, or seems to be." He looked at the assembled
young men with a sage expression. "We've that lamented,
quick and foolish temper, do we not? 'Tis a great shame in
so noble a people."

"You do not all have such a temper," a new voice said
firmly, and Niclas was glad to see Loris, Ffinian's adopted
ward, standing just outside the doorway, a large pitcher
cradled in both hands. She was a mere mortal, and Niclas
could feel her emotions. But this was generally a pleasure, for she was as sweet-natured and kind-hearted as
she was beautiful, and her feelings were usually gentle.

Usually. There was one exception, and that was whenever she was in Kian's company. Not that Kian didn't deserve Loris's wrath; he did very little to keep it at bay. In
truth, he seemed to do all he could to draw it out. But it
wouldn't have mattered if he was unfailingly sweet to her—
it wasn't possible for Loris to feel anything but animosity
for the lad. Magic had made it thus. Like himself, Loris was
living beneath a blood curse that, also like himself, had
never yet been repaired.

"Mister Niclas is above all things a gentleman," she stated. "I've never heard a cross word from him unless he's been driven beyond all reason by one of his less well mannered relatives. And even then"—she smiled warmly at Niclas—"he remains a gentleman."

"You would know best, dear Loris," Kian said mockingly. "You always do."

She sent him a dark look and tried to walk into the chamber, but it wasn't particularly easy; Kian stood in such a way as to oblige her to brush against him in order to move forward. But Loris was no wilting young maiden; she shifted the pitcher and put an elbow into Kian's stomach with such force that he nearly doubled over. Accordingly, he stepped aside, and Loris, ignoring whatever comment it was that Kian muttered beneath his breath as she passed, moved toward the bed with a satisfied smile that mirrored the pleasure Niclas felt emanating from her.

"I've brought fresh water," she said, pouring some into a bowl set near the bed. "Has she moved at all? No? Well, don't worry, Mister Seymour. She'll wake soon, I'm quite sure of it."

Niclas hoped she was right; Julia had been asleep for almost two full days following Kian's return from the other realm. Kian, waking immediately, had assured them that Julia's spirit had indeed been successfully retrieved, and that appeared to be true, for both color and warmth had begun to return to her body, and her breathing—which had become worrisomely shallow—had grown steadier and deeper.

Loris wet a cloth with a little of the fresh water and gently dabbed Julia's face and lips.

"She's smiling," she said softly. "Do you see, Cousin Niclas? I believe she must be having pleasant dreams."

"Do you think so?" Kian asked scornfully. "I imagine you know of such things. Your dreams are all so pleasant, are they not, dear Loris?"

Even before she looked up to spear Kian with a heated glare, Niclas could feel the young woman's fury. Although she was not able to harbor any affection for Kian, Niclas was still surprised by the keen hatred Loris felt for his younger cousin. The curse she was under didn't demand such virulence. And yet, there was something else there, too, running beneath her feelings; an emotion that confused him.

They were all odd people at Castle Tylluan; odd and bewildering. Niclas wasn't sure he would ever sort out the relationships and how they truly felt about each other.

Uncle Ffinian was perhaps the simplest to understand. He was merely a wild man, half-mad and entirely determined to have his own way in all things, no matter how insensible. Among Seymours he was the rarity who possessed no magic at all, though Niclas had often thought that his grizzled uncle's uncanny ability to charm females might possibly be tied to his Seymour blood. But he had proved, through the birth of his sons by a wife who'd been mere mortal, that powerful magic could be passed along despite a Seymour's lack of gifts.

Dyfed was a bit more complicated than his father, but not overly. He and Kian were identical in physical features, but entirely different otherwise. Dyfed was a gentle soul, patient and even-tempered. He wasn't above helping his older brother start riots or wreak havoc, but left to his own pursuits, Dyfed seldom caused trouble. He was a dreamer, thoughtful and bookish. More often than not he did his utmost to talk Kian out of the wilder pursuits that had made the brothers famous in London. The problem, so far as Niclas could tell, was that he didn't appear to possess the ability to extricate himself from such wildness once it had been set into motion.

Dyfed's gift, which Niclas had always thought one of the most welcome among their family, was that of being able to speak without words, directly into the mind, or minds, of anyone he wished—even those who were merely mortal. It had been a problem when he was a child, for Dyfed hadn't learned to speak until he was nearly seven years old, but had relied entirely upon his mental powers to make himself known.

Kian was the opposite of his brother. He was wild and boundlessly active, highly intelligent though not bookish, and never had the least difficulty accepting responsibility for his actions. Indeed, he actually seemed to glory in his misdeeds, save when some unfortunate bystander had been harmed. But despite the numerous times Niclas had been obliged to get him out of trouble, it was difficult not to admire the lad.

Kian possessed what Malachi called "a noble soul." He was neither cruel nor mean-spirited, save with Loris, and was ever quick to make friends with almost anyone he met. He had an open, generous, and affectionate nature and a searing wit that could either make one smile or send one scuttling for the nearest place of refuge.

As for magic, Kian was second in power among Seymours only to the earl of Graymar. But he was still a young man, and his abilities would continue to mature as he

aged. They were enough now, thankfully, to have successfully retrieved Julia, but one day he would possess almost
unimaginable powers.

As far as Niclas knew, extraordinary wizards never
reached any kind of finality in regard to the magic they
wielded, but continued to increase in strength until their
physical bodies died and they passed into the spirit realm.
In this manner no heir to the head of the Seymour clan
could successfully challenge the current head, for no matter how much the one increased, the other would increase,
as well.

Not that Niclas thought Kian would ever challenge
Malachi. For one thing, he wasn't exactly pleased at being heir to the earl of Graymar, and for another, he wor-
shipped the ground Malachi walked on. One day, Niclas
believed, Kian would make an excellent *Dewin Mawr*.

Loris was perhaps the most intriguing piece of the
puzzle to be found at Castle Tylluan. She had been orphaned at an early age and left in the care of a nefarious
innkeeper in London, and had been but thirteen when that
same innkeeper had decided to sell her into prostitution.
But Kian, who had then been seventeen (and already in
the bad habit of visiting the worst hells in town), had
challenged her new master to a game of dice and come
away with Loris as his prize. Malachi, who had become
involved, hadn't told Niclas everything, but evidently
the fellow who'd lost believed Kian guilty of cheating—
which was possible, of course, given that the boy had
used magic to win in such games before, though it was
strictly forbidden by the rules of their kind. A fight had
ensued and, in typical Seymour fashion, yet another tavern had been damaged. Kian had drawn blood on Loris's

behalf, and a blood curse had been placed on her, though she'd been entirely innocent of any of that night's events. Malachi had done everything in his power to lift the curse, just as he had for Niclas, but to no avail.

Loris had come to live at Castle Tylluan as Ffinian's ward and, despite her youth, had immediately taken up management of the estate. Tylluan had been in dire need of a female's knowing touch for a long while, ever since Niclas's aunt had died, and even at the age of thirteen Loris proved that she possessed the natural talents required for overseeing such a large dwelling with very few funds at her disposal. The castle was kept meticulously clean, despite the old and somewhat shabby furnishings, and the meals to be had at Tylluan were among the best in Wales. Ffinian, Kian, Dyfed, and all their men were kept well in line—which was something of a miracle, considering the wildness they displayed when left to themselves.

Loris was a sweet and mild-mannered young woman, and lovely to behold, tall and slender, with an elegance of form and face that had always made Niclas wonder who her family had been. There was nothing coarse or low in her manner, as might have been expected of a girl left orphaned in a filthy dockside tavern, and she was as beautiful as any diamond of the ton. Her dark hair, which she generally wore unbound, was long, thick, and curling, streaked with a multitude of golden strands that shimmered beneath light, sometimes giving the illusion as she moved that Loris was glowing. Her eyes were the color of cinnamon, neither brown nor rust nor gold, but a mixture of all three.

Loris and Dyfed had recently become betrothed, which surprised Niclas, for he had never been able to discern any particular passion between the two. Dyfed was certainly fond of the girl, as any observer could see, and Loris made a great show of affection for Dyfed, especially when Kian was present. But Niclas couldn't feel a matching emotion in her breast. Her strongest feelings were all reserved for Kian, and those were always far too angry and muddled for him to sort out.

"Look," Loris said, gazing at Julia, and he could feel excitement rise within her. "I think she's beginning to wake."

They all gathered near in anticipation, even Kian, who threw off his boredom and pushed away from the door to come close. Niclas gathered Julia's hands in his and leaned over her.

"Julia?"

She *was* smiling; Loris had been right about that.

"I've had the most wonderful dream," she said, and opened her eyes.

"Thank God," Niclas said as she blinked up at him. For one overwhelming moment he felt as if his eyes might start to fill with tears, he was so deeply relieved.

"There you are," she said sleepily, a tiny bit of chiding in her tone, though she smiled a little more widely. "I've been looking for you everywhere, Niclas."

"I'm here," he said. "I've been waiting for you."

"I know," she whispered, and pulled one of her hands free to touch his face. "I could hear your voice calling me. I tried so hard to find you, but you were always just a little too far away. But the search was so lovely, because you kept telling me that you—" She suddenly seemed to realize that they weren't alone. Blearily, she gazed at the other faces looming over her. She looked for a long moment at

Dyfed, then at Kian, finally saying, "Why, Mister Seymour, did you get back safely, then?"

Kian proffered one of his rare smiles. "I did, indeed," he replied warmly. "It's good to see you again, Miss Linley. Welcome to Castle Tylluan. I hope you've had a pleasant sleep."

"Thank you, sir," she said politely, if yet wearily. "I did. The best of my life. I had such lovely dreams." She closed her eyes and sighed, then looked about the room once more, taking in Ffinian, Loris, and Dyfed. Especially Dyfed, whom she looked at for a particularly long moment.

"Niclas," she murmured, touching his arm.

"Yes, Julia?"

"They're not like those other brothers, are they? The wolves?"

He laughed out loud, and Loris tried bravely to stifle a giggle. Behind them Ffinian harrumphed, Kian snorted, and Dyfed muttered something indistinguishable.

"Not exactly," Niclas said, grinning at Julia's disconcerted expression.

"They're worse," Loris said, laughing once more. "Much worse."

Julia looked at her questioningly, and Loris smiled. "No, they're not," she amended. "You have nothing to fear, Miss Linley. I'll make certain that they leave you in peace."

Niclas introduced all those in the room and then gave a brief explanation of what had transpired since they'd left Steffan's camp, of their hurried passage through the hills and of Kian's journey to the spirit world to find and bring Julia back, of his immediate return and Steffan's eventual return, and of the days of waiting for her to wake.

"And my aunt?" she asked. "You've contacted her?"

Niclas nodded. "She was here yesterday to visit you. Did you not hear her voice? She spoke to you for some length of time."

"No, I only heard you," she said, blushing slightly at the murmur of knowing approval from Ffinian and his sons. Niclas scowled at his relatives.

"Will she be coming again soon?" Julia asked. "I don't want her to worry. And Jane? Is she safe?"

"Jane is with your aunt, completely recovered," Niclas said soothingly, lightly rubbing the hand he yet held. "She and Abercraf are there together, and he's taking very good care of her. They both came yesterday with your aunt, and I promised that I would send word the moment you woke."

"I'll send a rider to my darling Alice at once," Ffinian said. "If I know my dear girl, she'll be here tomorrow, ready to scuttle you back to Glen Aur where you'll be protected from our wicked ways at Tylluan."

Niclas and Kian exchanged looks, and Kian said, with care, "I'm not certain that Miss Linley should leave Tylluan just yet, *tad*. She'll be safer here than at Glen Aur."

"Oh?" Ffinian remarked, glancing from his son to Niclas to Julia. "Of course, we should like nothing better, Miss Linley, if you would consent. Our dearest Loris would enjoy the company of another female, I vow."

"But—" Julia began.

"And Lady Alice may come and visit you as often as she desires," Niclas added quickly. Until he knew that Cadmaran had accepted the loss of Ceridwen, Julia would be staying where Kian's powers could keep her safe. The only problem was that the suggestion pleased his uncle far too well.

Ffinian straightened and looked at Julia in a fatherly manner. "You'll be staying at Tylluan until 'tis safe for you to leave, and that's that. I'll go now and send word to my beloved Alice, and you'll see her come the morrow. Come, my lads, and darling Loris. We'll leave these two lovers alone for a space, for 'tis clear Niclas is longing to kiss his lady fair—"

"Uncle!" Niclas uttered in disbelief, while his cousins laughed, Loris smiled, and Julia blushed hotly.

His uncle merely winked at him. "And is loath to do so before an audience. Welcome to Castle Tylluan, Miss Linley. When you've rested up fully from your ordeal we'll have a grand feast to celebrate your coming."

"Welcome to you, Miss Linley," Dyfed said in his usual charming manner, smiling and nodding as he left the chamber, and Kian followed suit, stopping a moment to lift one of Julia's hands and kiss it. Loris, gathering up her bowl and cloth, said, "I'll return in half an hour to help you bathe and dress, miss. Water is heating for a proper bath and your clothes have been cleaned. I'll bring some bread and wine and a thick broth when I come, for I'm sure you must be hungry."

"They're wonderful," Julia murmured when they'd gone. "And you led me to believe they were wild."

"They're a pain," Niclas replied, smiling down at her. "But my uncle was right in one thing. I am longing to kiss you."

"Are you, Niclas?" She stroked his cheek with the backs of her fingers. "Why haven't you, then?"

"I've been too busy being relieved at your waking. You've been asleep a long time, Miss Linley."

She grinned. "Then you'd best make me glad I came to, for I do hate to leave such lovely dreams behind."

Niclas lowered his mouth toward her own. "I'll do my very best," he murmured, "to make you forget them altogether."

Fourteen

"Are you certain you're feeling well enough to walk, my dear? We can sit here on this bench beneath the tree, if you like. It's rather shady for such a cool day, but the view is lovely."

"Oh, no, Aunt," Julia assured Lady Alice, who was strolling slowly beside her, her arm linked with Julia's. "It feels good to be out of doors and walking. It was such a strange, long sleep. I feel as if I've just returned from a lengthy journey." She glanced at her aunt. "Do you wish to sit, Aunt Alice? I should be glad to do so if you'd like to stop."

"For a few moments, perhaps," Lady Alice said, and Julia thought she detected a hint of relief in her tone. "If you don't mind."

"No, not at all."

Castle Tylluan was set on a hill, and the gardens, which were beautiful, if somewhat wild and overgrown, provided a view of the valley below, where Glen Aur lay.

"It is lovely," Lady Alice said at last, sighing. "I have

lived here for the better part of my life, yet I never grow weary of it. I'm glad you're able to enjoy this particular view, Julia, for you've never seen it before now, often as you've come to visit me."

"It is beautiful," Julia agreed. "Castle Tylluan was once very grand, was it not?"

Lady Alice nodded. "A long time ago, my dear. Hundreds of years ago it was counted among the finest castles in Wales, but it's fallen far from that glory, I fear. Ffinian wants to renew its splendor, but, unfortunately," she said with a chuckle, "he wants to use my money to do it, and I fear I can't allow that."

Julia gazed at her with surprise. "You don't intend to wed him, then?"

Lady Alice looked at her with surprise. "Who, Ffinian? Of course I don't. What put such an idea into your head, my dear?"

"Well, you did, for one," Julia replied, much shocked. "Or, rather, your last letter to Aunt Eunice did. I didn't read it myself, but she told me that you had described Baron Tylluan's increasingly determined attempts to press you into marriage. You said that you were beginning to grow weary of saying no to the man, so, naturally, Aunt Eunice thought—"

"That I was near to giving in to him simply for the sake of peace?" Lady Alice asked. "Does she truly believe me such a simpleton as that? But I suppose she does, for we've seldom agreed upon any matter. I was merely expressing my frustration with Ffinian in that missive. Nothing more. Surely she wasn't so foolish as to send you all the way to Wales because of a mere letter?"

"Not just because of that," said Julia. "There was the

baron's behavior, as well. Everyone in London, all of our friends and acquaintances, are gossiping and spreading tales that he's going to force you to the altar. The rumors are so widespread that we've all begun to worry that they were true."

"Even you?" Lady Alice asked, surprised.

Julia nodded.

"Why, Julia," Lady Alice scolded, "I know what the family, and especially Eunice, thinks of me, but I never expected that you would believe such nonsense. You have far more sense than that. Why on earth should I marry Ffinian Seymour when my relationship with him suits me very well? I keep him as a lover, and——"

"Aunt!"

"Yes, as my lover," Lady Alice repeated without a hint of embarrassment, "for I'm not so old as all that, no matter what you or my sister may think, but I certainly don't wish to take another husband. Not Ffinian or any man. That may change in time, but not now. And as for being forced, I should like to see any man who could get the better of me."

Embarrassment flushed over Julia from the top of her head to the soles of her feet, a hot, tingling sensation that was distinctly uncomfortable. She felt so foolish. Of course, she knew that Ffinian Seymour and her aunt were lovers; she had known it for months, and had long since gotten over her shock. She could scarcely claim to be surprised that her aunt didn't need rescuing. It was something that should have been obvious all the way back in London.

Lady Alice was, after all, a Linley. She was strong and bold and stubborn. No one could make her do what she didn't wish, not Baron Tylluan, and certainly not her family. In fact, she had never done what the family told her to do. Ever.

But even for a Linley she was unusual. For instance, she was incredibly beautiful. Not that other Linleys weren't, for many were. But Lady Alice was beautiful in the same way that silk was sensual. Age had whitened her dark hair, but though she was seventy, little else about her had changed. Her skin was as smooth as a young girl's and her bright blue eyes were yet undimmed. She was . . . luxuriant, Julia thought, unable to think of a more apt description, and so striking that it still made men stare as she passed by. With wit, charm, and wealth added to the mix, it was no wonder Ffinian Seymour sought Lady Alice as a wife.

"He seems terribly determined to make you change your mind," Julia said.

"He does," Lady Alice agreed, patting Julia's hand, "but, unlike my sister, I've had a great deal of experience in handling men, and I do not require the aid of the family in order to do so. Not that I'm sorry you've come, dear, for it's wonderful to see you again, but I do wish you'd not been sent on so foolish and useless an errand."

Julia stared at her gorgeous aunt in silence, thinking back over the past several days and all that she and Niclas had gone through.

"Niclas is going to hate me," she said. "And his entire family, too. Especially Lord Graymar." She groaned and lowered her face into her hands.

"Nonsense," Lady Alice said reassuringly. "Lord Graymar is a lovely young man, and I quite approve of

Niclas Seymour. He'll make a fine husband, for he clearly adores you, though goodness knows you'll have a terrible time with the family about it. Linleys are so superior that it's a wonder they ever find any suitable mates."

"Aunt—"

"You must follow your heart, my dear, even if it means angering the family. I can tell you from experience that if you love Niclas Seymour, you'll never regret choosing him over the life your relatives would keep you in. I never for a moment regretted making that same choice when I wed Hueil Morgan. He more than made up for what I lost." She took Julia's chin in her hand and looked directly into her eyes. "Eunice and your parents would never understand or agree with that, but you are not like them, my dear. And you never will be."

"I think you must be right," Julia said, "for I've always been a terrible disappointment. I've tried to be what they want, to do what they want, but it seems impossible. I must not be stubborn enough."

"How foolish," Aunt Alice said. "All Linleys are stubborn, love. It's in our blood, regardless of any other peculiarities. Now, I tell you what we'll do. You'll stay with me at Glen Aur for the remainder of the season, if you like, for I should enjoy it above all things. Your young man may stay here at Tylluan and you can see each other as often as you wish without any family interference— you must know that once you're beneath my sister's eye she'll never allow the two of you a private moment alone, even when you're properly betrothed."

"Niclas isn't my young màn, Aunt. He's—"

"And then," Lady Alice went on happily, "perhaps at the end of the summer—for it's always so dreadfully hot in town, and we'd be far more comfortable spending those months at Glen Aur—we'll go to London together. I'll assure your mother and father and Eunice that you and Mister Seymour saved me from Ffinian's wicked designs, and that if it hadn't been for your coming to Wales I might have been forced into an unwanted marriage."

"That would please them no end," Julia confessed. "Aunt Eunice should love the opportunity to scold you for being so foolish as to have ever come to Wales in the first place."

Aunt Alice laughed. "Wouldn't she, though? I can hear her now, and see her expression. She's always been frightfully angry with me for following my heart. But perhaps she'll be so pleased with you that she'll allow you to follow yours with little difficulty. If Eunice will give Niclas Seymour her blessing, your parents will surely follow."

"You're so kind to offer to do such a thing for me, Aunt," Julia said, "but I fear it would do no good. Niclas Seymour is not going to wed me."

"Of course he is," her aunt insisted. "I saw it the very moment when I first arrived at Tylluan to visit you while you yet slept. The boy was in such a state, and all his thoughts were of you. He hadn't taken a moment's rest while you were insensible, but stayed by your side constantly. It was immediately clear not only to me, but to everyone who saw him, what his feelings for you are. And what yours are for him, for that matter. Every time you hear his name you blush in the most delightfully youthful manner—you're doing it this very moment. It would be foolish to pretend that you don't love the boy."

Tears began to sting at the back of Julia's eyes, and she drew in a slow breath.

"I've loved Niclas Seymour for the past eight years, from the moment I set sight on him in London. It was at a ball, and he was dancing, and I— Well, it doesn't matter."

"But it does!" Lady Alice insisted. "Darling, what on earth could possibly keep the two of you apart? You don't truly care for what the family thinks and he's not already bound to another." She paused thoughtfully, then understanding filled her sparkling blue eyes, and she said, in a deep, almost angry tone, "Never tell me it's because of the magic?"

Julia blinked. "Do you know about that, too, Aunt? It makes sense, of course, for you've known Baron Tylluan these many years and haven't yet asked me why I was in the castle, sleeping for so many days. Anyone unused to such things would have been terribly distraught, I imagine."

"I knew of the magical families and their ways long before Ffinian and I began our relationship," her aunt replied. "My own dear Hueil was a sympathetic to such families, as many Welsh are. But how foolish of that boy to let anything so unimportant keep him from marriage. Surely he realizes, after all you've been through, that you'd never reveal the Seymours' secrets."

"It isn't that," she said. "There's something else. Something inside of him. I can't explain it to you, for I don't entirely know myself."

"Then you must ask him, my dear."

"I will," Julia promised. "But please, promise me that you'll say nothing to Niclas of not needing rescue from Baron Tylluan. He's come all this way, and for some reason it was very important to him. So important that he went to great trouble to convince Aunt Eunice to accept him as my escort in place of Lord Graymar. And the journey hasn't been the least simple or easy."

Lady Alice smiled warmly. "I shall do my best to play the lady in distress. But if it was as important to him as you say, he's going to realize the truth rather shortly."

Julia nodded. "I'll tell him the truth. Tonight. The baron has insisted upon a grand feast with all his men in attendance to welcome me to the castle properly, and as soon as it's over, I'll tell him."

"And afterward?"

"Afterward," Julia said, "he'll return to London, and if your kind offer to stay with you during the summer is still open, I'll come to Glen Aur."

"Look at them," Niclas said, standing at the window of his bedchamber, gazing down into the garden where Lady Alice and Julia were slowly strolling, arm in arm. "They have their heads together like two young girls chattering about the latest fashions. I wonder what they're talking about?"

"It's been several years since Miss Linley last saw her ladyship," Abercraf remarked from across the room, where he was deftly folding Niclas's freshly laundered clothes. "I imagine they have a great deal to discuss."

"Yes," Niclas murmured. "Just the events of the last few days will take some time to tell, I imagine. Fortunately, Lady Alice's late husband, Sir Hueil, was one of our sympathetics, so I doubt she'll be surprised by what she hears."

"If not because of that," said Abercraf, "then certainly from being in company with Baron Tylluan."

"Very true," Niclas murmured.

"Miss Linley seems to have come through very well, just as Jane did. I'm afraid, however, that Jane's quite angry about not being able to remain with Miss Linley. I don't know how to explain it to her."

"We went to a great deal of trouble to erase the knowledge of Seymour magic from her memories," Niclas said. "If Jane were to stay at Tylluan she'd discover it all over again in a very short time. I'm nervous about her being here even for a few hours, although I suppose there's little chance that she'll run into my uncle or cousins."

"No, no, she's quite busy repairing Miss Linley's garments and setting her bedchamber to order. It should keep her occupied until Lady Alice is ready to depart."

Niclas hoped that was the case. Neither Ffinian nor his sons made an effort to hide their talents, with the result that objects flew to their destinations, rather than being retrieved, doors opened without being touched, fires were lit without the help of a match, and, in Dyfed's case, a voice was heard in one's head without the use of speech.

Julia had held up remarkably well while being in company with the Tylluan Seymours for the past day and a half. Indeed, she'd not seemed to mind their odd ways at all, and had been readily and warmly received by them in kind. She and Loris appeared to get along especially well, which Niclas knew was a boon for the younger girl; Loris had very little female company at Castle Tylluan.

He only prayed that things would go well tonight, during the feast that Ffinian had been so merrily preparing. Niclas had attended several such feasts, and they had all started well and ended riotously.

"Do you require another draft of potion, sir?" Abercraf asked, offering to refill the empty glass in Niclas's hand.

"No, thank you," he replied, and set the glass aside. "It seems to work better than the last few Lord Graymar's made. And it doesn't taste quite so bad, either."

"You do look much improved from yesterday, sir," said Abercraf, picking up a neckcloth and approaching Niclas. "The rest you took, as well as the potion, appear to have done you a great deal of good."

"Yes, they have," Niclas agreed, standing still as Abercraf expertly arranged the cloth about his neck. "I almost feel myself again. Or as much as that's possible."

The truth was that he'd been so exhausted following Julia's return that he'd spent a full ten hours lying flat on a bed, eyes closed, murmuring the ancient chant Malachi had taught him. That, along with the potion, had proved so successful that it would probably be days before he'd need to rest again.

The trouble was, being well rested, and having the crisis surrounding Julia over, left Niclas with few excuses for not facing the truth about the uselessness of his attempt to lift the curse.

There was nothing to rescue Lady Alice from. Niclas had sensed what her feelings were when she'd come to Tylluan shortly after they had arrived, when Julia had still been insensible. Despite the intense concern she'd held for her niece, the emotions that she experienced in Ffinian's presence were still strong, and none of them was fear. Lady Alice felt love for Ffinian, tenderness, a little impatience and exasperation, but not fear.

There was nothing that he could do for the Linleys, for there had never truly been a problem. Malachi had tried to warn him that the effort wouldn't be enough to affect the curse, and Niclas had accepted that his cousin was probably right. But it wasn't until he'd actually come to Tylluan and seen for himself how matters stood between Ffinian and Lady Alice that he'd given up hope. Because this had been his last chance, and he had clung to it, not letting himself consider just how slim it truly was.

In the garden below, Julia and her aunt embraced, and then began to move slowly toward the gate that led to Lady Alice's waiting carriage.

There was still one matter to occupy him for a few days more. Cadmaran was yet a danger to them, at least until Malachi had Ceridwen safely married to Colonel Spar. Julia would have to remain at Tylluan until then, and Niclas would have to stay, as well, to make certain that she was safe. They would have a little time to enjoy each other's company before they had to begin their journey back to London, and before Niclas had to decide what he wanted to do. But he wasn't going to think about that now. Julia made him happy, and that was what he wanted to dwell on until their time was gone. It was a gift he would give himself.

"Lady Alice is about to leave," he murmured, turning from the window to allow Abercraf to help him into his jacket. "Jane will need to hurry and gather her things in order to accompany her back to Glen Aur."

"I'll go at once and tell her, sir," Abercraf said, smoothing the shoulders and lapels of the tight-fitting garment. "Shall I bring you a breakfast tray afterward?"

"No, thank you. I'm going downstairs to speak with Miss Linley."

At the bottom of the stairs Niclas came to a halt, arrested by a strong surge of emotions coming from a hallway just around the corner to his left. Low voices confirmed the presence of at least two persons who were hidden from his view, and what he felt coming from there made him wonder if he should proceed.

Panic, anger . . . and what else? The strength of the feelings made him think instantly of Loris, and the sound of her voice the next moment told him that he'd been right.

"Get out of my way."

"Why? You've plenty of room to pass, darling Loris."

"Don't call me that!"

"And why shouldn't I? Everyone else at Tylluan does. Darling Loris. Dearest Loris. Or is it only from my lips that you don't want to hear the words?"

"If you don't move—"

"Say my name first."

"—I'll kick you."

"Say my name. I want to hear it. You say Dyfed's name all the time. Why can't you say mine?"

"I'll count to three, and then—"

"Say it, Loris. Just once."

"One."

"Please."

She faltered for a moment, but then, a bit shakily, continued. "Two."

A lengthy silence followed, and Niclas knew that Kian had quieted her with a kiss. Her heart had filled with pain, longing, and despair, and they were so similar that he could scarce tell one from the other.

He slipped away from the stairs and across the hallway entrance, glancing only briefly to see Loris pinned against a wall by Kian's much larger figure. She wasn't fighting, she wasn't even resisting, and Kian's kiss appeared to be neither rough nor forceful. Whatever struggle was taking place between the two of them now was internal, and Niclas was quite certain that he wouldn't be able to figure it out.

He had just exited through one of the heavy main doors when another familiar voice hailed him.

"Ah, there you are, my lad," Uncle Ffinian said happily, stomping in his usual hearty manner from the direction of a copse of trees. He held a gun in one hand and a collection of motley dogs—not a one of them hunters—loped along at his side.

"Been out birding, have you, Uncle? Had any luck?"

"Nah, damned dogs scare them all away before I can get a shot."

"Then perhaps you shouldn't take them," Niclas advised, though he couldn't resist reaching down to scratch a couple of their soft, furry heads. They responded with slavish, wagging delight.

"Ah, well, they like coming along and I don't want to spoil their fun. And it doesn't matter, really," he said, grinning widely, "I can never hit the birds even when I do have time to aim. Kian and Dyfed keep fowl on the table. My own talent is with the fish."

"That's only because the faeries help you," Niclas teased.

Ffinian laughed and gave a shake of his head. "Aye, that's true, lad, very true. Now, where are you off to this fine morning? And where is Miss Linley?"

"Presently, she's by the garden gate, saying good-bye to Lady Alice. You didn't know she'd come?"

Ffinian's face lit up like a lamp. "Ah, she's come? So early? No, I didn't expect it, for she is given to coming after luncheon, if she comes at all. It's usually me who does all the going up and down the hill if I wish to have a little visit. But she's going away already, you say? I can't be having that," he said, setting his gun aside on a low wall. "Hurry! We can't let her get away!"

"Uncle, she's not a thief who needs catching, and I have no intention of—"

But his uncle strode down the driveway without listening, disappearing beyond the garden wall. Sighing, Niclas began to follow, and very nearly ran Julia down as she came hurrying from the place where his uncle had disappeared.

"Oh, I'm sorry!" she said as they just missed colliding. "I wasn't looking where I was going and didn't expect—"

With his hands on her shoulders, Niclas steadied her and said, "The fault is mine entirely. Please don't apologize."

She smiled up at him, searching his face. "You're looking much improved this morning. You must have slept well."

"As well as I generally do," he replied. "I was just coming to find you, Julia. If you're not yet weary of walking through my uncle's gardens—though I'm not entirely certain they can properly be called that—would you do me the honor of giving me your company?"

"I should be delighted," she said, her smile widening, "but my aunt is about to leave and I must fetch Jane."

"She'll be down shortly. Abercraf is getting her. This is probably her now," he said as one of the massive castle doors opened. They watched as Loris struggled to make her way outside, held back by Kian with a hand on her arm. She swung at him with her other hand, whacking him soundly on the shoulder and gaining her freedom. Then she strode off toward the stables and Kian went back inside, closing the door firmly behind him.

Niclas turned back to Julia. "Or perhaps it's only Kian and Loris having another fight."

Julia sighed and shook her head. "That," she said as Niclas began to lead her toward the nearest garden gate, "is a very complicated relationship. They clearly want to deny their feelings for each other. But it's odd, isn't it, that she should be betrothed to the brother when she really doesn't care for him as she does for Kian."

"Loris?" Niclas asked, much surprised by her comments. "You believe that Loris and Kian are in love?"

"It seems obvious to me that they are," she replied simply.

"That's impossible," Niclas told her.

"Why?" she asked, pausing as he opened the gate and then walking through it. "Because of the curse that was laid upon Loris? A blood curse, I believe she called it." She made a sound of distaste. "It sounds terrible, does it not?"

Niclas stopped just inside the gate and, freezing, stared at her. Panic threatened to overwhelm him, and he could scarce think of what to do or say.

She walked a few steps farther into the overgrown garden, but when she realized that he hadn't followed, she stopped and turned.

"Niclas?"

"Loris told you of it?" he asked, his voice thick in his throat.

Julia's blue eyes filled with regret, and she moved back to take one of his hands. "I'm sorry. I didn't realize it would upset you for me to know of such things. And truly, I know very little, for Loris only spoke of it briefly, as a way to explain her unruly relationship with Kian. I didn't even have the feeling that she believed it was true. She was quite dismissive about it."

Niclas squeezed her hand lightly and mastered himself.

"Aye, she is, and always has been. But some people," he said solemnly, "have difficulty accepting that their lives have been altered by some power outside their control."

"I understand," Julia said, searching his face. "Loris is a strong person, like my Aunt Eunice. She would not lightly accept any interference in her life. But is it true, then? Is there a curse on her? A blood curse?"

He drew in a tight breath and set her hand on his arm.

"Let's walk."

He shut the gate and they began to move, without any clear direction at first, and then Niclas found one of the paths that had nearly been overgrown with grass and led her that way.

"I apologize for the state of the gardens," he said. "For the entire castle, but especially for the gardens. I wish my uncle would at least keep them in some state of order. That only requires a little labor, not a fortune."

"Tylluan is terribly in need of repair, isn't it?" Julia replied conversationally, but he could hear the tension behind the words. "Loris has done admirably in making it as presentable as possible."

"She's kept it from falling down into a crumbling heap," Niclas agreed. "My uncle is a fine fellow, in his way, but he hasn't any interest in managing himself or his affairs in such a way as to actually make himself prosperous. Kian will do much better, once he's the baron."

"He does seem a capable young man," she said, and then they fell silent.

The far side of the garden came to an end at the top of a cliff, where a low wall gave way to a particularly spectacular view of the valley. An ancient stone bench set before the wall was the favorite spot of all who went into the gardens. Niclas had hoped to take Julia there because it would provide a private place where he might be completely alone with her and away from his prying family. They had so little time left; he didn't want to spend it speaking of the very thing that endlessly haunted him. But they would speak of it, even if he couldn't bring himself to confess the whole.

"Oh, how beautiful," she murmured as they neared the garden's edge. "You can see Glen Aur so well from here. How lovely it is."

She was lovely, he wanted to say aloud. She wore an alluring gown in a shade of blue that put him in mind of the awful garment she'd worn to the Dubrow ball, save that this gown was delightfully becoming. It was very feminine, as she was, and accentuated her slender, delicate frame in a most enticing manner. Niclas found it hard to keep from touching her. He made himself look at the view before them, instead.

"I've often imagined Ffinian standing here in the evenings, gazing down at the lights of Glen Aur," he said, "and thinking of your aunt. Missing her and wondering when he would see her again."

"I believe he must," she said. "He loves her. I'm certain of that. But I'm equally certain that the reason he wishes to wed her is her wealth."

"It's most likely," Niclas agreed. "Marriage never seemed to sit well with him, even when my aunt was alive. But she had a gift for keeping their wealth and making him even wealthier, and he adored her to her final day. Sadly, when she was gone, he lost nearly all she had gained for him and her sons."

"Is that why he loves my aunt, then?" she asked, troubled. "Because she has a way with money?"

He smiled and touched her cheek in a brief caress. "No, my dear. He wants to marry her because of her way with money, but he loves her for herself. Having met Lady Alice, I quite understand. In fact, I would think my uncle a fool if he did not love her. Come and sit."

He took one of her hands and led her to the bench, then sat close beside her. He didn't release her, but spent a quiet moment comparing the sizes of their hands, gently pressing their palms together. Lifting his other hand, he traced the lines of slender bones with a single fingertip, and felt her shiver slightly beneath the light touch.

"You are so delicate," he murmured. "So dainty and exquisite. Wizards—some wizards—are born with the ability to tap into supernatural strength, and this is one of the gifts I possess. Yet the power you wield over me makes that strength seem useless by comparison. I have felt great affection for a number of women in my life, but none has ever before captured my heart." He gazed at her fully. "You have both captured and conquered it, Julia."

"Niclas," she murmured, but he stopped her with a shake of his head.

"We shouldn't speak of it more. There is nothing I can offer you beyond my heart, as little as that may be worth," he told her. "I simply wanted you to know." Releasing her hand, he straightened and turned to look at the vista before them.

"Among my people, a blood curse is the worst kind of magic that can befall a group or individual. It's complicated to explain how such a curse works, for the circumstances surrounding each have a great deal to do with exactly what the curse will be. It's helpful that you've met the guardians and understand something of what they are. They are the ones who decide when an act worthy of punishment has been committed, and what that remedy should be."

"The guardians?" she asked. "They wield so great a power over your people?"

"It's a power that's been given to them by the ones who rule the world we were exiled from." When she raised her eyebrows, he said, "That story is far too long to tell. Suffice it to say that the guardians were given such power over us because they are very wise and can see all that occurs in this world.

"When a supernatural mortal uses his or her powers, either directly or indirectly, and blood is shed, the guardians make a judgment of guilt or innocence and, if they find guilt, decide upon a punishment. There are a great many variables, of course, such as in times of war or of an action taken in self-defense. Age and maturity play a part, too, for younger members of the Families are held to a lesser standard. But even then there are exceptions. Kian was but seventeen when he brought down the curse that plagues both Loris and himself, and it might well be argued that he acted in self-defense when blood was drawn. Yet the guardians judged him guilty, and he was punished accordingly."

"But wasn't the curse set upon Loris?" Julia asked. "So that she could never feel anything but hatred for him?"

"Loris was the one chosen for Kian, long before they met. She has never believed that, of course, but I think that's due to the curse. It has filled her with disbelief."

"Chosen?"

"To be his mate," Niclas said softly, sadness rising within him. "When one of my kind takes a mate, a special magic is invoked that creates a powerful bond, and they become what we call a *unoliaeth*, or oneness, to each other. In rare instances, however, the guardians select a mate, or *unoliaeth*, for one of our kind, and that choice cannot be altered. Kian's mate was decided for him before either he or Loris were even born, and now she is the only woman that Kian can ever love."

"Oh, no," Julia murmured. "And yet she cannot love him, because of the curse. Then the guardians have indeed punished him fully for whatever wrong he did." She looked deeply troubled. "They seemed such kind beings when I was with them. How could they condemn anyone to so terrible a fate? Can nothing be done to redeem such a curse?"

"Every blood curse is different," Niclas said, "but each can be lifted in some specific way. The challenge for the one who is cursed is to find that way. And that isn't always easy. The guardians tend to think on a mystical plane, and their idea of recompense is usually quite different from ours."

"But surely Lord Graymar would know how to lift such a curse? Or Steffan could go to the spirit realm and ask the guardians?"

Niclas smiled grimly. "Magic isn't always as easy as it may seem. In fact, it's often more trouble than help."

Julia reached out to touch his hand, lightly. "Are they lifted very often? Blood curses?"

"No," he said, and stood, strolling the few steps to the half-wall. "Not very often."

He gazed down into the valley and thought of a way to turn the topic. Any more talk of blood curses was going to lead to revelations that he wasn't yet ready for.

"Steffan is down there somewhere," he said, "though I don't suppose we can see his camp from here. It will be hidden by the trees."

"Steffan?" Julia asked, still seated on the bench. "I assumed that he and his men returned to their home camp."

"Not yet. There's a certain stream in the valley, not far from your aunt's estate, where particularly knowing water faeries live. Steffan has been encamped there with his men, reading the bowl and communicating to Malachi with their help. It requires a great deal of swimming, however, as the faeries can't come out of the water, so he's obliged to remain near the stream."

"Is he still trying to discover Cadmaran's whereabouts?"

He nodded. "Aye, but with no luck yet. Even Malachi doesn't know where he is, though my cousin Ceridwen is safe, regardless. Malachi's striving to get her wed to the man she's betrothed to, and once they're married there will be nothing Cadmaran can do. She'll be protected by a magic that he has no power against."

"Truly?" she asked, clearly surprised by this. "There are obviously many exceptions to magic that I know nothing about. But if marriage is the simple answer, then why should that be so difficult to arrange? Surely the earl of Graymar can procure a special license with ease."

"When someone in a magical family wishes to marry,"

he said, moving back to sit beside her, "they must first seek permission of what we call 'elders'—not because they're aged, but because they have attained great wisdom—who are selected from each of the families in our union. Especially when the proposed spouse is a mere mortal. Well," he amended thoughtfully, "I suppose that's not entirely true. Morcar Cadmaran asked for Ceridwen's hand in marriage and that was the most hotly contested proposal in family history, or so I hear tell. I don't know why it's taking so long for them to decide about Colonel Spar and Ceridwen. He's exactly the sort of sympathetic mortal that we need in the family."

"Colonel Adam Spar?" Julia asked, straightening. "He's to wed your cousin?"

"Do you know him?"

She laughed merrily. "Oh, indeed, I do. The poor fellow made the mistake of taking pity on me five seasons ago and asking me to dance. My family immediately tried to force him into marrying me, and he felt so sorry for me that I think he would have done it if I hadn't scolded him for giving way to them." She sighed at the memory. "He was a fine and handsome gentleman and I was so grateful for his kindness." She smiled up into Niclas's now scowling face. "I'm so glad he's to wed your cousin. She's a fortunate woman, and you must like him, too, knowing the kind of man he is. He'll be very good to her."

"I did like him," Niclas muttered irately. "I hate him now. I hate every man who ever danced with you, or smiled at you. Or even looked at you back then."

Julia didn't appear to be alarmed by his anger; she raised a hand and set it upon his chest.

"Don't be foolish," she chided gently. "They cared

nothing for such a little mouse, and I cared nothing for them."

"It should have been *me*," he said, not even knowing how to tell her what he felt. She had been there, for years, and he'd never known. It was as if he'd missed the most important thing in his life, never even aware of her. "It should have been me," he said again, and then, without considering whether it was wise or right, he gathered her up in his arms and kissed her.

It was impossible to be gentle when he was filled with such anger and desperation, but she murmured against his seeking lips and gentled him by degrees, fitting into the crook of the arm that was lashed about her and sliding her own arm about his neck.

His lips were just parting over her own when they heard Kian shouting.

"Hey, Niclas! Stop that! Let Miss Linley breathe for a moment, will you?"

Niclas made a growling sound and lifted his head. Julia laughed, and they both looked to see Kian standing not far off.

"He's heartless, that boy," he muttered. "I shall make him rue the day he was born."

To Kian he called, irately, "What is it?"

"Steffan's just arrived! He bears good tidings from Malachi."

Niclas was dragging Julia in the direction of the gate before Kian had finished speaking.

"What's happened?" he demanded sharply. "Is Ceridwen—"

"She's fine," Kian said happily. "She and Colonel Spar were married last night."

"So soon?" Niclas said, surprised. "How on earth did Malachi manage to convince the elders so quickly?" The relief he felt was mixed with a sense of dread. The precious time he'd hoped to have with Julia was suddenly fading.

"Is she safe, then?" Julia asked.

"Aye, as safe as she can possibly be," Kian answered. "Cadmaran can't touch her now. And Colonel Spar is safe, as well. To harm either of them would cause Lord Llew to lose many of his powers, and he won't chance that."

"Where has the earl of Llew gone, then?" Niclas asked. "Is he yet in London? Or does he come here, seeking revenge?"

"Steffan reports that he's merely begun his journey back to Castle Llew. It would do him no good to visit revenge on you now, Niclas, for he has nothing to gain and much to lose. Ceridwen is lost to him completely, now that she's wed. It's likely he's going home to lick his wounds. He'll give us no further trouble." He looked from one to the other, smiling his rare smile. "You're safe, now, Miss Linley," he said, and offered her his arm to escort her back into the castle. "We shall have much to celebrate at the feast this evening."

Fifteen

The rain had started not long after the feast ended. It put Niclas in mind of the night when he and Julia had escaped Cadmaran in Shrewsbury and made their way across the border to Wales. Enoch had safely carried them to Arionrhod's dwelling, and Julia had slept in Niclas's arms, warm and softly feminine, wrapped in his heavy coat.

A gust of cold, damp wind blew in through the tall open window where Niclas stood, ruffling the edges of his hair and chilling the flesh where his unbuttoned shirt lay open.

The chamber behind him was dark. He'd sent Abercraf to bed without letting him light a fire, then had blown out all the candles and lamps so that the atmosphere would match his mood. He had meant to go out riding, but the rain had put an end to his plans. It was one thing to force a beast out into such weather when it was absolutely necessary, but quite another to ask the creature to endure the same merely because a man wished to exhaust himself beyond all pain.

Lightning briefly lit the sky as well as the valley below, where the lights of Glen Aur twinkled merrily against the night's black cover. He hoped that Julia saw it from her window, as well. It would make a pretty memory to take home to London.

Tomorrow, if the rain stopped, they would begin their journey back. She was fully recovered from her visit to the spirit realm, and they were safe from Cadmaran. More importantly, there was nothing for them to accomplish here between her aunt and his uncle, and thus no reason to delay the return. The sooner he had her home again, the better. What he would do after that, Niclas wasn't yet sure.

The curse would not be lifted, and because of that, he could not allow himself to see her again once they were in London. And as he knew very well that he wouldn't be able to stay away from her if she was anywhere within hundreds of miles of his reach, Niclas had to either go far, far away, or find another solution.

The wind blew again, harder this time, so that rain swept inside the window to briefly shower both him and the floor. Niclas closed his eyes and wished the cold of the night might freeze him right through. Freeze away every thought, every feeling.

She'd been happy tonight. That's what he would think on. The grand feast that Ffinian and his untamed sons had given in Julia's honor. Niclas smiled just remembering.

It had been typical of the wild celebrations to be found at Castle Tylluan. There had been music and laughter and dancing and a bounty of fine food and drink. Ffinian had been his jovial, mad self, entertaining Julia, the guest of honor, with his tall tales and bawdy jokes, while Steffan,

Kian, and Dyfed had taken turns regaling her with a Seymour family history that almost had Niclas blushing.

She had laughed with real pleasure and thoroughly enjoyed herself, and Niclas had been relieved by her happy acceptance of his strange—but admittedly entertaining—family. There were few mere mortal women of his acquaintance who wouldn't have run screaming out the doors, but Julia, perhaps because of the Tarian, perhaps because of her recent experiences with magic, or perhaps because she was simply Julia, clearly had no trouble at all in the discovery of such people.

But then the celebration had changed, just as it always did after a few hours of drinking, and what had been entertaining became rather more dangerous.

Many of Ffinian's and some of Steffan's men were lesser wizards, and, though none possessed remarkable skills, some were capable of the common magic of levitating objects. Along with Kian, these men had devised a game that involved flying objects striking various other objects or places in the great hall for different points. A fork knocking down an empty bottle of wine was two points. A salt cellar striking a candlestick was five points. A spoon hitting the nose on a fading face in an old tapestry hanging upon the far wall was ten points. This alone was enough to make Niclas nervous, for any innocent individual might accidentally be struck by so many flying objects.

But then, as usual, it got worse.

Whoever could float a napkin the closest to a candle flame without it catching fire won twenty points, with the result that numerous cloths caught fire and sent small bits of glowing ash about the hall. After being obliged to pour a pitcher of water on a smoking curtain, Loris thankfully put an end to that particular aspect of the sport.

But that didn't dim the gamesters' spirits. Kian, half-drunk and more than a little angry at what he viewed as Loris's attempt to spoil their pleasure, jumped up on one of the tables and, ignoring Dyfed's pleas to get down, challenged the men to strike him with any object they could levitate.

Niclas had hurriedly grabbed Julia and moved her away from the table and to the other side of the hall, ducking as everything from plates to lamps began flying.

Loris remonstrated, Niclas remonstrated, and Dyfed made yet another attempt, but it was to no avail. Ffinian pounded gleefully on the table with a fist and Steffan clapped in time as Kian leaped and jumped out of harm's way, dancing up and down the length of the table, kicking food and platters and cups and pitchers out of his way and deflecting objects with both magic and athletic skill. Steffan's men, who had brought their instruments along, struck up a lively tune and raucous shouting and laughter filled the hall as the game grew increasingly fast and furious.

"Good heavens," Julia murmured, staring wide-eyed at the spectacle. "They're flinging knives at him. Are you sure he won't be hurt?"

"No, I'm not," Niclas said, dragging her down under the cover of a side table as a piece of crockery smashed against the wall above their heads. "But I'm going to make sure we aren't."

"Please tell me this isn't for my benefit alone," she said, burrowing close as Niclas's arms folded about her and a large silver platter struck the wall.

"No, this is what happens at every celebratory feast, I'm afraid. Loris will put a stop to it in a moment."

"*Loris?*" Julia said with disbelief.

"She's the only one who can. I've tried before, believe me, but it only makes them worse. Even Malachi can't make them stop unless it's by force, and we always pay for it later when Kian and Dyfed are in London. Look, she's had enough. She's going to stop them now."

He felt Julia lift her head just enough to watch as Loris made her way across the great hall, walking directly toward the table where Kian yet performed his skillful dance. She showed no fear of the objects flying in all directions, and deftly ducked and sidestepped as she made her way. At last, Kian saw Loris coming, and he fell still, breathing heavily with the exertion of the game. His smile and laughter died away and his expression, as he gazed at Loris, tightened. Reaching out a single hand, he brought the movement of all objects to a halt, so that those which were in midair fell harmlessly to the ground. Loris came to stand before him, placing her hands on her hips and meeting Kian's angry gaze with her own.

"Now, darling Loris," Ffinian said placatingly, still sitting in his place at the head of the long table. "We were only having a bit of fun."

"You've had your fun," she said, "as usual. And you've made a mess, as usual. And, as usual"—she turned her gaze to Ffinian—"you've broken that which we can't afford to replace. If this goes on we'll have nothing left to eat or drink with but our bare hands."

"Don't fret over a bit of broken crockery, dearest girl," Ffinian replied, failing miserably at looking contrite. "Once I've wed my dear Lady Alice we'll have plates of gold to dine upon. There's no need to be in such a taking."

"Loris is always in a taking, *tad*," Kian said, jumping lightly from the table to stand before her. Loris was tall for a female, yet she was obliged to tilt her head up to hold his gaze. "Are you not, darling Loris?"

"Not always," she replied evenly. "But if this mess isn't cleared away before the hour is out I shall be in a taking such as no Welshman has ever before seen."

The cleaning of the hall had immediately begun. Ffinian invited those guests who weren't involved in the chore to join him in the library, where he would no doubt continue drinking until he was too weary to go on. Steffan had readily accepted, but Julia, realizing that the presence of a lady would only dull the men's fun, had pleaded weariness. Tendering her good-nights, she had climbed the stairs to her bedchamber. Niclas had stayed with his cousins and uncle for two glasses of whisky, then had ignored their drunken insistences that he stay and excused himself. That had been three hours past, and the castle had grown quiet and dark, all those occupants who weren't on duty as guards having sought their beds.

It was a good night for sleeping, Niclas thought as yet another flash of lightning lit the sky. Cold, stormy nights always made a bed seem warmer, and a pillow softer. He glanced at the large, comfortable bed in the chamber. Abercraf had pulled the covers back and made it ready in case Niclas wished to lie down and rest. It was a game they played out every night, a way to maintain a semblance of normalcy. There had been a time when Niclas had thought it a good idea, a hope for the day when it would no longer be a farce. Now he could only view it with despair.

Sighing, he turned his gaze back out the open window.

It was going to be a long night, but at least he had the storm for company.

Julia shivered as she made her way down the dark hallway, the flame of her candle flickering in the chilly breeze that whistled its way in through the little cracks in the castle walls. The fire in her room had managed to keep her warm even after the storm began and the air grew colder, but the castle halls felt like the inside of a cave. The discomfort would be short-lived, though, once she found Niclas's chamber.

She thought, when she first pushed the heavy door open, that she had made a mistake. Loris must have been confused when she'd told her Niclas was using this room, for it was as cold as the hallway and completely dark. Julia very nearly went back out at once, pulling the door to shut it, but the sound of the rain and wind blowing through the chamber's open window made her stop.

She stepped back in and stood quietly, waiting. A flash of light from the storm revealed Niclas's tall form, and she shut the door behind her, then turned to throw the bolt.

He said nothing as she came near, clutching the shawl she'd thrown over her gown tightly about her neck and lifting the candle a bit higher to find her way.

"You shouldn't be here," he said softly, his face only partly illumined by the flickering candlelight.

"Why don't you have a fire?" she asked. "It's freezing in here. You'll catch a chill."

He made a movement toward her, saying, stiffly, "Let me take you back to your room," but she stepped back.

"No, Niclas. I've come to speak with you, and . . . and I don't plan to leave, even after that." She swallowed against the nervousness that trembled in her voice.

He stood where he was, silent. The fitful wind gusted, making the open window rattle and droplets of rain splatter on to the floor and walls—and on Niclas, as well. Julia shivered, and as her eyes grew used to the darkness, she could see that he wasn't wearing a jacket. Worse, the buttons of his shirt were undone, revealing the skin beneath.

"What are you doing?" she asked, feeling slightly aggravated. "You can't possibly be comfortable."

He shrugged. "I find it refreshing. What did you come to speak with me about so late at night? I imagined you long asleep by now."

"I was, for an hour or so," she confessed. "But then something woke me."

He looked at her curiously. "What?"

"A question," she said. "Or perhaps a realization. I should have known after you explained everything to me this afternoon, but my mind has been occupied with other matters. Niclas—" She moved closer, and the wind blew out her candle. "Please tell me. Has a curse been laid on you? A blood curse?"

She could scarcely make out his features without the help of the candle, but she both felt and heard the quiet sigh he gave.

"Stay here," he murmured, and took the candlestick out of her hand. He walked away and she heard a great deal of cloth rustling from the direction of the enormous bed that sat in the middle of the room. When he returned he enfolded Julia in a soft, heavy blanket, then drew her into his arms and settled again in front of the open window.

"Look," he said, cradling her so that her head rested upon his chest. "You can see the lights of Glen Aur from here, even in the storm."

Her shivering began to lessen in the blanket's comforting warmth. She could feel the strength of the arms lashed about her, and the gentleness, as well.

Cold air stung her cheeks as she looked to where he pointed. In the valley below the lights of Glen Aur twinkled invitingly, and she thought of her aunt there, safe and sleeping.

"It's beautiful," she whispered. "My aunt has asked me to stay with her through the rest of the Season. And the summer, as well."

"Has she?" he asked, a touch of surprise in his tone. "Perhaps that would be best."

She swallowed again, harder this time. "Do you think so, Niclas?"

"Yes," he said, his voice low. "I do. I would far rather leave you with Lady Alice, where I know you will be in pleasant company, than take you back to London and put you beneath Lady Eunice's hand again. I want you to be happy, Julia."

Rain blew in through the window again, and Julia closed her eyes and lifted her face to feel the cold drops on her skin.

"I am under a blood curse," he said softly, his arms tightening. "I came to Wales, brought you here, in the hope of lifting it by preventing my uncle from forcing himself upon your aunt. But as I'm sure you've discovered without my having to say it, there was nothing to be stopped. No unpleasant deed to be performed. Ffinian speaks of marrying your aunt, but Lady Alice clearly has him well in hand." He spoke tonelessly, without emotion, and Julia felt her heart breaking. "We came for nothing, Julia. You suffered this journey, and Cadmaran's spell, and were nearly lost to the spirit realm for nothing. Instead of performing a good deed for the Linleys, I've only added insult to injury. Except in this instance, if any lasting harm had come to you, I wouldn't have needed a curse to teach me sorrow."

She turned in his arms to look up at him, gazing into the light eyes, dimmed by the darkness.

"I don't understand," she said. "How could doing something for my family help to lift a curse? You've done nothing to us."

He lifted a hand and, with gentle fingertips, wiped the moisture from her face. Then he stroked the edges of her hair back upon her forehead, lightly, carefully.

"I caused the death of the man who for many years was my dearest friend. He was also a distant cousin of yours."

"Do you mean Andrew Payne?" she asked. When he nodded, she said, "But he was a very distant relation. I hardly even knew him. And you couldn't have had anything to do with his death, because he committed suicide over his wife's infidelities. He left a letter explaining everything."

"Everything except how he discovered that his wife was being unfaithful. They were both mere mortals, you know. I was able to read her feelings."

Shock stole Julia's voice, momentarily. Reaching up through the blanket, she gripped a handful of Niclas's shirt.

"You told him?"

He covered her hand with his own, squeezing hard.

"He loved Lucilla desperately, and he knew something was wrong. I thought I was being a friend by helping him, and assumed that he would simply put a stop to her affairs. The trouble was that I didn't bother to read his emotions before I told him. I could control the gift in those days. Far worse, I failed to tell him everything that I had felt from Lucilla, for fear that he would wonder how I knew."

"He didn't know about your gift?"

"I never revealed it to him, not even when we were at school together. As I said, it was easier to control my gifts in those days. But I wish I had taken the risk of his discovery, for if I'd only told him how deeply and truly Lucilla loved him, despite the other men, perhaps he never would have fallen into such despair."

"And perhaps he would," she said. "I didn't know Andrew Payne well, but I cannot believe that the guardians found you to blame for what was, in the end, his decision."

A particularly loud clap of thunder punctuated the words, and Julia turned to shout out the window, "No, I can't!"

She felt his hands, warm and gentle on her face, turning her back to him.

"I love you," he said, and kissed her until every ounce of indignation had disappeared. Lifting his head, he murmured, "I was afraid you would hate me. Andrew may have been a distant relative, but he was your cousin, all the same. I wouldn't have blamed you. God knows how I've hated and blamed myself. I don't think the guardians were wrong to punish me."

"What is the curse?" she asked. "Are you in pain? Is that why you always seem to be so weary?"

"I'm not in physical pain," he said, "but mental. I can no longer sleep as mortals must do, to rest my mind completely. My body rests and renews itself, but not my mind."

It took Julia several moments to comprehend what he'd said, and several more to consider just how great a punishment had been laid upon him.

"And this has been since Andrew died?" she asked. "You've not had a proper sleep for over *three years*?"

Through the darkness, she saw his nod.

"But how can that be? You would have gone mad by now. Any man would."

"Other men don't have Earl Graymar for a cousin," he said simply. "And, despite what he's been able to do for me, I am inexorably sliding toward madness. Magic can but slow the process, not stop it. Already I've lost the ability to control my gifts, so that when I'm with mere mortals I feel all their emotions without relief. In time I'll cease to be rational, and God alone knows where it will end."

"That is why you cannot marry," she said, touching his cheek. "I felt something inside of you, because of the Tarian, and accepted that we could never be together. Now I know what it is."

He kissed her again, then held her tightly as the wind gusted all about them. "I let myself hope, as we journeyed, when I knew I loved you, that by the time we returned to London the curse would be gone, that I could ask you to be my wife. But it became clear from the first day at Tylluan that there was nothing I could do to repay the debt I owe."

"Must it be repaid to my family? Or only to someone related to Andrew?"

"I don't know," he said. "No one ever knows precisely how the curse can be lifted, or what duty must be performed. The cursed one can only try, and keep trying, everything possible, to repay the blood they are guilty of."

"It was *not* your fault," she repeated emphatically. "Lucilla's foolish behavior had far more to do with it than you did, and Andrew's weakness in controlling her was even more to blame."

He shook his head. "I used magic to find out and tell him what I had no right to divulge. And Andrew would still be alive if I'd simply stayed out of the matter entirely. It was very wrong of me, Julia, and I accept that completely."

"Then let me help you to find the way to lift the curse," she said eagerly, pushing away enough to look up at him. The wind gusted in a curtain of rain, spotting them both with droplets, but she paid it no mind. "I know everything that's happening among all of the families Andrew was related to, and I can discover who all of Lucilla's relatives are, as well. Together we can take every opportunity to be of help or service, and in time surely we'll come across the right fix. Don't say no until you've had a chance to think upon it," she said when he began to shake his head.

"Darling, I love you far too much to take such a chance. Do you think I would bind you to me, only to watch as I descend into madness? To live with me night after night as I wander and roam until you begin to feel crazed, as well? And what if I should get you with child? Would you let our son or daughter grow up in a living nightmare? No, love. I know you would not, and I wouldn't ask you to make such a choice. Don't weep, Julia. Please."

"It's only the rain," she lied.

He bent and kissed both cheeks, several times, taking the moisture away.

"I'll take you to Glen Aur in the morning," he said, "and then Abercraf and I will depart."

"Will you go back to London?"

"I don't know," he murmured. "Perhaps I will. Malachi would come after me if I didn't. And there are matters that I must attend to in town. But regardless of what happens to me, Julia, you must promise that you'll live as fully and happily as you possibly can. Don't go back to Linley House to live with Lady Eunice, for, much as I respect her, I cannot believe you wish to remain with her for the rest of your life."

"I don't want to live alone, either," she whispered. "I hope you aren't going to say anything about my forgetting you and finding another man, because if you do, I'll strike you. And though you're much bigger and stronger, I shall do my best to make it hurt."

And then, embarrassingly, her trembling voice gave way and tears flowed. Niclas quickly gathered her close and murmured soothingly.

"I don't expect you to forget me," he said. "Just as I know I'll never be able to put you from my thoughts. But I don't want you to suffer or be alone. If you don't have sufficient funds of your own to set up your own house in London, I'll provide them. Jane can go with you, and I'm sure Lady Alice would far rather stay with you when she visits town than with her sister. You can go to parties and balls and dinners and the theater. You can live, Julia. That's what I want for you. To live and be as happy and content as you possibly can. Promise me, please, that you'll try."

She sniffled, sounding embarrassingly like a child to

her own ears, then wiped her face and looked up at him.

"I'll make you my promise, but only in exchange for something from you, first."

"I'll give you anything that I can so long as it brings you no harm," he said.

Julia's heart began to beat loudly in her ears, and she suddenly found that she wasn't drawing in enough breath. The storm outside had begun to lessen, and thunder rumbled in the distance.

"I want to know, just once . . ." she began, thankful that it was too dark for him to see how hot her cheeks had become. "I—I want to stay here with you tonight, and . . ."

A hand rose to cradle her face again. "I might get you with child, love."

"That would only ensure my happiness," she whispered. "I would never regret such a gift."

"You would not, I know, but the child would suffer. Society isn't kind to such children or their mothers, and I'll not leave either of you to such a fate. But there is another way for us to be as one, Julia." He kissed her, gently. "Come and lie with me."

Picking her up in his arms, he carried her, blanket and all, to the huge bed, and laid her gently upon it. Bending, he kissed her and said, "I'm going to light the fire."

Within moments a small blaze was burning in the hearth, dimly illuminating the room with its flickering light and spreading warmth into the chilled air. He closed the open window, shutting out the storm, and then moved back to the bed, sitting to remove first his boots, then to pull off his shirt and toss it aside.

Julia watched him in the glow of the firelight, her fingers clutching at the blanket and her breathing quickening.

She had never seen a man without a shirt on before. He was powerfully built, and his smooth skin glowed in the golden firelight, flowing tautly over his muscular frame. He also looked much bigger, suddenly, and when he sat beside her on the bed, Julia couldn't stop the nervous squeak that came out of her.

"Don't be afraid," he murmured, leaning to kiss her lips. "I love you, Julia. I want to be one with you. And I want to give you pleasure."

With careful movements he parted the blanket and pried her fingers free so that he could spread it out. She felt vulnerable, exposed, but then he slowly stretched out beside Julia and gathered her into his embrace. Tentatively she lifted a hand and laid it upon his shoulder, testing the strange new feeling of his bare flesh.

"You're so soft," she whispered, surprised, and heard him chuckle.

"Men aren't supposed to be soft," he said, "but I'm glad if it pleases you."

Growing bolder, she stroked him, and felt him shiver with pleasure. Then his hands began to move, too. Tilting her face up, he brought his mouth down to hers once more. Julia moaned and pressed closer, caressing his shoulders and neck and back, delighting in the warmth and silkiness of his skin.

One of Niclas's hands cupped the back of her head, his fingers rubbing lightly in her hair, and the other slid slowly down her back, then lower still. She felt the skirt of her nightgown rising inch by inch, seemingly endless in length, until she felt the warmth of his fingers on the skin beneath.

She moaned again and his mouth parted over her own,

his kiss demanding a response that Julia gladly gave.

His hands roamed over her body, caressing the swell of her breasts, her waist and hips.

Then he began to unbutton the top of her gown, making room for his hand to slip inside to cup and caress her breasts. He muttered when the Tarian got in the way, and impatiently pushed it aside.

Pleasure. Just as he'd said. That's what it was, and she had never really known it before, or even dreamed of it.

But it wasn't enough. Julia wanted—needed—something more from him, but didn't know how to ask.

"Niclas," she said, and he rose up and silenced her with a kiss. He was breathing harshly when he lifted his head and, gazing into her eyes, murmured, "Now we will be one."

He knelt in the middle of the bed and pulled Julia up to kneel before him. The gown, unbuttoned, slid from her shoulders to her hips. The Tarian hung between her breasts, its shimmering light dueling with the golden fire glow. It tingled against her skin in a manner that she'd only felt once before, just after Niclas had placed it on her, as if it had come to life.

Lifting her hands, Niclas folded them around the Tarian, then placed both his hands, strong and warm, over hers. The necklace glowed so brightly that their flesh was illuminated, and tiny slivers of light escaped through the folds of their clasped fingers.

"Hold the necklace tightly," he said. "Don't let go, no matter what you feel happening. We'll be safe, and together. Look at me, Julia, and keep looking at me."

He smiled, and she smiled in turn. And then he began to speak.

"I, Niclas Oliver Robert Seymour, declare this woman as my *unoliaeth*. My heart is hers, my strength is hers, all that I possess is hers, forever. I bind myself to her alone, and proclaim my love for her alone, forever. I have said it before the guardians and with the witness of the Tarian, and thus it will be from this moment on. Forever."

Before the final word was out of his mouth the room had begun to spin, or perhaps she and Niclas had begun to spin. The Tarian, beneath their joined hands, grew warm, and the sensation of tingling increased.

Once before the Tarian had pulled her out of her body, so that she wasn't afraid when it happened again. Except this time she wasn't pulled down, but lifted up. It was like being set free from invisible tethers and drifting away from Tylluan, from the earth, and into a weightless sphere composed of clouds and deep blue skies. She was floating, lifted to an entirely new realm that consisted of neither thought nor care, but only of feelings. And she wasn't alone. She was with Niclas. With him, but more than that. Entwined with him. One with him.

Pleasure. Yes, beyond all knowing. She could hear his voice inside her and feel his touch deep within. A rhythm of sensation pulsed around and through them, and they moved to it in a beautiful dance. And the pleasure grew, and spread, and at last took Julia completely. She cried out, but Niclas held her safe, murmuring gently as they drifted back, slowly, into warmth and darkness.

She woke sometime later to find herself in his arms, wrapped together in the blanket, lying on the bed before the fire in his chamber at Tylluan. He was watching her solemnly and lightly stroking her cheek. Julia was so sated and replete that she couldn't do more than smile.

She didn't think she had ever been more comfortable or relaxed in all her life.

"Go to sleep," he whispered. "I'll wake you in time to get you safely back to your room unseen. Sleep."

Happily, she did his bidding. Closing her eyes, she obediently slid into slumber.

Sixteen

$\mathcal{L}$ady Alice arrived the next morning before Loris had even finished helping Julia to pack her things. She had only come to visit her niece, and was delighted to find that she could take her back to Glen Aur. Neither Julia nor Niclas were quite as pleased, but could do nothing but agree that it was a happy coincidence that had brought her ladyship to Tylluan.

An hour later they had all converged at Tylluan's mighty castle doors, outside of which Lady Alice's carriage stood, to bid Julia good-bye. She was crushed by the men—especially Uncle Ffinian—and hugged by Loris. Steffan kissed her hand and then her cheek, claiming the privilege of special friendship as they had shared something of an adventure together. Kian, not to be outdone and insisting that, as he was the one who'd rescued her from the other world, his claim to friendship with Julia was far greater, kissed her on the hand and both cheeks.

Then, with rare tact, they stood back and gave Niclas a moment alone with her.

They had already said good-bye, when Niclas had awakened Julia at sunrise and taken her back to her chamber. There was very little they could say to each other now, but letting go of each other's hands seemed to be impossible. All those surrounding them looked on with open interest.

Julia pulled away first, lifting her hands to the back of her neck. "You must give this back to Lord Graymar," she said somewhat unsteadily, and with great care she removed the Tarian. Everyone present leaned forward to have a better look at the rare object, which all Seymours knew of but few had ever seen. "I'm sure I don't require its protection any longer, and I should be quite nervous to continue to wear it when you're not near."

Niclas was uneasy. "I wish you would keep it. Just in case. Lord Graymar will come to Glen Aur to retrieve it soon, and to see how you fare."

"It's too valuable," she said, and folded his fingers around the glowing stone. "If something should happen to it while it's in my care, the loss to your family would be too great. And I'm safe now. Please take it, Niclas."

Reluctantly, he pocketed the heavy necklace and turned his attention to Julia's lovely, upturned face.

"Good-bye," she murmured, very afraid that she was going to begin crying.

Niclas blinked at the sudden irritation of his own eyes, and nodded. "Don't forget the promise you made."

Her smile trembled slightly. "I won't."

He stood on the driveway long after they drove away, Abercraf at his side. The pain in his heart was dark, sharp, depthless. How did a person survive such loss?

"Have you packed all my things? Are we ready to depart?" he asked quietly.

"Yes, sir. I sent most of your things ahead with the coach, so there was very little to pack. Just enough changes to get us back to London, barring any delays."

"God help us, we had enough of those on the journey here." He gazed back at the road, where the dust from Lady Alice's coach had now settled. "But, I confess, Abercraf, that this was the most enjoyable journey of my life."

Ffinian wouldn't let him leave until after they'd enjoyed a hearty afternoon meal, and then his relatives delayed him further by treating him to the same sort of send-off that they'd given Julia earlier in the day.

"Will you be staying at Tylluan long, Steffan?" he asked as they clasped hands.

"Only the night, *cfender*. My men and I depart for our own dwellings first thing in the morn. We must be well in place before the season ends and travelers begin to leave town. There are always plenty of good potential victims on the roads then."

"I wish you'd stop robbing people. It's going to get you hung one of these days."

"Never," Steffan said with a laugh. "Malachi would save me first."

"Malachi needs to put a stop to your chosen vocation."

Steffan shrugged lightly. "He says it keeps me out of trouble."

"Keeps you out of—" Niclas gave up. "It sounds like his line of logic."

They rode away well before sundown, their saddlebags heavy with the food Loris had insisted upon sending with them.

"Is there any hope that we might return to this part of Wales during the summer months, sir, rather than going to Tawel Lle?" Abercraf asked as they guided their horses down the mountain with care. "I don't mean to speak out of turn, of course, but I should like to see Miss Jane again, if it would be at all possible."

"I'll make certain that you see her before long, Abercraf," Niclas vowed, making a silent note to see that all of his servants, especially Abercraf, were financially well settled before being released from his employ. "In truth, I believe I can promise that it will be well before summer arrives."

"Are you quite settled in now, dear?"

Julia turned to see her aunt coming out to the terrace on which she stood. It was growing dark, and the cold night mist was beginning to fill the valley and cover the stars in the sky.

"Yes, Aunt," she said. "Quite settled, thank you. I had forgotten how lovely Glen Aur is." She looked out across the estate to where a wide river flowed. A mountain rose above it, and near the top she could see the lights of Castle Tylluan, seeming very far away in the gathering mist.

"I stood at one of the castle windows last night and looked down into the valley," she said. "It was raining so hard, but I could see the lights of Glen Aur and thought of you here, and of the time I would spend in this beautiful place. Now I look up and see Castle Tylluan's lights, and think of a day when I might visit there again." She smiled at her aunt, who was gazing at her with understanding. "I never knew I was so fickle," Julia murmured.

"Those who love Tylluan and its occupants can't help but be drawn to it, my dear," Lady Alice said gently. "I believe that may be part of its magic. But the rest of it is simply the people. I always miss Ffinian terribly when he's there and I'm here, and I often stand in just this same spot and gaze up to see where he is."

"If you love him so very much," Julia asked, "why will you not marry him? Surely you don't mind about the money, and he truly loves you."

"I know he does, dear. But I could never live at Tylluan, and he hasn't yet come to accept that he must give it up. When that day comes, I'll welcome him here at Glen Aur and we shall see what kind of relationship would suit him best. I don't require marriage, you see. Only his company."

"But could he leave Tylluan?" Julia asked. "He's the baron, after all, and will be until he dies and Kian inherits."

"Ffinian isn't truly Baron Tylluan, though he calls himself by the title. Kian is, and has been since his mother passed away. Both the title and the estate are his."

"But how can that be?"

Lady Alice made a waving motion with one hand. "Seymours do things in their own peculiar way, and that includes the matter of inheritance. Ffinian's wife inherited the estate from her mother, and when she died it was passed down to her oldest child—Kian. Ffinian understood that he would never inherit when he married her. Such arrangements are often made when these unique families are involved. Kian has no interest in shouldering such responsibilities yet, and thus is content to let his father continue as he is. But the day will come when Ffinian must step down and let his son take his rightful place. And I shall be here, waiting, when he does. Though," she said, as she moved to sit upon the nearest bench, "I do hope it will be soon, for I'm not getting any younger, and I should like to do a bit of traveling before many more years pass. We should have such a lovely time traveling, Ffinian and I. Can you not imagine him charming women all over Europe?"

Julia smiled at the thought. "He'll have them swooning. He is indeed the most charming man. All Seymours seem to be," she said, her smile fading. "At least the ones I've met."

"As are those that I've known," said her aunt. "But I confess that your Niclas may be the most charming of all. He has such a thoughtful, gentlemanly manner, and is so very handsome. Were you able to settle the problems between you, my dear? He didn't give me a definite answer when I asked him to visit us soon."

Julia looked up at Tylluan again. "Yes," she said. "Everything has been settled."

"That's fine, then." Lady Alice pulled her shawl closer. "My, it's growing cold, isn't it? I believe we may have rain again tonight. Come, my love, and let's go in beside the fire. Dinner will be served soon, and then I'm sure you'll want to retire. You must be weary after the long day we've had."

A storm came up in the middle of the night. A fitful, thunderous storm that made the windowpanes rattle in their fittings.

A vivid bolt of lightning woke Julia, and the furious clap of thunder that followed had her sitting up and clutching the bed linens.

"Niclas," she murmured aloud, praying that he and Abercraf were safe at some wayside inn.

She lifted a hand to touch her neck, feeling the loss of the Tarian's weight there. It had been uncomfortable to wear while she slept, yet she missed it now. It had changed her in ways that she'd never known, being merely mortal, and now that it was gone she could feel those changes slipping away. Yet her senses were still heightened, as they'd been when she had worn the necklace, and as she slowly cast her gaze across the dim, fire-lit room, she knew that something was wrong.

Terribly wrong.

Run, she thought. Scream. *Now.*

She tossed the covers aside and, careless of her bare feet, ran to the bedroom door. But the handle refused to turn, and the key was frozen.

"Oh, no," she said, and lifted a fist to pound on the heavy wood.

A strong arm stopped her, and a large, gloved hand slipped over her mouth to quiet the scream she'd been about to emit. Even as she was lifted from the floor and pressed against the length of a tall, hard body, she knew who it was.

"Why, Miss Linley, were you going to run away so soon after my arrival? How unforgivably rude. And I thought Linleys were such pillars of society. I shall have to inform your aunt of your terrible failings as a hostess."

She fought with all her strength as he dragged her back across the room and flung her roughly onto the bed. Julia landed on her back but quickly scrambled upright, holding the neckline of her white cotton gown firmly in place.

The earl of Llew loomed over her, far taller than she had remembered but just as dark and frightening. He was clothed all in black, with a black multi-caped cloak sweeping from his broad shoulders almost to the floor. His hair was unbound and fell wildly about his dimly illuminated face, making him look fierce and even demonic. His black eyes pinned her with a penetrating stare, moving slowly from her face down the length of her body. He did nothing to hide what he was thinking, and Julia began to tremble.

"Such a pretty little gown you've worn to greet me in, I see." Reaching out a gloved hand, he stroked the exposed skin of her neck and shoulder. "It makes me think of all the things I should like to do to you, dearest Julia. And that would serve him especially well, would it not, to rape his lover while her sweet aunt sleeps but a few doors away?" He leaned closer, gripping Julia's chin between the vise of his forefinger and thumb to force her near. "But I'll not enjoy you just yet. We might be interrupted, and then I might be obliged to harm someone you love. And that would make you unhappy, would it not, dearest Julia? Not to mention that it would be a terrible way to begin our new life together."

She tried to scream, to twist away, but he held her tight. The vise on her chin squeezed so painfully that tears filled her eyes.

"What? Have I taken you by surprise, my sweet? Did you believe you would marry? Perhaps become wife to Niclas Seymour? Did you?" The fingers tightened and she groaned in pain, bending beneath his force. She was certain she was going to faint, and struggled to maintain her senses.

"I'm afraid I could never allow it," he said, bringing their faces so close that she could feel the heat of his breath as he spoke. "I want vengeance on Niclas Seymour. On all Seymours. They have denied me the wife I desired, and now I will do the same. Niclas Seymour shall not have you. He must live, instead, with the knowledge that his beloved Julia belongs to another man, is lying beneath another man and receiving his seed and pleasuring that other man in every way that he commands. And not as a cherished wife. No, not that. She will be my mistress. My whore. And all of society will know of it. Not that I care for that. I only care about making him suffer. And he will, my love. Oh, yes, he will.

"He'll know very well how I'll use you, and that your life will be a misery and a hell because of me. And he'll know, too, that you can never leave me, for I can force you to love me with sick desperation. I can. You'll soon discover that I speak the truth."

She reached up to grasp his hand with both of her own, digging her fingers into the leather of his glove and pulling hard in a bid for release. With an angry grunt he flung her back, and Julia crawled farther away, gasping for air and rubbing at the sharp pain in her face.

"I won't . . . love you," she managed to say. *"Ever."*

He chuckled with dark amusement. "You'll do whatever I tell you to do, Julia, just as you did once before. And if you struggle against my power, I'll make you very sorry. But come, my blushing virgin. It's time we're away." She felt a hand close over one of her ankles, and with one powerful tug she was dragged across the bed and onto the hard floor. The next moment he had taken a fistful of her hair and pulled her upright, holding her up just high enough that she had to stand on her toes to keep the strands from ripping out of her scalp. Using both fists she struck his chest and shoulders and face, whatever she could reach, but it had no effect whatsoever.

"Now, Julia, you're going to stop this foolishness and obey me," he said, and gave her a shake that sent rivulets of pain streaming over her scalp and face. "You're going to stop fighting and collect your shoes and a coat. We've many miles to journey until we reach Llew and I don't want my cherished mistress arriving in naught but her sleeping gown, pretty as it may be." With his free hand he reached out to caress her breast through the thin cloth, squeezing lightly and then a bit harder, and all the while Julia flailed at him, using both arms and legs now. And still it had no effect on the man. It was as if he were impervious to pain.

"Delightful," he declared with satisfaction, moving his hand lower, along the curve of her waist. "I believe you'll do quite nicely, Miss Linley. I shall soon have your belly swelling with child. My child. My bastard. And then I'll get you with another, and more after that, until we shall send half a dozen or more of our odd half-breeds out into the world to worry the Seymours."

She finally managed to land a solid blow to his face, smack on his cheek beneath his left eye. He gave a grunt of pain, which filled Julia with intense satisfaction for the moment she was allowed to enjoy it. With an oath he yanked her upward off her feet and sent his own hand flying toward her face. She saw it coming, but could never afterward remember receiving the blow.

Seventeen

$\mathscr{I}$t wasn't a clap of thunder or a bolt of lightning that woke Steffan. It was a dream—the kind that meant something particular to a mystic.

Within moments he was on his way out his bedchamber door, running barefooted down the hall toward his uncle's room. Half an hour after that he and his men were on their way, riding through the rain to find Niclas, while Ffinian, Kian, and Dyfed were readying their men for the long ride to Castle Llew.

"We'll have our dear Julia safely back, my lads, never fear," Ffinian declared over the noise of the rain as they made to mount their horses. "I only hope Steffan can run Niclas to ground before too much time has passed."

"We gave our word to Steffan that we'd wait for Niclas to arrive before we did anything, *tad*," Kian told him, "and we'll keep to that."

"Only for as long as we must, my boy," his father said, spurring his horse forward. "And after that we'll be fetching her out of Castle Llew on our own, and waiting be damned."

The storm didn't disturb Niclas, either. He'd been sitting in his room at the modest inn where he and Abercraf had settled, staring into the fire. Lightning illuminated the room from time to time and thunder filled the air with its ominous rumblings, but he paid little mind to either.

He was thinking of Julia and wondering whether she was sleeping and, if so, what she was dreaming of. Did she miss him as much as he already missed her? Was she afraid, as he was, of the days to come? Of the loneliness?

He would go back to London to settle matters and make plans. Malachi would agree to keep an eye on Julia, to make certain that she was well. He'd pester her into going out into society, even if she didn't wish to. The earl of Graymar was good at that.

Then Niclas heard something over the rain, and lifted his head. It was vaguely familiar. A sound? A voice?

Earlier, the inn had been loud with the noise of merrymakers in the tavern, but that had died away more than an hour before. This voice was different, urgent and angry and . . .

Niclas bolted out of the chair and fumbled for his shirt, which he tossed on without buttoning.

"Steffan!" he shouted, throwing his bedchamber door open and racing into the hall. "Steffan! I'm here!"

Abercraf's door opened across the hall, and the manservant stood there in his nightgown and bare feet, his hair all askew.

"Sir! Is something amiss?" he cried, but Niclas had already run past him toward the stairs.

"Steffan!"

"Niclas! Cousin!"

Steffan was at the entryway, barred by the innkeeper who held a gun aimed at him.

"Let him in!" Niclas demanded, rushing down the few remaining steps and physically pushing the innkeeper aside. "Get back. Put that thing away."

"Niclas," Steffan said, striving for breath as he and his men pushed their way inside. They were as wet as they could possibly be. "We've come to fetch you. It's Cadmaran."

Niclas knew that the silent moment that passed was much shorter than it seemed: shock made it feel as if it were an eternity.

"He has Julia," he said, the strained sound of his own voice foreign to him.

Steffan nodded. Reaching out, he clutched Niclas by the arm.

"He's taking her to Llew. Our uncle and cousins are already on their way with all their men. They believe it will be enough, but you and I both know the truth. We'll need Malachi if we're to get her back. Kian can't fight against the earl of Llew. He's simply not strong enough."

A particularly loud clap of thunder exploded above their heads. Niclas closed his eyes.

They needed Malachi. No one else could wrest her from Morcar Cadmaran's clutches.

"Can you call him?" he asked Steffan. "Is there any way at all to reach him?"

Steffan shook his head.

"I've been thinking on nothing else during our ride here. If I could send word through the water faeries, or if I only had time to read the bowl and send word from the spirit realm—but even then there's no assurance that he would know quickly enough and"—he squeezed Niclas's arm so hard that it hurt, and rare desperation filled his voice—"there simply isn't enough time. I dreamt of what was happening to Julia, and of what is to happen. We can't delay, and we can't wait for the *Dewin Mawr*."

"There's a way yet left to us," Niclas murmured.

"No," Steffan replied forcefully. *"No."*

"It's out of your hands," he said sharply. "Innkeeper!" he shouted, and that man appeared with his gun still in hand. "Put that away," Niclas said again, then waved a hand at his cousin and his men. "Give these men something to eat and drink. Quickly. We'll be leaving within fifteen minutes' time."

"But, sir," said the innkeeper, "you can't mean to go out in this storm? That's not at all wise, sir."

"Fifteen minutes," Niclas repeated as he made his way to the stairs. "I'll pay you twice what it's worth to make sure they're well filled by then."

"I don't like it," Ffinian said, giving a shake of his head. "I say it's best if we attack with full force, using all our men. If we can but overwhelm Cadmaran's forces—and keep him busy with defense—Kian might be able to take him by surprise."

"It won't work," Niclas said, accepting the cup of wine that Dyfed pressed into his hand. "Cadmaran's men outnumber us fivefold, and even if they didn't, he might very well use Julia as protection against whatever magic Kian might attempt. And don't forget that if we attack first, Cadmaran will gain the advantage. His powers will increase and Kian's will be lessened. Worse than that, Malachi will be able to do little to help us." He gazed solemnly at those assembled. "Cadmaran must be forced to attack, and there's only one way I can think of that he might be lured into doing just that."

He and Steffan and Steffan's men had just arrived at the place outside the earl of Llew's estate where Ffinian and his sons and men had set up a camp of sorts. The storm had diminished into a light, though steady, drizzle, and the tent where the men had gathered to discuss their plan was more than sufficient to protect them from the elements.

"At least let me go with you," Kian said.

"He'd never let you pass through the gates," Niclas replied. "I must go alone."

"He'll harm you," Steffan said, his face pale and his countenance shaken. "I can sense it. He's going to hurt you badly, Niclas. You must have someone to lend you aid."

"I hope that I shall," he said, finishing the last of the wine and setting the cup aside with finality. "Malachi will come once he senses I'm in danger."

"But that will take time, lad," Ffinian said. "What if he's delayed half an hour?"

"Then I shall be extremely put out with him," Niclas said with a grim smile. "Though I don't expect to be here to do anything about it."

In the corner where he stood, Steffan groaned out loud. "Don't speak of death," he pleaded. "I feel a great dread for what's to come. Don't tempt fate by making light of such matters, *cfender,* I pray you."

Niclas moved to set a comforting hand on his arm.

"Don't fear for me, Steffan. None of you," he said, looking at each of them, "must think of me, but keep your minds fixed on getting Julia safely away. If you bear me any love at all, promise me that. No matter what may happen, the end of this day must see her delivered. Give me your hands on it."

He set his hand in the middle of the circle they made and each laid his own upon it.

"Take every care, lad," Ffinian said. "Cadmaran's as dark and shifty as a demon. He cares only for himself and no other."

"I'll be careful," Niclas vowed. "And it's the earl of Llew's self-love that I'm counting on. It's the only thing, I believe, that can send all his caution fleeing."

Eighteen

It hadn't occurred to Niclas just how difficult it would be to get inside Castle Llew. He wasn't quite certain what it was he'd expected when he rode Enoch up to the massive front gates, but it wasn't to be informed that the earl of Llew had given strict instructions not to admit Niclas, or any Seymours, for any reason.

"Wonderful," he muttered, standing in the softly falling rain with Enoch's reins in his hand. "Now what?"

It made perfect sense, of course. Why should Lord Llew bid him enter when keeping him out might force Niclas to gather all his relatives about him for an attack? Cadmaran had nothing to lose by sitting safely behind his walls, and much to gain should an army of Seymours make the first move.

"Tell your master," Niclas said to the gatekeeper, "that I have come alone and unarmed. I have only brought with me something to bargain in exchange for Miss Linley's return."

"What is it?" asked the gatekeeper.

"I'll not speak of it to you," Niclas replied solemnly.

"Tell your master that it is ancient, from before memory, and that the lord of the Seymours would as soon see me dead as part with it."

Twenty minutes later, the gates opened, and Niclas, sending Enoch back to the camp, walked in alone.

The earl of Llew's estate was vast and beautiful, made grand by Cadmaran's wealth. Niclas thought it a bit pretentious, but, then, he couldn't help but compare it to Glain Tarran, the seat of the earl of Graymar. Malachi left it to grow as wild and natural as he possibly could without letting the land overrun the dwellings. Castle Llew, on the other hand, was so ruthlessly kept that not even the trees or bushes showed a hint of softness. Knowing Cadmaran, they were probably afraid to.

The castle was filled with people—fighting men and servants—and yet there was a strange, stark quiet in the place. Everyone was silent as they went about their work, so that all Niclas heard as he made his way from the outer bailey to the massive inner bailey and through the great castle doors that opened for him as he approached were footsteps, or the infrequent clatter of bowls and cups, or the scraping of a broom against a bare floor. No one looked at him as he passed, no one spoke to him, and their emotions were so shuttered that Niclas could feel very little emanating from them. The entire castle had clearly been cast beneath a deep and powerful spell. Did they even know what they did, these inhabitants of Llew? Did they know where they were, or how long they'd been there?

The castle itself had been maintained in a kind of medieval splendor, and Niclas could discern little in the way of modern furnishings or comforts. Torches, rather than lamps, lit the halls with their bright flames, and if the floors weren't covered with rushes, as they had been in times long past, the exquisite but faded carpets that lined them looked as if they hailed from a date no later than the Renaissance. As he walked toward two grand, tall wooden doors that surely led into the great hall, Niclas could imagine himself being transported back to the days of his ancestors, whose names and adventures he had learned of in his youth. Seymours had fought battles and sought peace in this same castle long, long ago. Now it was his turn to face their ancient enemy.

He stopped before the doors and drew in a deep breath, praying that the spirits of those long-past relatives would be with him in this moment.

The doors were heavy, but their hinges were well oiled. As Niclas pushed they slowly swung open without making a sound.

The great hall of Castle Llew was both enormous and dark. Tall windows on either side of the long room were covered by heavy red curtains, and the only sources of light were provided by the several large fireplaces set at intervals in the stone walls and more of those torches that Cadmaran clearly preferred. At the far end of the room was a dais, and upon the dais a chair that looked very much like a medieval throne. Cadmaran sat upon it, seeming to be very relaxed, with one leg stretched out.

Julia was before the lord of the castle, kneeling with her head bowed, silent, motionless, her hands folded in her lap. She looked as if she might be praying to him, though Niclas knew that was only how Cadmaran wanted it to appear. She was barefooted and dressed in a thin, white nightgown, a coat and a pair of shoes having been tossed on the floor not far away, and she looked very small and helpless compared to Cadmaran's large, dark person.

Slowly, Niclas began to walk toward the dais, not surprised when the doors closed unaided behind him. Though he was taller than most men, the size of the hall made him feel inconsequential, like a fly about to be swatted by an extremely large hand.

He tried not to think of the earl of Llew's powers; indeed, he tried not to think of anything other than the task at hand, but it was impossible. Memories of a particular day in his youth flooded all other thoughts away . . . memories of the very first time he'd met Morcar Cadmaran.

They had been boys, though Cadmaran had been closer to Malachi's age, and therefore a couple of years older. It had been at one of the large, important gatherings of the Families—a meeting of such scale that it only took place once every five years, and lasted a full week, during which time the various clans discussed all their concerns and made wide-ranging agreements.

Malachi had been twelve and already declared the heir to the earldom—which wasn't surprising, as his father was at that time the head of the Seymours. Unfortunately, he wasn't above being a bit cocky about it. He and Morcar, who was likewise aware that he would one day assume leadership of the Cadmarans, couldn't seem to help trying to best each other in displays of magic and skill.

Niclas, only ten, had tried to talk some sense into them, but as each day of the gathering passed the boys' dares had grown more dangerous. Finally, Morcar had challenged Malachi to accompany him to a nearby village, where they would see who could perform the greatest magic without being caught by mere mortals. Niclas, filled with foreboding, had tagged along at Malachi's insistence.

It had started innocently enough, with Morcar sending little rocks scooting in front of villagers as they walked and Malachi blowing breezes to make windows rattle and business doors fly open.

But it had escalated rapidly, until Malachi was making cats fly and Morcar was sending barrels rolling through the village center, careless of the people walking there.

And then, Morcar had decided to turn his magic on the villagers themselves.

First it had been making girls' skirts fly, then sending a stray dog barking after a group of boys, then pelting two men with acorns from a nearby tree, and then . . . with a suddenness that had taken both Niclas and Malachi by surprise, Morcar had begun lifting people into the air and sending them flying, having very little concern for where they landed or if they were hurt. He'd sent one luckless man straight into the side of a building, and the poor fellow had fallen senseless to the ground. Niclas, to his shame, had begun to babble incoherently until Malachi put a hand over his mouth and forced him to run away.

The sound of Morcar's laughter followed them for what seemed like an eternity, until they finally hid in a gathering of rocks and struggled to catch their breath.

Niclas had trembled like a foolish infant despite his cousin's comforting arm about him, and for long minutes all Malachi could say, over and over, guilt heavy in his voice, was, "I could have stopped him," for even then his powers had been superior.

Morcar Cadmaran escaped punishment that day, probably because of his youth, but he had never again gotten the better of the present earl of Graymar.

"You're more foolhardy than I suspected," Lord Llew

said now as Niclas approached. "You came without your cousin to defend you. How noble." The last two words were uttered so derisively that there was no doubt as to their meaning.

"You have never loved as I have," Niclas replied. "A man who has waited his entire life for such a miracle doesn't treat it lightly. I've come to get Julia back."

Cadmaran smiled. "I'm sorry to disappoint you, but she doesn't want to go. She is here to take the place of the wife I was promised, though I don't intend to wed her. Shall I tell you what I do intend?"

"No," Niclas said flatly, glancing to where Julia was kneeling. She hadn't moved an inch, not even having heard his voice.

"Miss Linley," the earl of Llew said, smiling, "wishes to become my mistress. Is that not so, my love?"

A long moment passed before she replied, without emotion, "Yes, my lord."

"Any man would be fortunate to possess so lovely a woman for his own pleasure, would he not?" he asked. "And it has occurred to me that it would be wrong to keep sweet Julia here at Llew for my eyes alone. In order to be entirely fair, I must share her with society." Cadmaran sat forward. "And that means taking her to London."

Yes, that was just the sort of thing Cadmaran would do, Niclas thought. He would parade Julia about in public, showing her plainly as his possession, forcing her through magic to behave with perfect obedience, perhaps even dressing her in a manner that would openly declare her new, lowered status as his mistress. Nothing would be more degrading to Julia, or more painful to him. As far as vengeance went, it was perfect.

But it wasn't going to come to that. Niclas was going to make certain of it.

"Her family might have something to say about that," he murmured, taking special note of his surroundings. The earl of Llew had filled his castle with grand and valuable ornaments, probably to caress his massive ego. Some of those ornaments were tied to magic, some were simply impressive. Niclas made a mental map of where things stood, what to avoid and what to aim for, particularly good spots that might provide momentary shelter in the coming onslaught. There were, thankfully, a number of tables and chairs and, interestingly, empty suits of medieval armor. "It's unlikely that the Linleys would sit by in silence while one of their own is publicly humiliated."

"I don't care in the least what either the Linleys or anyone else thinks, says, or does. They may object all they wish, or act against me at their peril. I have no fear of them. What I care about," Cadmaran said, looking very directly at Niclas, "is what you think. Does my plan meet with your approval?"

Niclas came to a halt at the bottom of the dais. Three tall steps led up to the throne where Cadmaran sat, and to where Julia knelt.

Her face was turned away from him, and her long, shining brown hair hung loose down the length of her back, falling to her waist.

"You know it doesn't," Niclas replied, his gaze held fast on Julia's still form. "Which is precisely why you propose it. You mean to make me suffer for the loss of Ceridwen. I understand that well enough. But I've not come to exchange thoughts and ideas with you. I've come to gain Julia's freedom."

The earl of Llew chuckled. "Then you've come in vain, Mister Seymour. Julia doesn't wish to leave me, do you, my love?"

Her reply, like the last, only came after a moment of silence.

"No, my lord."

"But he doesn't believe you, pet," Cadmaran told her, and reached out one long, elegant finger to turn her chin. "You must look at him quite directly and convince him of your sincerity."

A tingle of shock coursed through Niclas at the sight of her face; one of her eyes and most of her cheek were heavily bruised and swollen.

"Julia," he murmured, and took an involuntary step forward before stopping himself. He had to maintain complete control of his thoughts and actions, or he'd be giving Cadmaran a great advantage.

"Go on, my sweet," Cadmaran ordered, holding Julia's face toward Niclas. "Tell him."

Another short silence, but it was enough to confirm the hope that had taken root in Niclas's heart. She was fighting Cadmaran this time.

"I wish to remain here with my lord, Earl Llew," she said tonelessly, but Niclas saw the spark of something else behind her eyes.

"Nonetheless," Niclas said, and reluctantly turned his gaze to Cadmaran. "I'm going to take her out of here."

The earl of Llew sat back in his chair and indolently crossed his long legs. He regarded Niclas from his imperial height with unveiled disdain.

"You can't," he said. "You haven't the means, certainly not the power. Lord Graymar might attempt it, but then he should have to challenge me, and if he challenges me and uses magic, I can kill him, and no one, not even the guardians, can hold it against me."

"The laws of England would," Niclas reminded him, but Cadmaran only laughed.

"We don't live by the laws of England, or, rather, we shouldn't. But even if Seymours are so foolish that they do, that has nothing to do with me. If Malachi Seymour challenges me, I will kill him."

"Then, if your mind is set, it will do you no harm to consider my proposal."

"I suppose I might find it amusing to hear what you have to say," Cadmaran admitted. He gave a wave of one elegant hand. "Proceed, Mister Seymour."

"I've brought something of value," he began, but the earl of Llew uttered a snort and said, "What could you possibly have that would be of interest to me? You don't even possess proper magic."

"No, I don't," Niclas confessed. "But I do have this." He reached up to untie the sodden cloth about his neck and cast it aside. With careful fingers he pulled the chain out from beneath his shirt, all the while watching Cadmaran's reaction. The moment the glowing medallion appeared he saw what he had hoped for: recognition, then a fleeting moment of shock, followed by an even briefer flash of unbridled lust. By the time the Tarian slid to lie openly upon Niclas's chest, the earl of Llew had mastered himself, though Niclas thought he detected a slight rise in the other man's breathing.

"I'm sure you know what this is, Earl Llew."

"It's a fake," Cadmaran said curtly. "Malachi would never let it leave Mervaille, let alone put it in your keeping.

And he'd certainly never exchange it for the sake of a mere female, not even if she was his love, rather than yours. He's not that great a fool."

"It's not a fake," Niclas said softly. "You can feel its power."

The only sign that this was true was the way Cadmaran's fingers clutched the arms of his grand chair. His face, however, was admirably schooled into nonchalance.

"You wish to trade the Tarian for Miss Linley? Very well, it's agreed." He sat forward and held out a hand. "Let me have it and you can both go in peace."

Niclas shook his head. "I can't part with it that easily. The Tarian is far too valuable. I brought it because I knew you'd never fight me for Miss Linley otherwise. But you'll fight for the Tarian."

Cadmaran managed to drag his gaze away from the necklace. He looked at Niclas with amazement, and then he laughed.

"You wish to fight me? *You?*" He eyed Niclas up and down and clearly found him lacking. "For the Tarian? Oh, come now. You must think me a dunce to fall for such a jest."

"For the Tarian, aye," Niclas said, "but Julia is to be the prize. If I win, I keep the Tarian and Julia comes away with me, completely free of your spell, but if you win—"

"I understand," the earl of Llew said rather breathlessly, slowly standing. It seemed to take forever for him to gain full height, and when he did, he was even more imposing. Niclas swallowed and wondered why he could never remember just how tall the man was. "If I win, I get the Tarian." He began to descend the steps one by one, ignoring Julia completely as he passed her, his eyes fixed intently on the glowing necklace. "The Tarian," he whispered. "I shall possess its power, as will my heirs to come. The Seymours shall bemoan its loss for generations, and your name will be cursed as the feckless fool who lost it simply because you were so weak as to put a woman above your family. And not even a woman worth thinking of, but a common mortal." As he came closer he lifted a hand, reaching his fingers toward the Tarian, as if to touch it. "A mortal of middling beauty and ordinary character, with nothing in the least superior to recommend her to our kind. For this," he said as Niclas stepped back to avoid his touch, "you would lose so valuable an object?"

"You don't know that I'll lose it," Niclas said.

"Oh, yes," Cadmaran murmured. "I do. And should Malachi challenge me for it, it will be too late. The Tarian will make me far more powerful. He shall never again be able to defeat me."

His hand, which had yet been reaching out toward Niclas, suddenly waved away toward one of the walls.

"How shall we conduct our battle, then? Which weapons do you prefer? They're all here," he said, indicating the various weapons mounted about the hall. "You've but to name your preferred manner of defeat."

"You agree to my terms in full?" Niclas asked. "You must speak them out loud, so that the guardians have a record in case I should—"

"What?" Cadmaran asked, smiling. "Fail? As indeed you will. I have no trouble speaking it aloud. I will fight you, Niclas Seymour, for the Tarian and Miss Linley. Winner takes all."

"There is one thing you must know before we begin, however," Niclas said. "The Tarian cannot be taken from

the one who possesses it unless that one freely removes
and gives it away, or," he added, "unless that one is dead.
If that is the case, it may be removed, and becomes the
sole property of the new possessor."

"And?" Cadmaran said. "Did you think me unaware of
its properties?"

"No," Niclas said, and was unsettled to feel his palms
starting to sweat. "I merely thought you should know that
I don't intend to give you the necklace, and that you cannot remove it if I'm merely insensible. If you intend to
possess the Tarian, you must kill me."

That gave the earl of Llew a moment of pause. He
gazed at Niclas for a long, considering moment.

"I see," he said at last. "Then I must necessarily refrain
from using magic, lest I call down a curse upon my head.
That is indeed a fate to avoid at all costs. But," he went on,
circling Niclas slowly, "if I gain the Tarian, no curse will
be able to dim my powers. The earl of Graymar would be
allowed to call me out to avenge your death, but if I possess the Tarian, he can have no hope of success. Either
way, the risk is well worth taking." He came to a halt and
faced Niclas. "I confirm my agreement to the terms, and
the guardians are my judges. Choose your weapons."

It occurred to Niclas, briefly, that the other man had
shown shockingly little regard for the taking of another's
life, but perhaps he'd expected too much from the earl of
Llew.

His silence appeared to provoke Cadmaran, who was all
eagerness for the contest to begin. As he removed the elegant black coat he'd been wearing, he said, "We can fancy
ourselves medieval warriors and use swords, or stand firmly

in our modern time and choose pistols. Rapiers would be an elegant choice. Have you studied fencing? But of course you must have," he said with a slight smile. "Your cousin is accounted among the greatest swordsmen in England. Surely you picked up a few tricks from him along the way."

Niclas was an acceptable swordsman, but far too much time had passed since he'd practiced the sport. There was only one skill Niclas had excelled at in the past three years, and that was because he'd found it to be a way of relaxing and quieting the racket in his brain.

"Fists," he said.

"Pardon me?" Cadmaran inclined his ear.

Niclas felt a flush of embarrassment. It struck him just how odd it was to have to repeat the method with which he was inviting Cadmaran to annihilate him.

"Fisticuffs," he said more loudly.

He appeared to have genuinely surprised the other man.

"Fisticuffs?" Cadmaran repeated. "Boxing, do you mean? The London Prize Ring rules?"

"No," Niclas replied, and began to remove his own wet coat. "I mean fisticuffs. No rules, save for no magic." He thought with regret that he'd not be able to call upon his gift of supernatural strength, either.

"I don't know why I should be surprised," Cadmaran said, sneering. "It's a common sport for a common wizard. This is what the Seymours get for marrying mere—"

Niclas was a good two inches shorter than Cadmaran, but he was able to land a solid blow to the face that sent the earl of Llew sprawling. The other man landed unceremoniously on his back, his expression a mixture of shock and pain.

"You talk too much," Niclas told him, letting himself enjoy a brief moment of satisfaction. He'd only been able to land that blow because he'd taken Cadmaran by surprise. The moment his opponent gained his feet, Niclas knew he'd be in trouble. But that was precisely why he'd come. "No doubt because you love the sound of your own voice so dearly."

He was right. Cadmaran came off the ground with a roar of fury and ran at him full force. He sent a fist flying toward Niclas's face, but Niclas hadn't spent so many nights brawling on London's docks for nothing. He ducked the blow with ease and sent his own fist into the earl of Llew's belly, keeping his knuckles tight to deliver the greatest impact. Cadmaran doubled over but managed to keep his balance, and by the time he'd swung about Niclas had moved away to the other side of the room.

"Julia!" he shouted as the other man gathered himself for a fresh attack. "I know you can hear me. I've come to take you out, but you've got to fight!"

Cadmaran didn't run at him this time, but moved with greater care. Niclas backed away with equal caution, still speaking to Julia, who remained quiet and passive on the dais.

"You fought him once before," he said aloud. "Do you remember? But that time you didn't know what you were up against. Now you do, and you have the power to win."

Cadmaran lunged and swung at him, and again Niclas easily bounced away, this time sending both fists into his opponent's lower back, which he knew from experience was particularly painful.

It went on for long minutes; not once did Cadmaran manage to land a blow, but expended himself chasing Niclas about, while Niclas did little more than jump aside and take every opportunity afterward to strike. He knew the fight couldn't go on like this forever, but while it did, he continued to address Julia, encouraging her to resist the spell she was under.

"Be quiet!" Cadmaran shouted furiously, breathing harshly now as they circled each other. "She can't hear you and she certainly can't obey you. She's *mine*."

"She *can* hear me," Niclas told him. "She hears my voice because she is my *unoliaeth*, and nothing but death can break that bond. Julia! I know you're listening! Fight hard! Come back to me!"

Cadmaran made the mistake of glancing toward Julia, and Niclas put his head down and ran forward, actually lifting the bigger man off his feet for a second or two before shoving him away. For the second time, Cadmaran landed on his back, sprawling in a most undignified manner, which Niclas hoped would sufficiently prick his pride. But just to be certain, he said, "No wonder you wanted to use weapons. You clearly need all the help you can get, my lord Llew. Do you wish to rest a little before going on?" As Cadmaran awkwardly pushed to his feet, Niclas raised his voice. "Do you see how easily he can be fought, Julia? There is nothing to fear in casting aside the spell he's placed you under."

As he rose, Cadmaran's expression was tight with rage. His black eyes speared Niclas with a look of hatred, and he knew at last that the moment had come. He had pushed the earl of Llew over the edge, beyond sense or reason. Niclas straightened and tried to ready himself for what was to come.

It began slowly. Objects in the hall started to shake, mirroring the wrath of the master of Castle Llew. The curtains swayed and the torches trembled in their holders, causing the light in the hall to flicker violently. Cups, plates, tables, chairs, and all the fine ornaments began to rattle loudly. Candlesticks dropped to the ground and several of the vacant suits of armor fell over with a loud crash. Weapons mounted on the wall came loose from their moorings and clattered to the ground.

"Very impressive," Niclas called out. "I shouldn't wish to be the one to clean up this mess, however."

Cadmaran again did that odd thing that Niclas had occasionally observed, and appeared to grow taller. He lifted a hand and pointed it at Niclas, clearly intending to strike him with some spell or other—but he had forgotten about the Tarian.

"Your magic is useless on me," Niclas informed him with as much of a sneer as he could manage. "And since you can't seem to fight as well as a mere mortal man, perhaps you should admit defeat now."

"The Tarian protects you from the power of magic," the earl of Llew managed between harsh breaths, "but it does not protect you from the results of magic. Those you must save yourself from"—a thin smile formed on his lips—"if you can."

The earl tilted one long finger and a sword yet mounted on the far wall began to shake violently. The next moment it had come free altogether and shot directly toward Niclas, point out. He barely had time to throw himself aside before it arrived, the blade skimming so close that it sliced through the upper part of his arm.

Blood began to seep before Niclas became aware of the stinging pain that followed and, rather than fear, he felt a resounding relief.

Blood had been spilled, and now Malachi would come. He would rescue Julia, regardless of what happened to Niclas. All he had to do now was stay alive long enough so that Cadmaran wouldn't have a chance to inflict any harm on her before the lord of the Seymours arrived.

Objects began to fly from all directions, axes and knives and more swords. One of the empty knights lost his javelin as it became a spear aimed at Niclas's heart.

Rolling, he leaped to his feet and ran, just managing to overturn a sturdy wooden table and hide behind it before the weapons struck with loud, angry thuds.

"Hurry, Malachi," Niclas murmured aloud. An ominous clattering drew his attention. Two large shields mounted above him were about to strike. Niclas rolled tightly against the table, tucking his legs in as the heavy objects fell.

"I always knew he wasn't very clever," Niclas said, grabbing one of the shields to use for a cover as he ran out from behind the table. A number of things struck the shield, hard, but fell harmlessly away, and he could hear Cadmaran cursing from the center of the hall.

It seemed to take forever, but Niclas managed to get behind another table and push it over, too.

Now there was a curious silence. Niclas waited, striving to control his breath, listening intently for Cadmaran's footsteps, but none came. But letting a powerful wizard have too long to think was a mistake, for within a few moments he might devise any number of plans. Such as using Julia's life to bargain with.

Grasping the shield, Niclas gingerly looked over the table's edge, and saw that Cadmaran was indeed standing very still, thinking. Julia, however, had moved off the dais, and was standing in the far corner of the hall. She was watching the unfolding events without any discernible emotion on her face, but the fact that she'd moved anywhere at all of her own free will was, to Niclas, an extraordinarily good sign.

Cadmaran was standing quite still, blinking. He lifted a hand in front of his face and moved it slowly. Then, just as slowly, he turned toward the now empty dais, and kept looking, searching, most likely, for Julia.

Niclas shot up to his full height, purposely holding the shield away in order to draw Cadmaran's attention, and shouted, "Ready to cede defeat yet?"

He never even saw the knives that struck him. Cadmaran had left a dozen of them, of various eras, lengths, and blades, drifting almost to the ceiling, ready to strike the moment Niclas showed himself. Four struck him to the hilt: one in his left shoulder, one in his right arm, one in his left thigh, and one almost in the center of his belly. He brought the shield up just in time to deflect one aimed directly at his heart. The others skimmed past, slicing a cheek, shoulder, and arm, striking the wall behind him with a loud clattering.

Niclas fell to his knees, then, as the pain began, collapsed onto his back. He lay there behind the table, feeling the shock and thinking, belatedly, *He's not quite as stupid as I believed.*

He had three of the daggers out by the time Cadmaran's face loomed over him, and had managed to pull the fourth from his belly before Cadmaran knelt.

"I'm going blind," the earl of Llew said quietly as one of his large hands closed over Niclas's throat. "I've been cursed, just as you knew I would be when you drove me to lose my temper. You've cost me a great deal." His long fingers began to squeeze.

Niclas lifted both his hands to grasp the earl's wrists, but his strength seemed to have drained away with the blood he'd lost. He could feel it pouring from his wounds, making a wet, warm pool beneath him.

"But I won't need my sight once I have the Tarian." It will be better than sight to me, and I shall cheer myself with the knowledge of how Julia will suffer beneath my hands in your absence, but always for your sake." His other hand joined the first about Niclas's neck, squeezing lightly.

"I'm going to kill you slowly," Cadmaran murmured, bending close. "My sight dims with each passing moment, but I can still feel your life pulsing beneath my hands. I shall enjoy the seconds as I feel the flow of your blood slowing beneath my fingers. And stopping."

Julia, Niclas thought, struggling as mightily as he could. *Malachi, make sure she's safe . . .*

He couldn't fight any longer. Or breathe. His eyes closed, and he heard Cadmaran chuckling. Fleetingly he thought about the Tarian, but that remorse couldn't hold him.

He could only think of Julia, and how much he regretted leaving her at Cadmaran's mercy.

And then, of a sudden, the vise about his neck was

gone. Air rushed into his lungs and, gasping, he surfaced from the heavy blackness to find Julia standing over him, an enormous axe drooping in her delicate hands. Cadmaran was lying crumpled to one side, perfectly still.

"I . . . I only struck him with the flat of the blade," she said, staring wide-eyed down at Niclas. Her face had gone white, and she was visibly trembling. "I hope I didn't kill him. Oh, Niclas."

Weakly, he reached out a hand and she fell to her knees, shoving the axe aside and pressing herself into the crook of his arm. With a smile, he set his hand upon her head.

"It's all right, love. Malachi will be here soon. He'll take care of everything."

As if he'd been announced, the most powerful wizard in Europe arrived. Niclas had expected something spectacular, but this was among his cousin's better entrances. It sounded as if a tremendous, violent storm had started up inside the house.

"Stay down," Niclas told Julia, just as a furious blast of wind shot through the entire castle like an explosion, shattering windows and slamming doors open and sending objects flying. It was sufficiently frightening to cause even Cadmaran's spell-restrained servants to start screaming and shouting.

The heavy doors to the great hall had slammed open and were swinging back and forth, banging against the walls. But as the earl of Graymar entered the room they began to shudder loudly, broke off their hinges and fell with a crash to the floor.

"He always has to make such a fuss over these things.

And noise." Niclas laughed weakly and closed his eyes. "No, stay down, love. He's not done yet."

"Niclas!" It came out as an unearthly roar rather than anything human. The very walls and floor shook. *"Morcar!"*

"Better tell him we're here, Julia," Niclas whispered, "before he tears the whole castle down."

And then, for the first time in over three years, he slid into complete blackness, and slept.

Nineteen

"Niclas?"

He felt a cool cloth on his forehead.

"Niclas?"

It was Julia, and she sounded anxious—and very far away, as if she were part of a dream and he couldn't reach her.

"Come along, *cfender*. Stop lolling about and wake up. You've cosseted yourself long enough."

That was Malachi. Which meant this wasn't a dream, for Niclas would never let Malachi into any dream that Julia was already in.

"I was sleeping," Niclas muttered groggily, his eyes still closed. "And I want to keep sleeping. For a month."

"Three days is more than sufficient to make up for what you've missed," the earl of Graymar stated imperiously. "And I should think you'd want to celebrate the lifting of the curse. Which you can do much better if you're awake."

If Malachi had spent more than three years of his life endlessly awake, he would have developed a deep appreciation for the bliss that only sleep could bring.

The curse was gone. Niclas was giddy with the realization.

"Look at him," Malachi said. "He's smiling. If you're able to smile, then you're able to awaken."

"You stayed in Wales all this time just to yell at me?" Niclas said, slowly dragging his eyelids open. Julia was hovering over him, gazing at him with concern. He smiled and tried to lift a hand to touch her face, but discovered that it hurt too much. "Your bruise is better," he murmured, thankful that Malachi was such a gifted healer. "I could have killed Cadmaran for that alone."

"You mustn't move for a little while," she said, tears brightening her blue eyes. "Lord Graymar has tended your wounds with some of his special potions, and he vows that you'll mend quickly, but you must lie abed for a few days. You're safe at Glen Aur."

Lie in bed for a few days, he repeated silently. How delightful. He would spend all of it sleeping, unless he could convince Julia to join him.

"Where's Cadmaran?" he asked.

Malachi's blond head popped into view, his crystalline blue eyes peering down at Niclas from over Julia's shoulder.

"At Castle Llew, where he should remain for some time. The elders are considering a punishment apart from what the guardians have already done, but we'll have no trouble from him for a long while, regardless. He called a blood curse down upon his head, and was blinded. Not as

Steffan is blind, but in the manner of mere mortals. He must now learn to live in this new way."

"His powers?"

"They remain undimmed, so far as I can tell, which perhaps isn't what either of us might have wished, but it is far preferable to his gaining the Tarian."

Niclas came awake more fully. "The Tarian," he said anxiously. "I had forgotten. Is it safe?"

Malachi smiled. "I have it. Morcar couldn't have taken it from you unless you were dead, and thanks to Miss Linley"—he set an approving hand on her shoulder—"he wasn't able to accomplish the deed. He did, however, get close enough to cause the curse to be lifted. The guardians were clearly convinced that you were ready to make the ultimate sacrifice for Miss Linley's sake."

Niclas looked back into Julia's face. "You broke the spell," he said, and was struck anew by how much he loved her. "You fought him."

"It wasn't like the last time," she said, tears spilling down her cheeks. "I heard your voice so clearly, and my own longing gave me the strength to follow your urging."

"You are my *unoliaeth* now," he murmured, ignoring the interested sound that his cousin made in the background. "We will always be able to hear each other, no matter how far apart we may be."

"But I should have fought harder, for then you might not have been so terribly wounded." A sob escaped her trembling lips. "He almost killed you, Niclas. I would have l-lost you forever."

He did reach up then, damning the bandages on his arms, and pulled her down to lie—very carefully—upon his also bandaged chest.

"Hush, love. It's over now, and though Cadmaran never would have wished to do us good, he was the means through which the curse has been lifted. We will never be parted again, in this world or the next. We're going to be married, and you will be my life. You and whatever children God may bless us with."

He looked at Malachi, who was gazing down at them with a very large smile upon his face.

"What?" Niclas said suspiciously.

"I had a feeling, even before you left London with Miss Linley, that this would be the outcome. Not about the curse being lifted, of course, but that Miss Linley was your *unoliaeth*."

Niclas didn't know why he was surprised, for since they'd been boys Malachi had known everything. Julia, however, stiffened and slowly sat up, wiping her face and turning to look at him.

"What do you mean, my lord? How could you know?"

"Niclas told me that he couldn't feel your emotions," Malachi explained. "And there could be only two explanations for that. Either you possess magic in your blood, even a little, or you were always intended for him. Predestined, you might say."

"And there is no magic in my family," Julia said.

Malachi shook his head. "None that I can find. And that leaves only the *unoliaeth* to explain why Niclas can't feel your emotions. He cannot feel anyone to whom he is related—and he is already, in a manner, related to you. I suspected that this was the reason even before you left London together."

"Yet you saw fit not to say anything to me about it?" Niclas asked.

"What could I have said?" Malachi asked. "And if I had, what would you have thought? You wanted a chance to lift the curse, and if I'd told you of my suspicions, you might not have gone. And, although I had my reservations about the wisdom of your escorting Miss Linley in my place, I felt that I had to give you the opportunity you sought."

"But—"

"And I couldn't be sure, yet. It was something only you could discover, for such a predestined union is very rare among lesser wizards, as you know. I saw that you were attracted to Julia," he said, "but that wasn't proof enough." He held his hands out in a gesture of resignation. "I sent you off to Wales knowing what might happen, and having already determined that if Julia was to be your wife, I could do nothing but accept it. But you must believe me, Niclas, and dear Julia," he added, smiling warmly at her, "that I am not unhappy about this turn of events. Indeed, quite the opposite. I am most pleased, especially to know that Julia will be one of us, and my new cousin." Bending, he kissed her cheek.

Niclas smiled. "Thank you, Malachi. We shall be married as soon as possible, if that pleases Julia."

"It pleases me very much," she told him. "Though I fear my family will give us a good deal of trouble. My aunt Eunice—"

"Leave it to me, why don't you?" Malachi suggested. "I'll call upon my, ah, particular talents to convince her of the rightness of the union. I believe I can assure you that Lady Eunice will not only agree to the marriage, but be utterly delighted with it."

Niclas and Julia exchanged looks. "I'm not certain we should ask it of you."

Malachi waved the words away. "Consider it a wedding gift. I shall be glad to do it, if only to see you safely wed. Now, as to the elders—"

"I'll speak with them," Niclas said.

Malachi's eyes widened only slightly at the words, but enough for Niclas to see that he'd surprised him.

"That has always been the task of the *Dewin Mawr*," Earl Graymar said. "I don't know what they would think if you were to approach them. Or what they would say."

"It doesn't really matter," Niclas told him. "I'm not going to ask their permission. I'm only going to tell them, as a courtesy, that Julia and I are to wed."

If it was possible, he had managed to surprise his cousin even more. Malachi looked, for a moment, as if he would argue, but after a few silent seconds, he said, calmly, "I see. Well. I perceive that Julia has had a more positive influence on you than I had hoped. If I ever meet such a woman who can have a like influence on me, I shall count myself a fortunate man." He set a hand on Julia's shoulder and squeezed lightly. "I'll leave the two of you alone, then, to make your plans."

"You look more exhausted than I feel," Niclas murmured once his cousin had departed. "Have you slept at all since Castle Llew?"

"Enough," she said, and he knew she was lying.

"Lie down with me here."

"Oh, no, dear. There isn't enough room."

Niclas stared at her for a blissful moment. "You called me 'dear,'" he said.

She looked at him fondly, a little amused. "Does that mean you liked it? Or would you prefer me to call you by some other endearment?"

"I liked it. But feel free to call me any and every endearment that you can think of. I shall like all of them. Lie down, love. There's room enough for us both."

She did, but slowly and with great care.

"Am I hurting you?" She gingerly rested her head on the pillow and clasped one of his hands.

He closed his eyes with pleasure. "You make me feel wonderful. Having you here makes me want to get well more quickly. I think we may spend the first year of our married life more in bed than out. Sleeping a good deal, I grant you, but many other things, as well." He turned his head to smile into her eyes. "Julia, are you quite certain that you want to wed me?"

"Niclas, darling," she replied calmly, "do you want me to get up and hit you very hard?"

"No."

"Then don't ever ask me such a foolish question again. Dear."

"I only want to make certain that you've considered what it means to marry into a family such as mine. There are challenges to face that you've never had to think about before. Above all, to keep anyone from discovering that people like your own husband and children are incredibly different."

"It sounds much more delightful than accompanying my aunt Eunice to card parties. I wonder what sorts of gifts our children will have? Won't it be wonderful discovering their unique talents?"

If Niclas thought he had loved her before, his heart swelled painfully with the feeling just now.

"It isn't a simple thing for a child to discover that he's different from the vast majority of others. For most of my life—from the moment I realized just how unusual I was—I've longed for something that could give me peace. Not just in the way of my gift, but from all that I am, all that my family is. I dreamed of it, but my life hasn't been such that fantasies could play a part. After a time," he said, "I had to put all dreams aside. Until I met you. It sounds trite to say it, but it's true, Julia. You've made my dreams come true."

Her slow smile warmed him all the way through.

"I haven't dreamed all my life," she murmured, "or even for much of it. My people have always been terribly sensible, and dreams were strictly discouraged. The truth is, I've only ever had one dream, and I've been careful to keep it very secret in my heart since it came to life on the night when I first saw you. There was never any hope that it would come true, but I kept it all the same. And then, a wonderful thing happened."

"Your dream came true?" he asked hopefully, thinking of kissing her.

"Magic came into my life in a most unexpected way," she replied. "And because of it, my dream came true."

Niclas thought a moment, then met her knowing smile.

"Yes," he said, "that's true, isn't it? I believe this must be the first time in my entire life that I've been truly thankful to be a Seymour."

She laughed merrily and leaned to kiss him, promising, "I shall do everything possible to keep you, and our children, feeling that way."

And then, lying close, hands entwined, they did the most wonderful, pleasurable thing that Niclas could think of, at least until his bandages came off, and, wishing each other pleasant dreams, they went to sleep.

Turn the page for a sneak peek at the next thrilling book

Touch of Passion

Coming soon
from St. Martin's Paperbacks

$\mathcal{H}$e would come tonight. Loris knew he would, regardless how she locked her doors or windows. He would find a way in. He always did.

The question she wished she could answer, as she gazed at her reflection in the mirror, was which feeling was most prominent in her heart—fear, or anticipation?

Lifting a hand, she touched her lips with her fingertips, remembering the way he had kissed her the night before. No one had ever kissed her like that. Not even Dyfed. Kian . . . Kian had sometimes kissed her in a similar manner, but with a good deal more difficulty, for she'd never received his attentions willingly. At least not initially. Much to her annoyance, she never seemed to be able to keep her senses for very long once he'd set his mouth against hers—due, most likely, to some magic he used. But even those kisses hadn't been like the ones she'd shared with the strange young man who came to her at night.

She didn't know his name, wasn't even precisely certain what he was, whether angel or demon, and yet when he'd taken her into his arms and kissed her, she'd felt as if they were connected in some unfathomable way. They had become one—it sounded foolish now to think such a thing, but there was no other way to describe it. There had been a feeling of wholeness, of rightness . . . and of intense pleasure.

"God forgive me," Loris whispered, her hand moving to cover her heated cheek. She was ashamed to think now of her response to him. And a little frightened. She hadn't been able to stop him, and hadn't wanted to.

No, she silently chided. That wasn't being honest. The truth was that she hadn't wanted to stop him. If he hadn't left her chamber by his own determination, she surely wouldn't have made him do so.

"You've got to do better tonight, Loris," she instructed her reflection firmly. "He's a complete stranger to you, after all. It's terribly wrong. All of it."

She believed herself, and vowed to resist him better. But in her heart she knew she wouldn't.

Moonlight streamed through the open window, giving enough light for Kian to see himself in the full-length mirror. As many times as he'd made the transformation before, he hadn't yet grown bored of watching the changes that came over his face and coloring and clothes. It was so odd, becoming someone who didn't exist. But it was necessary.

He had to be near Loris. No, not just near her, for he was close enough each day to feel the hatred for him that the curse had placed in her heart. But she was his *unoliaeth.* His oneness. They had been fated, and could never love another. If the curse kept her from recognizing him as her true mate while he was Kian, it didn't seem to stop her from at least liking him in another guise. For more than that, he didn't hope.

She'd let him kiss her last night, and, better still, had kissed him in return. Kian had thought he might reel from the sheer wonder of it. That was how it would have been between them if the curse had never been placed. Her love was his by right, and if it wasn't precisely noble of him to take it by deception, then nobility would have to go by the wayside. His need for her smile, her touch, was akin to obsession.

The change took but moments. His lengthy blond hair grew shorter and darkened until it was almost black. The lightness of his blue eyes darkened, until they were the same color as his hair. His finer features grew bolder, his nose lengthened slightly, and his shoulders widened a fraction. He looked a little like one of his dark-haired Seymour cousins. His garments took a few moments longer to complete the transition, taking on a mien similar to the fair folk who dwelled in the woods. It had seemed a good choice when he'd first decided to make these secret visits to Loris. It wasn't unusual for faeries to sneak into the dwellings of mortals at night, either to take something they desired or to lay blessings or curses upon the family within. Or even to simply cause mischief. Unfortunately, Loris wasn't yet familiar enough with the magic folk who lived in and around Tylluan to identify the garments. She had no idea what to make of him, save that he was a stranger who couldn't stop visiting her at night, and who, when he was with her, couldn't keep his hands off her. Or his lips, either.

He thought of the embrace they'd shared the night

before, and imagined what the coming hours would bring. Expectation made his breathing quicken—and that made him smile. How incredible that he, Kian Seymour, who'd bedded his first female before he'd reached the age of thirteen, should feel so foolishly light-headed at the mere idea of being with a woman. He'd been warned that love was like that, and had scoffed. But Loris made him believe. She'd changed everything for him.

The night was dark and cold as he made his way to the small balcony outside his window. A fitful wind lifted his hair at the ends and fluttered the edges of his tunic. Kian took a deep breath and let the anticipation within him rise.

She was waiting for him. He could feel it.

She had locked the windows and bolted the doors, but Loris knew it wouldn't do any good. He would come, and apart from running away, all she could do was wait. Minutes passed, and then an hour. She was weary from a day filled with keeping the castle, and longed to lie down upon her soft bed. But she couldn't bring herself to do so. It would make her feel too . . . vulnerable. Apart from that, it was disturbing to drop into a restless slumber, only to be wakened by a stranger standing over her bed. She knew because he had wakened her in such a manner before.

Weariness at last won out, and she settled into one of the large chairs near the fire. Leaning her head against the cushions, she closed her eyes and let her thoughts drift. Sleep beckoned, but she was too wary to follow.

"When will he come?" she murmured aloud.

"I'm here."

Loris opened her eyes and saw him standing there, having suddenly and silently appeared, as he was sometimes given to doing. He was leaning in a relaxed pose against the mantel, gazing down at her.

The stranger was darkly handsome, tall and muscular. His demeanor, as she had discovered during his previous visits, was charming, thoughtful, and well-spoken. He was sometimes somber, often amused, always gentle and considerate.

And yet she knew almost nothing else about him.

"Why do you come here?" she asked, looking fully into his dark eyes. "Why to me?"

He smiled. "You know why," he said, and pushed from the mantel. "You're tired, Loris." Slowly, he moved to kneel before the chair, and took her hands in his own. "You've had a difficult day?"

She ignored the question.

"No, I don't know why you come," she said, searching his face by the dim light of the fire. "I don't even know who you are. Or what you are."

"Is it Kian Seymour who wearies you so?" he asked. "He's cruel and unkind. I know how greatly you hate him."

"I don't hate Kian," she told him firmly. "He can be difficult and obstinate, but I don't hate him for it."

"Then perhaps it's his brother, Dyfed. His attentions are too demanding."

"It isn't any of them," she said impatiently. "But if it were, at least I would have a name to accuse them by. Why do you come here and . . . and spend time with me, yet not tell me who you are? Do you live at Tylluan? In some secret room in the castle that I've not yet found? Are you a Seymour? Are you even human?" She pulled her hands free and set them on either side of his face.

"You feel real enough, but there are spirits who can take on the form of mortals. But if you were not welcome here, if you were an intruder or an enemy, Kian would surely know. Unless you're as powerful a wizard as he is."

"I'm not your enemy, Loris," he said, lifting one hand to stroke the backs of his fingers gently down her cheek. "And I'm not Kian Seymour's enemy. I mean no harm to anyone at Tylluan. Most especially not to you."

With a sigh she pushed his hand away and stood, pulling her night robe more tightly about her waist and stepping around the stranger's kneeling form.

"You should go," she said. "And never come back."

He didn't move. Didn't rise to his feet. Didn't even look at her. Loris bit her lip and turned away, toward the fire, and prayed that she wouldn't start crying.

"Do you want me to go?" he asked in a low voice.

She didn't answer. Silence stretched out for a long moment, and then she finally heard him. His hands, warm and strong, fell upon her shoulders and gently turned him to face her. Searching her face, he asked once more, "Do you want me to go, Loris?"

"I want to know who you are."

He lowered his head and softly kissed her lips, a brief and tender caress.

"In your heart, you already know who I am," he murmured.

Loris shook her head in denial, but he kissed her again, more deeply, and she felt once more the rightness that was between them. She pressed closer to the solid warmth of his body, sliding her arms up about his neck.

When it ended, they were quiet again, holding each other, swaying slightly back and forth. His cheek was pressed against the top of her head, and she could feel his breath against her hair.

"Won't you tell me something about yourself?" she whispered. "Just your name will be enough. Please."

His arms tightened, and he sighed.

"On the day, or night, that you speak my true name, I will forever after be banished from Tylluan. Until that time, you may call me whatever you wish."

Loris looked up at him.

"Banished?" she said, dismayed. "But why? Who are you?"

He stroked her hair back from her face, and said, "I am one who wants to be near you always. I will never harm nor dishonor you. I want to come to you freely, without fear, without shame, and give you pleasure and respite. I want to be the one you tell your secrets to, your dreams, all of the things that you can tell no one else. I want to hear of your days and be part of your nights, to hold and touch you, to be touched by you in turn. I want to hear your voice and carry the memory of it away with me until I'm with you once more." He kissed her again, slowly, deeply. "This is who I am, Loris." His hand cradled her face. "Is it enough?"

"Yes," she whispered, drawing him back down to her. "It's enough."

Join top authors for the ultimate cruise experience. Spend 7 days in the Mexican Riviera aboard the luxurious Carnival Pride℠. Start in Los Angeles/Long Beach, CA and visit Puerto Vallarta, Mazatlan and Cabo San Lucas. Enjoy all this with a ship full of authors and book lovers on the **"Authors at Sea Cruise"** April 2 - 9, 2006.

Mail in this coupon with proof of purchase* to receive $250 per person off the regular **"Authors at Sea Cruise"** price. One coupon per person required to receive $250 discount. For complete details call **1-877-ADV-NTGE** or visit **www.AuthorsAtSea.com**

PRICES STARTING AT $749 PER PERSON WITH COUPON!

*proof of purchase is original sales receipt with this book purchased circled.
**plus applicable taxes, fees and gratuities

Carnival The Most Popular Cruise Line in the World!

GET $250 OFF

Name   (Please Print)

Address   Apt. No.

City   State   Zip

E-Mail Address

See Following Page For Terms & Conditions.

**For booking form and complete information
go to www.AuthorsAtSea.com or call 1-877-ADV-NTGE**

Carnival Pride℠
April 2 - 9, 2006.

7 Day Exotic Mexican Riviera Itinerary

DAY	PORT	ARRIVE	DEPART
Sun	Los Angeles/Long Beach, CA		4:00 P.M.
Mon	"Book Lover's" Day at Sea		
Tue	"Book Lover's" Day at Sea		
Wed	Puerto Vallarta, Mexico	8:00 A.M.	10:00 P.M.
Thu	Mazatlan, Mexico	9:00 A.M.	6:00 P.M.
Fri	Cabo San Lucas, Mexico	7:00 A.M.	4:00 P.M.
Sat	"Book Lover's" Day at Sea		
Sun	Los Angeles/Long Beach, CA	9:00 A.M.	

ports of call subject to weather conditions

TERMS AND CONDITIONS

PAYMENT SCHEDULE:
50% due upon booking
Full and final payment due by February 10, 2006

Acceptable forms of payment are Visa, MasterCard, American Express, Discover and checks. The cardholder must be one of the passengers traveling. A fee of $25 will apply for all returned checks. Check payments must be made payable to **Advantage International, LLC** and sent to: **Advantage International, LLC, 195 North Harbor Drive, Suite 4206, Chicago, IL 60601**

CHANGE/CANCELLATION:
Notice of change/cancellation must be made in writing to Advantage International, LLC.

Change:
Changes in cabin category may be requested and can result in increased rate and penalties. A name change is permitted 60 days or more prior to departure and will incur a penalty of $50 per name change. Deviation from the group schedule and package is a cancellation.

Cancellation:

181 days or more prior to departure	$250 per person
121 - 180 days prior to departure	50% of the package price
120 - 61 days prior to departure	75% of the package price
60 days or less prior to departure	100% of the package price (nonrefundable)

US and Canadian citizens are required to present a valid passport or the original birth certificate and state issued photo ID (drivers license). All other nationalities must contact the consulate of the various ports that are visited for verification of documentation.

We strongly recommend trip cancellation insurance!

For complete details call 1-877-ADV-NTGE or visit www.AuthorsAtSea.com

---

This coupon does not constitute an offer from St. Martin's Press LLC

For booking form and complete information
go to **www.AuthorsAtSea.com** or call **1-877-ADV-NTGE**

Complete coupon and booking form and mail both to:
**Advantage International, LLC,
195 North Harbor Drive, Suite 4206, Chicago, IL 60601**